Genesis of the Hunter

Book 2

By
Joshua Martyr

Chapter One

Siege
I

Little light from the moon and stars reached the earth this night, for blackened clouds, heavy with rain, had drifted across the sky. Clothed in the robe of a monk, he gazed out from within the hood, his face quite shrouded by the recess of shadow within. He had left Colin and Ober in the distance some time ago and the feeling of leaving them behind had been a rather unsettling one, for it was not solely his friends whom he left behind, but all that they represented – the cherished merriment, camaraderie, and love that had oft been what had made life worth living in times of sorrow and hardship. The life he had known before he was changed in body was yet so fresh in his mind – so tangible. It made his new world of night seem as some horrid dream from which he could not wake; yet, somehow, sitting astride the great bay and riding over the rolling plains of Northumberland made him feel like the man he had been but a little while past.

He regarded the bay and the black mare, which, tethered to the bay's saddle by a rope lead, dutifully followed his snorting mount. He found himself strangely comforted by the two steeds – comforted by their indiscriminate trust, affection, and even their very presence with him on his journey. He rode westward, mirroring the river, Tweed, as he made his way inland, just as he had done whilst journeying to the lair of the demon he had slain. He knew he could not stay in Berwick, nor reside in any place at length for that matter. Bronwyn's death was grim evidence of this fact, and he was unsure if he would ever relinquish the guilt he carried, as he bore it like a great weight over his shoulders. He reasoned that death had found Bronwyn solely as a result of his seeking her and that if he had but remained interred in the ground, she would breathe still. He had come to learn that his days of merriment, of enjoying the company of friends and loved ones, of even standing in the light of day, were at an end.

Indeed, were he not compelled to do what he understood as

God's work, he might have ended his own life some time ago. Now, all he had, all he gave, was death – death from which, he beseeched of himself, the innocent must be spared, and by which only the wicked should suffer, lest he risk what little was left of his soul. He feared death would eventually find those he held dear, those with whom he fraternized, and thus he wandered through the night, alone with his beasts beneath the dark firmament above.

Somewhere beneath this selfsame sky, the white demons stalked the haunts of men, for in days past he had chanced upon traces of more of their kind as he roamed. He had also found that to hunt these creatures, he might often find himself within these aforementioned haunts of men, and at present, his roguish, feral appearance was not conducive to any kind of inconspicuous mingling. He had found, however, that his look was such that if he remained aloof, composed, reserved, and discreetly mindful of how people observed him, he was, for the most part, passable as a man; and, as garbs often proclaim the man, he reasoned that Colin's suggestion of a change of attire might prove useful in this endeavor.

* * * *

Berwick Castle grew larger as he approached, and when he had drawn near as he dared on horseback, he drew back his hood, dismounted, and led the horses into the natural alcove of a nearby thicket. This small island of shrubs and trees rose more than high enough from the grassy plain to conceal the horses, shrouding the animals' forms in deep, unfathomable shadow. The sentry tied the bay's reins to a slender tree and watched as it tossed its head somewhat nervously, evidently unsure about its dark, confined surroundings. He steadied the beast with a firm grip of its reins beneath the bit and stroked its neck and mane with his free hand. He spoke to it in a smooth, soothing voice.

"Calm yourself, friend, calm yourself. Be calm...shhhh...I shall return shortly."

The black mare that, being led, was less agitated, nuzzled the sentry as he rested his face upon one side of her neck, stroking her flank. He removed one of the large, empty sacks from the small load upon its back and slung it over his shoulder as he patted the mare's side a final time. The sack, like the others, was fastened with a thick drawstring, woven through a series of grommets near the mouth of the sack. This caused the mouth of the sack to tighten and close when the sack was hung from the drawstring whilst weighted with contents. He tied the drawstring into a noose, which he slung over one shoulder and under the opposite arm so that the sack draped off his back next to where the hood of his robe hung below his shoulders. Shortly thereafter, the sentry left the safety of the thicket, adorning the great hood of his priest's habit as he made his way up the steepening slope towards Berwick Castle.

In the days since his inception into the world of night, he had found himself drawing ever closer to castles, towns, and villages as he ranged; less afeared of being seen by others, and increasingly confident in his ability to move amidst them unseen.

It was not long before he reached the outer bailey, and slinking over it, he made his way to the castle. He dared not venture near the entranceway into the castle, for there he would surely be spotted. Instead, he gazed upwards at the nine towers, many of differing girth, structure, and height, which loomed above the main bulk of the castle, rising from curtain walls, encompassing the courtyard within. He observed them, deciding which would be best suited for entry. It would most certainly not be the slender Hog's Tower, for he had heard told that it was naught but a dungeon high above the castle. Eyeing the small, lone window near its crown, he intuited that the massive, lofty keep would serve his purposes.

He skulked towards the side of the castle from which he could access the keep most readily. The arched window was set with glass – a rarity indeed; its presence indicating wealth, perhaps even betraying the abode of the town lord himself, for no other window he observed from his position bore the sheen of glass. The crown of the keep was mounted by four, squat, crenellated towers, and upon each, a single guard was stationed.

Rain began to spit from above and it was not long before it fell in torrents: a symphony of spattering droplets, almost obscuring the castle that rose before him. Moving silently and patiently, he eluded the eyes of the stationed guards, for, as was his habit, he clung to the darkest shadows wherever he could, and thusly, reached the castle itself. When he was beneath the keep, he placed his pale, bare hands and feet against the mortared stones of the castle and began to climb. The castle stones were slick with rain, yet he clung to the glistening rock with ease. The black claws upon his hands and feet hooked and gripped against the stones, to which, equal to the task, his fingers and palms held fast.

Sweeping under his hood, rain whipped against his face as he ascended, and his yellow eyes blinked and squinted through the deluge. He moved silently and steadily, the faint scratching of his clawed fingers and toes drowned by the incessant tumult of the rain. Now and again the hilt and pommel of his sword would scrape against the stone from beneath his robe, and he paused for a moment to shift his belt and scabbard before continuing his ascension. Slowly, cautiously, his eyes searching the surrounding towers for vigilant guards, he pulled himself onto the castle wall. Moving in a deep crouch, he stalked towards the darkest side of the keep, and here, hidden in the blackest of shadows, he scaled the stone structure.

The keep was a large, rectangular column, nearly as tall again as the curtain walls of the castle that enclosed the courtyard, which was now clearly visible from where he clung to the keep. He looked down at the river Tweed and saw the White Wall, the great wall that ran from the port at the Tweed's bank, up the steep motte and adjoined to the castle. Alongside this wall, ran a set of stairs, the Breakneck Stairs he had heard them called. From above, muffled by the wind and rain, he heard the voices of the guards atop the four corner towers of the keep. They murmured amongst one another intermittently as they endured the weather above.

Still a little distance from the crown of keep, he reached the window – the sole window upon this face of the keep above where it rose from the castle wall. He reached upwards and took hold of the windowsill, first with one hand, then the other. Slowly, he pulled his head up towards the window to peer into the room beyond. He kept much of his face hidden below the sill and behind one side of the frame, so that he stared out through a single eye from the bottom corner of the window. He was dismayed to find an ornate iron grating built into the masonry within the aperture. The grating was set in the stone frame a hand's breadth from the glass, effectively barring the window. He slipped the fingers of his right hand through the swirling, almost floral patterns of iron, and clasped the grating.

He pulled then pushed against the grating, but it was solidly fixed into the masonry. Even if he were able to shake it loose and finally wrench it from the window with brute force, it would cause far too much noise for too long, and most assuredly alert the four guards above to his presence. He looked past the grating and stared into the room. It was dark, but his keen eyes pierced the shadows. The room was relatively large, its occupants elsewhere. Against the wall to his right was the head of a large bed, neatly covered with patterned sheets, and held above the wooden floor by a lavish, wooden bed frame. Just beyond the window was a writing desk and chair, and against the far wall, off to the right, was an enormous wardrobe. Other furnishings and ornamentations filled the room, but what caught the sentry's eye was the large window directly ahead of him, across the room on the far wall.

The window was considerably larger than the one through which he now peered, and it was barred neither by grating or by glass. Most fortuitously, its hinged, wooden shutters had been left wide open to allow fresh air into the room. He noted that he could not see open sky, or the opposite wing of the castle through the open window. Strangely enough, all he saw beyond the opening was a stone wall, as though the window opened into some kind of dark hollow or shaft in the center of the keep. He began to contemplate what might lie beyond the open window and determined that regardless of what it was, he must find a way into it to access the window and gain entry to the room. If the shaft were indeed what he suspected, then he would have to enter it from the very roof of the keep.

He ascended the remaining distance to the top of the keep with cat-like whid, and peeked out over the roof from where the stone floor of the roof met the base of one of the squat, corner towers. Rain swept over the keep on the back of a strong wind, which howled softly as it roiled about the four towers. His robe barely thrashed in the wind, so heavy was it with rain. The guards dipped their heads and squinted their eyes, rain rapping against their conical helms and dribbling down the metal nose guards, which jutted down from the brow of each helm. Upon occasion, a guard would look about ineffectually, though much of their time was spent with their chins tucked and shoulders hunched, attempting to keep their bodies warm under their rain soaked cloaks, tunics and undergarments. They strained to peer out over the surrounding land through the deluge.

The sentry did not feel their chill. He hauled himself onto the top of the keep and pressed his back against the small tower beside him. The towers were not even so high as Colin's smithy, yet the darkness, pooling shadows, and masking rain, hid the sentry from the guards' eyes. Just as he had thought, there was a large, squarish opening in the stone floor near the center of the keep. Its diameter was nearly twice his own length and its edges were somewhat beveled, though by design or wear he was not sure.

It was a lightwell, a lengthy shaft that descended into the very bowels of the castle, bringing light and fresh air into areas that might otherwise be altogether devoid of both. It was this lightwell that the unbolted window opened into, and in descending into it he could gain entry into the room. He turned his attention to the tower at his back, craning his neck to stare upwards at its crenellated top. From its base, he could not see the guard stationed above, and he was leery of being spotted. Should the guard be facing him as he made his move towards the lightwell, he would not reach the guard before he alerted the others.

Time was short, however, and the sentry had the worrisome feeling that the other guards, whose backs were to him at the moment, would soon turn round for whatever reason and spot him. Thus, gambling with the position of the guard above him, he stole towards the center of the roof, his eye upon the top of the tower as he left its base. After a few agonizing moments, the guard came into view, his back to the sentry, his arms huddled together for warmth. Relieved, and moving quickly and silently across the keep, the sentry returned his gaze to the lightwell. Rain fell into the dark opening, and rainwater ran over its edges, trickling down into the depths of the stone shaft. As he neared the verge of the lightwell, he spotted the sill of the open window below. He did not hesitate, nor even break stride as he lunged over the edge of the lightwell and dropped into the darkened shaft.

He twisted in the air, orienting his body so that he faced the window below. His robe billowed and he heard the low whoosh of air it created as he descended into the lightwell. He watched as the sill rushed up towards him and he extended his pale hands and feet. He alighted softly, with an effortless grace: his hands finding purchase upon the sill itself, his feet bracing themselves below against the wall of the shaft. There was a hushed grating of claw over stone, and all was silent once more, save the wind and rain overhead.

Stark still, he hung from the sill for a moment, listening for something: anything; his heart beating excitedly within him. He peered down into the depths of the lightwell. From far below, he could hear the muted, roisterous gabble of revelry. He presumed that the castle's great hall lay somewhere beneath him. He also caught the trace scent of a putrid stench that wafted from the bowels of the castle, and surmised that, via a system of chutes below, the rainwater was being utilized to purge the castle latrines. He drew in a deep calming breath, exhaled, and then pulled himself into the open window. He crouched upon the windowsill, and there paused briefly, his amber eyes searching the room once over before he dropped from the sill into the dark room.

The room was quiet. The sounds of the storm seemed distant as the heavens themselves. He removed his dripping hood and brushed a few stray strands of rain-slicked hair from his face. Ahead was the barred window and wooden writing desk. To his right was the door to the room. He approached it and listened, hearing nothing immediately beyond the door. He turned from the door to glance at the wardrobe, and then hurried towards it. He opened its large, double doors, which creaked faintly as they were swung apart. Inside hung a wealth of clothing and he rifled through them. Some were overly lavish, vibrant, and ornate for his purposes, but there were those that met his specifications. He slung the sack off his back, and crouching, placed it on the floor between his legs. He loosened the drawstring and opened the mouth of the sack. From the assemblage of clothes, he took two hooded cloaks, one black, one a deep brown, and tucked them into the sack. He pilfered a few other articles of clothing, and two pairs of leather boots, which he knew would be snug, and stuffed them into the sack with the cloaks.

He was in the process of snatching up some trinkets from a jewelry box on a large bedside nightstand, when he saw his reflection upon the burnished, metal surface of a silver hand mirror lying next to the jewelry box. The mirror was propped against the stone wall behind the nightstand, so that its reflective surface was angled somewhat towards him. He went quite still as he stared disgustedly into his own lurid eyes, the eyes of a thief and murderer. Suddenly plagued with shame, he reached out towards the mirror, pulled it away from the wall and placed it face down upon the top of the nightstand. He bowed his head and closed his eyes, then, rousing himself from his self-loathing, he knelt to a knee to cram the last of the trinkets into the sack. He was about to tie the sack closed once more, when he perceived a subtle glint from the corner of his eye.

It came from the floor where it met the wall, just next to the base of the nightstand. The shining thing was small, no larger than a pea. He reached out and picked it up between his thumb and forefinger. It was a faceted gem, one which might have once been affixed to a necklace or ring. He was wondering if, in his haste, he had jarred the gem loose from one of the effects he had taken from the jewelry box, when he noticed something peculiar. He stared beyond the gem between his fingers, observing the wall next to where he had found the little jewel. It appeared that the mortar surrounding a particularly large stone slab in the base of the wall had been chiseled away.

It seemed unlikely that the passage of time was the cause of the worn mortar, for the rest of the wall was relatively pristine. Indeed, the entire assemblage of walls which constituted the room looked to be as perfect in condition as one could expect. In the absence of mortar, the large stone was bordered by a dark, gaping crack, suggesting that the stone might be dislodged from the wall if one were so inclined. The stone was more than half covered by the base of the nightstand and so, after dropping the tiny gem into the sack, he grasped the nightstand with both hands and moved it aside. He then squatted by the bedside once more, examining the stone.

The crack ringing the stone was large enough that he could wedge the very tops of his fingertips into it. Gripping the stone as best he could, he began to pull. The stone slid free from the wall quite easily, leaving a dark hollow at the base of the wall where it had rested. He put the stone aside and stared into the hollow, in which he saw a wooden chest. It was not a large chest, just over two hands' breadths in length and perhaps one in both width and height. He drew the chest from the hollow with both hands, and giving it a gentle shake, heard the distinct clinking of a mass of coins within. The chest was locked, and he decided against opening it there and then. He placed the chest in the sack and slid the stone back into place, sealing the hollow. He stood, moved the nightstand back where it had been, then crouched to take hold of the drawstring. He lifted the bundle and the rope went taut under the newfound weight of the sack, safely enclosing the spoils within it as the drawstring pulled the mouth of the sack closed.

The sentry slung the sack over his back and was in the process of securing the rope noose under his arm and over the other shoulder, when he realized he was unsure of how exactly he was to leave the castle. He stared at the grated window, dismissed it as a viable option, and walked towards the other window. Bracing himself with his left arm, he leaned out the open window as far as he could and twisted his head and neck to peer up at the mouth of the lightwell. His eyelids tightened as rainwater cascaded upon him, and through the narrow vista above he watched blackened storm clouds roll by. He reached up with his free hand and placed his palm against the wall of the shaft.

Rainwater, which coated the shaft like glistening, liquescent glass, poured through his fingers and streamed down his arm. The masonry under his palm was relatively smooth, a smoothness made slick by the rainwater that ran down is length. He clutched at a stone, his fine claws seeking purchase in the mortar filled crannies surrounding it. He attempted to pull himself upwards, but his hand slid from the stone with a harsh, wet scrape. His side thumped against the sill and the coins and trinkets in the sack jingled audibly. He pulled himself back into the chamber and wiped the rain and his dripping hair from his eyes. He looked about the chamber, distressed. His eyes fell upon the door, and though he knew there was little choice in the matter, he was immediately reluctant to attempt withdrawing from the castle by the chamber door.

He was indecisive, and for a few moments he did naught but stare at the door with a look of foreboding upon his face. Finally, he approached the door and put his ear to it. He listened intently, but heard nothing. He opened the door gradually with the utmost patience and care, wincing as the hinges creaked and whined. The door led to a small landing, from which a stone staircase spiraled downwards. Silent and wary, his left arm bent awkwardly behind his back to keep the sack from swaying, he made his way down the twisting stairs.

II

With its narrow walls and low ceiling, the stairwell was quite confined. Small torches were hung few and far between at intermittent points along one wall, so that the cramped stairwell was vaguely aglow with dim, dancing firelight. He continued down the steps, which, after one last turn, eventually led him to an arched, stone doorway that opened into the span of a poorly lit hall. He moved his bare feet over the remaining stone stairs beneath him with noiseless, tentative steps. He heard the delicate sound of a torch flickering near his ear and the murmur of distant voices within the castle. As he neared the door, he heard a faint sound of movement and came to a sudden halt, sniffing the air. He caught the scent of a man, two men, on either side of the doorway. With his free hand, he slowly pulled his hood over his head. In doing so, he was suddenly aware that he had betrayed his presence to them.

* * * *

The two guards stood with their backs to the stone wall, each to one side of the open doorway. One had a short, blond beard, the other, a younger man, was essentially clean shaven. They stood statuesque and resolute at their stations, paragons of the discipline befitting an English castle garrison. A wavering pool of warm light spilled betwixt them from within the doorway, an arch-shaped fiery glow, which stretched along the stone-tiled floor; its origin a flickering torch, hung at the base of the stairwell. Mere paces from the elder guard's left foot, within the pool of torchlight, a silent, supple shadow glided into view on the hallway floor, only just beyond the threshold of the doorway. The shadow was indistinct, the movement brief, but enough to warrant his complete attention. The elder guard turned his head and leaned in towards the doorway, his eyes darting to where the shadow had retreated behind the threshold. The guard craned his neck so that he might glance a little ways beyond the doorway.

Though it had remained unapparent to his eyes at first glance, he was quick to discern that the shadow he had seen was a sleeved arm, and that the large body of amorphous shadow into which it had coalesced was the intimation of a presence that had somehow found its way into the stairwell behind him and his younger compatriot. He took a step to his left and leaned into the doorway, far enough that his helmed head and left shoulder were canted into the doorway. The guard peered into the stairwell and what he saw caused his breath to freeze in his breast and his body to tighten with fear. Before him, bathed in torchlight and shadow, shrouded in hood and habit, was a strange, fearsome man, who gazed out from beneath his hood with the icy, emotionless glare of a serpent. For what seemed an interminable instant in time, their eyes locked, each holding the other's gaze in a deathly silence. The guard took a hesitant step away from the wall, unable to tear his gaze from strange man before him.

"You there! Halt!"

He had only just managed to blurt his command before the robed man rushed towards him with terrifying speed.

The young guard had, with rising curiosity, noted his bearded compatriot's change in body language from the corner of his eye. The youngster turned his head to observe the fellow at his right. He was more than trepidatious however, when he saw the elder guard shy from the doorway with an affrighted look upon his face, crying out to what seemed vacant air. No sooner had his comrade cried out, than, accompanied by a rush of air, a large hooded figure in dark, billowing garbs burst forth from the doorway. The young guard's heart caught in his throat, and so startled was he by this spectral form that his body clenched tight in distress. The hooded figure attacked without warning, without mercy and without a sound. The hooded man, for man it must be, was upon his bearded companion in the time it took the young guard to blink.

He could do naught but watch as the hooded man swung his right arm in a rising arc from his hip with menacing purpose, the back of his pale fist striking the face of the elder guard with terrible force. The elder guard's head shuddered and reeled under the brutal impact, blood and spittle bursting from his face in a rubescent spray, accompanied by a loud, wet crack. The elder guard flew backward and his limp body spun in the air before he struck the far wall with a clatter of mail. As his comrade slid from the wall, the young guard saw that his compatriot's jaw hung disjointed and slack, and that bloodied gaps now yawned in his mouth where teeth had once been. The nose-bridge of his helm was naught but a piece of twisted metal, which had torn into the flesh of his face, and his eyes, glassy and rolling as if in a delirium, stared into nothingness as he collapsed to the ground.

Instinctually, the youngster had clasped his sword and, seeing that the hooded man had given him his back for an instant, sought to run his compatriot's assailant through whilst the man remained unawares. He had only just begun to draw his sword, when the hooded man whirled round with frightening speed and clutched his sword arm about the wrist. He grunted in anguish, for the hooded man's grip crushed his wrist like an iron manacle, and glancing down, he saw that the monstrous hand had caught his sword arm before his blade was even half drawn. Grimacing, his eyes lifted to those of the hooded man, a look of pain and disbelief upon his face.

The hooded man was already dropping his clenched fist down upon the young guard like a smith's hammer, and it tore through the air to bash the guard's helm with chilling savagery.

* * * *

The sentry watched the guard's lifeless body slump to the ground at his feet, his right arm still raised where his clenched fist had pummeled the guard's skull. He was, in some measure, taken aback by the effect and degree of his ferocity, yet somehow empowered by the propensity. He heard rising calls to arms within the castle, and his head bolted upright within his hood to stare down the hallway before him. He heard the echoes of approaching footfalls at a run, and the clinking of mail and weaponry. He heard the same from some other chamber or hall behind him, yet held his gaze down the hallway before him, and for good reason. Some thirty paces from where he was poised over the fallen guard's body, past a few mounted torches, built into the stone wall on the right side of the hallway, was the portal to his salvation.

It was a small, open window, its top arched like those in the lord's chamber. A little distance from the hallway window, from around a corner that might have led into another hallway or stairwell, tempestuous cries and resounding footfalls drew dangerously near. The sentry sprang to life once more, propelling himself forth into an outright sprint, his laden sack jingling as it swung to and fro across his back. The footfalls and voices of men drew ever nearer from beyond the far corner and from behind him, yet he was unwavering in his purpose, his eyes fixed upon the open window. He was not yet half way to the window when three guards, their red cloaks streaming out behind them, burst into the hallway in front of him, rounding the corner with swords drawn. The lead guard was evidently fleeter of foot than the others and seeing the sentry, he quickened his pace further still.

"Halt, cur!" The lead guard's voice was a throaty bellow, and seeing two of his fellow guards so horridly felled by the robed assailant before him, his face twisted into a disdainful scowl under his helm.

The lead guard was unprepared for the rapidity with which the robed assailant gained the ground between them, nor had he expected the robed man to continue in his path towards himself and his fellow guards unarmed as he was. The lead guard pressed onward and drew back his sword arm.

The window lay between the onrushing guards and the sentry, who staying his course with unfaltering resolution, streaked towards the charging guards head on. He had hoped to escape through the window before the guards could reach him, but he saw now that he must clash with the armed men if he was to make good said escape. He could hear their breaths heaving in their chests and smell the odor of the bodies. To his glinting, amber eyes, the penultimate moment before they would meet seemed to linger. In that moment, he observed the way the torchlight shone with a dim glow upon their helms and mail. He studied their faces and the fortitude of their wills: he saw the whites of their eyes trained upon him, the grim intent behind them, and the fear some sought to hide. His eyes met those of the lead guard and fixed themselves upon him.

To either side of the sentry, torches whipped by. The very walls seemed little more than blurs of motion; such was his speed. He and the first of the guards were separated by mere paces and an instant thereafter were separated by naught at all.

The sentry watched as the first of the guards lunged forward with his sword, seeking to drive the blade into his chest. In one seamless motion, the sentry pivoted on a foot and lunged sideward, so that he slipped by the guard's blade unscathed in a single, deft stride. The guard's blade whisked past the sentry's chest, followed by the guard's outstretched arm. Bent at the elbow, the sentry thrust out his right arm, ramming the ridge of his forearm into the lead guard's head as he hurtled into him sidelong. The guard's head slung backward at a harsh angle and his feet catapulted out from underneath him. The man's slack body drifted through the air feet first before it tumbled once over across the stone floor, his sword clattering loudly as it slid across the hallway.

The guard's body had not yet even come to ground before the sentry had turned to face the remaining guards. Keeping close to one another, these attacked in a somewhat staggered alignment. His sword raised, the first of the two slashed downward at the sentry in an attempt to cleave his head from his shoulders. The sentry crouched low and, darting to one side, dipped under the blade, slipping past the man to pounce upon the other guard, who trailed just beyond the one he had bypassed. This last guard was unprepared for the sentry's sudden attack, and was barely able to lift his sword before the sentry was upon him. The sentry caught the guard's sword arm in a powerful grip, and violently thrust the white palm of his right hand into the stricken guard's face. In that same, single movement, wherein the guard's head jolted under the prodigious impetus, the sentry seized the man's face, lifted him, and drove the back of the man's head into the wall adjacent the window.

A low clang resounded throughout the hallway as the back of the guard's helm dented inwards. Eyes half closed and lolling, pinned against the stone wall by the sentry's fearsome talon, the guard hung limp from his head, his face flattened by the sentry's white palm. The sentry heard vigorous movement at his back, and knowing it was the last of the guards, left the body of the senseless guard in his clutch to slide from the wall and topple to the ground.

He spun round with frightening speed, in time to see the guard's sword tearing through the air towards him. He veered and twisted away from the blade, narrowly escaping a split skull. He was not able to avoid the blade entirely, however, and it hissed by his head to score a gash across his left shoulder. The sentry backed into the opposite wall with some force. He glanced at the window next to him, then at his wounded shoulder, and then his eyes shot to those of the guard, who, at that very moment, had caught his first real glance of the face of the robed man before him. The sentry felt his lips curl into a snarl and heard a quiet, animal growl rumble in his throat.

The guard's eyes widened in alarm and fear gnawed at his guts. For a moment, the guard hesitated; he froze, numbed by the fiendish sight before him. In that moment, the sentry tore a torch off the wall next to him and swung it at the guard. The torch swept through the air with a deep, forceful whoosh, leaving a trail of flame in its wake. The guard began to lift his sword arm to parry, but to no avail. The sentry brought the flaming end of the torch down upon the guard with terrible might, and it burst into a flitting cascade of glowing embers and flame as he bashed the guard's skull. The felled guard pitched to one side and hit the stone floor with a heavy thud, while his helm tumbled down the hallway with a clatter. The sentry dropped the torch, adjusted the rope and sack he had harnessed to himself, and headed for the open window.

From the opposite end of the hall, four other guards, led by their captain, hastened into the hallway. Following their captain's lead, they all came to a sudden halt, all bearing looks of utter dismay; for in the hallway lay the scattered, bloodied bodies of five of their compatriots. All was still save the flickering flames of torches and a single, rolling helm, which, tinkling softly as it wobbled about, came to rest near the captain's feet. The captain peered down at the helm with a perturbed yet bewildered expression, and then looked up, staring at the empty hallway.

* * * *

The sentry had backed out of the window, his visage facing the dark, clouded sky so that the rain, which had diminished to a light drizzle, spattered delicately over his face. He had first forced the sack through the stone aperture, then followed the dangling sack with his head. Reaching for the portion of stony wall above the window with his clasping talons, he had then pulled himself upwards, sliding his waist and legs out through the window so that his clawed feet could find purchase on the wet, stone wall.

The courtyard below, which the window had opened over, stretched out behind him as he ascended. The scent of dampened hay and the scents of the lord's beasts rose from the darkened courtyard and lingered in the moist air. He knew not what stone structure he scaled, only that it backed into the courtyard, that its roof rose to a height just below that of the curtain wall of the castle against which it was built, and that it was evidently conjoined to the lower half of the keep. He could hear the hard nails at his fingertips grating softly against the stone as he ascended the wall, as well as the infrequent, subdued clink of the trinkets within the sack. The wind keened above, and below, from within the castle, came the melded, riotous cries of men. The guards atop the towers paced and looked about searchingly from their posts, yet he had thus far remained unseen.

Though nerve-wracking, the climb to the top of the structure was not an overly lengthy one, and he was soon hauling himself onto the roof. Crouched as low as he was able, he made his way across the roof to the curtain wall of the castle, the parapet walk of which was a few arms' breadths above the roof. He came to rest against the wall, looking about anxiously, and wondering if he had been spotted. His heart was pounding and he took a deep breath to calm himself. He looked up at the parapet walk above him, and before he was truly aware of what he was doing, he leapt up onto the parapet walk.

The contents of his sack tinkled as he alighted upon the cold stone, and once again, he slung his left arm behind his back to staunch the movement of the valuables within the sack. His keen eyes fossicked his surroundings, searching for the fastest means of escape. He peered over one of the wall crenels and saw the winding waters of the Tweed down below, skirting the shore beyond the southern portion of the grassy motte upon which the castle was built. He thought of chancing a climb back down the outside of the wall, but then observed what he believed would be a faster withdrawal from the castle.

From where he crouched upon the parapet, he broke into a run, moving swiftly atop the castle wall. With billowing hood and robe, faintly silhouetted as he raced over the castle wall, he appeared in a way otherworldly. With such speed did his shadowy form sweep across the crenellated wall that, at first glance, it seemed as though he flew phantom-like atop the castle. He was rapidly approaching the Breakneck Stairs, which from the south wall of the castle, wound their way to the port upon the Tweed. Alongside the stairs entire length, ran the great White Wall. The sentry eyed the White Wall as he sped forth. Where the White Wall was adjoined to the castle, it rose nearly halfway up the curtain wall before dropping downhill. As he was eying the White Wall, a man's voice echoed over the whirling wind.

"There! Upon the wall! The south wall is besieged!"

The sentry's eyes darted upward to a small, crenel-crowned guard tower next to the lofty corner tower, both some distance from him. Upon the guard tower, one of the garrisons was yelling, pointing at him with a gloved hand. Quite abruptly, the guard ceased his shouts and began to make his way down the external stairs which wound round the little guard tower. The sentry heard the rapid, scraping staccato of the guard's boots upon the wet, stone steps as the guard disappeared behind the tower whilst following their winding course. The guard reemerged from behind the tower, his feet firmly planted upon the parapet walk. The guard drew his sword and broke into a steady run towards the sentry. The discordant ring of an alarm bell resounded from somewhere below, and the sentry arrowed towards the guard with an air of desperation.

As he ran, the sentry let go the sack with his left arm, leaving it to dangle at his back as pulled up his robe to his waist, uncovering the sword beneath. With his right hand he grasped the hilt of the Tizona, then pulled the great blade free of its scabbard to clasp the hilt with both hands. The guard's face seemed to lose its hardened appearance upon sight of the sentry's sword, betraying his budding apprehension. Both the sentry and the guard charged one another upon the narrow parapet walk. No longer driven by logic and reason, possessed solely by a frantic instinct to survive, the sentry hefted his blade into the air with a wild fervor. The two men met upon the wall, the sentry's great muscles straining beneath the robe as he heaved his sword towards the guard with all his might.

His assault was not the refined swing of a swordsman, but that of a mace-wielding barbarian, seeking to crush the bones of his adversary. The blade hurtled towards the guard with a deep rush of air. The guard was only just able to put his sword up in time, but the blow struck with such awesome power that the great blade battered through the guard's parry with a strident clang and a shower of sparks. The sentry's blade hammered into the guard's body with a sound like distant thunder, accompanied by the crack of bone. An arc of spattered blood erupted from high upon the guard's chest, followed by ruptured links of chain mail. The guard flew backward and to one side, a gargled yelp forced from his caved chest. The guard's sword lanced over the castle wall as the guard's hewed body jounced off a stone crenel and toppled from the wall into the courtyard far below.

Sheathing his sword, the sentry continued on, racing along the wall, arrows suddenly whizzing by him sporadically. He reached the point where the White Wall intersected the castle wall below. He hopped up into an interstice between two crenels and lowered his body down along the outer wall of the castle. He let go of wall with his left hand and hung for moment, held solely by his right arm. He cocked his head, seemingly evaluating the precipitous drop to the narrow White Wall below. He had never fallen from so high, yet some innate understanding convinced him that he could. He hesitated a moment longer, then let himself drop from the castle wall. His robe flapped and rustled turbulently as he plummeted downwards, and what had once appeared so far below, rushed upwards ominously to meet him. Yet he had found a sort of calm as he plunged into the night, attuned to a sort of balance in his body as it fell. His arms spread wide, and legs extended below him, he hurtled Christ-like to the narrow White Wall.

The impact was abrupt and jolting, a painful shudder which shook his very bones. He tried to balance after the jarring landing, but he could not, and the added, shifting weight of the sack made the task all the more difficult. He pitched forward, but saved himself from dropping to the Breakneck Stairs with a single hand, which shot out and clasped the top of the wall. He took hold of the White Wall with his other hand then yanked himself back atop it. He rose to his feet quickly, and without a moment's hesitation, began to run along the top of the White Wall towards where it terminated at the port. He was aware of a sharp pain in his ankle, one that lamed him in the slightest as he made his way down the motte atop the narrow wall. He could still hear the commotion of the castle, but he had begun to distance himself from it.

The port drew nearer as he raced along the White Wall, and he finally reached the bank of the Tweed. It was from where the White Wall terminated at the port, where it overlooked the dark water of the Tweed that the sentry leapt from the top of the wall towards the river below. For a time, he soared through the air and then he descended into the calm waters of the Tweed. The laden sack and his waterlogged garbs dragged him downward, yet still he swam, pulling himself frog-like along the bank beneath the river. Strangely enough, his lungs were not urgent to call for breath, nor did his heart quicken its beat. The disturbed water where he had plunged, bubbled, roiled, and then calmed, and the Tweed became as dark glass once more.

* * * *

The big bay whinnied its displeasure at a sudden rustling in the underbrush of the thicket surrounding it. Equally wary, the black mare snorted and tossed its head. A robed, hooded form appeared in the shadowy alcove where the horses were tethered.

"Ah, ah...be still," the sentry crooned in a gentle voice as he limped towards them. "Be still."

The sentry drew back his soaked hood and approached the two horses. He placed himself between them and stroked their broad necks, while the black mare nuzzled the sack that hung upon his back.

Chapter Two

Perceptions
I

The web of time seemed to spin itself all around him, as though it intended to leave him untouched by its silks of ages. It was no doubt the will of God, a sign that he had not yet fulfilled his ordained purpose. The days had become weeks and then months. Months had coalesced into years, then decades, the third of which, since his birth into a world of night, was but a clutch of seasons away. The century had turned nearly a score of years after his change, the fifteenth following the death of Christ.

Death: once strange and disturbing in both sight and concept, it had wound its way into his reality such that the prospect and carnality of it was, to him, troublingly mundane. He was unsure when he had accepted death, unsure when it had become commonplace. His mind did not seem to shed the faces of those he had killed, nor did their images dwindle. Just as his mind recalled, in perfect detail, the lands throughout which he had traveled, so, too, did it recall all the faces of those whose lives he had taken, whose blood had rushed past his lips. He remembered the way their bodies had wilted under his savagery, as death took its hold upon them. He reviled each deed, and not in so much as to feel disgust for the deed itself, but of his growing insensitivity to its performance.

The mighty huntsman, till the last, dignified and restrained, had passed some years ago. At some point, Colin had become an old man in the wake of time. His bright, red hair had dimmed in luster, thinned, and become overrun with whites and greys. So many whom the sentry had known, laughed with over ale, or fought along side, were dead, or at the very least approaching the brink of death.

Long ago, in the wilds surrounding Berwick, he had come across the great wolf in the night. It had lain upon its side, as still and hard as stone: its dried jowls twisted into an empty snarl, its eyes shrunken into its skull, its coat swaying in the gentle breeze. Never again did he see a wolf in English forests, nor in the wilds of its surrounding lands. His pack horse, the black mare, had passed sixteen years after his raid of Berwick Castle, and the big bay had grown unfit to ride a few years thereafter. He had grown fond of the two horses, accustomed to their company during the otherwise lonely nights. Together they had journeyed much of England and France as he sought the haunts of the white demons.

The horses, namely the mare, had oft been laden with treasures from the spoils the white demons tended to amass within their lairs. Infrequently, he would plunder riches from some of the vulnerable castles he came across in his travels throughout the land. After having secured valuables by either means, he would stow them in various caches throughout Northumberland; the first and largest of these being the old demon cave upon the rocky hillock, wherein he had found his first demon horde. In summation, he had begun to accumulate a substantial trove of riches, yet regardless of his growing wealth, he lived a nomadic existence, at all times upon the trail of his quarry.

Never before had he hunted such cunning and illusive prey. At first, it had seemed as though the white demons could slink out of existence, leaving only the faintest scents and traces of their presence, and he was hard pressed to detect even these. During his first two years on the hunt, he had caught and slain only one of the fiendish creatures. What was worse, he had come across the thing more by happenstance than by his skill as a tracker. The innumerable nights of fruitless hunting began to take its toll upon him, and he had suffered from maddening frustration. As the hunt had become his life, it had also become his obsession: his means of absolution, for only through it could he prove his worth to God; and those many years ago, he had seen himself as inadequate to the task in his charge from on high.

He became introspective, examining the nuances of his own nocturnal proclivities, and the more he understood about himself, the more he began to intuit about that which he hunted. Then, it was as though a veil had had been lifted from his eyes and the creatures revealed themselves to him. He learned where to look, how, when, and what for, and he was amazed by how many of them actually moved through the night. For how long had these demons crept through the dark unseen? A generation, centuries, he did not know. Equally alarming was how close he had seen them come to village and town folk as they stalked their quarries – a macabre sight indeed to see them lurking in the shadows so.

In the years that followed, he would glimpse them skulking through the dark like rats, crouched low to the ground, sniffing about with heads cocking in small spastic movements at each new sight and sound. They were wary, artful predators, nearly impossible to follow without detection. Thus, he could learn little else of them before he was forced to burst from hiding to give chase and bring them down before they vanished into the night. They seemed increasingly able to hide in plain sight – to, in a way, adopt, or a least for a time, mimic certain habits of men in order to draw near to them. In short, what he had learned, what he was learning, was that they were more intelligent than he had once thought; yet even having adopted this insight into his conception of the demon, nothing could have prepared him for what he was to discover outside the Scottish village of Cille Martainn.

II

A keen, Scottish boy of twelve years, the stableboy was short for his age, but stout of stature. Not wanting to disappoint his father, nor cause him displeasure, he had gone about his chores fastidiously. Having tended to his duties, he sat on a stool under a thatch-roofed awning built into one side of his home, adjacent to the stables. The other hostler had left for the evening, yet he remained, watching the setting sun. He tore dry morsels of bread from a small loaf, eating them with a piece of old goat cheese. The general din of clucking chickens, bleating goats and sheep, and bustling village folk had finally begun to peter. He gazed out at the open countryside surrounding the little village, and at the dense forests and mountainous hills which ringed much of the horizon. The leaves had begun to turn color, but their splendor was diminished in the fading sunlight.

It was then that he noticed a rider approaching from the south, his mount moving at a brisk walk. As the man neared, the stableboy saw that he wore a black, hooded cloak. The hood hid his features and the cloak flowed over the horse's back and haunches, undulating in the gentle autumn breeze. The man also wore a long-skirted, black tunic, a thick, dark-brown, embroidered, leather jerkin, and matching leather boots and gloves. The rider's finery proclaimed him to be a man of status, a noble of some sort perhaps; indeed his beasts were magnificent animals. The nobleman rode upon a large, dark, roan with sorrel mane and tail. Trailing behind the roan, and tethered to its saddle, was a lissome, wide-eyed, chestnut horse, with sacks secured over its back with rope.

The stableboy wondered why a noble of such evident prestige should travel the countryside without armed escort, and in the growing dark no less, when roving vagabonds, or worse, might see fit to dispossess him of his belongings. The nobleman rode into the village, an imposing figure upon the large roan. The hooves of the roan and chestnut sank into the soft earth with, deep, moist thumps that reached his ears as they approached. One of the horses discharged an airy snort as the nobleman steered them in his direction. The stableboy rose from the stool and placed the remains of his platter of food upon it. Wiping his hands on his grubby clothes, he stepped out from under the awning. The nobleman drew ever nearer until he was but a few paces from the stableboy, whereupon he brought the roan to a halt. The boy was nervous. Partly because he was in the presence of a noble and partly because the man had an eerie quality about him, the source of which he could not place. The man was imposing to say the least, a trait reinforced by the lengthy, ornate sword which, sheathed in its scabbard, hung from the man's belt. The nobleman stared down at him from atop the roan and beckoned him. The stableboy approached timidly.

"What place is this boy?" The noble inquired in a calm, solemn voice. There was something about the nobleman's stare that was so piercing that the young hostler wished to avert his eyes; yet he held the man's gaze.

"Tis...tis the village Cille Martainn, mi'lord," managed the boy. The man turned from the stableboy, looked about, then stared down at him once more.

"You shall tend to my horses."

The stableboy nodded as he spoke.

"See that they are groomed and their hooves tended to. Give them hay, clean water, and much grain. Leave their loads untouched and their bridles as they are. Should any of my possessions go astray, you and your family shall be held accountable."

"Aye, mi'lord," said the stableboy, keeping his composure as best he could. The nobleman reached into a small pouch and produced a small handful of coins.

"I trust this will be enough for their care." The man said as he outstretched his gloved hand to drop the coins into the stableboy's cupped hands. The stableboy stared at the coins wide-eyed.

"Oh...aye, mi'lord... but tis more than mi' father bade me take," he explained, but saw that the nobleman made no move to take any of the coins back. "I...I'll ne let a thing happen te yer horses, er yer goods." The stableboy said sincerely.

"See that nothing does and there shall be more coin for you and your family when I depart."

"Aye, mi'lord." The stableboy said with a smile.

* * * *

The sentry sat unmoving atop the steeple of the old church, his hood drawn back from his face, a gentle breeze caressing his black locks. Though he could not see into the stables, the barn itself was well within range of his sharp eyes. The boy tended to his horses in the stables, unaware that the sentry sat in wait nearby. From his position, he could keep a vigil of sorts upon his beasts and belongings, whilst from the vantage the steeple afforded, he could scour a moderate portion of the village and the land beyond, as he awaited the coming of demons. His eyes panned the horizon. The village was built upon a relatively flat, grassy expanse of field. Ensconced within a natural alcove, the field was half encompassed by dense forest. Beyond, wooded hillocks and grass-covered, mountainous rises loomed above the tree line. He studied the hilly landscape, examining its lofty contours. Whether it be a pair of the creatures, or a solitary demon on the prowl, if any demon did indeed hunt this village, it, or they, would approach from one of the distant hills.

He reasoned that if there were a den nearby, it would likely be atop the colossal rise to the north of the village. Of course, there was the chance he was incorrect; however, a lair upon such a rise was a safe distance from the village, and relatively inaccessible to a demon's quarry during the day, when men were most likely to happen upon a lair and find the white demons in their death-like slumber within. Perhaps the demons would use such a rise to search the darkness below, unseen from on high, much as he did now. He waited.

The sun had set a while past, yet a few people still puttered about the village. There were clouds in the sky and the moonlight was dim. He heard a vague, distant sound, one of the wooden doors being closed somewhere below him, and he watched as the boy withdrew from the stables. The boy's clothes did not sag, nor bulge with the weight of stolen coin. He was a good boy, an honest boy; he had seen it in the young one's eyes. He turned his attention to the edge of the forest, occasionally whispering to himself as he ruminated, his eyes following the winding fringes of the forest. He knew that he could not observe all sides of the village from a single vantage, and that if the lair were on one of the smaller hills on the opposite side of the village, there was a considerable possibility that a demon might stalk into the village unseen.

The thought irked him, but given the lay of the land, his reason and experience dictated that he had chosen the most feasible position from which he might intercept an encroaching demon. Thus, he sat motionless upon the steeple, gazing out at the surrounding wilds. Besides, he could only watch the entire village from atop the tallest of the surrounding rises, and doing so would place him too far from the village itself when the moment came, if it came; and so he waited.

Patience was an invaluable virtue in hunting these creatures, one which he had come to learn most arduously. Foresight and understanding, gained by means of an intimate knowledge of the creatures; these were the attributes he possessed which told him where to look and how to find them, but it was patience that was paramount in the hunt. The creatures hunted three or even four days apart, and even then might not hunt the same village or town twice in a row if there were other settlements nearby. The waiting was the hardest part – night after endless night whilst the hunt was afoot. Patience was of the essence, and so he waited further still.

The world around him had grown tranquil and quiet as he sat alone with his thoughts. Save the subtle turns of his head and his flitting, searching eyes, he was as a stone gargoyle atop the steeple, safeguarding the village throughout the night. His awareness of the passage of time was not the result of conscious effort, but rather, an innate sensation with which he kept commune. He sensed the night's denouement through the natural rhythm within him, and knew it would not be immoderately long before the first trace of light in the east. Still, there was no sign of the creatures. That they had not yet even begun their hunt with the morn so near was unlikely. Either no demon hunted the village this night, or it, they, however many there were, had already skulked into the village unseen.

If this was so, the lair was likely not where he had anticipated, though precious little could be spoken of in absolutes. Either way, his vigil had come to a close. For the first time since he had settled upon the steeple, his body began to move. He rose to his feet, took a purposeful step out into the vacant air and let himself drop to the roof of the church, his cloak splayed and flailing as it trailed him downward. He alighted in a silent crouch, and peering over the verge of the roof, leaped to the bare earth below. Drawing the black hood over his head, he began to make his way through the village.

He wound past scores of thatched huts and stinking pens. He moved noiselessly, peering around every corner, his eyes scouring the dark for the slightest movements. He slinked past a few more hovels and came to a stop near a small, dilapidated barn. From under the door and through the cracks in the wood, dim, amber light wavered from within. He was about to steer clear of the little barn, when he heard what might have been a rasping grunt, followed by a fainter utterance. Though the barn walls had fallen into disrepair, the sounds that emanated from therein were still so subdued that he could barely hear them. He wondered if a demon had brought down some innocent who had awakened to check on their beasts in the night, and so he crept towards the barn door. The outer latch had been left unfastened and it deepened his suspicion. He placed the palm of his left hand upon the wooden door. He smelt the sweet, rank odor of swine within, and heard a distinct rustling of scattered hay. Moreover, he heard a weak, guttural groan: the groan of a man. Slowly, quietly, he drew his sword, gave the door a gentle push, and then watched as it swung open inwardly.

He was so taken aback by what he saw before him that, for a moment, he could do naught but furrow his brow and squint in disbelief. The opening door revealed a large pigsty lit by a large candle. Held erect in a copper holder with a wide dish for a base, the candle had been placed upon a bail of hay. Just outside the sty itself, a scraggly-haired man, well past his prime, half stood, half squatted over a large sow, which was tethered to a gatepost by the neck. The sentry could not see much of the man's face, as his back was to him. What he did note was that the man's trousers were bunched about his ankles, his bare, wrinkled rump exposed below his slovenly shirt. What was most distressing was not his nakedness, but his clumsy, wriggling advances upon the sow, his hands clutching the haunches of the corpulent swine.

The door creaked, then moaned as it opened to its limit, and the man's head spun round to peer over his shoulder. He stared dumbstruck at the figure that had suddenly appeared in the doorway. The man's lips trembled and he blinked stupidly. The man cast his eyes to his fallen trousers, licked his lips spastically, then pursed them. His eyes now blinking with odd rapidity, he chanced a nervous, sidelong glance at the sow then looked up expectantly, fearfully, at the sentry.

The sentry's face was the picture of stolid disapproval beneath the hood, and he simply stared at the bizarre spectacle before him. He had seen strange fair in his time, but nothing so obscene as this. Whilst the two gazed at each other, the sow squealed vehemently and gave a sudden tug against its restraint. Again, the man glanced down at the sow and, with a guilty countenance, stared up at the sentry once more. The sentry turned from the man without expression and stepped out of the doorway back into night. He paused for a moment, and then turned his head as if to peer at the man over his shoulder, though he made no real effort to look upon the wretch.

"Your name is...Brian?" he inquired in a casual, somber tone.

The man licked his lips and blinked anxiously as he stammered in reply.

"Ah...ah...B...Biron...m...my lord."

The sentry faced forward and stole back out into the village. He fought to hold back a smile. Colin had gotten his name right after all.

* * * *

The sentry made his way through what appeared to be a more prosperous quarter of Cille Martainn. As was his way, he skirted the domiciles and rickety shops in absolute silence, clinging to the shadows they cast in the moonlit village, moving through the darkest of darks to remain unseen. Once unsettled, perhaps even timorous during such prowls, he moved through Cille Martainn masterfully, with the utmost poise and confidence. He neared a large, rectangular structure fashioned out of halved logs. As he was downwind of the structure, he detected the acrid scent of aging ale from within it almost instantaneously, and assumed it must be a tavern. Slumbering with his back propped against the wall of the tavern was a drunken vagrant, whose heavy stink reached his nostrils with equal immediacy. From where he stood in the shadows, his back nearly pressed against a large thatched hut, the sentry observed the vagrant.

The man's face was smeared with grime, and his beard was a filthy brownish tangle. So scrawny was he that he appeared half starved, his gaunt face revealing the contours of his skull. The vagrant's mouth hung agape as he slept and he drooled ale-tainted spittle upon his tattered, muddied clothes. A part of him felt pity for this enfeebled unfortunate, whilst another part of him, an iniquitous, instinctual side, felt something else entirely. He combated the instinct and repressed it, as he had done countless times before whilst the compulsion was manageable; and he would restrain himself thus until the instinct became an inescapable necessity.

He registered a sudden movement out of the corner of his eye, which divorced him from his thoughts. He turned his head in the direction he had perceived movement, and seeing naught but the darkened village before him, leaned out from where he was concealed for a broader scope of things. Still, he saw nothing. Then, quite abruptly, a man appeared between two large, wooden sheds. The sheds were no more than fifty paces from the tavern, perhaps another twenty from where he stood with his back to the hut. The man was blanketed in darkness between the sheds, but the sentry's sharp eyes could still make out his form, though the man's face was shrouded in a copious, dark hood. His garbs were those of a peasant, but they were torn and looked to be horribly squalid from what he could discern. Conceivably, the man was another vagrant, another drunkard stumbling about the vicinity of the tavern, addled with ale.

Nonetheless, he could not help but feel that there was something awry, something strange about man in the shadows. It was the way he moved, his stooped, feline poise: the way his head would cock at the subtlest sounds, like an attentive falcon on the wing, the way he seemed to sniff at the night air, the nimble, deft manner with which he crept through the darkness. The sentry watched the hooded figure steal forth from the shadows and warily emerge into the pale moonlight. It was then that he saw the bare feet and hands, pale as the very moonlight which bathed them, and tipped with menacing, black claws: a demon on the scent of its prey.

The demon rounded the shed nearest the tavern and came to

an abrupt halt. It took a step back towards the shadows, crouched low, then cocked its head. Though he could not see the thing's face, he was well aware that it was staring intently at the sleeping vagrant. The thing was eerie to look upon, and not simply because he knew what it intended, but because he had never seen one of the creatures masquerade as man so cleverly as this one. Even with what little he had come to understand of these creatures, there was little doubt they possessed some capacity to think and learn, and it was this that disturbed him most.

The sentry observed a change in the demon's posture, in the very attitude of its body. The demon leaned forward from where it crouched, half hidden in the shadow of the shed, regarding the vagrant with keen interest. Then, it took a measured, purposeful step forward, locking its hooded gaze upon the slumbering drunkard with unwavering focus.

The sentry knew that having spotted its quarry, it would not be long before the demon was upon the vagrant; yet he dared not move with the demon still so distant from where he hid, lest he send it scurrying into the darkness with he too far upon its heels. He watched as the thing stalked forward, closing on its prey in silence and with increasing rapidity until, driven to frenzy by the primal instincts within it, it sprang into a mad dash, not a score of paces from the vagrant. The thing launched itself so suddenly, that even as the sentry burst from the shadows beyond the hut at full tilt, the demon had all but closed the gap between it and the sleeping man. The demon must have spotted him from the corner of its eye, for it dug its clawed feet into the dirt, tossing up flecks of earth and swirling dust as it came to an abrupt halt.

The thing crouched low once more and took a few hesitant steps away from the onrushing sentry. Much like others he had hunted, the thing was confounded, unsure what to make of him. It appeared to be torn between fight or flight, uncertain if he were prey, fellow, or foe. It seemed to study him as he gained the distance between them, and just as he reached for the hilt of his sword, it emitted a feral growl from under the hood, turned tail, and darted for the sheds. Knowing he would need the full measure of his speed, the sentry released the hilt to free his hand and sprinted after the fleeing creature. It hastened into the dark passage between the two sheds with the sentry trailing close behind, his cloak streaming out after him as a thing in flight.

The sentry turned into the passage in time to see the white demon scamper out of view to the left. The sentry followed, erupting from the passage at a sharp angle, kicking up dust from under his boots. He caught sight of the demon as he rounded the corner of the shed, and saw that it was headed towards a dense assemblage of dwellings. He pressed the chase with the tenacity of a hound on the heels of a fox as they swept through the village. The demon veered in amongst the villager's homes in what seemed to be an attempt to elude the sentry, who followed at an unshakeable pace as they raced amidst the dwellings. The chase became a series of abrupt twists and turns as the sentry followed the demon's erratic path.

Upon occasion, he would lose sight of the demon for the briefest of instants as it weaved amidst the darkened passages, and he was forced to catch sight of it once more as he burst into and out of the passages himself. He had only just glimpsed the demon after one such evasion when, in mid stride, the demon made a sudden leap upwards to one side. Its tattered garb fluttered behind it as it rose into the air, and he nearly lost sight of it beyond a nearby roof as it alighted upon the slate shingles in an agile crouch on the far side of the rooftop. He reacted instinctually, without thought, or reason, simply following his prey wherever it might run.

Abruptly, he too propelled himself skyward, lifting into air above the roof. The demon spun round where it had hunkered atop the roof; their eyes met as he soared through the air towards it, his lofty form silhouetted by the moon. The demon leapt towards an adjacent roof as the sentry descended where the thing had been crouched an instant before. The wooden supports beneath the shingles creaked as he landed, and again as he sprang from the verge of the roof in pursuit of the demon.

They were as dark specters, leaping from roof to roof with preternatural speed and ability as they traversed the village high above the ground. They were fleeting forms lancing through the night, ethereally illumined by the moon above. The sentry's heaving breaths left him in vaporous plumes, which, albescent in the moonlight, swirled and dispersed in his wake. Hard as he tried, he could not close upon the demon, nor could it outdistance him. Still, he pursued the thing relentlessly, as though he would chase it to the ends of the earth, and though the demon never looked back, it heard the tireless footfalls at its heels, and so it too kept on.

The sentry watched as the demon sprang high from a stout hut up towards the rooftop of a large, wooden construct. Invariably, he followed its path. The demon had appeared to vanish beyond the edge of the roof and as he himself ascended into the air; clearing the thatch upon the roof of the construct, he saw why. The weight of the alighting demon had collapsed a trough-sized portion of the roof, through which one of its legs had sunk to the waist. The demon partially righted itself upon its arms and its sole, free shank, and with frantic effort, began to withdraw its leg from where it had punched through the roof as the sentry dropped from the night sky mere arm spans from it. As the sentry touched down upon the thatch, his eyes fixed upon his fallen quarry with murderous intent, a distinct splintering sound erupted from the wooden framework of the roof beneath them, and an expanse of the roof suddenly gave way under their weights.

They fell into the darkened room below amidst a cascade of thatch and broken timber. The sentry came to ground upon hand and foot, causing a sparse cloud of dust to rise from the hard, earthen floor beneath him. He tucked his head into his chest as the last of the debris rained down upon him from above. He heard something weighty fall to the ground nearby, accompanied by what sounded to be the clatter of metal implements. When he looked up, he spied the demon bringing itself to a crouch beside a wrecked, overturned rack of metalwork, which it must have struck as it fell. Its back partially facing him, the demon seemed to be grasping at something that lay on the ground beneath a scattering of debris.

He allowed himself a brief assessment of his surroundings, and presumed that they had fallen into what must be a storage room for the village smithy. The sentry rose to his feet, sending a flurry of dust and strands of thatch drifting to the ground from his cloak. He was about to charge the demon when, to his utter surprise, it whirled round with a sword in hand, which it must have found laying near the fallen rack of metalwork. For a moment, the sentry went still, the point of the blade wavering mere hands' breadths from his face. The demon remained in a low, wary crouch, its back arched and hackles raised like a cornered cat. The large hood had fallen from its head, revealing its animalistic countenance, upon which emotion was undeniably writ. He saw fear in the demon's vivid, gleaming eyes, and the bestial hand which held the sword aloft, trembled ever so faintly.

Never before had a demon confronted him with weapon in hand, and yet it was not trepidation he felt as he looked upon the creature, but something entirely contrary. The demon gripped the sword in a most unbalanced, unpracticed manner, holding out the blade as a hunched mendicant would hold a begging pan in the streets. The demon appeared to have no real understanding in the art of a sword, and he wondered why it should choose to face him with a weapon it had no mastery of. He realized that just as the demon clothed itself in the garbs of men through its propensity for mimicry, so too did it seek to defend itself in a fashion it had seen performed, but did not truly comprehend. It was not unlike a child that took up its father's blade, standing fearful in the midst of marauding, seasoned warriors.

Wary of the sentry, the demon took an awkward step forward, slashed at him clumsily, then lowered back into its defensive crouch. The sentry easily evaded the wild swing, taking a deft, sidelong step and tilting his hooded head to one side. There was a sudden, rising commotion from a brick-walled antechamber behind him, and he turned his head to peer over his shoulder. The tumult was somewhat dampened, for it sounded from beyond a closed door, and thus he did not see the affrighted villagers. Undoubtedly the startled shouts were those of the resident blacksmith, and the shriller cries those of his wife and child. The din had prompted the demon into instantaneous flight, so that even before the sentry turned his head to face the demon once more, the creature made a sudden dash for a nearby door.

Upon reaching the door it did not slow it the slightest, but dipped as it ran, and with tremendous force, battered the door with its shoulder. With a loud crack and a splintering of wood, the busted door swung wide open into the night, hanging limply from its remaining, demolished hinge as the demon streaked past. The sentry bounded into a sprint, following the demon through the doorway and into the night.

* * * *

Once more, the demon weaved its way through the village with the sentry at its heels. For a short time, the demon carried the sword it had taken with it, as though the mere possession of it might protect it like some holy relic. With one arm outstretched, the creature dragged the sword behind it carelessly, the blade flailing about, its tip jouncing over the dirt. Carrying the blade in this manner hampered the demon's movement, and it soon abandoned the weapon as the sentry began to close upon it. The sentry drove the demon past the fringes of the village and on into Cille Martainn Glen, a glen of green fields and the ancient standing stones of Celts long dead.

As before, the sentry could not gain the distance between him and the fleeing demon, and it seemed as though they were locked in a hunt eternal. He was inclined to believe that this demon was more fleet of foot than any he had ever encountered. Never before had he been on the chase so long, and he knew that they could both continue thus till daybreak, but to what end. He pursued the demon through the glen, through a surrounding forest and over increasingly hilly landscape, until the inevitable occurred; the east was suffused with the light of the coming morn.

The western skyline at their back was still dark as they raced up the face of a lofty, grassy rise. Both were breathing heavily now, their hearts pounding within their chests, their muscles stiffening from their exertion. Beyond the rise, the sun had but barely begun to lift itself from the earth. Upon the face of the rise, still shaded by the fading night, the demon reached the summit with the sentry close behind. The sentry watched as the demon leapt the remained distance to the peak of the rise. It was suddenly illuminated by a fiery, pastel brilliance as it burst up over the summit. So close was he to the demon, that in the next instant, he too was bathed in the rich radiance. Before him, the demon yowled in agony, a throaty, mated sound of man and beast. It turned from the burgeoning light of the east, its eyes tightly shut, its pale, clawed hands clutched over its eyes and heavily muscled brow. The light caused his own eyes discomfort as well, yet so infantile a sunrise as this did not render him so stricken as the writhing demon before him.

The thing staggered about blindly for a moment, and seeing his opportunity, the sentry drew his sword. It sang as it was slid free of his scabbard. In what must have been an act of desperation, the demon, snarling impotently, forced its eyes to open into narrow slits as the sentry lunged towards it. Gripping the hilt of the great Tizona with both hands, and pointing the blade outward, he quickly leveled the sword at his waist and then drove the blade forward into the demon's chest. He thrust the blade up under the demon's breastbone until the sharp tip ground to a halt within the thing, as it lodged against its spine. The demon's mouth opened wide, its fangs bared, a look of pain and rage upon its fearsome aspect. A horrid, rasping howl erupted from its throat, and with both its ashen talons, it seized the length of blade that had not been impelled into its body.

The demon strained to free itself from the sword upon which it was impaled, but the sentry strode forward, his sword held in an iron grip as he shifted the blade within the thing, driving it upwards in its chest, as though he intended to lift the demon from its feet. The demon roared, sending forth dark flecks of blood from the gullet of its yawning maw, as it glared at him vengefully through quivering, narrowed slits. With sudden fury, it lurched forward and slashed at him with its claws, gashing him along the jaw. The sentry's head reeled to one side, and the black hood fell away from his dark locks. His lips curled into a daunting snarl, and a sonorous, rumbling growl resonated from his throat.

The demon's body jerked violently as the sentry twisted the blade within it with savage force, and the thing hunched forward in agony. The jolt shook the tip of the blade free from the demon's spine, and as the sentry drove the sword forward a final time, the blade slipped between the thing's ribs, bore through flesh and cloth, and jutted out from its back. He ran the blade clean through the demon, so that they stood with their faces a mere hand's breadth apart. The demon's blood ran in rivulets down the hilt of the sword and over the sentry's hands. It clutched the sentry's forearms in an icy, unmoving grip, as though it were bracing itself for the death he would soon deliver. The demon's limbs began to tremble, and its breaths had become shallow gasps. It was as though some of the ferocity had left the creature, and most disturbingly, it seemed to stare at him with a look he could only interpret as betrayal.

The demon slumped to its knees, still gazing upon him with its vivid, yellow eyes, the pupils within shrunken to mere pinpricks in morning light. The sentry hauled his sword free of the demon's body, releasing a stream of its warm blood. He tore his arm free of the demon's clutches and seized it by its mane, whilst, with his sword arm, he lifted his gore-streaked blade into the air. The demon simply stared up at him with glassy, liquescent eyes, its tongue lolling within its hanging jaw. A harsh, grating sound came forth from the demon's throat, and to his utter astonishment, the demon spoke.

"Q...quahkd nutrihkt...d...de...detrihkt."

The sentry could do naught but listen to the strange, chilling words which the white demon spoke. With his sword poised in the air, he froze in disbelief, and stared down at the demon wide-eyed. He hesitated a moment longer, then twice brought the blade down upon it with merciless savagery whilst he held it firmly by the mane, sundering its head from its body. The demon's lifeless body toppled to a side, blood pulsing from the hewed neck. The sentry let the head drop at his feet, his mind tortured by the sound of the demon's rasping voice as he recalled its strange words. The sentry stared down at the gruesome carcass at his feet, and pulled his hood over his head to avert the light of the dawn. He wiped his blade clean on the demon's pilfered garbs, and then sheathed it in his scabbard. He turned from the summit, from the bloodied body atop it, and began to walk down the dark face of the rise. He looked about him, then up towards the brightening sky, and saw that he would not have time to find shelter in the lands surrounding Cille Martainn. He quickly removed his gloves and pocketed them, turned, spread his legs, and stooped towards the ground.

He began to dig into the face of the rise, frantically tearing into the earth like a clawed beast. He slung showers of grass and soil through his legs, and he had soon formed a gaping, earthy depression on the face of the rise. He burrowed deeper and deeper into the soil, until his whole body could fit inside the hollow. Still, he kept on, digging indefatigably, tossing cool, dark earth upwards as he bore downwards into the ground. When he reached an acceptable depth, he backed out of the burrow. He squinted painfully in the light. By the brightness of the sky, the sun was nearly half risen. He lowered to the ground, half scooping, half embracing the large pile of earth which had accumulated near the mouth of burrow, and slid into the opening backwards, hauling much of the soil with him. With this soil and damper earth from within, he firmly occluded the opening to the burrow, and then lay to rest in the darkness.

His last thoughts were of the demon's words, unlike anything he ever heard, and yet somehow familiar. He felt that its words were, in a sense, comparable to Latin, and with this thought he unraveled the mystery of the demon's words.

"Quahkd nutrihkt detrihkt," he whispered to himself. "Quad me nutrit me destruit...that which nourishes me, also destroys me."

It had spoken in a base and most rudimentary manner, yet its words had held undeniable meaning. He closed his eyes and his breathing softened. The beat of his heart slowed to a single, languid pulse, and all thought was lost.

Chapter Three

I Am Gabriel

Sebastian Klyne stirred torpidly before taking a deep, somnolent inhalation. His eyes opened rather slowly, and he allowed them to do so with considerable disappointment. This had been one of the only nights he had been able to lay down without pain, from his neck in particular. Only days earlier, with irritating regularity, he had been waking in the dead of night with throbbing pains in his neck or leg from any untoward movement he had made in his sleep. He had hoped to sleep through the night, to get up feeling at least moderately refreshed the next morning; but it seemed this was not to be. It was not even pain, or discomfort that had awakened him, but the routine of his recent sleeping pattern; his body, it seemed, had simply roused itself out of habit. He put a hand to his neck to insure he had not disturbed the position of the large gauze pad in his sleep. Dr. Canterberry had removed the spongy neck brace a few days ago and substituted it with a gauze pad secured by large bandages. This new dressing allowed Sebastian much greater mobility of his neck, and was not nearly so stifling and irritating as the neck brace.

It had been well over a week since the beginning of his convalescence at the facility, and thus far, his stay had been more than pleasant, if somewhat restricted. He had been confined to his bed with an intravenous feed until such time as Dr. Canterberry had felt that he was safely past any risk of anemia. He had then been transferred from the hospice room to one of the few sleeping quarters in the opposite wing of the building, on the opposite side of the steel doors. Dr. Canterberry, and perhaps even the doctor's employer, had seen that his room was furnished with all the creature comforts he required, including a laptop – though he could not access the Internet: a television, an alarm clock, clothes, food, and various toiletries, and he discovered that the facility itself boasted a number of amenities. He was, however, confined to the third floor: a floor solely accessible to employees with level-three clearance. Dr. Canterberry explained that it was simply a measure to keep his presence at the facility secret from those members of staff who were a level-two clearance or lower, which was essentially everyone else in the facility. In the time he had spent at the facility, he had only spoken to two people. There was, of course, Dr. Canterberry, with whom he chatted daily, and, to a significantly lesser degree, he would converse with the comparatively reserved Dr. Ling, the geneticist who often worked with Dr. Canterberry.

Sebastian turned his head on the pillow gingerly and glanced at the alarm clock on the night table; it read three-twenty in the morning. The red glow from the digital numbers limned the smooth surface of the night table and the edges of his pillow, covers, and bed in a soft scarlet. It was the only source of light at the moment, for the room had no windows to let in the city lights. He tried to force himself back into slumber, but ended up doing nothing more than stirring his thoughts into further wakefulness. He stared up at the ceiling for a while, and after emitting a defeated exhalation, he came to grips with the fact that he could not sleep and eased himself into a sitting position against the headboard with a pillow propped up behind him.

He grabbed a remote from where it lay beside the alarm clock and turned on the television. The television blipped on and, to some degree, illuminated the room with its fluctuating phosphorescence. Sebastian began to flip through the stations, yawning as he did so. He stopped on a news station, in which a female newscaster, with a flattering suit, was recounting a recent sting operation in the typical, removed intonation befitting a newscaster. What had made him stop on the channel was that in the background behind the newscaster, in the upper, right-hand quadrant of the television screen, one of his commanding officers was giving an interview. The interview had obviously taken place prior to this particular airing, as the officer was doing the interview in broad daylight. Sebastian could only just hear the officer's deep drawl beyond the newscaster's domineering voice. The interview soon became the prime focus and the screen changed accordingly, in that the officer's face now occupied the full expanse of the screen, and the newscaster had fallen silent.

Sebastian had a sudden desire for the English tea Dr. Canterberry had introduced him to, and decided he would indulge himself. He uncovered himself, tossing the covers to one side with a single hand. He then swiveled his legs off the bed with some care until he was sitting upright on the edge of the bed. He was reaching for the crutches Dr. Canterberry had given him a little while ago, when he heard the newscaster speak his name. He looked up at the television screen and saw that the newscaster had taken center stage once more. He also noted the still photograph of his face in the upper, right-hand quadrant of the screen, where the officer's interview had initially taken place. For a moment, he sat and stared. Of course he knew that the state, perhaps even a moderate portion of the country presumed him missing, Dr. Canterberry had made him aware of that fact some time ago, and had assured him that the situation would soon be addressed.

The day following his first night at the facility, Dr. Canterberry had gone over a general plan for his resurfacing into the public eye. However, it was his first time seeing this particular account of the Haitian sting on television and it was strange to hear the newscaster speak about him as though he were dead when he was in fact watching the newscast in relative comfort. He wondered how some of the boys at work would react when he simply showed up one day, and with that thought, he recalled Dr. Canterberry's proposition:

"You are to call your station to tell them you are alive and well," Dr. Canterberry had begun. "You will take a taxi and call the station en route, from the driver's cell phone. We will give you money for the taxi, and for the added incentive to coerce the driver into letting you use his phone. When your superiors inquire as to where you have been, you will tell them that two Russian men, one—"

"Because of the Russian mob involvement in the sting?" Sebastian had asked.

"Precisely." The doctor had answered. "Two men, one tall and somewhat slender, the other shorter and stockier, happened to run into you after you...ahm...saw to that Haitian fellow. It would be prudent to say that one of the Russians shot you in the thigh and that they then took you hostage for leverage in case they did not make it out of the secured perimeter without getting caught... ahm...in their car of course...black car don't forget to mention, because we were seen and followed...though I am not sure you would recall, poor chap. Ahm...anyhow, it should follow that a while after they cleared the perimeter, you tried to escape and were shot in the neck as you did. Perhaps you wrestle with the gun as you fight to unlock the car door or something the like, so that in the end, you are catapulted out of the moving vehicle, out into the dark somewhere. Either way, they leave you for dead.

Then, fortunate for you, a caring citizen, a former doctor no less, who is adamant on remaining anonymous because of prior malpractice suits, happens to find you and takes you to his private clinic. You wake from a coma a week and some days later. The doctor agrees to drive you somewhere close to home, but requests that you be blindfolded to save himself from the possibility of any future hassles, and you oblige out of courtesy for his hospice... ahm...because if you didn't, then the police would simply ask you to lead them to this doctor for questioning, and seeing how said doctor does not actually exist, it might bring some degree of suspicion down upon you. Well then...the doctor then drops you off at a payphone, one that we will designate at a later date. You call the taxi from the payphone and...well...there you have it."

Sebastian let his thoughts slip from his mind and was reawakened to his current hankering for a hot cup of the doctor's tea. Sebastian took the crutches from where they were propped against the wall near the bedside and rose to his feet using his good leg. He slipped a crutch under each of his armpits and, leaving the television on, made his way to the door. He hobbled through a stretch of the dimly lit hallway towards the third floor lounge. There was no door into the lounge; on one side, the hallway simply opened into a lavish, warmly lit alcove, semicircular in design. A large plasma screen television was mounted on the concavity that was the inner wall of the lounge and a collection of soft couches sat before it. Along the curved wall, to either side of the television, were cupboards filled with life's necessities and comforts, as well as an array of kitchen appliances and two burnished countertops, which conformed to the bend of the wall.

He hobbled over to the cupboard in which the Earl Grey was kept, and took a single teabag. He removed a teapot from a cupboard beneath one of the counters and filled it with water at the closest sink. He left the water to boil on the stove and made his way to the couch nearest the remote. He sank into the couch with some relief and lifted his injured leg to rest it along the length of the couch. He set down the crutches then picked up the remote from the glass coffee table beside him. He turned on the television and began to flip through the channels. He stopped when he saw a night scene from Jurassic Park, in which Ian Malcolm, played by Jeff Goldblum, demanded, in a most comical fashion, that the driver of their jeep go faster to escape a pursuing tyrannosaurus. He had only been watching the movie for a short while when the teapot began to whistle. Using a single crutch to free one of his hands, he limped to the stove, removed the teapot, and prepared his tea. He was back on the couch in five minutes with a steaming cup of Earl Grey on the glass coffee table next to him. He drank the tea in small sips, and watched the movie through to its climax.

His restlessness began to diminish and he welcomed his sudden fatigue. He tidied the lounge and then hobbled back to his room through the dimly lit hallway. He had left the door open and so he heard the faint rambling of voices from the television even before he entered his room. He ambled through the doorway, and quite by accident, knocked over the small garbage can to the right of the door with a crutch. He let a mild curse slip, and removing the crutches from under his arms, he lowered himself to the floor on his good leg. He righted the garbage can and was in the process of rising to his feet, when he heard a hard, solemn voice from somewhere within the room behind him. The room was not an extremely large one, and the proximity of the voice startled him as it imposed itself upon the relative quiet of the room.

"Trouble sleeping, Officer Klyne?"

Sebastian spun around awkwardly, heedful of his knitting wounds. Against the wall opposite the bed, a few meters from the television, was a table upon which he had placed the laptop Dr. Canterberry had given him. Sitting on the table, in a most casual fashion, with one foot on the seat of a chair and the other resting flat on the floor, was a formidable-looking man dressed all in black. The man remained absolutely still, and in his long, flowing, black coat, which served to obscure his form in the meager light, he seemed able to blend into the shadows. The man's elbows were rested overtop of his single, bent knee, his forearms crossed in a manner which denoted a limitless patience.

The man sat where the television did not cast its dim, flickering glow directly upon him, yet even so veiled by diaphanous shadow, Sebastian had the vague sense that the man's hands and face were rather pale in a way; and when he met the man's piercing gaze, he noted the strange quality his eyes bore in the partial darkness. This was without doubt the proprietor of the facility. Sebastian's eyes were unnaturally wide, and his jaw hung slack.

"Oh...um...y...you must be...um...Gabriel," Sebastian stammered as he clumsily tucked the crutches under his arms once more. Sebastian was understandably shaken given the man's dining predilection, and Gabriel's presence was so stately and eerie that Sebastian was inclined to take a step away from him. He did so unconsciously, and awkwardly, for his body had stiffened with fright. One of his crutches stubbed against something and he stumbled backward, wincing from the immediate pain his neck and thigh issued in response to his sudden, reflexive movements. He lost his balance and was about to topple when his back struck the length of wall next to the door, which kept him on his feet, albeit jarringly.

As he struck the wall, Sebastian felt a slight prominence at his back give with a soft click, and the room was suddenly flooded with light from above. He blinked as his eyes adjusted to the light, and he turned to find Gabriel with his head averted, his torso twisted to one side, and his eyes buried in the crook of his right arm so that his black locks fell about his hidden face. With his legs in the same, casual position, he calmly lifted his left arm and pointed directly past Sebastian with the dark-clawed forefinger of his pale hand.

"I would appreciate it if you turned that off," said Gabriel in a nonchalant tone. Sebastian simply stared at Gabriel for a moment, wanting to apologize, but too horrified by the thought that he might have angered Gabriel to do so. Sebastian leaned away from the wall and reached for the light switch with his left hand, finally managing a nearly incoherent apology.

"Uh...sorry," uttered Sebastian. "Sorry about that," he reasserted after clearing his throat once the lights were out again. Gabriel assumed his former poise. For Sebastian, the brief silence that followed was far too awkward for him to bear and he blurted the first thing that came to mind.

"I...uh...thought that the only...I thought that sunlight was the thing that was bad for...you guys."

"Any visible light past a certain degree of intensity is unfavorable to nocturnal eyes," Gabriel responded flatly.

"Oh...yeah...of course."

Gabriel touched the pointed tips of his blackish nails to the laptop, which lay beside him on the table. He glanced at it then returned his stern gaze to Sebastian.

"I trust that all the conveniences you require have been seen to thus far?"

"Yeah...yeah, Doctor C has been great. He's gone out of his way to help me from the very beginning. He's been great to talk to as well. He's allowed me to understand so much about things I had no idea about... Dr. Ling too, when I see him. I...um...I have to thank you for all you have provided me with, I mean this is your facility, so...thanks for having me...and...um...not eating me."

As Gabriel raised a single hand and gestured towards the bed, Sebastian thought he saw the slightest trace of what might have been amusement on his shadowed face.

"No need to stand on ceremony, Officer Klyne, especially with such injuries. Please...make yourself comfortable."

Sebastian secured the crutches underneath him and hobbled to the bedside. He lowered himself on the edge of the bed and lifted his legs onto it, propping his back against the headboard as he had done earlier.

"How are you feeling today, Officer Klyne?"

"Better...um...yeah, pretty good." Sebastian replied.

"Good, because we can't hide you from the world forever. I find myself in a precarious position," Gabriel began. "I have taken great care to keep the secrets of this facility from the outside world, insuring the safety of this place and of its employees. It is no easy thing to hide in plain sight, to avoid the suspicions of this metropolis with which I must interact in multifarious ways. It has taken me more lifetimes than you could ever dream to live to establish this enterprise and all its intricacies. You..." Sebastian's jaw tightened and his stomach began to knot upon Gabriel's sudden reference to him, "stumbled upon something extraordinary to your experience, something which you were not meant to see. Nigel is a saint with regards to his morality, and I cannot rebuke him for it, but if not for his compunctions, you would never have been brought here, and but for his carelessness, you were not to have seen what you have. Last week, Nigel discussed with me the prospect of your employment; he spoke highly of you and somehow convinced me to acquiesce. He told me later that you had whole-heartedly accepted what we might offer, and I do trust his judgment...but you...you, I do not know. You potentially jeopardize all that we have."

Gabriel fell silent, staring into the depths of Sebastian's eyes in such an austere, expectant manner, that this time the silence was more than awkward for Sebastian; it was nothing short of terrifying. Sebastian felt his chest tensing, and his breaths grew somewhat tremulous.

"I...uh...I understand where you're coming from," he swallowed. "I realize that all this is bigger than me, and that you don't have any real, concrete reason to trust me...yet. But, like I told Dr. C, I can be part of this...I want to know about this world inside my world, I need to know. I mean, come on, I'm SWAT, I live a life of action and I know how to keep a secret. In the past week, I've learned things people haven't known for...I don't even know how long. I want to do this. I will do whatever I have to do to prove myself. I'll call in and quit my job right now if you want me to... whatever it takes, man."

"Whatever it takes?" Gabriel repeated as he eyed Sebastian with some scrutiny.

"Well...as long as it doesn't involve me killing some innocent civilian or something...yeah."

Gabriel nodded slowly, as though he were satisfied by this single reply.

"And why should I take such a risk?"

Sebastian breathed in deeply and stared down at floor contemplatively. After a brief moment's hesitation he looked back up at Gabriel.

"You say you trust Dr. C...that trust had to begin somewhere. Now, I know that you didn't just run into him like it happened with me. He told me you had been observing him for some time, analyzing his background, studying who he was and weighing out whether he would be the one for you to put some faith in...I know... I get it...but Dr. C must have told you about my background. You can check it out for yourself, though I'm sure you already have. Listen, all I have is my job and my shitty apartment. My dad died about three years ago, my mother left us when I was three, I'm an only child...I haven't even had a date for like five weeks...I've got no baggage, nothing to hold me back and besides...it's better pay." Gabriel subtly raised a single eyebrow. "I'm just saying," Sebastian said defensively, with both hands raised in exclamation. "I'm in. I'm in in a way that counts...I...I'm in...Gabriel."

Gabriel simply stared at him, and it appeared as though his frightening eyes were peering straight through him, to detect his whitest of lies, to uncover his deepest of secrets. After a time, the intensity in Gabriel's eyes and upon his countenance seemed to diminish. At this, Sebastian released the breath that had been trapped in his lungs.

"You will be monitored by those who wittingly or unwittingly work for me. You will follow my directions and heed all the rules of conduct to which ranking employees of this facility adhere. If you deliberately place the safety of this facility or its employees in danger, you must be prepared to face certain consequences."

"I'm sure I don't want to know," Sebastian said earnestly. "But like I said...I'm in."

"Good," Gabriel answered with a sudden calm in voice. "You start your first assignment tomorrow night."

Sebastian's face sank in disbelief.

"Tomorrow?"

"Problem?" Gabriel inquired innocently.

"Um...no...but I hope you don't need me in the field or something," said Sebastian as he glanced at the wound on his thigh. "I'm still kind of handicapped at the moment."

"That won't be a problem," Gabriel assured him. "As I'm sure you are aware, the subject of your recent absence has made the news, not exactly front page stuff, but your face is in the media nonetheless. We are going to have to return you to everyday life so that any ongoing investigations into your disappearance are halted immediately, and so that we can get you out of the news as quickly as possible. You won't have to quit your job. I want you in place over there, at least for now. I trust Nigel was thorough in his rendition of how it is you are to...reappear."

"Yeah...I...um...I've got it."

"There are a few details that have been ironed out, but those can wait till morning. In the meantime, I suggest you get some sleep, Officer Klyne."

Gabriel turned from Sebastian and began to lift himself from the table.

"Sebastian," offered the young officer.

Gabriel returned his gaze to Officer Klyne.

"I mean...if that's cool with you...just call me Sebastian."

"All right," Gabriel answered impartially after seemingly inspecting him for a moment with his chilling eyes. "Sebastian."

Gabriel rose from the table.

"Hey...um," Sebastian exclaimed hesitantly. "Could I ask you something? Maybe a couple things, actually."

Gabriel faced Sebastian once more, stared at him briefly, his aspect unexpressive as he slowly sank back into his previous sitting position. Gabriel said nothing in response, but regarded Sebastian unwaveringly and expectantly.

"I do have an intelligent question after this one...really...but I just have to know this first. I'm curious, if I had kept the lights on, would your skin have, like, charred into dust or something? What's...how does that work?"

"Hm," Gabriel uttered disapprovingly, with a near-imperceptible shake of his head. "Obviously, Nigel didn't do as good a job in explaining things as I thought he would." He paused, perhaps collecting his thoughts. "As I mentioned earlier, it is what light does to our inner eye that is immediately damaging. Artificial light in general does not have an overly ravaging effect on exposed skin...some blotchiness and general topical irritation over a substantial amount of time, not much else. We are still simply creatures of flesh and blood after all, so logic would dictate that we would not simply...disintegrate...or what have you, when exposed to light. However, Nigel and I have found that the sun and certain other forms of more intense radiation, to which our essentially pigmentless skins have no defense, elicit the formation of severe, bleeding rashes and suppurative sores on flesh exposed to said radiation for longer than six hours.

"Oh," Sebastian replied contemplatively. "Could that kill you or..."

Gabriel shook his head dismissively.

"Aside from the fact that you would never find them or I out during the day, all that is needed is to feed and fall into diapause, allowing the body to heal and rejuvenate. Nigel must have spoken to you about the restive state in which the diurnal hours are spent."

Sebastian nodded.

"What Dr. C didn't cover is what I want to ask you now." Sebastian cleared his throat as he repositioned himself on the bed. "Dr. C told me that the vampires are a distinct species, and that, within the range of...I guess...individual variability, they are all like the one you guys keep up here in that lab to run tests on. By the way, that thing was a sight I won't ever forget...scary as hell. It looked so...kind of like an animal or something...that face, the pointed ears...it looked...I don't know. And you...you share so many of their characteristics...I mean, basically you are like them; you are a vampire, but at the same time, you're not. Like...your skin tone is not that much lighter than some Eastern Europeans I've known...other than that and a couple other features, you look exactly like any dude I might see at the gym or something."

Sebastian regarded Gabriel attentively, evidently hoping for some explanation that could resolve his confusion. Gabriel stared at him steadily, his face inexpressive, but behind his eyes he seemed thoughtful, as though he were recalling memories long past.

"I was not always what I am now. I was born into the world of men...human. I was...much like you at your age. Far from here, long before you were born, a hunting vampire came to me in the night. I was battered, broken, and mangled. However, during the course of our struggle, I inflicted grievous wounds on the thing, and from its ruptured flesh and veins, its leprous blood flowed into the gashes it had torn into me. My fate was sealed then." Gabriel's eyes seemed to regain their composed, even cold, purposeful stare. "It is not their bite, or even their blood alone that can have this...effect." He gestured at his own body with the short, pointed claws of his hands. "It is the cells of their underlying tissue, hidden within their flesh, the primordial cells Nigel has spoken of, the vampires' archaic essence. I had hewed the vampire to such a depth, that these primordial cells were torn free from their vacuoles, and spilled into the vampire's flowing blood, which, serving as a vector, carried the cells into my open wounds."

"So, how did that collection of the vampire's primordial cells... change you?" asked Sebastian.

"In the vampire, the replication of primordial cells is mediated and kept in check by the surrounding vampiric cells and various other inhibitors unique to the vampire. If, by chance, a mutation occurs after a primordial cell division, the resultant aberrant cell, or cells are identified and destroyed. In my body, however, a more...accommodating environment...the primordial cells began to divide without such restrictions, and as far as Nigel can tell, somehow, for some reason, an aberrant strain arose, which, self-replicating like some immortal culture of bacteria, began to proliferate within me. These primordial cells ran rampant through my body, infecting every cell in every organ inside me. In the same way that the vampires' primordial cells augment themselves through imposition upon the genetic components of the human cells to become vampiric cells, this variant strain of primordial cells began to commandeer my own cells. My human cells were attacked and, over time, changed into vampiric cells; my physiology, and to a significant degree, my very organs, were changed accordingly." Gabriel had a distant, contemplative look in his eyes. "It was a strange sensation. To feel my strength, my body, ebbing away as though I were being leeched upon and consumed from within, dying slowly from the inside out...it was most...unpleasant."

Gabriel's eyes, like dim embers in the faint dark, returned to Sebastian's. Gabriel rose from where he sat upon the table and adjusted his open coat.

"I have business to attend to. Get some sleep, much is expected of you tomorrow."

"Hey, Gabriel...um...you said something about those cells inside you being like an immortal bacterial culture. Dr. C said that vampires usually live to around two-hundred, but that you...you've lived much longer than that...that you might even be immortal."

"Hm," Gabriel scoffed softly. "Nigel is often...presumptuous with his findings, and we have deliberated this point on more than one occasion. I am in tune with my being in a way none can understand; I have remembered my body's each and every subtle change since I became what I am. I am not immortal. I can be killed, I can bleed, and one day...one day I will die. But not today."

Gabriel pivoted around and headed towards the door, his coat flowing out behind.

"Jesus," Sebastian whispered. Gabriel halted and half turned to peer at Sebastian over his shoulder. "You really are a freakin' vampire...I was hanging out...with a vampire."

Gabriel turned towards the door once more and made his way towards it.

"Goodnight, Sebastian," he offered somberly before he exited the room, closing the door behind him.

Chapter Four

The Lord Moxica
I

Winter had come early, blanketing the rolling, Scottish landscapes and forest canopies with thick, powdery snow. Ponderous snowflakes drifted copiously through the night air, carried by a cold, gentle wind. In all directions, the earthen horizons faded into albescence, the winter white standing in stark contrast to the cloudy, black sky. Night had fallen not long ago, and the moon and stars colored the snow-covered hinterland a vibrant, bluish-silver. Slight in stature, with windswept, grizzled hair and a short, scruffy beard, the steward, Finnigan, approached the door of the inn. He and the four soldiers assigned to guard him, on return from their business to the north, had reached the inn shortly after entering Edinburgh. With their horses seen to, and they, weary and chilled from their journey in the cold, a warm inn was a most welcome and inviting sight. The subdued sounds of music and revelry sounded from within, and as Finnigan opened the door, the raucous, yet pleasing merriment filled his ears.

His cohort followed him in, their mail gleaming dimly beneath their surcoats in the firelight, which, emanating from the hearth and torches, suffused the inn with a rich, wavering glow. Finnigan approached the innkeeper, and after exchanging a few pleasantries through the din, he and his cohort were soon partaking in the merriment with two flagons of ale between them, and a cordial wench in their midst. From where they sat at the long, wooden table, they cheered on the singing minstrel and the lively Scot who played upon the pipe. They drank from their gourds and lost themselves in the gaiety.

Finnigan brought his gourd to his mouth and let the frothy ale trickle past his lips. Unlike one or two of the soldiers who were seated close by, he still had his wits about him, though he was aware of the first inklings of drunkenness. He wiped his mouth with the back of his hand and placed the gourd on the table. He leaned back on the bench and glanced about the inn, observing some of the more buxom serving maids as they attended to their duties. He was, without discretion, staring at one such wench, when something a short distance behind her caught his eye. In the darkest corner of the mess hall, shrouded in a black cloak and hood, a formidable-looking man sat alone at a small round table. Upon the table was a single gourd of ale, its contents untouched as evidenced by the shimmering dark liquid and traces of foam that still ringed the brim of the gourd. He was, without question, of noble bearing, as his attire suggested, and he sat silent and unmoving, far removed from the merrymaking throng. Finnigan wondered how long the hooded man had been present in that dark corner, for up till now, the man had remained unseen to him; and, as Finnigan regarded the gaggle of fellow Scots cavorting about him, it seemed that they too were generally unaware of the mirthless figure.

Though the man's face was made tenebrous by the hood and the deep shadow cast within it, there was something distinctly familiar about the hooded man. It was, Finnigan thought, the hooded man's manner and poise – his aloofness and indifference to those around him that was so decisively familiar. It was the way the man kept to the shadows – the way he observed the world around him from them. Though Finnigan could not see the man's eyes beneath the hood, he had the sense that the man was staring at something on the opposite side of the mess hall. Finnigan turned on the bench and, to the best of his ability, followed the hooded man's gaze. He turned in time to see a thickly set, half-drunken man, with braids in his ruddy beard, headed towards the inn door. Under his arm was the cordial wench that had been in Finnigan's company but a short time ago, and the ruddy-bearded man held her close to his side as he chuckled and guffawed lasciviously in her ear.

She did not respond in kind, but it seemed she was not entirely repulsed by his advances, nor by the sizable pouch of coin on his belt. The man opened the door with his free hand, and the two stepped out into winter night. Finnigan returned his gaze to the hooded man and saw, in so far as he could tell, that the man still stared intently and unmoving in the same direction. Finnigan peered over his shoulder, once again following what he believed to be the hooded man's line of sight. He spied three men – peasants or derelicts, and by their look, devious characters all. It appeared that the wench had not been the only one to catch a glimpse of bearded man's pouch beneath his cloak, and Finnigan watched as the three men followed the pair out the door and into the cold. Once again, Finnigan turned to observe the hooded man, only to find a vacant stool in the dark corner, and the untouched gourd, standing where it had been left atop the little table still brimming with ale. Surprised, Finnigan searched the mess hall for the dark figure, and barely caught sight of the hooded man moving purposefully towards the door. The man moved discreetly, walking along the wall until he reached the door, whereupon he too slipped out into the chill darkness.

Finnigan had noted the slight pallor of the man's lips and chin in the firelight, and was reasonably certain of the man's identity. Finnigan rose from the long table, stepped over the bench, and made his way to the door. Those of his cohort who were still reasonably coherent, stood to follow their charge, but Finnigan waved that they be seated and withdrew from the inn alone.

* * * *

It was not a biting cold per se, but it was by no means comfortable, and Finnigan wrapped his cloak tightly about his frail form, his footfalls crunching softly in the snow. Outside the inn, the snow was littered with footprints, meandering in a myriad of directions. He was unsure where the hooded man had gone, and was about to head back into the inn, when he heard a stifled, shrill cry, which sounded to have been cut short. The cry had come from somewhere within the sizeable alley between the inn and its neighboring structure to the left, and Finnigan hastened to the corner wall of the inn. As he approached the mouth of the alley, he heard movement in the snow from around the corner, a kind of frantic scuffling, accompanied by effortful grunts and breaths. From where he had pressed himself against the corner wall, Finnigan leaned to one side and peered into the alley.

In what moonlight that shone into the alley, he spied the three rogues and the victims of their villainy: the wench and the bearded man. One of the rogues, a man whose head was bald and shiny as a ripe apple, save for the feathery hairs along the sides and back of his head, had his hand over the stricken wench's mouth, gripping her delicate jaw and stifling her with brutal disregard. His other arm was snaked about her waist, holding her to him, his hand clutching her breasts. Looming over the felled body of the bearded man, his back to Finnigan, his hands balled into fists, was another of the rogues, a bull of a man with a shaggy cloak and boots, both fashioned of bear fur. The third rogue, taller than the rest, and thinner even than Finnigan, looked on with his back to the steward as well. Finnigan watched as the big man began to untie the bearded man's coin purse from the leather belt to which it was fastened, while the others watched, waiting to divide the spoils, and perhaps have their way with the wench as well.

From over the inn, the moonlight shone into the alley on an angle, illuminating one wall with its dim glow and consequentially casting the opposite side of the alley in deep shadow. Within this narrow fringe of darkness, which spanned the length of alley, Finnigan was suddenly aware of a subtle movement in the dark near the tall rogue, a silent, obscure form stealing forth from where it had moved unseen alongside the wall: a fleeting shadow, within shadow. Finnigan strained to perceive this form, and was reasonably certain that it was the tenebrous figure of a man: a figure shrouded by darkness, by hood and cloak. There was then an impression of movement in the blackness, and what was once shadow sprung to light, as the hooded man lunged from the dark that had concealed him.

The attack was sudden, startlingly quick, and vicious – a leveling blow to the tall man's temple, which resounded with a horrid, hollow crack. The impact caused the man's head to snap and keel to one side, the blow jolting the man's body with such force, that he was hurtled, headlong and limp, into the far wall, from which he jounced and then crumpled into a heap in the snow. His back to Finnigan, the hooded man turned to the bald rogue, who after a few moments hesitation, his face betraying his mounting fear, flung the wench aside and swung at the hooded man with his fist. With the quickness of an asp, the hooded man raised his left arm and caught the bald rogue's bare fist about the knuckles with a gloved hand, halting the blow dead in his palm. For an instant, the two were unmoving, their gazes locked, and in that brief moment, whilst the rogue stared into the depths of the dark hood, his face sank in despair. With his free hand, the hooded man delivered the rogue a single blow that might have brought an ox to its knees.

The hooded man assailed the rogue with such speed, that Finnigan was barely able to convince himself with certainty that he had actually seen the hooded man move at all. The rogue's bald head arced backward, followed in kind by a spray of blood from his caved nose. The bald man reeled backwards, and his limp body collapsed to the ground.

Even as the hooded man had caught the bald rogue's fist, the big man's attention had already been diverted from his senseless victim's pouch to the plight of his fellow bandits. He had risen from where had been crouched over the bearded man, evidentially taller and larger than the hooded man before him. Upon glimpsing this eerie, hooded figure, the big man had hesitated on his feet for a moment; but seeing his fellows so brutally dispatched, and emboldened by the recognition of his great size as compared to that of the hooded man's, the big man bellowed and charged.

The hooded man stood his ground before the onrushing giant: statue still. Only when the big man swung his heavy fist, did the hooded man move, crouching low and lunging towards the big man with wicked speed. The hooded man slipped under the big man's massive arm, battering the man's side with his shoulder, clutching him about the waist and legs with his arms. The hooded man hammered into the giant with such power, that not only did he stop the big man dead in his tracks, he drove the man backwards, lifting him from his feet as might a charging bull.

A heavy thud sounded through the alley and, grimacing as his breath was forced from his lungs, the big man folded over the hooded man's shoulder as his body was carried towards the moonlit wall with ominous force. Before he released him, the hooded man dashed the giant's hefty body against the wall with force enough to make the timbers rattle and crack, a sound which seemed to echo in Finnigan's ears. The big man's body quaked as it struck the wall sidelong, and then it was left to drop to the cold, snowy ground next to where the whimpering wench had, in abject fright, curled herself against the wall with her hands about her face.

Finnigan watched the big man come to ground with the hooded man standing over him like a headstone. Quite suddenly, the hooded man spun around, and though, as before, he could not see the man's eyes within the hood, Finnigan was painfully aware that the hooded man was staring directly at him. Finnigan's breath froze in his chest. For an instant, they merely regarded one another.

The big man, it appeared, was as sturdy as he looked, and albeit shakily, he brought himself to his knees. The hooded man seemed reluctant to take his sight from Finnigan, and so turned from him slowly, breaking gaze with him at the penultimate moment before returning his attention to the man who rose before him. Even as the hooded man turned round, the big man had lunged forward, swinging at the hooded man once more with a wild blow, which arced downwards towards his shrouded countenance. The hooded man made a subtle, deft movement to one side, and the big man's fist whisked by his hooded face, narrowly grazing his chest as it crossed him. Evidently a seasoned brawler, and surprisingly quick for his size, the big man transitioned his prior folly into another assault.

Maintaining his lurching, forward motion, he reared his thick neck, and grunting, butted the hooded man's face with his broad brow. The hooded man appeared caught off guard, yet indifferent to the man's attack, and he seemed to simply accept the blow. The hooded man's head rocked back in the slightest, and the man took a single rearward step to regain his prior poise. Finnigan heard what he thought might have been a soft growl sound from within the man's hood.

The hooded man's right arm shot out as fast as Finnigan could blink, his gloved hand seizing the big man by the throat. The hooded man drove the big brawler backward, buffeting him against the wall once more and pinning him there with his single, outstretched arm. He had evidently begun to crush the brawling rogue's throat, for the big man gripped the hooded man's forearm with both hands in an attempt to free himself from the hooded man's grasp. The big brawler's eyes began to stand out from their sockets, his face flushed deep red, and his tongue lolled out whilst a few horrid rasps escaped his throat.

The one-sided skirmish would have been a strange and unlikely spectacle to any onlooker; save to Finnigan, who had seen something the like before; and he witnessed the big man held fast by the hooded man's single hand.

His furred boots firmly planted upon the ground, the big man struggled and writhed, kicking up wisps of powdery snow as he strained vainly to free himself from the hooded man's grip, which must have clenched his throat like an iron vice. From where he stood, Finnigan heard a faint, wet series of cracks, and shortly thereafter the big man's body went still and was left to slide lifelessly from the wall and slump to the frozen earth.

Finnigan watched as the shivering wench, sobbing and stricken with emotion, rose to her knees and reverently took the hooded man's hand in her own hands, and clutched it to her chest. She brought her lips to the top of his hand so that they were pressed against the leather of his glove, and spoke into his hand as though she were in prayer, with her tearing eyes tightly shut.

"Oh...thank ye, mi'lord...thank ye. God...God bless ye, mi'lord... God bless ye te come te the aid o'common folk such as mi'self." She managed as she sobbed her heartfelt thanks. The hooded man stood over her, almost, it seemed, unsure of what to do. He had begun to withdraw his hand from the woman's ever tightening grip when she bowed submissively before him, still clutching his hand to her breast. Finnigan stared wide-eyed, as the hooded man's hand slid free from the glove, revealing pale, hoary skin, and fingers tipped with short, blackened claws, the likes of which he had only ever seen upon one other. Immediately, the hooded man concealed his exposed hand within his long, black cloak, and reclaimed the glove he had been divested of with his other hand. When the wench looked up at him with her wet, fawn's eyes, the hooded man was already sliding his hand back into the glove under cover of his cloak. With comparatively strange gentility, he lifted his freshly gloved hand to the woman's face and stroked her tear-streaked cheek with his fingertips.

"Go home, child," he whispered. Sniffling, the young woman nodded sheepishly and rose to her feet. As she did, Finnigan stepped out from behind the wall, and with slow, measured steps, walked into the alley towards the hooded man.

* * * *

The sentry recognized the man who had peered at him from the mouth of the alley as the traveler who had entered the inn with a small contingent of men. Beyond this however, he was sure he had not laid eyes on the man before, yet the man seemed to regard him as though they were acquainted. From the corner of his eye, the sentry had seen the man emerge from where he had been hidden, and half turned to observe the man as he approached, purposefully keeping his face obscured within his shadowy hood.

Though she was startled to see this man, whomsoever he may be, the young woman gave the man a brief bow and curtsy as she passed him, and then hastened from the alley, likely back towards the inn. The man eyed her as she slipped by him, then, coming to a stop a few paces from the sentry, the man fell to a knee and bowed ingratiatingly.

"Mi'lord, master," the man said reverently. "I did'ne know ye'd be away from the castle. I hope yer lordship was ne concerned about the matter fer which ye sent me abroad. We were delayed solely by the ice and snow...ne a thing else has gone untoward, I swear it."

The sentry was baffled by the man's address, and wondered if he were not a madman, some poor soul at the end of his wits. Why should this man, in light of all that he had just witnessed, mistake him for another? The idea seemed simply preposterous. Hoping to glean further information from the ready-tongued man, the sentry said nothing to him in reply, but stared at him in silence through the dark shadow that veiled much of his face beneath the hood. In the winter quiet that followed, the wind moaning faintly above them, the man raised his bowed head slowly, a puzzled, fearful look upon his face.

"Why does yer lordship nay speak? Have I committed some offense o'which I am ne aware?"

The sentry hesitated a moment longer, then, speaking under his breath so that the true timbre and quality of his voice was somewhat indeterminate, he addressed the man.

"Of what color are my eyes?" The sentry whispered austerely, knowing that the man could not truly see his eyes in the dim moonlight that lit the alley. The man, who had bowed his head a second time, lifted his gaze to the sentry once more, his eyes narrowed in confusion. It seemed that the man's uncertainty was wrought by both the nature of the question, and the unfamiliarity in his would be master's voice.

"They...they are the color o'the heavenly flame...made so when yer lordship was sanctified by the holy chalice...as...as yer lordship has told."

The man opened his mouth as though he desired to say something more, but instead he remained silent, as a look of concern claimed his weathered countenance. The sentry was taken aback, for the man did indeed seem to possess some vague familiarity with what he had become those many years past, yet the man's talk of things hallowed was as perplexing as the man's conviction that he was his loyal servant. The sentry turned so that he faced the man head on, and then reached for the brim of his hood with his right hand. He clenched the supple, black cloth in his gloved fist and drew back the hood, revealing his face for the first time in what seemed an eternity. Standing stark against his flowing black locks and the pale counters of his visage, the sentry's lurid eyes stared into those of the genuflecting man with chilling severity.

"Do you still think me to be your master?" The sentry inquired in an emotionless, probing tone. For a moment, the man simply stared at him wide-eyed, his mouth agape. Then, quite abruptly, he averted the sentry's gaze, and once again bowed his head in reverence.

"F...Forgive me, mi'lord...ye are ne mi'master...but sure as I breathe...y...ye are one o'the old knights o'Jerusalem like mi'master, and like him, ye have touched the holy chalice." The man stated worshipfully.

"Why say you this? How did you come to be so informed?" The sentry demanded.

"I...I am a man of no great import, mi'lord, but...I am the steward of mi'master, and like him, ye are blessed, changed by the grail, made more than man."

As before, the sentry was silent for a short while, as he pondered over what he had heard.

"I should like to meet your master," the sentry said finally. The man's spirits seemed suddenly lifted, and he regarded the sentry almost amicably.

"Surely, mi'lord, yer visit would nay doubt please mi'master."

"What are you called?"

"Finnigan, mi'lord."

"And to where do you journey come the morrow?" asked the sentry.

"Te Rosslyn, mi'lord...Rosslyn Castle...te return te mi'master."

"Then you shall take me to your master," bade the sentry. "Rest your horses and your men, for I have...matters...to attend to this night, and will not be ready for travel till late in the day."

The sentry regarded Finnigan with unapparent scrutiny, observing the man's reaction to his slight untruth, and to his decision to travel through the following night. Finnigan did not seem skeptical of his reasoning in the slightest, and the sentry wondered what actual knowledge this man might possess pertaining to demon kind, and why it should pass that he know anything at all.

"I shall meet with you and your guard at the inn come sunset tomorrow," the sentry continued, "and thereafter we shall ride to Rosslyn."

"Aye, mi'lord," Finnigan concurred with a subtle nod of his head.

"Go now," the sentry said calmly. "I shall seek you at dusk."

Finnigan rose to his feet and bowed a final time before turning from the sentry. He departed from the alley at a brisk pace, hastening back to the inn to escape the winter cold. The sentry watched him go and then drew his hood back over his head. The tall rogue stirred slightly in the snow and the sentry took a few slow steps towards him. He crouched next to the man's felled body, and reaching out with a single, gloved hand, clutched him tightly by the hair of his scalp. A weak, listless moan escaped the rogue's lips as the sentry dragged him headlong into the darkness.

II

Though a chilling wind keened softly above, whirling about flakes of snow which continued to cascade from the dark, cloudy sky, to one such as the sentry, with tough, pallid flesh, the sting of the winter cold was rendered a mere spring evening's cool. Still garbed in his hood and cloak, mounted upon the large roan, the sentry traversed the rolling lands beyond Edinburgh. The roan's massive hooves thumped against the snow-covered ground, accompanied by the falling hooves of the trailing chestnut mare, which, tethered to the roan, was laden with two sacks of miscellaneous riches. The sentry kept the beasts at a brisk walk, hot breath steaming from their moist nostrils as he drove them onward. The sentry fully intended to convene with the man who called himself Finnigan, though not before he stowed his most recent of spoils in one of the caches he had established in Scotland, the nearest of which was half a night's travel south of Edinburgh. This night, he would cache the spoils and then return to Edinburgh, where he would stable the horses. Come sunrise, he would find or dig some sanctuary in which to take refuge from the sun during the day, and then emerge at sunset to join Finnigan and his cohort after having saddled and bridled the roan once more.

Not wanting to leave a painfully visible trail in the snow that might lead others to sight of his horde, the sentry dismounted some distance from the cache and, leaving the horses tethered and concealed in a wood, made his way to the cache on foot. He carried a sack on either shoulder, the treasures within tinkling softly as he made his way up a gentle, forested slope. Even so weighted by his burden, he moved with uncanny agility, often using trees, boulders, and fallen timber to travel across, lest he leave a distinct trail in his wake. Now high upon the snowy hilltop, the sentry came to a small, dark hollow beneath a tangle of giant roots, which were chaotically splayed below a large, gnarled tree. The hollow was large enough that one might gain entrance into it if one so desired, but the meager entrance and the darkness of it belied the capaciousness of the chamber that had been dug within. The sentry crammed the sacks into the depths of the hollow and then made his way back down the forested hill.

As he had done whilst he ascended, the sentry traversed the treetops and leapt from boulder to boulder as he made his way down the slope, leaving a ghost of a trail behind him. He moved with masterful silence and practiced art, a slinking wraith winding through the winter night. The sentry sprang from a large boulder into the fork of a tree between two towering branches, and then leapt down onto the massive trunk of an old, fallen tree. He was nearly halfway across the rotting timber, when, for the briefest of instants, he heard what was akin to mewling. The sound was somewhat shrill and unthreatening, yet there was a familiar rasp to the sound that put the sentry on edge. He froze upon the fallen tree and pricked his ears, his head tilting subtly from one side to the other.

Once again he heard the strange sound, this time more faint and briefer even than the first time. He searched amidst the trees and shadows with his eyes, staring downhill in the direction from which the sound had come. He dropped noiselessly onto the snowy hillside from the toppled tree, immediately assuming his predatory crouch as he stalked forward towards the source of the sound. He wound his way through the sparse forest until he reached a small clearing at the base of the hill. Therein, the moonlight shone brightest, unimpeded by the trees and reflected by the snow-covered ground as it was. The sentry halted, searching the forest with his wide, piercing eyes. Through the trees, which stood between him and the clearing, the sentry was quite certain he could perceive subtle movements from beyond. A moment later he caught the faintest trace of his sworn prey on the wind, and his demeanor became suddenly grimmer.

His eyes fixed straight ahead with unwavering focus, the sentry made his way towards the clearing. He oriented himself so that he approached downwind of the clearing, and drew near enough that he could peer into the clearing without having his view terribly compromised by the now leafless flora. He lowered himself behind a patch of icicle-laden shrubbery and a few bare, gnarled trees. Once settled, he went stalk still: seeing yet unseen, an omniscient presence hidden amidst the trees and shadows. That which had moved beyond the trees slowly came into view and the sentry watched wide-eyed as the moving thing took form.

Keeping to the fringe of wood within the clearing, a she-demon strode through the snow. He had hunted she-demons before, and in his experience they were a less common blight upon the earth than the larger demons he had oft come upon: those whose bodies bore the semblance of men. It, unlike other she-demons he had encountered, was not clothed in the old, soiled garbs of past prey. Instead, unabashed by its nakedness as white demons seemed inclined to be, the she-demon's bare, ashen body was exposed to the winter night. The demoness was a lithe yet notably muscular creature, smooth of skin, with long, coarse, raven-black hair, dappled with large flakes of snow, which drifted downwards from the dark firmament.

Its breasts were naught but meager approximations of womanhood overtop a sinuously muscular chest. Though the prominence of its features were greatly subdued, its face still bore the same bestial excrescences of the larger male demons he had hunted, and as it drew nearer to where he hid beyond the fringe of the clearing, he marked its lurid eyes. In so much as what it was by nature, the demoness repulsed him, sickened him, and yet in observing its elegant symmetry, its natural grace and poise, some atavistic part of him conceived that the demoness was in some way beautiful. He dismissed the thought, and reaching for the hilt of his sword, slowly, silently, he began to draw his blade.

It was then that, beyond the meager span of frost-coated trees and underbrush before him, another movement caught his eye. He trained his gaze upon the moving thing, and perceived that whatever it was, it was rather small, and that it moved silently and nimbly through the snow. The diminutive thing, which seemed to be trailing the she-demon, moved into view from where it had remained obscured behind a short stretch of frozen bush. The sentry went still and simply stared in disbelief, his blade poised where it had begun to be unsheathed from its scabbard. The thing that followed the demoness was a child, a demon child. If such a thing was remotely comparable to the children of mankind, then it was, to his eye, a youngling of no more than four or five years. It too was bare bodied and pallid of skin, and it bore, though in a most immature form, those same features that most readily denoted its kind. A faint mewl escaped the little demon as it loped after its dam upon hands and feet, and coming to a standstill, the she-demon turned its torso to peer back at the youngling.

The she-demon's lips curled back into a snarl that was somehow unthreatening, even inviting, despite it having revealed its pearly fangs. With an expression that was almost tender, the demoness emitted a soft sound that was both coo and purr. The youngling scrambled to the she-demon's side, and using the short, pointed claws on its hands and feet, it scrambled up the she-demon's flank then climbed towards the she-demon's shoulder. The demoness did not flinch, nor baulk as the youngling's claws found purchase over her pale hide. Instead, she turned her head to nuzzle the youngling as it neared her face, it having clung to the demoness' shoulder and to her long, thick mane.

The sentry regarded the demoness with confused emotion. He was unsure when this creature had become 'she' in his mind, unsure when he had personified her as something so like a woman. He had never seen such behavior amongst demons – such compassion. He had also never stumbled upon the things so serendipitously – never truly observed their way outside the hunt. He had of late been unable to ignore the traces of humanity that the white demons seemed to possess, a perception undoubtedly elicited by the demon that had spoken to him in its familiar tongue, before he had silenced it forever. Before then, he had been loath to consider demon-kind anything more than upright beasts that skulked the darkness. However, since that dawn at Cille Martainn Glen, the burning hate he had once felt for the hellish things had dwindled to a dull flame, and the immense, savage satisfaction he had once derived from their slaughter was similarly diminished. It seemed now that he hunted and killed less out of anger or vengeance, than out of a sense duty; that he was simply fulfilling his ordained role from on high.

The sentry watched as the youngling clambered about atop its mother, and watched as she, with such patience and gentility, steadied the boisterous youngster with a hand, as she allowed it to frolic upon her. With her young one fidgeting about her shoulders, the demoness continued on in the direction she had been walking. Still keeping to the furthermost limits of the clearing, skirting the edge of the forest, the demoness drew ever nearer to the spot where the sentry hid mere paces within the snowy wood. The sentry's grip tightened about the hilt of his sword as he readied himself to ambush the two demons. He would strike down the she-demon first, and then attend to young one. He waited until the demoness crossed his face, at which point she was closest to him. When, in the next instant, her smooth back was to him, he found himself hesitating in lieu of what should have been a quick and easy kill.

A part of him wanted nothing more than to take the life of the she-demon, and yet another part of him, a stronger more compelling part, wanted something more of her. Having only just walked past the hidden sentry, the gentle she-demon allowed her youngster its play a short while longer, then, taking the little creature by the wrist, she hoisted it from her shoulders with a single hand, and then lowered the chittering youngster back into the snow. Confused by his feelings, and inwardly cursing himself for faltering in his duty, his lips curled into a noiseless snarl and slowly, exasperatedly, he slid the unsheathed length of his blade back into his scabbard.

Shortly thereafter, the demoness straightened abruptly and sniffed at the vacant air. The winds had changed. The sentry remained motionless behind the ice-encrusted underbrush as the demoness turned round, nearly facing the hidden sentry directly. Seeking the source of the scent she had caught, she peered into the shadowy wood with her vivid, golden eyes, her head cocked, suggesting her pointed ears were pricked beneath her long, inky mane. Her eyes never leaving the general spot whereabouts the sentry was concealed, the demoness issued a faint, raspy sound meant for the ears of the youngling demon, an utterance that might well have been words.

Either way, the utterance carried some meaning, for, upon hearing it, the youngling shrank away from its mother and lowered itself into the snow to hide from whatever it was its mother now stalked. Cautiously, quietly, the demoness approached the sentry's position, her eyes searching the darkness amidst the trees and bush. Investigatory, she moved slowly along the fringe of the wood until she stood immediately before where the sentry lurked within the forest. Here, she placed a hand upon the trunk of a tree and leaned forward almost timidly, scenting and fossicking the gloom. Piercing through the dark, and through the tangle of bare flora, her keen eyes settled upon the sentry, and from him they did not stray.

The relative calm with which this she-demon had approached gave the sentry the ironic impression that it was he who was the hunted. After a moment's hesitation, knowing full well that the demoness was more than aware of his presence, the unmoving sentry stirred. Ever so slowly, he rose from under cover of the brush, revealing himself in his entirety to the she-demon, who regarded him with what seemed both curiosity and trepidation.

For a time, they simply stared at one another, each in their fashion attempting to discern the intent of the other. Then the she-demon took a few, wary steps towards the sentry, and in doing so, moved from the moonlit clearing into the wood. Once again she came to a stop, her head tilting to a side as she observed the sentry.

The sentry felt paralyzed by the duality of his convictions. A part of him was certain he should take hold of his sword once more and fell the she-demon before him, and yet another part of him was placated by her presence, and by her sudden, in some way alluring, change in scent. It was not a strong scent. It was a delicate, sweet musk carried upon the gentle breeze, which percolated amidst the trees. Subtle as it was, upon entering his nostrils it spoke most forcefully to some deep-seeded part of him, stirring a repressed, instinctual side of him to life. His breaths slowed and deepened, and the she-demon, her leeriness dwindling, began to move towards him once again, sniffing the air as though she too had caught some riveting scent. She stopped mere paces from him, marbled in moonlight and shadow.

Conflicting thoughts and emotions pervaded the sentry, and quite suddenly, with a seemingly tortured grimace up his face, he turned from the she-demon and hastened towards the solace of dark forest. He was compelled, though he knew not why, to peer back at the demoness over his shoulder. She stood exactly where he had left her, her head tilted curiously to one side as she watched him vanish back into the woods. He turned from her tenebrous, naked form and continued on along the base of the wooded hill, making his way back towards his tethered horses.

III

He had barely made the return journey to Edinburgh before sunrise. Upon arrival, he immediately had his horses stabled and tended to, and had then sought shelter from the rising sun in a windowless room at the inn. Having revivified himself therein, he had risen from the bed, left the confines of the room, and then made his way to the stables as dusk descended upon the land. He had the big roan readied for travel and paid the hostler to attend to the chestnut mare in his absence. Only after having seen to these necessities, did the sentry then make his way to inn.

The setting sun drowned the near cloudless, western sky in scarlet and orange, bathing and coloring the snow-covered ground with its rich effulgence. Similarly tinged by the evening hue, the roan's hot breath plumed from its nostrils into the cold air, whilst the sentry kept the big stallion at a brisk walk. The sentry's keen eyes, his pupils mere pinpricks in the fading light, spied Finnigan and his company by the roadside near the inn long before they were aware of his presence. It was one of Finnigan's men who first caught sight of the approaching sentry. He turned to the steward, Finnigan, and following some brief remark, pointed in the sentry's direction. Finnigan exhorted his horse into a smooth canter, riding on an intercept path towards the sentry. The four guards subsequently followed suit, but trailed the steward at hastened trots atop their mounts. The sentry brought the roan to a halt, and Finnigan reined his horse a mere arms length from the big stallion.

"Good'even, mi'lord," Finnigan addressed him with a slight bow of his head.

"Evening," the sentry greeted placidly in reply.

"We shall depart post-haste if yer lordship is so inclined," proposed the steward. The sentry gave Finnigan a reserved, stately nod of his hooded head. Looking to his approaching cohort, Finnigan made a gesture with a single upraised hand and called out to the armed men.

"Te us," he ordered casually. The steward kicked his horse into a walk, turned it about, and brought it alongside the sentry's roan. The steward's company fell in along the flanks of the meager cavalcade, aligning themselves so that two men, one behind the other, guarded either side. Finnigan chanced an expectant glance upon the sentry, who squeezed the roan's sides with his heels in turn. Seeing that the sentry was indeed prepared to embark, Finnigan also goaded his horse into a walk. With their two mounts traveling abreast, ever flanked by Finnigan's company, the cavalcade began their journey to Rossyln.

They traveled south from Edinburgh, through Midlothlian. His vision keen for one of his age, the steward, Finnigan, squinted in the moonlight as he led the cavalcade across the hinterland, whilst the four soldiers watched their path for brigands. Though outwardly he seemed inattentive and perhaps even self-absorbed, the sentry, unmoved, discreet, and silent, also observed the passing landscape. It was he who, with his raptorial vision scouring the darkness, truly safeguarded the party, albeit unknown to those about him, save perhaps the enigmatic steward. Much of their journey was made in silence, for though he was ready tongued, Finnigan, in abidance of a servant's conduct in the presence of a noble, would only speak when spoken to, and the sentry had no interest in inane banter.

However, now and again the sentry would converse with the steward, though solely for the purpose of ascertaining what breadth of knowledge Finnigan possessed, and to learn more of the steward's arcane master. The sentry's few questions were subtly and indirectly weaved into his formal parlance. He learned that Finnigan had served under his master from a tender age: that the steward's master was a keeper of records of sorts at Rosslyn Castle, and that in spite of his circuitous interrogation he could not dissipate the air of mystery surrounding this master. Indeed, the steward was reticent, even fearful to answer further lines of inquiry, and made it tacitly understood that his master's idiosyncrasies could not be discussed in the presence of the four guards, and that he was forbade doing so.

The small cavalcade traveled into the dead of night, and yet the hinterland was pleasantly lit, for the moon above imparted its pale glow unto the snow, which covered the rolling, frozen landscape. The ink-black sky was heavy with stars, and wisps of dark clouds drifted through the sky. As they rode forth, the steward spoke over the breeze that moaned faintly about them, his most unexpected voice shattering the winter silence. Following a minute turn of his head, the sentry glanced at Finnigan from beneath his shadowy hood. He saw that the steward had raised one hand, and was pointing towards the tenebrous stretch of uneven prominences that lined the horizon before them. Somewhat to the west, similarly cloaked by the darkness, was a large village through which it seemed they would pass.

"Rosslyn, mi'lord, and yonder lays Rossyln castle, atop one o'the cliffs o'the glen."

As they rode through the wilds of Rosslyn, the surrounding terrain became increasingly hilly and wooded. Skirting the north bank of a river Finnigan had called the Esk, the cavalcade entered the lofty, thickly forested system of promontories that was Rosslyn Glen. Looming above one such promontory, the stone of its vast curtain walls silhouetted against the starry firmament, was Rosslyn castle. This single promontory, and hence the castle upon it, was accessible only by means of a drawbridge. Consequently, Finnigan led the company up a large, wooded hillside, which rose a short distance from the Esk. Having ascended the rise, the meager cavalcade rode on towards the drawbridge, drawing ever nearer to the great castle that towered beyond it. Now high above the river Esk, the sentry looked down upon the untamed expanse that was Rosslyn Glen. He noted the tree-covered chasms that scarred the precipitous land, in particular the dark gorge, which surrounded much of the castle.

Indeed, as they approached the citadel, the sentry saw that the drawbridge served to span a sizeable fissure in the land between the rise they were atop and the promontory which held the castle aloft. The cavalcade came to a halt at the drawbridge, for it had been raised for the night. Finnigan exchanged a few words and pleasantrics with a soldier in a nearby guard tower, and soon afterward, the drawbridge began to lower. The deep, metallic staccato of the drawbridge's extending chains was somewhat abrasive to the sentry's sensitive ears, and the drawbridge creaked and groaned until finally it touched down before them with a boom, which resounded throughout the glen below. Finnigan bade the soldier in the guard tower farewell with a gesture of his hand, and then the meager cavalcade made their way over the drawbridge and into Rossyln castle.

* * * *

The sentry followed Finnigan up a seemingly unending, spiral staircase. A series of torches, mounted on the wall, lit their way as they ascended, the warm light wavering over the surface of the cold stone that surrounded them. The passage was rather narrow, steeply inclined, and harbored the scent of the burning torches.

Having consigned their horses to attendants upon entrance into the courtyard, Finnigan had dismissed his guard and led the sentry to the east wing of the castle. Opposite the keep side, the east side of the castle boasted a few towers along the curtain wall and overlooked a cliff face that was little more than a sheer drop into the glen below. It was one of these towers that they ascended at present, diligently climbing the winding stairs within. They were undoubtedly near the top of the tower, for they had been coursing the stairway for some time. Through the distinctive odor of the torches, the sentry caught the scent of a man out of sight around the inner wall of the meandering stairway. A second sniff of the air told him that two men were lying in wait close by.

Indeed, after climbing one last helical segment of steps, two guards came into view from behind the curve of the inner wall. Their backs faced either side of the stairway. They were dressed in the same surcoats the steward's men had been: long garbs with Rosslyn standards on the chest. They too wore chain mail beneath their surcoats, and both were armed with swords. They stiffened at the sight of the hooded sentry, each making a subtle, yet deliberate movement towards the center of the stairway to block the passage – their sword hands upon the hilts of their blades. Finnigan gave them an appeasing, yet commanding wave of his hand, to which one of the guards issued the steward a curt nod in return. Both guards then resumed their posts, allowing Finnigan and the sentry to pass between them on the narrow stairs.

Continuing their climb, they rounded one final bend in the stairway, whereafter they arrived at a large, wooden door at the top of the stairwell – no doubt the uppermost chamber of the tower. The door was ornately engraved and fixed with a large, iron knocker, held in the mouth of a mounted, iron, lion head. A large symbol was carved upon the very top of the door: a great, staring eye, backdropped by the rays of a sun in splendor. The sentry examined a second emblem – a circular etching at the very center of the door. The inner border of the engraved circle was ringed with Latin characters and depicted within the annulus were two knights upon a single horse. Each knight bore both lance and shield, each shield marked with a single crucifix. The sentry turned his attention to Finnigan as the steward reached for the iron knocker, pulled it back, and then struck the door a single time. The sound echoed in the stairway before relinquishing it to silence once more. From beyond the door, a deep, dour, reserved voice filled that silence, the single word drawn out with what seemed a calm displeasure.

"Enter."

His one hand still gripping the iron knocker, his face somewhat tightened with what might have been anxiety, the steward glanced over his shoulder at the sentry and then turned back to the door. The steward placed the palm of his free hand against the elaborate door, and leaning forward, pushed against it. The heavy door budged forward, allowing a sliver of dim light to play lambently over the steward's face. A rumbling creak issued from the door and then it groaned as the steward swung it open steadily. The steward stepped through the doorway, and then, in a most deferential fashion, moved to one side of the threshold with a modest bow, allowing the sentry to pass him by. The sentry strode into the chamber and came to a halt a few paces beyond the door.

The chamber beyond the door was surprisingly large and was lit by an arrangement of candles and torches. To the sentry's night eyes, the chamber was bright, though not uncomfortably so. Flickering amber firelight set the surrounding walls aglow, and even quivered vaguely upon the ceiling high above. Towering wooden bookcases occupied much of the space along the four walls. These boasted an assortment of old texts and scrolls, which were fastidiously arranged within the shelves. Upon the walls to either side of him, was a single, shuttered window. Ahead, two sizable stone pillars, some distance from one another and equidistant from the center of the chamber, rose from the smooth floor into the lofty ceiling. Between the two pillars, and beyond them, set against the far wall betwixt two colossal shelves, was a broad, inclined writing desk. To one side of the desk, and rising well above it, stood a tall, iron candle stand, which bore a host of small candles, tiny flames dancing upon their wicks.

Ancient parchments littered one side of the desk, and upon the other was a large, open book, the writings upon one of its exposed pages unfinished. Sitting before the desk, in a high-backed, imperial, wooden chair of exquisite design, was a man of regal bearing. His back to the sentry, the man did not so much as turn his head to look upon those who had entered his chamber. Beneath his copious, silky, black cloak, the man was broad of shoulder. Like some perfect, black liquescence, the man's long hair flowed past his shoulders; much of it tied taut and high atop his head, so that the thick mane cascaded to the man's back over his cloak, like a stallion's tail. The sentry was aware of a faint, wet scratching, which sounded from the unfinished page of the open book as a masterful hand continued to move an inky quill across the brittle paper. The hand was a formidable one, adorned with golden, gem-set rings, and was pale as dry ash.

Presently, the scratching abated, the feathers of the quill ceased to tremble, and the now motionless hand held the quill poised above the paper. In an even tone of powerful timbre, the man spoke once more. The man had a strange manner of speaking. The nature of the man's words, or so the sentry was inclined to believe, was indicative of the tongue of men from the Holy Land, or conceivably of the Ottoman Empire: men whom the sentry had encountered in his travels and sojourns of war. It seemed however, that tongues of other nations influenced the man's speech, perhaps even the tongue of his native Spain.

"Finnigan," the man addressed the steward, still preoccupied with the written works before him. "I hope dat, for your sake, der is both a significant and convincing reason," his tone seemed to graduated in severity, "for you to have brought another into my presence, into my sanctum, without my request, or consent."

Still standing next to the door, his manner most obsequious, the steward cleared his throat in a fashion that betrayed a modicum of apprehension.

"I...I have, mi'lord master..."

The steward breathed in as though he desired to say something further, but fell silent as the sentry began to walk forward once more. Finnigan eyed the sentry as he neared the center of the chamber in approach of the steward's master. Having heard the sentry's quiet footfalls, the steward's master straightened in his chair more than he had been, his head rising attentively from the text upon the writing desk. In a most unconcerned fashion, the master placed his quill in a small inkwell, and then in an unhurried, yet purposeful motion, he rose from where he sat. At this, the sentry slowed, and then came to a standstill between the two pillars, staring intently at the steward's master from beneath his hood.

His form concealed behind his long, flowing cloak, the steward's master took a single step to one side of his chair, and with the dignified air of a monarch, turned to face the sentry. The sentry watched as a pallid face came about from behind the man's great, black mane. The face did not bare the bestial excrescences of those creatures that were his prey, nor was it set on either side with sharply pointed ears. On the contrary, the face, if perhaps foreign in appearance, was one as handsome and refined as was to be found amongst men. Yet, like his own, the face was pale and smooth, with lurid eyes that gleamed like golden gems.

His expression both stolid and intrigued, the steward's master took a few deliberate steps towards the sentry and then stopped a short distance from him, scrutinizing the hooded man before him with a piercing gaze. He was not quite so tall as the sentry, but he was most assuredly broader and more heavily muscled. Beneath the cloak, the steward's master was garbed in a lengthy, black tunic of the utmost finery, studded with gold and made of leather. A strange, thin, curved blade with a lengthy hilt hung at his side, the scabbard and rounded guard ornamented with serpentine, golden dragons. The chamber had fallen into such silence that the flickering flames of the torches and candles seemed to tickle the air with a vague, susurration. In this silence, the steward's master regarded the sentry, almost expectantly so.

Slowly, the sentry raised a single hand to his brow, and taking hold of his hood, drew it back from his face, revealing himself to the steward's master. For what seemed an indeterminate amount of time, each man held the unwavering gaze of the other. Their expressions composed, yet severe and knowing, they stood before one other like forbidding statues with glaring eyes, which glistened like vivid, amber pools in the firelight. His gaze never leaving that of the sentry, the steward's master raised his right hand high into the air, the copious, billowing sleeve of the black undergarment he wore beneath the tunic swaying as it slid a little ways from his wrist, revealing a ghostly, muscular forearm. He gestured ever so subtly to Finnigan, who still stood next to the door awaiting his master's bidding.

"Leave us," said steward's master in a placid, sovereign tone. Finnigan bowed his head and withdrew from the chamber, pulling the hefty door closed behind him. As it shut, a heavy reverberation filled the chamber. The echo lessened and then faded, returning the chamber to its former quiet. Perfectly still, and alone in the chamber, the sentry and the steward's master observed one other patiently.

* * * *

It was the sentry who finally broke the silence between them, speaking in a voice devoid of mirth.

"Who are you?" he inquired of the steward's master.

"I...have been given many names," he replied, his eyes growing distant as they looked off into nothingness. The steward's master then leveled his eyes upon the sentry once more.

"Though I would imagine dat it is not so much who I am, but what, dat is of particular interest at present...yes?" The hard face of the steward's master seemed to soften, perhaps divulging what might have been the slightest hint of amusement.

"Nonetheless, I do not presume to know your mind, and so I shall acquiesce to your query. I...am Moxica."

Admittedly, since he had been ushered into the world of night, the sentry had seen many a strange sight, but for some reason the presence of this Moxica before him, a man, a being, so like himself, evoked in him some sense of the surreal. Moxica lowered his head in the slightest as he eyed the sentry, provoking a few locks of his silky black mane to slide forth from his shoulders.

"And you," he continued, "you who have found your way into dis most secret place." He casually gestured to the chamber surrounding them. "Who...are you?"

The sentry had not spoken his own name, nor heard it spoken for so long, that its utterance was peculiar to his own ears even as it crossed his lips.

"I...am Gabriel," he said.

"Well...Gabriel, I am pleased to make your acquaintance. As you can imagine, it is not often dat I happen upon one with whom I share such...kinship; in truth, you are de only other I have encountered, save of course de vampir demselves."

"Vampir," Gabriel repeated, his mind seeking some representation for the word. "The demons? Do you speak of the white demons?"

The minute trace of a wry smile crept across Moxica's pale lips.

"Dey are not demons, my friend. Tell me, when was it dat you were made more den man? When did it come to pass dat de night became yours to roam?"

"Some fifty years past," Gabriel replied, the vivid memories of countless nights flooding his mind.

"Ah, you are but a child unto dis existence, it is little wonder den why you still possess such...naivety."

Outwardly composed, Gabriel retorted with an assuredness that was exemplified by the gravity of his gaze.

"I know that I was faced with the blackest of deaths and survived by God's grace. Through some power, through some divine whim, I was created anew: birthed from the earth itself, changed into what I am, given the strength to purge this world of the demons that walk it. Those whom I have loved have passed into heaven, but it seems that God will not let me die, for I have sworn to rid the world of these beasts of the pit, and perhaps I shall not see heaven's gate until I do. I see my path—my destiny—clearly; for it is my sole salvation."

"You see nothing," Moxica replied casually. "You are blinded by de fog of vengeance and ignorance. I say dis not to insult you my friend, but to bring de truth to light. Many lifetimes ago, I was as you are now, lost in confusion and contempt...dis will soon pass, perhaps somewhere deep within you, de veil has already begun to lift. Surely, if as you say, you have hunted de vampir, as I once did, you must have seen dat dey are more den mere beasts."

Reluctant as he was to acknowledge Moxica's words, Gabriel could not help but recall the demon that had spoken to him in its moribund moment of life, nor could he prevent the image of the lissome she-demon from haunting his thoughts. Moxica continued, recapturing Gabriel's attention.

"What has happened to you is not God's doing, nor is de retribution you reap His will. You are what you are because of de vampir and de capricious nature of life itself." Moxica paused for a moment and glanced down at his hand, curling the dark claws of his fingertips into his palm. "It is something inside dem, coursing in der veins, like a poison, like a blessing. It changes one from within, whittles and destroys what is man, and leaves in its place...dis," he indicated Gabriel's body with a wave of the same hand, as he met the sentry's gaze once more. "Ages ago, when, like you, I was still wrathful and impetuous, I caught one of dese vampir, but did not slay it. Not understanding what dey truly were, I caged it, like an animal. De tortured sorrow upon its face from what pains I inflicted upon de creature..." He hesitated a moment before speaking anew. "I came to learn much dat was simply...unexpected."

"Your own steward does not share this rendition of things," said Gabriel in a rather austere manner. "And so I am inclined to believe that you have filled his head with lies. If that is so, then I can, if I choose, consider what you have said, but have no reason to give your words credence, regardless of our likeness. The steward...Finnigan...he believes you to be an old knight of Jerusalem – one who has touched the Holy Grail of Christ. He believes that it was a miracle of the chalice that made you what you are, and you, one who denies the workings of the divine, have led him to this belief."

"Hmm," Moxica crooned thoughtfully as he turned from Gabriel and proceeded to wander a little ways from him, his head tilted pensively. "I...have told many untruths to many men," said Moxica, as he turned his head to face Gabriel once more. "For I have found dat in de face of some truths, truths dat are de most revelational and unspeakable, de minds of men fare better with de untruth dan with de truth itself. Dese truths shake de foundation of de world man has come to know, and hence, man cannot reconcile with de reality dese truths represent, thus birthing unrest and anarchy amongst dem. And so it is often true dat mankind's ignorance is der bliss; surely, at least dis you have come to understand. You yourself hide what you truly are beneath de borrowed robes of wealthy men, and so, even remaining silent, you proclaim to de world dat you are something you are not.

"It may be dat you still feel shame for what you are, but I know dat you do dis, guise yourself as man amidst men, because you know de fear and chaos de truth of what you are would create amongst de people." Moxica eyed Gabriel searchingly, as a tradesman might observe a learning apprentice. "However," he carried on, regaining his former affability, "much of what my steward has told you is indeed de truth. Long ago, my wanderings, lead me to Jerusalem. I had followed a vast migration of pilgrims to de Holy Land, taking those who strayed or lagged behind to feed upon. I soon found myself in a desert kingdom, and so I acquainted myself with de great city and dwelled der for some time. I would, as a habit, take refuge from de sun outside of de city, seeking respite in small caves within de desert mountains, or by digging into de sands demselves. Those nights when de compulsion to feed was maddening, I hunted, of course, but, during de nights between, I explored de Kingdom of Jerusalem, over time discovering its many secrets and hidden treasures.

"It came to pass dat a small army of French knights arrived in Jerusalem, de Order of de Poor Knights of Christ dey called demselves. Dese knights proclaimed it was der mandate to protect de pilgrimage routes into de Holy Land, and so a great many of dem encamped outside de city. Nine knights of de order, perhaps seeking shelter from de desert sun, perhaps seeking entombed riches, strayed from de rest and discovered one of de caves I spoke of. Venturing into de depths of dis cave, with torches to light der way, dey happened upon me whilst I lay in stillness in de darkness. As I have told you, I once hunted de vampir as well. When dese knights found me, my clothes and flesh were still bloodied from a particularly...savage...encounter I had with two vampir in de night. De knights believed me a dead man and, being pious Christians, thought it best to remove me from de cave so dat dey might bury me in de earth...after, of course, relieving me of what coin I had upon my person and thieving de valuables I had kept in de cave.

"Inevitably, as dey dragged me from where I lay, I stirred from my torpor. Thinking me possessed, dey shrank from me as I arose, der blades drawn and dey mad with fear. Der, in de close quarters of de cave, unhealed, addled and weakened as I was, I would have been hard pressed to dispatch nine wary, armed knights, not to mention what number of der brethren dat might have been alerted to de cries and sounds of battle. I reasoned dat, in actuality, dese knights presented me a novel opportunity, one dat I would not have previously considered at dat time, but one which, in de clarity of dat moment, I decided to pursue.

"In short, I struck an accord with dem, namely with de foremost of de knights, Hughes de Payen and Andre de Montbard, both long dead now. Dis order of knights came to be known as de Templar, and were, in some respects, an extension of my influence, accomplishing for me dat which I could not have in de daylight world of men. Dey swore me into der order, kept my existence secret, and provided me with what amenities I requested. De nine knights formed an inner circle within de order – an alliance of which I was a part. In return I gave dem riches, riches dat made dem men of power.

"It was I who led dese knights to de secret Stables of Solomon, and dey who, for nine years, dug beneath de desert to plunder all de sacred treasures and ancient writings within. In de end, de order gained such knowledge and wealth as to unsettle both de church and monarchy, and so de church declared dese knights heretics, and de Templar were persecuted mercilessly. Dey were hunted down, tortured, and forced into hiding. Despite de sudden siege upon de order, in which most of de knights were captured in France, a small fleet of ships laden with riches and de last of de Templar...I amongst dem...fled here to Scotland to escape de persecution of de church and de King of France.

"Here...still...my existence is kept secret in dis castle, dis clandestine scriptorium, and it is I who still translate de knowledge of de ancients, rewriting de scrolls and parchments, as I have done for centuries." Moxica took a few, measured steps back towards Gabriel, who seemed entirely unmoved yet distinctively attentive. "So...Gabriel...I am indeed de ancient knight I am chronicled to be, and I have indeed held de Holy Grail, as it was one of de sacred treasures I found so long ago, though I am sorry to disclose dat it was naught more den an archaic cup fashioned of simple, desert clay."

Gabriel glanced about the room once more, as though it held new meaning for him.

"You have not been made a prisoner in this castle?" Gabriel asked as he looked to the large writing desk and the parchments upon it. Moxica grinned sardonically, revealing for the first time the dagger points of his ivory fangs.

"Hardly, my friend. I remain here only because it suits me to do so. Knowledge is power and, de wisdom of my years aside, I have learned much from dese ancient writings." he gestured at the litter upon the writing desk. "How civilizations were maintained, how dey were controlled, accounts of voyages and maps to places dat were once uncharted. At such a time dat I feel I have finished with dis place, den I shall vanish from it and begin anew elsewhere, as I have done before."

"And what of the Grail?" Gabriel inquired with evident interest.

"Ah...yes. What of it?"

"Surely you were not so remiss as to let such a thing slip from your grasp indefinitely."

"De Grail," Moxica replied, following a deep, patient inspiration, "is safely secreted in a reliquary. Dis...cup...is meaningless to me. Its only true value, is what influence it has over men, de power to make armies war in its name.

"Blasphemy springs quite readily from your tongue," Gabriel said grimly.

"It is simply another matter of truth: de discrepancy between it and what man has been made to believe. I know de man Jesus once lived, though I certainly do not understand him in de same capacity dat one such as you might. I have seen how truths become embellished, how a common man becomes legend, and how a great man becomes deified. I am no god, yet, ages ago, it came to pass dat I was worshipped as such." Moxica's eyes narrowed with a sudden sternness. "God...is a name, a titled tool used by men of worth to extend de limits of der own power; de threat of inexorable judgment, and so a methodology for de implementation of fear and consequent desire for salvation in de masses, making dem little more den sheep; de means by which mankind is granted some vague understanding of, and connection to, de mysteries of dis world; an instrument to give hope and purpose to de wayward, pathetic, peasant multitude, and unit dem in common cause – a cause governed by de greed twisted whims of kings, lords and bishops.

"In my time upon dis world, I have seen de greatest of evils, the most abominable of atrocities man can commit, done in de name of God, yet I have never seen dis...God, nor any other god in whose name men fall to der knees, and I have watched and waited for a sign of de divine for some time. You...Gabriel, have made a pact with a being dat shall never hear your pleas."

Silence followed, and once again, albeit it briefly, each held the stony gaze of the other.

"Believe what you will," said Gabriel finally, "but I have given my oath, and that I have given my sworn word in itself is enough to hold me to it."

Moxica chuckled dryly under his breath.

"A most holy pact you have with dis most munificent God of yours. Why are you so certain dis is de path you must take?"

Gabriel's voice raised, his tone stinging.

"Because these creatures are a scourge, a blight upon the world of men. They prey upon the innocent, upon women and children.

Moxica glared at Gabriel so probingly, it was as though he were peering into his very soul.

"And so you shall hunt dese lands, all lands, until de last of de vampir has let slip its last breath under your blade?"

"Yes."

"And you shall feel no remorse?"

"I will do what is needed to rid the world of this evil."

"Dey are not evil," Moxica stated disapprovingly. "Dey simply are. One does not dub de falcon evil because of its inborn ability to kill, nor de wolf, or de lion. Like dem, de vampir seeks only to survive in a world of men."

"The price of their survival is too great. These are the lives of the innocent, lives taken each night so long as these creatures lurk in the darkness."

"Are you so different from dem?" Moxica questioned astutely. "Do you yourself not take de lives of men to keep your own heart beating in your chest?" his voice was suddenly hard. "Have you not killed a thousand times over, and a thousand times again?"

A myriad of faces flashed through Gabriel's mind, as he envisioned the teeming multitude of those whose lives he had taken, whose blood he had drunk.

"I do not kill for killing's sake, and never have I taken the life of an innocent. Thieves, those that would rape and torture and kill, the wretched dregs of mankind, only these have perished by my hand, regardless of my hunger."

"You do not see, nor understand de purpose of de vampir. Like you, dey better mankind. You prey upon de villainous, dey prey upon de weak, de sick, de dull, those dat are de denigration of de race of man. You are dem. And so what shall you do when you have slain dem all? Will you den turn your blade on yourself?"

"Yes," Gabriel replied gravely.

"Ah, den it is clear, since I am no different from you, dat by your logic you must destroy me as well."

Gabriel hesitated, though only for a moment.

"I...will do what is needed. I have sworn to it, it is my destiny."

"I was being...facetious," warned Moxica.

Gabriel did not reply. Instead, his gloved hand betrayed the subtlest of movements towards the hilt of his sword. Suddenly aflame, Moxica's sharp eyes shot to the sentry's sword hand. Slowly, he lifted his eyes, glaring at Gabriel, his countenance admonishing and forbidding.

"I...would not advise dat."

Silence fell over the chamber once more, and a palpable tension hung in the air. As they had begun, they stood motionless before one another. Outwardly expressionless, they were as two cobras, poised to strike at the slightest twitch of the other. Though they uttered no words, their eyes, deadly and baleful, spoke volumes; each pair a set of angry, amber gems, which glinted in the ubiquitous candlelight. One could not so much as hear their breaths, though their chests would rise and fall as they filled and loosed their lungs. It was as though they were frozen, eyes locked, in this single, ominous moment. Then, with a chilling suddenness, Gabriel brought their standstill to a close.

In a single motion, Gabriel grasped the hilt of his sword and tore it from his scabbard. No sooner did Gabriel move, than the lord Moxica sprang to life, freeing his own blade with wicked speed, not a heartbeat after the sentry had drawn. Gabriel lunged forward, his sword hissing through the air as he swung the great blade. His long mane flailing like a lion's, Moxica fell into a crouch and raised his curved sword in time to clash it against the underside of the sentry's Tizona, so that the heavy sword swept by a mere hand's breadth above the ancient Lord's head. Gabriel did not falter, nor even break stride, but strode forward, continuing his assault. Reasoning that Moxica would be hard pressed to parry his blows with so slender a blade, he swung his sword with rending force, striving to breach the ancient lord's guard.

Evidently skilled with his blade, Moxica did not seek to meet and halt the sentry's flourishing sword with his own blade, but rather, with both hands clasping the lengthy hilt of his sword, he would bow under the force of Gabriel's heavy blows like a willow tree in a tempest wind, redirecting each clout with his curved blade so that they were rendered glancing. Again and again, with the sound of clashing steel ringing throughout the chamber, Gabriel swung the great blade, driving Moxica backward, yet unable to smite him. Upon seeing one of the stone pillars a short distance beyond Moxica, Gabriel sought to impel his adversary towards it, pin him against the stone column unawares, and there strike him down.

A moment later, they were mere paces from the pillar, and Gabriel closed on the ancient Lord. It was apparent however, that Moxica was more than aware of his surroundings, for as Gabriel swept the Tizona at his adversary's legs, Moxica sprang away from the glinting steel, turning from Gabriel whilst he lifted from the floor so that he came to face the pillar as he rose into the air. Moxica lifted the sole of his foot to the stone pillar, and then, with a powerful thrust of his single leg, he propelled himself from the pillar, his black cloak swirling as it trailed him. Gabriel's eyes quickly lifted to trace Moxica's sudden leap, and the ancient lord began to yaw and upend as he traveled through the air above Gabriel, his black cloak billowing and flailing at his back.

There was a sudden brandishing of curved steel and, incredibly, Moxica assailed the sentry from the air, slashing at him as he wheeled deftly above him. Gabriel was caught off guard, and though he attempted to evade the attack, he was still barely able to raise his sword to his brow to protect his skull. The curved blade clanged against his sword as Moxica sailed by upturned in the air. Gabriel winced, for, forced to parry so dangerously close to own face, the clashing steel rang painfully in his acute ears.

Gabriel followed Moxica with his eyes, as the looming, cloaked form of his adversary passed overhead and began to drop from view off to one side behind him. Gabriel turned his head to peer over his shoulder as not to lose sight of his foe. With a swift, catlike swivel, Moxica righted himself as he descended from above behind Gabriel, alighting upon the burnished floor as Gabriel spun round to face him. No sooner did Moxica come to ground, than with alarming speed, he lunged at Gabriel, closing on him instantly. Once again, Gabriel was hard pressed to parry Moxica's attack, and with sudden angst, he realized it was now he who was being driven back, harried by Moxica's swift, fluid strokes. Where the size of Gabriel's Tizona's made it a formidable weapon with which to sunder his opponents, the weighty blade, though deftly employed under the sentry's might, could not be wielded at the speed with which Moxica managed his slender blade.

Thus, as he was forced backward in the face of Moxica's relentless attack, Gabriel was scarcely able to raise his sword to keep Moxica's curved blade from biting into his flesh. It seemed as though each successive slash came faster and harder, lessening

Gabriel's time to react so that each parry was increasingly cramped and inefficacious. Gabriel attempted to sidestep Moxica's rush to gain much needed distance from his adversary, but, reacting nearly instantaneously, Moxica simply mirrored his dodge, smothering his evasion and pressing the attack. Moxica drove Gabriel past the pillar and back towards the wall upon which the great wooden door was set. Moxica delivered a final, vicious slash, which Gabriel was only just able to parry, meeting Moxica's blade with his own, a mere hand's breadth from his face.

The blow unbalanced Gabriel in the slightest and, in that moment, following the sweep of his blade into a tight spin, Moxica pivoted on a single foot with remarkable quickness. His other leg shot out from beneath the fringes of his billowing cloak, the sole of his leather boot thudding into Gabriel's chest with terrible force. Gabriel's breath left him as the impact jarred his ribs, and he felt his feet leave the floor as his body was lifted into the air. He was somewhat disquieted by how fast the blow had come, and he thought, as he was hurled backwards and headlong, that it was as though he had been kicked by the weighty hoof of a carthorse. Gabriel twisted in the air in an attempt to right himself, but still came to ground heavily upon the back of his head and neck, rolling over a single shoulder onto his side, whereupon he slid across the smooth floor. Sword in hand, he glided over the polished stone until he was not a few paces from the wall. Even before Gabriel could rise, Moxica had launched himself at the sentry once more, his blade poised to strike.

Somewhat shaken from having his skull dashed against the floor, Gabriel turned over and, addled as he was, immediately brought himself to a knee. He heard the approaching footfalls of the onrushing Moxica close behind him, and caught a fleeting glimpse of a large, dark form streaking towards him from his periphery. Now fully cognizant of his adversary's speed, Gabriel knew a mere instant's hesitation might well spell his demise and so, without so much as turning his head to face the ancient lord, he heaved his sword about with all his might. His sword clasped tightly in both hands, and his arms outstretched, he whirled round, wide-eyed and snarling like a cornered beast, slashing blindly at where he knew the ancient lord to be. Gabriel spun in time to see Moxica suddenly drop his curved blade to his chest defensively, readying himself to parry the unanticipated attack.

Moxica arched backward at the spine and sprang to one side in an attempt absorb and redirect the blow as he had done before.

Indeed, the lord Moxica skillfully evaded the full and tremendous force of the clout, but was unable to deflect Gabriel's blade so deftly as to render the blow a glancing one. As such, Gabriel's weighty sword battered Moxica's guard with strength enough to jolt the ancient Lord's heavily muscled body and unbalance him. Moxica took a few purposeful steps backward to regain his footing, allowing Gabriel a vital moment of respite. Recouped from his brief disorientation, and seeing that, to a degree, Moxica had given him his back, Gabriel was upon his feet in an instant. Hoisting his sword high above his head, he lunged at Moxica, seeking to cleave him head to foot.

Gabriel brought the Tizona down upon Moxica with a fury, but at the penultimate moment, Moxica raised his blade to meet the Tizona and stepping to one side whilst pivoting on a single foot, he spun away from the blow, slipping underneath the heavy blade to gain Gabriel's back. As he spun behind Gabriel, Moxica lashed out with his blade, extending the reach of his curved sword by slashing with it gripped in a single, outstretched hand. Having skimmed harmlessly alongside Moxica, Gabriel's sword hammered against the floor with a deafening clang, sending polished flecks of stone scattering across the chamber.

It was then that Gabriel's body shuddered under the abrupt and painful swipe of Moxica's blade, as it gashed the width of his back. His eyes narrowed into fiery slits, Gabriel grimaced and, with his fangs bared, he let loose a sound from his open maw that was nothing short of a roar. He raised his sword from the pulverized floor and whirled round to face Moxica with vengeance in his eyes, lashing out wildly with his blade as he did. Still clutching the curved blade in his outstretched sword hand, his aspect composed and fierce, Moxica stepped away from Gabriel, and then circled him slowly with arms widespread, as though goading the sentry to attack once more. With mounting rage Gabriel obliged, though not without method. Gabriel lunged forward, his sword held high as though he sought to bring it down upon his foe.

Instead, he swept the blade low, intending to cripple his adversary at the shanks, the weighty Tizona humming menacingly as it was swung to. It was an impossible blow to sidestep, and Gabriel knew this full well. It was apparent, however, that the lord Moxica had intuited his predicament no differently, for as Gabriel's blade neared its mark the ancient Lord leap skyward, lifting high into the air with arms and blade outstretched. Gabriel's blade tore the vacant air where Moxica had stood moments before, and he watched as Moxica's rising form began to arc backward and away from him above. With his fluent black garbs and mane undulating about him, the ancient Lord began to upend in the air, so that when finally he began his descent from whence he had soared, he plummeted to earth headlong, with arms widespread like a fallen angel; and when it seemed as though Moxica might strike the floor poised thus, he drew in his limbs and righted himself in the air at the penultimate moment, alighting upon the smooth stone on the soles of his boots, in a debonair crouch.

Even before Moxica had come to ground, Gabriel had charged the ancient lord, hoping to catch his foe unawares. It was as though the lord Moxica had anticipated Gabriel's attack, for the instant Moxica's heels touched the polished floor, his eyes shot up from beneath his lowered head, his curved sword raised defensively to deflect an immanent blow. The clang of steel resounded throughout the chamber anew and, once more, Moxica only narrowly escaped Gabriel's blade. Gabriel knew he could not allow Moxica to fall into rhythm with his lighter and more maneuverable blade; that he must mount a constant offensive to batter Moxica into submission and prevent him from employing his evidently seasoned craft with this strange, curved sword.

Gabriel swung at Moxica at oblique angles, using the farthest reaches of his blade, thus keeping Moxica at a distance and avoiding his deadly counterstrokes. Gabriel was soon aware of the warm blood soaking the top of his tunic and cloak, and felt the comparatively cool air of the chamber over the open wound upon his back. He paid the wound no heed however, and continued to accost the lord Moxica with heaving strokes of his sword. As he had before, Moxica would ever escape the brunt of Gabriel's furious swings, shedding the blows as best he could with deflective parries and a masterful elusiveness. Nonetheless, Moxica, artful swordsman that he was, seemed temporarily held at bay by this fresh assault. Seeing this, Gabriel's resolve was strengthened, and he surged forth, pressing his attack.

He drove Moxica backwards, past the broad writing desk and the iron candle stand, gradually angling the ancient lord towards the wall beyond. For the briefest of moments, Moxica seemed staggered by the sentry's newfound vigor, and sensing this, Gabriel lunged at Moxica, his sword poised threateningly above his head as though he might attempt to cleave the ancient lord from crown to foot once more. In truth, this was not the sentry's ambition, but merely a posturing to guise his intent. His sword gripped firmly in both hands, Gabriel began to bring the blade down upon Moxica in an arcing stroke. In this single moment, Gabriel thought he observed a change in his adversary's demeanor: a subtle, preparatory shift of weight, a stance which betrayed a certain readiness, and a look of calm anticipation in the ancient lord's golden eyes as he waited for the blade to descend.

It was clear that Moxica sought to shed the impending blow and deliver the sentry a deft counterstroke in return. This was precisely the sort of complacence Gabriel had hoped to foster in his foe. Moments before his blade fell upon that of Moxica's, Gabriel let his sword hand slip from the hilt of Tizona, so that he bore the sword downwards with a single arm. Held thus, the Tizona was less unyielding to Moxica's tactful parries, and so with one adroit movement, the ancient lord rendered the blow a glancing one. Accompanied by the shrill grating of steel, Gabriel felt the path of his blade deviate, as Moxica deflected the Tizona away from his person with his own sword. Gabriel watched as the Tizona, guided over the length of Moxica's curved blade, hissed through the air alongside Moxica, mere hands' breadths from the ancient lord. Even as Gabriel's blade sank towards the floor, the lord Moxica began to reorient his sword. With a nimble movement of his wrist, Moxica had shed Gabriel's blade and was poised to strike.

Gabriel had been rendered vulnerable. In effect, he had allowed himself to be made so, momentarily sacrificing his defenses for an opportunity to fell the lord Moxica. He knew that his vulnerability would not have escaped Moxica's attention, and he used this knowledge to bait his foe. Indeed, the sentry had been more than cognizant of the fact that if his stroke were parried to a side, he would be unable to lift the Tizona with his single arm fast enough to fend off Moxica's swift counterstroke.

So focused was the lord Moxica on avoiding the sentry's blade and exploiting the resultant opening in the sentry's defense, that he lost sight of, or perhaps simply failed to acknowledge the sentry's free hand. Emerging from behind the sentry's head and shoulders, the hand followed in the arcing path of the sentry's blade, clenching into a fist whilst it was hurtled at the ancient lord with tremendous force.

Resolute in his purpose and unwilling to squander the briefest of instants, Moxica thrust his blade forth from his crouched stance, seeking to impale the sentry's exposed side; but even as he endeavored to gore the sentry, he was met with a savage clout to one side of his head.

Extending himself to the fullest – the taut muscles of his body straining with monumental effort – an animal roar rumbled in Gabriel's throat as he channeled all his might into this single, reaching blow. The ancient Lord dipped his head in a belated attempt to avoid the sentry's fist, but to no avail. Gabriel struck Moxica high upon the temple, with strength enough to bring a stallion to his haunches. The sound of a heavy impact filled the chamber and Moxica's head reeled backwards under force of the blow, his inky locks flailing. His thrust having been robbed of its venom and aim, the ancient lord's blade grazed by Gabriel's side. His hand still balled into a fist, Gabriel looked on as Moxica keeled backwards, and watched as the ancient lord's feet left the floor.

Impelled by the sentry's blow, Moxica was momentarily lifted into the air, propelled headlong towards the wall of bookcases at his back. Accompanied by the sharp cracking of splintering wood, Moxica struck a looming bookcase headlong, the rear of his head, neck, and shoulders bashing against the aged timber with force enough quake the structure from its very foundations. Moxica jounced against the bookcase and collapsed on his side upon the stone floor at the foot of the wooden structure. Jarred loose from where they had been so neatly placed, a collection of archaic scrolls, books, and parchments toppled from the shelves and tumbled upon and about Moxica. A pall of dust unfurled from the shelves above and swirled as it descended, promising to settle upon the disarray below.

Having been guided downwards, Gabriel's sword had clanged against the smooth floor, and he drew it up, grasping it firmly in both hands once more. The instant Gabriel hefted the weapon, he set upon the fallen lord afresh, primed to finish the ancient lord where he lay. Moxica seemed disoriented by the blow he had taken, however, even as Gabriel began to close upon him, the ancient lord lifted himself from the floor; he rose to his feet abruptly with sword in hand, causing the cloud of dust that lingered about him to swirl chaotically. Moxica snarled menacingly. His fangs bared, he was a haunting, tenebrous figure in the scattering dust. His curved sword raised, Moxica sprang forth from the pall with alarming speed, wisps of dust trailing from his cloak and flowing black locks.

Moxica's blade glinted as it tore through the air towards the sentry, and he, caught off guard by Moxica's sudden assault, maneuvered his sword to meet the attack. Moxica's golden eyes burned like embers and his curved blade hissed with vengeance. Gabriel saw that the lord Moxica intended no less than to decapitate him with this wicked blow, and so just as the curved blade neared his own sword he abruptly dipped into a tight crouch. Moxica's blade whined by above the sentry's head, whilst the sentry leveled his blade at Moxica.

Gabriel drove his blade at Moxica's unguarded gut, thrusting the blade forth with all the strength and speed he could summon. The Tizona knifed through the vacant air between them, and when it seemed that the blade would surely find its mark, Moxica denied the sentry his victory. Moving impossibly, Moxica contorted his body away from the thrust with a deft, evasive twist, causing the sentry's blade to spear harmlessly into his billowing cloak.

Moxica was unhesitating and precise. Before Gabriel could even retract his blade, Moxica assailed him in return. Gabriel witnessed the rippling sway of black garbs before him and perceived the briefest flourish of Moxica's curved blade: a glimpse of gleaming steel resplendent with firelight. There was a sound of movement, of something whisking towards him, and then he felt the hot pain of Moxica's blade as it impaled him. Gabriel fell to a knee. For a moment he was unable to breath, unable to move, and with mouth agape, he simply stared up at Moxica who stared back into his eyes in return. Whatever emotion had briefly pervaded the ancient lord seemed to have quelled, for not a trace of anger was to be found upon his pale physiognomy, simply a cold, anguine look in his demon eyes. Even as, with cruel gradualness, Moxica forced the curved blade deeper into Gabriel's chest, the ancient lord's face remained vapid.

Still holding Moxica's remorseless gaze, Gabriel felt his breath leave him, felt the cold blade grate painfully against his ribs as it slid betwixt them, and felt a radiating agony within him as the blade punctured his lungs. Gabriel shook himself from his moribund stupor, and with what was an act of sheer will, he rose to his feet. Grimacing with pain, he swung his sword as best he could with a single hand, and felt sharp steel grind torturously against bone and flesh inside him.

Moxica recoiled, arcing his head and chest backwards, tilting to one side to avoid the sentry's desperate slash. Gabriel felt a sudden, wrenching throb within him as Moxica abruptly withdrew his blade from his insides whilst he moved clear of the Tizona. Gabriel watched as Moxica took a few steps away from him, eyeing him all the while. Moxica stood still and lowered his sword, the blade shimmering with rivulets of blood. Gabriel clutched his wounded side with his free hand. From the perforated flesh came a flow of blood that seeped into the garb beneath his leather tunic, leaking between his pale fingers and along the back of his hand. His breaths were rasping and painful, and his heart had begun to beat thunderously in his chest. He felt and tasted his own blood as it burbled upwards in his throat and trickled from one corner of his mouth. Still, the ancient lord and the sentry stood unmoving, each staring into the eyes of the other. Presently, Moxica spoke: a single word, a single chance to prevent further bloodshed.

"Yield," uttered Moxica in an assured yet placid tone. Gabriel did not reply, but removed his bloodied left hand from his wound and replaced it upon the hilt of the Tizona alongside his sword hand. Though the wound pained him horribly, and though it yet remained a gory slit of a wound, it had nearly ceased to bleed. Indeed, even as Gabriel stood staring at Moxica from beneath his lowered brow, the pain within him began to dwindle in the slightest, a sign that his body was already attempting to mend. Gritting his teeth against the searing sensation within him, Gabriel hoisted his sword and lunged at Moxica, a blood dampened growl in his throat.

Gabriel had but to twitch to trigger Moxica's swift attack, and so even as Gabriel took a single step towards the ancient lord, Moxica raised his own blade and launched himself at the sentry. The two combatants met with a strident clash of steel, their blades colliding above them. Though jolted by the weight of the sentry's blow, Moxica redirected the deadly Tizona as he slipped beneath and spun from the great blade as he had done before. Gaining the sentry's back once more, Moxica lashed out with his sword, the blade outstretched in a single hand. Hindered by his wound, Gabriel was slow to react to the ancient lord's deft movements. Even as he turned to face his foe, he knew he would be unable to defend himself. Gabriel caught a glimpse of flashing steel, which was followed by a deafening crack that erupted in his ears.

Gabriel's vision darkened and blurred, and an intense pain made itself known as Moxica's blade nearly split his skull along one side of his head, a jolt he felt through his entire being. A spray of blood spurted from Gabriel's riven scalp as his head listed to a side in the wake of Moxica's blade. Gabriel's sword felt suddenly heavy in his hands, and it was through his own volition that he was able to keep his sword raised at all. Though staggered and disoriented by the blow, still Gabriel stood his ground.

With a continuous, fluid flourish of his sword, Moxica spun swiftly and swept his blade low at the sentry's legs, hacking open a length of sinew, behind one of the sentry's knees, to the bone. Gabriel's legs buckled, and he fell to a knee. Wincing with pain, and using the Tizona to brace himself, Gabriel attempted to stand, the tip of his blade scraping unstably against the smooth, stone floor. He had barely begun to lift himself when Moxica tore into him with his curved blade once more. Moxica swung the sword downwards with terrifying force, the blade cleaving Gabriel's flesh and bone at the wrist, severing his sword hand from his forearm. Gabriel collapsed upon both knees, and it seemed that the passage of time slowed as he watched his ashen hand, its fingers unfurling from the hilt of the Tizona, fall to the stone floor with a wet thud, accompanied by the clatter of his fallen blade. Gabriel felt a pulsating agony spread from the end of his forearm. With a look of disbelief, he gazed before him at the bleeding, raw, hewed stump where his hand had been only moments before.

Gabriel curled his severed forearm against his body, leaving his left arm to fall at his side and, once more, Gabriel lifted his eyes to meet those of the ancient lord. Again, Moxica's face was emotionless and indifferent, even as he thrust his blade into Gabriel's gut and ran him through. Gabriel emitted a horrible, airy rasp. He lurched as the curved sword drove into his stomach, and he clutched at the blade with his remaining hand, his eyes never leaving those of Moxica.

The chamber was a soundless void, save for Gabriel's own labored breaths. The lord Moxica had debilitated him, broken him. Indeed, so great was his suffering that a part of him hoped for death. Moxica slid the curved blade free of Gabriel's gut, and a gush of thick blood followed its egress, splattering upon the floor between Gabriel's knees. Gabriel grasped at the wound with his remaining hand and the gore coursed through his fingers. Without warning, and with utter disregard, Moxica drove his foot into Gabriel's chest with brutal force, jolting the sentry's limp body, and sending it hurtling backwards through the air towards the center of the chamber. Gabriel lost what little breath he had in his ruptured lungs as he was lifted from the floor.

Gabriel's body shook as he impacted against one of the lofty pillars in the center of the chamber, the base of his skull and the length of his back thudding heavily against the stone. Barely conscious, Gabriel slid down the pillar, leaving a sanguineous streak, and came to rest upon the floor with his back propped against the stone. His head hanging feebly, blood-matted tendrils of hair hanging in his face, Gabriel peered up at the ancient lord. He saw that Moxica was not facing him, nor even heeding his presence in any real respect. Instead, the ancient lord was flippantly preoccupied with something he was carrying in the pocket of his tunic. Shortly, Moxica produced a black handkerchief, and placed it about the base of his curved blade, clasping it against the steel with his thumb and forefinger. With a single, measured pull of the cloth over the curved steel, he proceeded to wipe the blade clean of Gabriel's blood. Once finished, Moxica appeared to inspect the blade, and finally lifted his eyes from it, observing Gabriel casually.

His back rested against the stone pillar, Gabriel remained motionless, his remaining hand still clutching his pierced gut, from which rivulets of blood continued to stream betwixt his fingers. Deeply rubescent droplets ran down much of his ichor-slicked hair from where his scalp had been hewed into the bone. These droplets cumulated into globules at the ends of his locks, eventually falling to the stone floor. Gabriel's eyes wavered from Moxica to glance despairingly at the severed hand that lay upon the floor a short distance from him, and beyond it, his fallen sword. Gabriel's breaths had become forced and slow, and certain of his limbs had begun to tingle in the slightest. A great pool of blood had begun to form about him on the smooth floor, a coalescence of his bleeding wounds.

The most profuse of these was his maimed forearm, which lay awkwardly upon his lap, letting his blood in gentle pulses from its severed end. Though all his bleeding wounds had begun to ebb, his body felt strange, weakened and listless. His body began to tremble, most notably his remaining hand. His vision had begun to cloud and spot, and his limbs seemed distant and leaden. So drained was he of the vital blood within him, infirmity had set upon him, hand in hand with another sensation. The instinct, the need to feed burgeoned within him, compelling him nearly as powerfully as the first time he had ever felt the bestial impulse. Gabriel's heart began to beat with a sudden, intensified pace, a last recourse to prolong his endangered life.

His fluid, black cloak swaying subtly as he moved, Moxica approached the spot where Gabriel had come to rest with slow, purposeful strides. When he was mere paces from the fallen sentry,

Moxica came to a halt. From where he stood, he outstretched his sword arm and lifted his curved blade so that the tip was but a hand's breadth from Gabriel, and leveled at the sentry's throat.

Gabriel stared at the end of Moxica's blade, a detached, beaten look upon his aspect. Slowly lifting his eyes from the burnished blade, Gabriel returned his gaze to the lord Moxica. Moxica regarded him impassively, and yet there was some vague quality about his face which spoke of pity. For a time, Moxica simply stood glaring at Gabriel with his blade poised, until finally, in a voice both dour and reserved, Moxica spoke.

"You have much to learn, my young friend: about de ways of men and de ways of de world, of de vampir, of what you yourself arc. You are misled in your conceptions, misled by your own self, your own ignorance. Like men, de vampir possess attributes unique to de commonplace creatures of dis world, but dey are not demons, nor are you, nor I. Great is der longevity when compared to mankind, but like men dey are born and grow old...dey live and dey die. I understand your mind, for in my beginning der was much I did not comprehend, and der is much I have yet to learn; but heed all dat I have said, heed de lessons you have learned dis day. Wisdom is wrought of age, and so in time you shall come to understand de wisdom of my words...dat is of course if I so choose to give you your leave from dis place."

With disdain upon his visage, Moxica's lips moved as though he might say something further, but a noise from the door diverted the attention of the ancient Lord. Moxica chanced a slight turn of his head towards the entrance of the chamber. The great wooden door groaned as it swung open, the sound reverberating throughout the silent chamber. The steward, Finnigan, emerged from behind the door, his face stiffened with apprehension. Upon witnessing the grim spectacle within the chamber, his apprehension became horror, and he froze in his tracks.

"Em...mi...mi'lord...I beg yer forgiveness fer mi'intrusion," Finnigan stammered uneasily, his eyes flitting from his master to Gabriel's mutilated, bloodied form, "but I'd come te...te see if ye had need o'me and...and heard commotion from..."

As the steward fumbled with his words, Moxica raised his free hand, a subtle yet commanding demand for his steward to be silent, and Finnigan immediately obeyed.

Gabriel felt his body and mind surrendering to his instinct to survive, his atavistic compulsion for blood. His pounding heart awakened his body anew, giving him strength enough to bid his weakened body stand. His bleeding wounds had subsided to mere trickles and his vision had cleared. Gabriel glared at Finnigan with a lupine stare, the scent and sight of prey rousing the predator in him. He desired nothing more than to feed upon the stricken steward, yet he knew to make a single move in Moxica's direction would spell his end. Though his bleeding had abated, he was painfully aware that his body had but barely begun to heal. He would be hard pressed to lift himself from the floor, let alone confront the lord Moxica a second time. Gabriel reasoned that he must flee, or be left to the mercy of the ancient lord, and that he must soon feed, or perish.

Before Moxica returned his gaze to him, Gabriel batted the curved blade from his face, and summoning what vitality remained in his ravaged body, he braced his back and the palm of his remaining hand against the pillar behind him and rose to his feet in a single, if unsteady, motion. Gabriel saw Moxica's head whip about to face him once more with a threatening, piercing gaze. Gabriel slid rearward from the pillar and staggered backward, nearly losing balance. As he retreated, Gabriel took a final glance at his fallen hand and sword, the Tizona his father had given him. He looked to Moxica one last time, and their burning, amber eyes met, their aspects stolid. Then, Gabriel turned from the ancient lord and took flight toward one of the chamber windows.

Gabriel was horribly lame, yet still he rushed towards the window, grimacing with agony as he willed his butchered body onward. Moxica took a single step forward as though he might attempt to thwart the sentry's escape, but instead he halted, and simply watched as Gabriel leaped at the chamber window. Gabriel hammered against the wooden shutters with a shoulder, his good arm raised protectively over his lowered head. There was a piercing crack as the shutters gave, and Gabriel burst through them and out into the winter night with a cascade of broken, splintered wood.

* * * *

Cold wind howled in his ears as he soared outward and then plummeted downwards along the sheer wall of the castle. His cloak billowed and flailed, trailing his descent, and his matted locks blew clear of his pallid face. The snow-covered ground had begun to rise to meet him, and directly below him, he could see the verge of the precipice atop which the castle was built. A dreadful sensation gripped him, a merging of fear and foreboding, a knotting of his innards as he hurtled to the niveous earth. A great expanse of sloping crags wound their way downwards into the shadowy gorge that was Rosslyn Glen. Bare, ice-encrusted trees rose from the shadows between the crags, reaching up at the falling sentry with their branches. Like a stooping falcon, Gabriel fell from the black firmament towards the gnarled, outstretched limbs.

Gabriel crashed through several splintering branches, and was buffeted by others as he hurtled into the sparse canopy. He felt his bones tremor and his body jolted about. He fell through the snow-limned trees and struck the edge of the precipice as he dropped into the gorge, causing him to spin violently before jouncing painfully against the side of a jutting crag below the verge. An avalanche of snow and debris accompanied him as he toppled erratically – end over end down into the glen below. The cold rock gouged him and battered him as he fell amidst and the crags. Pain filled his being until finally his broken body went limp and his senses left him. Gabriel's lifeless, torn body tumbled out of sight into the shadows of Rosslyn Glen below.

High above, in the tower chamber of Rosslyn Castle, Moxica and his steward stared after the sentry. Unmoving, Moxica stared out into the darkness through the remnants of what had once been shutters. Tiny snowflakes drifted into the chamber from beyond the open window and alighted upon the stone floor. Finnigan, who had not moved from where he stood near the door, glanced at the window and then looked to his master warily. Continuing to stare out the window, Moxica remained stone still, an incredulous look upon his face. Finnigan fidgeted nervously, for it had been he who had taken the hooded stranger to his master's chamber, and he knew not what consequence he might face given his master's arcane, unpredictable nature. The chamber was deathly silent save for the faint murmur of wind from beyond the window, and it was more than the fretful steward could bear. Regarding his master, who had yet to blink, much less move or speak, Finnigan eventually found his voice.

"Em...y...yer ne goin' te...te kill me are ye...mi'lord?"

For a time, the ancient lord said nothing and during this time Finnigan's inner turmoil was overwhelming. Presently, Moxica lifted his free hand and pointed at the open window with a single, ringed forefinger.

"I...did not anticipate dat," he said in a placid, thoughtful tone. Finnigan, whose throat had gone completely dry, swallowed forcibly. He waited to hear more from his master, but the ancient lord remained standing in the center of the chamber with his eyes upon the window. Finnigan mustered up what little was left of his courage and cleared his throat.

"Em...Master?...Master? Y...yer ne—"

"No," Moxica interrupted casually, after what had seemed a moment of genuine consideration.

"Oh...oh...thank ye, Jesus," Finnigan muttered to himself as his eyes lifted to the ceiling. The steward bowed quickly and slipped back out through the door into the stairwell, pulling the heavy door shut behind him with resounding boom.

In the chamber, the barest trace of amusement made itself known upon Moxica's face. He raised his eyebrows, exhaled reflectively, and turned from the open window.

Chapter Five

To the New World
I

His mind was devoid of thought, devoid at least of any cogent thought. Gradually, his addled senses began to clear. His conscious mind was roused from its wakelessness, and he began to gain a certain, if muddled, awareness of his body. Pain was the first sensation he was to realize, a body besieged by agonies multifarious in nature. Where these pains were most excruciating, a warm wetness, which was cooling rapidly in the winter cold, made his flesh slick beneath his tattered robes.

He stirred, and wincing as he did so, Gabriel opened his eyes wearily. His breaths were labored and painful, and he noted that his body was trembling strangely—uncontrollably. The spasmodic tremors did not seem to be induced by the cold per se, but by the dire state of his ruined body. His weakened limbs tingled, and areas of his flesh felt numbed. He was gripped by an ominously moribund sensation, as though death were waiting to take him from within, biding its time like a vulture on the wing. He could hear his heart beating, struggling to keep life in his veins.

A wind drifted through the glen, a near noiseless sound accompanied by the subtle burbling of water nearby. Where Gabriel lay, much of the white snow fringing his fallen body was stained a deep red. With slow, painful, incremental movements, Gabriel began to lift himself from the snowy ground. It was not reason, perhaps not even his will that bade him rise, for his thoughts were erratic and confused. More than anything else, it was instinct that commanded his mind: a compulsion to survive at all cost.

Maneuvering his maimed forearm clumsily beneath him, slowly, gingerly, he brought himself to his elbows and knees. He remained thus for some time, breathing, waiting, hoping that his body might heal from its trauma. He was uncertain what length of time he had passed laying senseless, but he reasoned it had not been overly long, for the bleeding of his freshest of wounds had only just begun to abate. Having been dashed upon crags and branches during his descent into Rosslyn Glen, the flesh over his head and limbs had been gashed in many a spot. Undoubtedly, he had broken bones, for he felt a sharp, brittle stabbing from his ribs on one side, and the same from the wrist of his remaining hand. Gritting his teeth against the enfeebling pain of his body, Gabriel rose to his feet.

For a few moments, he simply stood where he had risen, his posture guarded and stiff as he observed his wooded, snow-covered surroundings. The sky was dark, yet the few stars that sparkled from beyond the black, clouded firmament sent a faint, pale glow into the basin of the gorge. The meager light illumined his warm breath as he exhaled into the cold, night air. Presently, he chanced a few measured steps, limping pronouncedly upon his lamed leg. His body still shook convulsively at times, and his limbs were increasingly benumbed as he grew ever weaker. He felt sickly and unsteady, as though he might topple at any time. He felt as though his drained body were relying upon its last reserves of strength. His thoughts were increasingly incoherent and ruled by his instinct. He was certain of one thing however, if he did not soon feed he might well collapse to the snowy ground, and if he did, it would mean his life. Keeping his maimed forearm to his chest, and clutching his black cloak to his body with his other arm, he hobbled onward as best he could. Driven forth by some innate compulsion to survive, Gabriel made his way through the glen towards Rosslyn village.

The forest was still and silent as he made his way through it, as though the snow and ice had brought all life within to a standstill. His gait was awkward and unstable, and so he did not move amidst the trees and icy, deadened brambles with his usual stealth. Instead, he stumbled about through the bare underbrush with twigs and branches snapping in his wake, his pace hopelessly slow. Perhaps if his ambulation had been quieter, he would have heard movement nearby in the pitch-black forest: heard the sounds of presences that had made themselves known in the cold air as he neared Rosslyn village. Oblivious to the eyes that watched him from the darkness, Gabriel urged himself onward, his head hung low. He had only taken a few steps further, when his lamed leg buckled beneath him and he fell to a knee. He grimaced under the abrupt pain, and with his eyes half shut, his head lolled exhaustedly. It was in this moment of sudden silence that his keen ears detected the subtlest of sounds from amidst the trees close by. The notion of some unseen presence roused him from his mindless state, and he searched the darkness with his sharp, fiery eyes.

He heard soft, tentative footfalls in the snow and forest litter, and his eyes darted to their source. He saw an obscure figure move amidst the trees deep in the darkness, and perceived that it was carrying a sizeable bundle of sorts upon its shoulders. The figure seemed to be observing him, and rather suddenly it let the bundle it held fall from its shoulders with a certain indifference. The strange bundle struck the frozen earth with a heavy thump, lifting wisps of powdery snow from the forest floor. The figure moved closer to Gabriel, winding gracefully betwixt the trees. As it approached from the near utter blackness, Gabriel caught glimpses of a gracile, pallid, nude form: of long, thick, raven-black mane, of animal eyes which glinted in the delicate starlight that trickled through the clouded firmament and through the snowy canopy. Gabriel remained still, and simply watched as the lissome she-demon emerged from beyond the trees.

The she-demon came to a halt some paces from him and cocked her head to one side as she regarded him. Gabriel did not sense any threat from the she-demon; in fact, the she-demon appeared hesitant to approach further. Nonetheless, Gabriel endeavored to rise to his feet, for he knew not what to expect of this creature before him, this vampir, as the lord Moxica had called it. As he rose, his leg buckled once more, and he toppled backwards over an old rotted log into the trunk of a large tree. His battered body thudded painfully against the sturdy trunk and he collapsed to the cold ground wincing, his back propped against the tree. The she-demon cocked her head to the opposite side, her haunting eyes playing over the sentry's mauled body. Weakened as he was, Gabriel merely stared blankly at the demoness as she observed him. He became aware of some movement a few paces beyond the she-demon, and he spied her youngling creeping towards its mother warily in a low crouch.

The she-demon tilted her head towards the youngling, issued a reassuring coo, and returned her piercing gaze to the sentry. With practiced predatory stealth and poise, the youngling skulked forth from where it had hidden in the shadows until it came abreast with its mother. It then hunkered in the snow, chittering inquisitively as it too observed the sentry. Slowly, the she-demon moved towards Gabriel anew, leaving the youngling where it had come to rest in the snow. She came to a standstill little more than an arm's breadth from where he lay against the tree, and he could not help but remark her powerful, sinuous body. Her silky, naked form loomed statuesque before him, and with her head tilted curiously to one side, she gazed down at him in a fashion that spoke to the side of him that was man. Her fierce visage seemed to reveal some understanding of his plight – perhaps conveying pity, or even compassion. Still, the she-demon remained wary, though her aloofness seemed to be diminishing quite rapidly. The demoness moved even closer to the sentry, and gradually lowered herself next to him. Gabriel had yet to move after having fallen.

He peered at the she-demon beside him from the corners of his eyes and watched as she, resting her haunches upon the backs of her shanks, leaned her face in close to his. She met his gaze and held it, her eyes curious, alert, and undeniably intelligent. She raised a single, ashen hand to his face and touched it to his brow, regarding it with the intrigue of a child. She ran her fingers over a half-healed gash upon his brow. Her sharp, blackish claws drew up some of the drying blood encrusted about the wound, and she brought her finger to her nostrils and sniffed the ichor. She looked over his torn body and tattered clothes once more, and then met his gaze again. The she-demon leaned closer still until not a hand's breadth separated their faces. He felt the heat of her breath upon him, and her earthy, sweetish scent danced in his nostrils. The she-demon began to sniff him, slowly moving her head along his face and neck with a concentrated look in her eye.

Still, Gabriel did not move; indeed he was unsure of what to do, even what to think. A moment later, the she-demon drew her face away from his and stood. She turned from him and walked back from whence she had come. The she-demon walked by her vampir youngling, which peered up at her and watched her pass, but stayed where it crouched upon the snow-covered ground. The she-demon's form grew tenebrous once more as she made her way back into the darkness amidst the trees. When the she-demon reached the indistinct bundle that she had let drop to the ground, she stooped and clasped it with a single hand. The she-demon proceeded to haul the bundle back towards the fallen sentry.

As the she-demon snatched up the bundle in her clutch, Gabriel realized it was no mere bundle at all. Indeed, what the she-demon towed behind her outstretched arm was a man – a commoner who had wrapped himself in numerous garbs to keep the winter cold from chilling his bones. Holding the man firmly about the ankle, the she-demon dragged the man's limp body through the snow callously, allowing the slack head and arms to buffet the roots and trunks of trees as the body was hauled through the underbrush. From where it sat upon its haunches, the vampir youngling leaned out towards the man's body and mewled softly, sniffing the body eagerly as it was dragged past. Gabriel saw that the man was a cripple, missing one of his legs below the knee. The cripple was gaunt and emaciated in appearance, his leathery skin soiled with soot, likely from a fire he had been curled next to for warmth.

The she-demon pulled the cripple alongside Gabriel, released the cripple's remaining shank, and left the body next to Gabriel. Cocking her head to one side, she watched him, curiously, expectantly. Gabriel understood her intent, yet it troubled him to come to grips with the meaning behind this sole act. Undeniably, unequivocally this was some base form of selflessness, an act of kindness, a virtue he had always believed unique to the nature of man alone. Gabriel stared down at the crippled wretch beside him, and then lifted his eyes to meet the she-demon's intense gaze. He saw her mouth open in the slightest and caught a fleeting glimpse of her sharp fangs. He watched in awe as her pale lips moved and a single word issued from her throat.

"Vehk'or."

Her voice, her spoken word, was strange, grating, effortful, and slurred. Nonetheless, there was no question that the she-demon had spoken – spoken a word that held some meaning for her and her kind, just as the other had those many years past. Gabriel simply stared at the she-demon in astonishment, struggling to focus his wandering mind so that he might discern what the she-demon had said. As before, he likened the vampir's harsh utterance to Latin, and his eyes widened with sudden comprehension. The Latin root was 'vescor'. The she-demon had told him to feed.

Gabriel held the she-demon's gaze for a few moments longer, his face searching and incredulous. Having invaded his nostrils some time before, the cripple's scent brought his mortal need for blood to the forefront of his being once more. He broke the she-demon's steady gaze and eyed the cripple with primal intent. Thin trickles of blood leaked from two puncture wounds on the cripple's neck, and from two smaller puncture wounds on the man's wrist. The flesh surrounding these was bruised, swollen, and raw, for the two vampir had fed on the cripple earlier in the night. However, the cripple was still clinging to life, for his heart still beat, albeit feebly, and there was breath yet in his tired lungs. Yielding himself entirely to his instincts, Gabriel clasped the scruff of the cripple's neck with his single tremulous hand, and hauled the limp body up towards him. Resting the cripple's back against his chest, Gabriel clutched him under the jaw, and jerked the lolling head backwards at a painful angle, exposing the soft of the cripple's throat.

The scent of blood was maddening and Gabriel fell into a feral trance. He lowered his head towards the cripple's barely pulsing neck, clamped his jaws about the man's throat, and bit down into the soft flesh. A muffled, wet, hollow crunch issued from the depths of the cripple's throat, as the sentry's powerful jaws compacted the man's neck. In the same instant, his dagger-like fangs plunged themselves deep into the man's weathered flesh, boring forth into the vital vessel beneath. Holding the cripple to him thus, he was still for some moments: his eyes distant and cold like a serpent's.

His jaws remained locked about the cripple's throat, as his fangs retracted from the punctured flesh. Blood welled in the wounds, pulsing into his waiting maw, and he imbibed the scarlet nectar with wolfish eagerness. He felt the lifeblood filling him, coursing through his veins, nourishing his starved flesh: the beginnings of revitalization within his debilitated body. His eyes looked as though they might shut, so entranced was he by his primordial instincts, by the tingling warmth that coursed through his body. He remained thus for some time, and the she-demon simply watched him all the while, standing next to him with her head tilted to one side. Gradually, the flow of blood began to ebb, concomitant with the cripple's very life. When the sentry finally exsanguinated the body, his eyes became alert and attentive once more, and he lifted his head from the cripple's throat. He breathed in deeply and then gazed down at the cripple's ghastly, gaunt body, which hung limp in his arms.

Once, long ago, such a sight would have caused his gorge rise in his throat, but his sensitivity to such things had changed. His heart had hardened, and his understanding, his perspective of life and death, was revised and detached. Gabriel released the cripple's dead body, and it slid lifelessly from his chest, slumping against a portion of the tree trunk before it toppled over onto the winter ground.

Though he had taken all that he could from the cripple, Gabriel was not yet satiated by what blood had remained in the wretch. Indeed, his compulsion for blood lingered still, and ravenously so. Nonetheless, a certain strength had already returned to him, pulling him from what he had felt to be the brink of death. The strange tremors that had afflicted his body began to subside and soon ceased. His powerful muscles no longer felt distant and leaden, and sensation returned to his numbed limbs. Entirely engrossed in the sensation of his body, Gabriel closed his eyes and rested his head against the tree at his back, his breaths slow and deep.

The she-demon's youngling, which had also been observing the sentry, leaned forward from where it was crouched, positioning itself upon its hands and feet. Its trepidation waning, it crept towards the sentry on all fours, though not without some hesitance. When it neared the sentry's feet, it came to a halt and issued a single inquisitive chitter. Gabriel opened his eyes and met the youngling's gaze. The sinewy muscles beneath the youngling's naked, ashen flesh tensed, as though it might then leap for safety. Instead, after staring at the sentry warily for a short time, the youngling relaxed its taut muscles and crept alongside the sentry in a most feline manner, its wide eyes never leaving his. The youngling came to a halt a second time, and passed between the sentry and its mother, its unblinking eyes seemingly searching the sentry's countenance.

From high above, a raven cawed, and the youngling lifted its amber eyes to the lofty treetop. Spotting the raven, which had alighted upon one of the uppermost branches, the youngling cocked its head, its eyes and ears pricked; then, quite abruptly, the youngling leapt towards the tree trunk and clung to the bark with the dark claws upon its hands and feet. It then scuttled up the tree towards the bare canopy.

The she-demon appeared disinterested with her young one's antics, for her eyes had not yet left the sentry, who turned to meet the vampir's gaze anew. Her bright eyes seemed to convey some sort of meaning, and he watched as the she-demon slowly crouched down beside him once more. Her eyes did not waver from his in the slightest, and the proximity of her presence elicited deep-seeded stirrings within him. A short while ago his instinct to survive had consumed his mind. With this need moderately fulfilled, another instinct burgeoned in its place, ushering itself into the forefront of his thoughts.

Part of him, the part that was man, which employed reason,

discretion, and thought, wanted to turn from the she-demon in disgust. It was another part of him, a deeper, baser side, which held his golden eyes to her naked skin. As he had noted in their first encounter, the she-demon's scent suddenly changed. The scent was intoxicating, a sweetish, gentle aroma, which allured him forcibly nonetheless, clearing his mind of thought and letting his instinct govern him. Gabriel forgot the pains of his body and his need for blood.

Sensing the change that had taken place within the sentry, the she-demon lowered her head to his, so that their cheeks all but touched. Warily extending a single, clawed hand, the she-demon cradled one side of the sentry's face in the cup of her palm. Presently, quietly, the she-demon sniffed him along his neck. Her state became increasingly roused the more of him she breathed in, her inspirations quicker and more frequent. It was as though the vampir had lost all inhibitions, for the she-demon began to nuzzle the sentry's face, a sound like purring resonant in her chest.

Gabriel's face was expressionless – vapid, so enrapt was he with what he was confronted with. He could feel the subtle warmth of her hand upon his face; the heat of her lips and breath, the caress of the smooth skin of her face upon his cheek. Now and again, surges of revulsion flooded his mind, only to be subsumed by the dominion of his instinct. The she-demon moved herself before him, crouching over him, straddling his loins. Her eyes searched him frenetically. Abruptly, the she-demon reached beneath his tunic with both hands, tearing his garbs below his belt with her claws. The she-demon lowered her nakedness upon him, once more emitting her strange purring as she did.

* * * *

The dark clouds that had begun to blanket the night sky drifted towards the northern horizon, allowing the glow of the moon and stars to filter through the thinning, residual wisps of cloud above. Below, still sitting with his back propped against the tree, Gabriel observed the she-demon with a sidelong glance. Their courtship had come to a close a little while past, and the she-demon now returned her attention to her youngling. Having risen to her feet at the base of the tree, the vampir gazed skyward, her demeanor serene and peaceable. In the branches high above, the youngling sat upon its haunches, rocking almost indiscernibly, as though in some sort of trance. As the raven had taken flight some time ago, the youngling simply gazed up at the increasingly starry firmament, its white body vaguely silhouetted in the dim light. The she-demon was staring at the youngling.

Her expression was one, Gabriel thought, that might bear a quality of endearment. A sound that was both a croon and a mewl resonated from the she-demon's throat, and the youngling turned from the night sky and peered down at its mother. Quite promptly thereafter, the youngling began to make its way down through the branches with surprising agility. It then clambered down the tree trunk, its claws scraping noisily against the rough bark. The youngling leapt to the ground and landed quietly in the snow. It immediately turned its attention to the body of the dead cripple and began to circle the corpse on all fours, sniffing it curiously. Quite abruptly, the thing seized the dead cripple by the scalp with both of its little hands. Gabriel watched disquietedly, as the tiny creature began to haul the dead cripple towards a patch of bare shrubs. The she-demon casually observed the youngling for a short while, and then turned from her young one and gently placed both of her palms upon the trunk of the great tree. The she-demon's claws caught on the bark, and she arced her back. She yawned serenely, exposing her fanged maw as she stretched her lissome musculature, which stood out definitively from beneath her ashen hide.

Gabriel watched the she-demon as she scratched at the bark whilst she extended herself. This sight disturbed him more than that of the youngster dragging the dead cripple. The driving instinct to mate had left Gabriel and his rationality had returned. It was with the clarity of this reason that he condemned himself for what he had done. He was so shamed, that even to look upon the she-demon's nudity repulsed him. His act dishonored him, and prayer would not absolve him, for it was sacrilege to have thus succumbed to the lust of this succubus. His disdain mounted, both for himself and the she-demon, and he wanted nothing more than to be gone from the midst of her and her young one.

Bracing himself against the tree trunk with his back and good arm, he began to lift himself from the cold ground. His maimed forearm cradled to his chest, he winced under the pain that still afflicted much of his body, and he rose to his feet gingerly. Peering at him inquisitively, the she-demon ceased her cattish display and removed her palms from the tree. The she-demon was suddenly still and merely stared at Gabriel with some intrigue. Beyond the icicle-laced patch of shrubs, the chary youngling looked up from the dead cripple for an instant and then returned its attention to the corpse. For a brief moment Gabriel regarded the she-demon, his aspect fierce and daunting. Sickened, he turned from her and limped off into the dark forest.

* * * *

Gabriel wound his way through the trees. Those tissues of his body that had been severed and battered had begun to knit, as had his broken flesh and bone. Regardless of his preternatural ability to mend, pain still pervaded his body, yet he perceived that the throbbing sensations had dulled in intensity. The rear of his previously hewn knee felt stiffened and somewhat unstable beneath the coagulated mass of scar tissue, and so his progress through the wood was atypically slow, albeit steady. He looked down at his mutilated forearm and stopped abruptly in his tracks. He was suddenly cognizant of the grim reality he faced: that because of his rashness, he must now live out the rest of his already cursed days without his hand. Still staring at his disabled appendage, he hung his head low so that his black locks fell over his face, and he shook his head in utter disbelief. He emitted a throaty, derisive snort as he observed the dried cap of blood and twisted, mending flesh that remained where his favored hand had once been. He roared with sudden rage, and balling his remaining hand, he bashed the outer side of his fist against the trunk of a tree. Gabriel's bestial ululation resounded through the quiet, winter forest.

When the wood fell silent once more, Gabriel heard movement through the snow and forest litter behind him. Even as he turned, he caught the scent of the she-demon. He spied her naked form as she slipped through the trees towards him, her youngling scampering about aimlessly some paces beyond her. It was clear the she-demon had followed him. Whether by scent, by sight, or trail, it mattered not; what concerned him was why. He wondered if the demoness, skilled huntress that she must be, had tracked him since their very first encounter. To have stumbled upon the she-demon by happenstance so far whence he had first seen her seemed increasingly unlikely. Gabriel reasoned that she had indeed followed him from Midlothlian to the fringes of Rosslyn Glen, but had not dared set foot into Rosslyn Castle.

The she-demon's eyes gleamed periodically as she passed through filtered beams of moon and starlight, and she stared calmly at Gabriel as she approached him devotedly. Gabriel's piercing eyes were alive with contempt, his face hard and unwelcoming. A bestial side of him voiced his intolerance, and he growled at her threateningly, a deep, harsh sound. Startled, the she-demon recoiled and froze in her tracks, as did her youngling, who then leapt for the safety of a tree. The she-demon cocked her head to a side, regarding him for a few moments with a saddened, bemused look upon her haunting face. They stood still for some time, each staring into the eyes of the other. Then, with a soft, defeated snarl, the reluctant she-demon turned from Gabriel slowly and began to make her way back through the darkened forest.

Her youngling leapt down from the crook of the tree in which it had sought refuge, and trotted along at her heels. Gabriel stood his ground and watched them go. Only once did the she-demon turn to look upon him a final time. Shortly thereafter, the she-demon turned to the dark wood once more, and she and her youngling evanesced into the consuming shadows beyond the trees. Gabriel turned from their vanished forms and continued on his way. Strangely, he felt something inside him that was reminiscent of regret, though he could not truly reason why.

II

The years of his ever-night rolled on. Inevitably, the years became decades, and in time, these coalesced into nigh a dyad of centuries. Yet the ravages of time passed him by, as though he were an unmoving, unyielding rock in the river of time, impervious to its inexorable flow. He made his way through many distant lands, encountering many different peoples, and seeing many strange and beautiful sights. The remarkable ability of his vampir mind allowed him to recall that which he had seen and heard with uncanny clarity, and so he would oft come to understand the tongues of the peoples he happened upon, those whom he hunted.

The world had changed. New roads scored once wild lands, and new villages and towns sprouted throughout like meadow flowers. To Gabriel, the changes he witnessed seemed inextricably linked to the greed of men, rather than progress for the sake of progress. Each man-made wonder served to bring gain, each innovation a testament both to man's creativity and avarice. War and conquest were the catalyst of grand invention. Longbows were replaced by rifles, crossbows replaced by muskets, men toiling through the night to forge that which might best take the life of other men, their ingenuity driven by the boundless covetousness of empires. Indeed, much had changed; yet to Gabriel, whose great many years afforded him unique lucidity and wisdom, much had remained the same.

With regard to his views and values, his conceptions of right and wrong, and his understanding of the world, Gabriel himself was much changed. Even his desire to hunt the vampir had steadily dwindled, and consequentially, the nights he devoted to the hunt waned as well. In the first place, he had hunted the vampir so tenaciously over the numerous decades that it oft took him years to find hide or hair of even one. Secondly, and he was somewhat loath to admit it to himself, he increasingly believed that the lord Moxica's notions of the vampir: of mankind, of many things, held significantly greater credence than he once thought. Moxica had spoken of his ignorance, of the wisdom he would in time possess, and the more Gabriel learned of the world, the more the ancient lord's words appeared to hold true.

Indeed, his own body was yet a mystery to him, for he had been alarmed and amazed when, in the year following his meeting with Moxica, a new hand had begun to grow in place of the one he had lost. At first, he had paid the small, boney lumps beneath the flesh of his useless stump no heed. In fact, his crippled sword arm had caused him such despair for a time that he had declined to look upon it. However, when the boney protuberances began to enlarge, project, and became sensitive to the touch, he could not help but mark their gradual development. The protuberances began to project increasingly, and had then segmented beneath his flesh, becoming crude, miniscule fingers. Some time later, a definitive, functional hand was birthed where mutilated flesh had once been, albeit undersized and feeble. Following a change in season with progressive use of the new appendage, Gabriel had found himself with a matured hand remade in the image of the one he had lost, as strong and sturdy as his favored hand had ever been.

To hunt the vampir had once been his sole reason to live, his sole salvation, as he had understood it. He had believed that his continued existence had some reason, served some ordained purpose. Countless nights had passed since his rebirth as a creature nocturnal, and his devout faith, his pious convictions, had begun to dissipate like river fog under a rising sun. He had lived to kill, and he killed to live, and he wondered if, with each life taken, he was not somehow robbed of some modicum of his humanity. If it was any consolation to his soul, if indeed one was harbored within him, he had ultimately been able to relinquish one of these two vices. In the past, his obsession to rid all lands of the vampir had consumed him, and he had dedicated the night to this purpose. Without this preoccupation to distract him, his nights were often spent in thought: contemplations of his past, present, and future, of the world, and his place in it.

It was strange to be in the world and yet not of it, to be a man and yet not truly so. Certainly, attired in his finery, he walked amongst them with practiced pretense, even spoke to them briefly in the dead of night, and they to him. Still, he existed along the fringes of society, a fleeting presence in the night, a whisper, a derelict. Since he had become what he now was, he had inevitably distanced himself from the bygone life he had once known. Bronwyn's death, the deaths of his friends, Ober, Colin and others he had known, had further severed his connection to the world of men. There was no merrymaking, nor tales over ale: no lengthy discussion by the fire, no warmth, no trust, no love. He simply was. Yet, aloof as he had become, his mastered skill of mingling with peoples in the night, or remaining unseen amidst them, allowed him some mocking semblance of his old life, which he cherished in a way. It made him wonder if he might be able to live amongst his once fellow man anew, still hidden in plain sight in a fashion, but on a grander more liberal scale. He pondered where he might begin his life afresh, and his ruminations led him to envision a distant place, an infant nation. It was during this time that he set his sights upon the New World.

He had learned of the New World from tales he had heard during his travels. He foresaw new opportunity there and was curious to voyage to this distant land. In truth there was naught but the treasures he had stowed to hold him to his home territories, for the place and time that he had known, the time wherein he had known love and laughter, had passed. He knew not what remained of his unnatural longevity, and so he undertook to set foot upon this far off place before death found him, if ever it did. It came to pass that in the year 1693, anno domani, Gabriel began preparations for his journey to the New World.

The collection of his scattered wealth had been a most tedious endeavor, as he had a number of small caches throughout both England and Scotland. He acquired three horses for the purpose, one to be ridden and scantily laden, and two to be tethered in tow strictly as beasts of burden. The tethered animals were immense, heavy-hoofed creatures, carthorses that were bred for such labor. These were each fitted with harnesses for carriage, and with capacious sacks, which hung two to a side like large saddlebags. With these animals at his aid, he would travel throughout the nights, locating each of his old caches by memory. It had been his plan to empty each of his caches, transport what he could south, and amass the treasures at a hidden location near port upon the northeast mouth of the English Channel. Those few caches he had in foreign lands he simply left behind. Nonetheless, he had been unable to carry out the ordeal in a single journey due to the sheer amount of wealth he had accumulated, and so the task had spanned a turn of the seasons.

He knew the Scottish and English lands well, and he had plotted his courses with the foresight that his exact memory afforded him. During the day, whilst he lay interred in the earth, the beasts and their precious loads had been hidden in what densely wooded areas he could find, as far removed from towns and traveled roads as was possible. Still, his possessions were susceptible to the thievery of roving bands and passers by that might stumble upon his laden horses by happenstance. As guileful as he was at concealing both himself and his belongings, he was fortunate never to have lost any of the loads, or the horses transporting them for that matter, for those who would steal any thing at any turn did abound. Indeed, more than once he would arrive at a cache in the night only to find that it had been looted of the treasure it had once held; and more than once, he had been forced to fend off bandits as he traveled the hinterland roads at night, much to the surprise and horror of the would-be thieves who incurred his wrath. It had been risky business to be sure, but in the end, his losses notwithstanding, he had still assembled a staggering fortune.

What had, at first, seemed an insurmountable dilemma, was how he was to survive a voyage across the great ocean. Keeping his bodily exertion to a minimum, or even remaining motionless in place of his usual nocturnal activity, he might last eight, perhaps nine days without feeding, but no more. Even if he managed such a feat, such infrequent feeding would leave his body weak and torpid. He was unwilling to stay the course of the voyage in so vulnerable a state during the night, for his predicament would be precarious enough as it was given his quiescent state during the day. Where he would shelter himself from the sun, undisturbed, was another conundrum altogether. The ship's crew was also a concern. It was Gabriel's habit to dispose of his prey once he had fed, leaving no trace of the occurrence. Even in the rare cases that he had been forced to flee in haste without his kill, he would tear out his victim's throat with his teeth, making it seem as though some animal had been at the body, masking the conspicuous puncture wounds upon their throats.

He would not be able to employ such a diversion upon a ship, no matter how great the vessel's size. Strange deaths and vanished crewmembers would arouse suspicions and superstitions, and the crew would undoubtedly scour the ship for a stowaway if their fear did not turn them on one another first. Preying upon the crew would detract from their ability to operate the ship, and eventually, if it were a small ship, there would be no crew left to speak of. Gabriel could not take the helm himself unless he set anchor during the day, a strategy that would lengthen the voyage two fold, and leave him starving to death upon an empty ship. After much deliberation, Gabriel had reasoned that the answer to his quandary lay in the Dark Continent.

* * * *

It was then that Gabriel had made his way to France, the first nation he was to pass through as he journeyed south. In the guise of a merchant, he chartered a barge upon which he, with his horses and cargo, crossed the English Channel in the night. It had not been the first time he had left England in such a fashion, yet he was wary nonetheless. He had instructed the small crew to come ashore away from any known ports to keep his presence secret, and as he had paid them handsomely to do so, they obliged quite readily. They reached the French shore at a remote location under cover of night, the outskirts of the port town Calais. There, he had disembarked and continued onwards into the south of France, and thence into his old homeland of Spain.

Much was not as he remembered, yet there was a poignant nostalgia to the place that he could not ignore. He had tried not to linger upon the oft painful memories of his youth, of his mother and father, but to no avail. It seemed that his humanity had not entirely left him after all.

He traveled as he had done whilst gathering his riches in Britain. He moved at night, keeping from main roads as best he could, hiding his beasts and cargo during the day in what wooded and mountainous areas he would happen upon. He had purchased a small, two-wheeled cart in France, to which he had harnessed the two carthorses, thus enabling his entire fortune to be transported in a single trek. In time, he had reached the southernmost tip of Spain, and there chartered another barge to cross the Strait of Gibraltar. Following a night's crossing of the strait, he had come to ground upon the Dark Continent, the great mass of land they called Africa.

III

Gabriel had ridden westward after disembarking on the African shore. The climate of the land was hotter even than his native Spain, and the earth more arid. Strange fauna inhabited the African plains, beasts both predator and prey. He had oft found the latter variety in herds of staggering size, their ranks meandering about the grasslands nearly so far as his keen eyes could see. Unlike the English skies, the African firmament had been largely cloudless and clear, and the moon and stars had shone from above with astonishing brilliance.

He had continued west until he neared the coast, and then headed south along it, keeping some distance inland from the shoreline. Night after night he had ridden south thus, until one night, he finally found what he sought.

* * * *

Far to the west, the torrid African sun had already begun to sink into the vast ocean beyond the barren shore; and the undulating water glowed like molten iron, so vibrantly did it reflect the vermillion blaze of the waning sun. Inland, to the east, the plains had grown dark, yet the world immediately about him was still bathed in a dim, fiery glow. Gabriel had but barely begun his evening travel. Though his anxious mount was inclined to quicken its pace, he kept the three horses at a brisk walk. His mount snorted warily, yet he paid it no mind, for he too had caught the scent and heard the strange whoopings and ululations of the devilish laughing beasts which prowled the plains. Fearsome hunters and scavengers though they were, Gabriel knew they would not dare come within ten paces of his horses, nor would he allow them if they grew so bold.

He paid the skulking creatures no real heed, but he observed them for a while nonetheless, watching them as they moved about in the dark, the glare from the moon giving their staring eyes a lurid, hellish quality. It was a quality of night creatures that chilled his blood no longer, a gaze, he thought, that he had seen many times before, even whilst staring down at his own reflection in a still pond under the stars.

Gabriel turned from the plains and gazed out at the ocean. Distant in the southwestern horizon, its swaying mast and broad, rocking hull partially silhouetted by the dwindling sun, a great ship sat upon the rolling, shimmering water some few-hundred paces from the shore. As far away as it was, Gabriel spotted the vessel immediately, for it broke the evenness of the horizon so distinctively. Indeed, he wondered how he had not seen it sooner. His eyes searched the length of shore nearest the ship, and saw that four rowboats had come to ground upon the beach. The rowboats were empty, but two men were standing in the vicinity of the beached vessels. Some distance further inland a sizable camp had been pitched, and as he rode closer he saw that there was some commotion thereabouts. Cries of anguish were carried to him upon the wind and, soon thereafter, so were the scents of blood and offal. A few campfires were ablaze, and these illumined the campsite with a flickering, golden effulgence. Smoke and dust whirled and rose from the camp.

Though he could see them, Gabriel knew he was too far from the gaggle of men to be seen himself. Regardless of this fact, he steered his mount inland, dismounted, and after securing the horses to a solitary tree, he proceeded the rest of way to the camp on foot. With his black, leather gloves and boots: his long dusky-grey cloak and black garments beneath, he was a vague form upon the increasingly dark landscape. The scents and sounds of the campsite intensified, and as he neared the camp he adorned the hood of his cloak, casting much of his face in shadow. He moved across the plain almost noiselessly, winding his way through the shrubs that dotted the arid land. The sun had nearly dipped beyond the ocean, and night had begun to take hold of the African plain.

His dark cloak gently billowing and flapping in the soft breeze, Gabriel was as a wandering phantom upon the plains, an indistinct, haunting figure. Lowering into his stealthy crouch, the shadows hid him further still, and he crept closer to the camp until he was no more than some fifty paces from it. He reached a patch of bush, and there lowered himself to a knee, observing the ensuing chaos from behind the shrubs. There he watched a great atrocity unfold before his eyes.

In the general center of the camp, groups of bewildered, terrified men, women, and children were huddled together in a teeming, erratic mass. They were dark skinned, the black peoples of Africa. Some clothed only in meager garbs that covered their loins, and others wholly naked, they were some hundred or more in number. All were bound or shackled in irons. Some were fettered at the neck and, from there, held in a line by long wooden poles to which their fetters were linked. Some were barracooned; others leashed in chains like dogs, and shackled together like beasts of burden. Black, iron manacles bit into the flesh of their ankles and wrists, and the jingling and clinking of iron chains accompanied their movements.

Women with tear-streaked faces screamed and wailed, whilst beaten, bloodied, scourged men reached out with their hands to those they had been torn from, their eyes wide and wild, shimmering with suffering. It was clear that they had been captured, snatched from their villages to be made slaves of a nation they had no kinship with. A handful of naval officers, Englishmen by their tongue and white-faced, red coats, shouted over the tormented cries. They and their crew, many with a whip in hand, had begun to drive the shackled groups of slaves towards the shore in coffles. Impeded by their fetters, the slaves staggered forth under the whips of the English slavers. Remaining where he had hid, Gabriel watched as the grim procession gradually made its way to the beach. A few of the crew remained behind, disassembling tents and gathering the supplies they were to take back to the ship.

Gabriel looked out over the ocean to the ship itself, and then returned his gaze to the slavers and their captives. The sight troubled him. For how many years, decades, had he hunted the vampir, decimating their number to insure they would never again take the lives of men? Life: precious life, the lives of the innocent, of men, women, children, and infants. Yet, it was apparent that man was no less a plague upon itself than the vampir. Throughout his many years, even before his rebirth, Gabriel had seen what horrors men would commit for their greed, guised as acts for God and country. He recalled Moxica's words, those concerning the heinous atrocities the ancient lord had seen man commit in the name of the divine. Staring at the anguished multitude of African peoples, Gabriel understood that he was bearing witness to a form of cruelty and suffering no vampir would ever inflict upon mankind. He understood that man had the perpetual capacity to treat his fellow man with less compassion and deference than a vampir would treat its prey.

His thoughts were by no means revelational, for he had thought them long before, nor was the horrid spectacle he witnessed unforeseen. The capture of slaves and the mass transport of this living cargo was what had drawn him from the north. This was the lure of the Dark Continent for many nations, and it was also the answer to his quandary: how he was to survive the ocean crossing. All that remained was how he was to transport his sizeable fortune. A swift decision was of the essence, for having captured so many of the African tribesmen; the English ship would not tarry long on the coast before setting sail to the New World.

His countrymen's greed for wealth insured they would stow his riches onboard. Even if their cargo-hold were overfull, they would find room to accommodate the wealth he possessed. He need do little more than offer his fortune, and it would most assuredly be taken without question. It would then be a simple matter of making his way onboard the ship himself, unseen under cover of night. Gabriel decided that this would be his best course of action, and he quietly made his way back across the expanse of open plain between the camp and his waiting horses. He untied the horses from the tree, loaded them and the small cart with their loads once more, and rode off towards the campsite with the carthorses in tow.

* * * *

At the camp, three other crewmen joined the two that had remained behind. All were packing away the last of their supplies and campsite paraphernalia. The crackling campfires helped put them at ease, for the flames kept the lurking beasts of the African night at bay. Presently, a subtle tinkling was audible over the burning timber, accompanied by the sound of hooves thumping heavily against the parched, dusty ground. A man on horseback, formidable in appearance, emerged from the darkness beyond the fires, and rode his steed into the center of the camp. The man wore a great, grey cloak and black garbs. The man was hooded, so that even in the firelight, his face was somewhat obscured. An ornate cutlass hung at his side, sheathed in a beautifully engraved wooden scabbard, and the hilt of a dagger protruded from a sheath at his opposite side.

Tethered to the man's steed were two impressive animals, to which a cart had been harnessed. Both the horses and the cart were laden with some manner of goods, which were stowed in thick sacks. No longer attentive to what tasks each had each been engaged with, the crewmen turned to face the lone rider. They eyed him nervously, their hands poised by their respective muskets and rapiers. From beneath the hood, the man's eyes seemed to scrutinize them, a piercing stare that, for them, spanned a progressively uncomfortable length of time. Some of the crewmen looked to one another searchingly, unsure what to make of the silent, unmoving rider. They watched as the hooded man casually dismounted, his stare unwavering. Still, the man said nothing, but silently turned his back to the crewmen and walked towards the horse-drawn cart. He reached into the cart and hauled up a sack from within it, righting it so that its drawstrings faced upwards.

The big sack jingled with the muffled sound of coin. The hooded man untied the sack, hefted it out of the cart, and turned to face the mystified crewmen once more, clutching the open sack in a single hand. Quite abruptly, the hooded man tossed the heavy sack to their feet, and it struck the bare ground with a heavy thud and a loud clinking. The sack toppled over, spilling coins and trinkets at the crewmen's feet. The crewmen gazed at the treasure before them with wonder. They peered up at the hooded man's remaining cargo with awe and then, with quizzical countenances, they regarded the hooded man anew. In a voice that was both reserved and commanding, the hooded man finally spoke.

"Gentlemen...I have a proposal."

* * * *

Gabriel told the crewmen that he was a traveling merchant in desperate need of a vessel to transport his riches. He had promised a quarter of his fortune should they accommodate him, and they immediately dispatched one crewman to send word to their captain. The captain readily obliged, and had sent his commanding officer and an additional two crewman back to the campsite for reasons of both diplomacy and labor assistance. The commander had offered Gabriel lodgings upon the ship on behalf of the captain, but Gabriel declined the offer, insisting that he had further business to attend to on the African coast. Gabriel had explained that a notable acquaintance of his, an heir of the Drake family, was expecting his shipment of riches and had representatives, accompanied by armed cavalcades, at all known ports to meet the ship when it reached port in the New World.

This acquaintance, Gabriel had informed them, or one of the aforementioned representatives, would see to his belongings. Albeit entirely fictitious, the commander had accepted his rational, but Gabriel knew that it was likely that neither the captain, nor his officers had any intention of giving up the horde he had entrusted to them. Perhaps the captain's word had held some merit, but when pitted against greed, in his experience, it was greed that prevailed over honor. Furthermore, there would have been no actual cavalcades to meet the English vessel, and it would only behoove the captain to have kept the unclaimed wealth. In any case, all that Gabriel actually desired was to, by any means, get his fortune aboard the ship and have it reach the shores of the New World.

Gabriel had left the Englishmen to their devices and ridden out into the African night upon his mount at a brisk canter. Near the outskirts of the campsite he had heard a fiendish ululation, and spotted one of the laughing beasts, its belly swollen, feasting on a black-skinned body left behind by the English. The yowling thing was joined by another, and then another, and the beasts had torn the body limb from limb. Gabriel rode on. Shortly thereafter, he had reached a rocky promontory upon the coast that overlooked the ocean, from which vantage point he observed the English slavers and their captives. Unbeknownst to the slavers, he had watched them load their rowboats with the forlorn Africans, and watched as time and again, the English departed to the great ship with a boatload of slaves and returned to the shore to take yet another load of the natives. Sitting still and a quiet atop his mount, he had watched as they loaded his possessions, and watched still as the last boat, carrying the last load, left shore for the massive ship.

No sooner was the beach cleared of all persons, than Gabriel had wheeled his steed from the cliff face and exhorted the animal into a rapid gallop. Pushing the animal to the limit of its speed, Gabriel had made his way down the barren slope where the land permitted descent. Upon reaching the beach, he had urged his frothing mount onward, and they tore across the sand and into the surf, sending a burst of shimmering droplets surging into the air. The horse had plowed flank-deep into the cool, ocean water when Gabriel suddenly dismounted into the churning blackness. Having unsheathed his dagger, he had slashed the horse free of its bridle and saddle, and watched as the freed animal turned back to shore. This done, he had turned to the looming ship, and plunging beneath the waves, swam out into the dark ocean waters.

* * * *

The milky glow of the moon and stars danced in shimmering wrinkles over the ocean surface, the bright, wavering reflections standing in stark contrast to the black water. Slow-moving waves thumped against the hull of the English ship, gently rocking the vessel, causing the woodwork to creak and groan. A colossal, iron, mooring chain rose from the black depths to the deck above, where a portion of its length remained raveled upon a sizeable reel. The sway of the ship caused the heavy chain to grind within the hawsepipe, and clank delicately against the hull. At the opposite end, the mooring chain was linked to the anchor, which still clung to the ocean floor. Near where the chain met the surface of the water, something moved beneath the dark liquescence. The water roiled in the slightest, and the thing emerged from the blackness.

* * * *

Gabriel stared up at the ship and the starry expanse of sky beyond, his fierce lupine eyes assessing, plotting. Presently, he lifted one gloved hand from the water and gently clasped the mooring chain. He took hold of the chain with his other hand and then hauled himself from the ocean. Water dribbled from his dangling locks and cloak, falling like rain upon the undulating surface below. The noise of the ocean and the rocking ship drowned the subtle sounds of his presence. Slowly, silently, hand over hand, Gabriel climbed the rusted iron links, holding his legs to the mooring chain with the delicate purchase of his feet. Reaching the point whereat the chain vanished into the hawsepipe, Gabriel ceased to climb, and twisted about upon the chain so that he faced the hull of the ship. Slowly, he then coiled his legs so that his thighs nearly touched his chest, bracing the soles of his feet against the hull whilst still firmly gripping the mooring chain with both hands.

Simultaneously hauling himself upwards with his arms and propelling himself from the hull with a thrust of his legs, he nimbly leapt up from the chain to the gunwale of the ship. For a short while he did not move, and simply clung to the gunwale, listening for footfalls upon the wooden deck. He then pulled himself upwards slowly, enough to allow his eyes to lift above the level of the gunwale and peer out over the deck. A foul stench, one of fear, sweat, excrement, and urine hung in air. It rose from an open, metal hatch leading to the hold below deck, as did the muffled lamentations of the imprisoned Africans. A handful of English officers and crewmen were engaged in their perfunctory duties above deck, some occasionally murmuring to one another in the darkness. Gabriel surmised that the crew would soon retire for the night, and then perhaps set sail at first light.

Gabriel observed the men further, and then examined the lay of the deck. In a single, noiseless motion, he flung himself over the gunwale and onto the deck. Slinking beneath rigging lines and around a few of the ships cannons, Gabriel crept out over the deck unseen, like some shadowy wraith in the moonlight. Upon reaching the hatch, Gabriel looked about above deck a final time and then dropped into the hold below.

* * * *

All around Gabriel, the African slaves had muttered and cried in the darkness. Some had seen him descend into the hold and they had seemed unsure of what to make of him. Regardless, they could not speak the tongue of the English to report his presence, and so Gabriel had made his way to the rear of the hold where it was darkest. The hatch had eventually been closed, and so little light filtered through the thick grates that comprised the hatch, that the shackled natives were made to feel about blindly in the all-consuming dark. Gabriel had remained below deck even after the English had slid the bolt to lock the hatch. In the dead of night whilst all was still, Gabriel had methodically torn into floorboards with his blade in one corner of the hold next to the aft bulkhead. Though he did not know their tongue, he had heard fear in the voices of the slaves.

Having realized that something lurked in the utter darkness with them, they had begun to chatter anxiously amongst one another. Breaching the floorboards, he had slid himself beneath the dislodged planks, and then replaced the loose floorboards where they had lain in attempts to conceal what he had done. He had then wormed his way through the deathly narrow space between the floorboards and the timber below, passing beneath the aft bulkhead. This cramped, dank crevice was to be his sole refuge for what time the ship would sail in daylight to the New World.

Many slaves died of starvation and disease, and so, those nights when he was forced to leave his hideaway to feed, Gabriel would take those closest to death. Their lives served to preserve his, and he saw that he was no better than the vampir, just as Moxica had once said. Indeed, those whom he preyed upon were the sick and the weak, and his selection weeded them from the rest, as a wolf would a sickly stag. Once Gabriel had fed, he would tear the throats of his victims, masking the deep puncture wounds his fangs inflicted.

Many of the crew believed the slaves had turned to cannibalism, and so they muzzled them to prevent any further mutilations. Yet every so often another mauled, drained, dead body would be found strewn upon the floor of the hold, and the crew's superstitions soon made them restless. The affrighted slaves knew not what plagued them so, nor could they voice their fears to their English captors.

Throughout the voyage, the slaves were kept in a condition filthier than that of swine in a sty. The choking miasma reached him even beneath the floorboards beyond the bulkhead, as did the putrid refuse, which had leaked into the floor timbers below the hold. Throughout the voyage, he more often heard rather than saw the helpless slaves raped, beaten, tortured, and abused. Some went mad, others took their own lives. The English broke families apart and exhibited a disregard for their fellow man that Gabriel had never experienced, even upon the battlefield in heat of war. Contempt and anger grew in Gabriel's heart, and even he struggled to keep his sanity, interred as he was beneath the stinking hold. When, one night, after what seemed an eternity at sea, shouts of 'land ho,' sounded from above deck, Gabriel crept forth from the bowels of the ship.

He heard the heavy rumbling of the mooring chain as it tumbled from its reel, pulled into the depths by the anchor, which the English had cast into the ocean. Shortly thereafter, Gabriel emerged from his hole and made his way through the stricken slaves towards the hatch upon the wooden ceiling above.

****

The preoccupied crew and its officers did not notice the sullied, tattered, shrouded figure that rose from the hatch with an air of grim intent. When finally they did note the cloaked stranger, it was far too late to flee. Gabriel unleashed his rage upon the terrified English, and his vengeance was swift and merciless. None escaped, nor lived to see the rise of the sun.

When all was still and quiet atop the bloodied deck, Gabriel removed his musty clothes, tossed them overboard, and then commandeered the ship. The sinewy muscles beneath his slicked, pale flesh stood out markedly in the moon and starlight as he raised the anchor. Securing the rigging, he left the sails to billow once more, and the great vessel lurched forth through the waves. As the ship cruised through the swells, Gabriel searched for his stowed trove. Breaking down its locked door, he gained entry into the forecastle of the ship, and from therein, hauled out over half his stockpile of riches onto the deck. He then similarly forced his way into the captain's cabin, where he found the remaining portion of his fortune. After helping himself to a sack full of the captain's finery and leisure clothes, he lugged the last of his wealth out onto the deck. Littered with the scattered bodies of the English dead, and with Gabriel forbiddingly poised at the helm atop the quarter deck, a heap of treasures upon the deck below, the ship coasted towards the shore of the New World.

Gabriel had let the sails billow to their fullest, and did not slow the vessel's mounting speed, for it was his intent to run the ship aground. The ship came to a violent, grinding halt upon a sandy shore and, below deck, the shackled Africans had shouted wildly as they were battered and shaken about by the jarring impact. When the ship settled, Gabriel had heaped half the treasure into one of the English rowboats and then loaded another as he had the first. From atop the deck he had lowered first one boat and then the other into the shallows below. Having dropped from the prow of the ship into the frothing surf, he had then hauled the laden boats across the sand in two separate treks, dragging each into the steaming jungle beyond the sandy shore. Taking precautions against would-be thieves, he had buried his riches in the jungle and effaced the tracks he had left in the sand using large palm branches.

Long after the ship was beached upon the coast, Gabriel had

returned to the vessel, dropped down through the hatch a final time, and freed the terrified slaves. This done, he had risen from the dank hold with a single leap and, in the eyes of the petrified slaves, had vanished from sight above, beyond the hatch. When the emancipated Africans finally braved a climb above deck they had been horrified by the morbid, charnel sight that met them. Confused and frightened, they had wandered about the deck aimlessly for a time. They finally left the ship and made their way along the beach away from the wreck, never to set eyes upon their ghostly liberator again.

* * * *

Dressed in the informal vestments of an English captain, his sacks of riches safely cached in the jungle and awaiting his return, Gabriel began to make his way north in the New World.

Chapter Six

Return of the Ancient

I

A collection of clouds drifted across the Virginia sky. The bright midday sun remained unobscured by the passing clouds, and its radiance illumined their vaporous, protean forms. Gazing through his immense office window, Director of National Intelligence, Andrew Sinclair, stared out at the blue sky beyond the glass. His elbow was propped on the arm of his chair, his chin rested between his thumb and forefinger. He had allowed himself to recline into the thickly padded, leather backrest, at least as far as the chair allowed. He was, in effect, the picture of contemplation, his mind distant from the lavish office and the amenities within it.

It had been well over a month since the Haitian sting, and he was no closer to finding a significant lead to the whereabouts of the man in black the sniper had described. Still gazing into the vast blue of the sky, Sinclair wondered if the methodology he and his compatriots had employed to narrow the search might have been an oversight in some way. He had at least entertained other possibilities of course, but the main thrust of the search effort lay in the method by which John Smith had been originally been found: essentially a money trail. John Smith: the white-faced man, the face that had plagued his childhood dreams.

Sinclair sat in his chair, unmoving save for the rise and fall of his chest. His mind remained engaged in other avenues of thought for some time, until the ring of his desk phone roused him from his musings: a call on his private line. He glanced at the call display, and then lifted the phone to his ear.

"This is Sinclair. You have something for me Reynolds?"

"Not exactly what you were looking for sir, and let me assure you it hasn't been for lack of trying. We've essentially dipped into the archived records of all the relevant institutions at our disposal, sourcing transactions involving antiquities, and analyzing banking records. We still have a lot to go over, but as of yet we don't really have anything. So far, the majority of our findings from this investigation point to notable families, some even in our own guild, and to public figures all of whose backgrounds have already been checked out in one way or another. I mean, it's no secret that a whole lot of us come from families that struck it rich a long time ago and...well...that single fact is pretty much all we're getting back for all our efforts on this end. Had a couple leads...dead ends...both turned out to be amateur treasure hunters of sorts. Now...we've been keeping tabs on officers involved in that sting in Queens like you asked. We haven't gotten anything of interest over the phone taps, but...well...it's not much, but that SWAT officer who resurfaced a few weeks back...Klyne...his account has undergone a sudden increase in funds, and not from bonuses, perks or—"

"From what source?" Sinclair interrupted.

"Don't know. The deposits were made in cash."

"Anything else?" asked Sinclair sternly.

"Nothing of merit...yet...but we've already started trying to get through dummy accounts we've encountered along the way, hopefully we'll find something soon."

"All right, keep on it. That will be all, thank you."

"Yes, sir."

Andrew Sinclair replaced the phone and went still as he fell into deep thought for a few moments, staring down at the office floor at nothing in particular. Abruptly, he snatched up the phone again and dialed a number. Kenton Bruce picked up on the other end.

"Andrew...just give me a second."

Sinclair waited in silence, a stern expression upon his face. Shortly, Kenton's voice issued from the phone once more.

"Andrew?" Kenton spoke Sinclair's name as if he was insuring that Sinclair was still present one the other line.

"Anything on your end?" Sinclair inquired quickly.

"No...nothing new."

"All right...I want you to bring in Sebastian Klyne."

"You sure? I mean...I read Klyne's report too. It's riddled with coincidence...improbable, yes...but plausible as well. You don't think he was in on it? He was shot, remember...twice."

"I had 'im monitored while he was debriefed," Sinclair explained. "A few subtle movements of his eyes suggested that he was not simply accessing long term memory, but tapping into creative centers."

"That kind of assessment is not exactly foolproof," Kenton stated somewhat dismissively.

"It's all the little things, Kenton, the little details that become significant when compiled. It's highly unlikely that the black car, allegedly driven by two additional Russian traffickers, got inside a secured perimeter undetected during the sting, and they sure as hell didn't get out without some kind of help. That means whoever was in that damn car probably knew that the sting was going down well before hand, which implies a leak from the ranks of the officers. Now, the suspect on the roof was spotted heading the same way as Klyne, and it just so happens that the officers in pursuit of this mystery car that Klyne ended up in had an air conditioning unit fall onto the hood of their cruiser. Be judicious, Kenton...Klyne reappears a couple weeks later, his circumstances having apparently been made such that he is incapable of divulging his whereabouts for the time he was missing?"

"Well..." Kenton began.

"And I just found out from Reynolds that following the sting, Klyne has been receiving untraceable cash deposits into his account. Deposits unrelated to his occupation," continued Sinclair.

"Okay...all right...so when you say bring him in..." Kenton responded questioningly.

"Nothing soft, no sweating for intel. I want 'im locked down in a military installation by tonight...hardball from the get go. Send three agents to bring him in. I want it covert and discreet. Klyne lives in Brooklyn, so have 'em bring him to Fort Hamilton... and insure they keep 'im in sensory deprivation during transport. Also, wrangle me a team of ten from the black ops personnel list, as well as a chopper with pilots and a door gunner. If Klyne gives us the info we need on our subject, I'm gonna be ready to get 'im, and I want to be prepared in case he's got armed persons with 'im. I also don't want to give our target the opportunity to be forewarned, or to escape."

"I'm assuming the personnel involved won't be fully briefed on the actual objective of this mission," Kenton ascertained.

"No...just throw 'em a bone. The hounds don't need to know what their masters want with the fox," said Sinclair metaphorically.

"All right. I'll handle the interrogation myself and send word when I'm done."

"No need, Kenton," Sinclair said assuredly. "I'm going to see to Klyne's interrogation personally. You don't need to be in the field for this one. I'll arrange for Fort Hamilton to accommodate myself and the team, and then I'll fly up there soon as I can. I'll likely be there before 'em, so you just make sure they get prepped, and have 'em meet me there. Oh, and insure the team is transported in civilian vehicles...again...I don't want any tip-offs, and if we're going to leave Klyne breathing, I don't want him suspecting anything that he shouldn't when it comes time to get after the target."

"Okay," Kenton replied. "I'll get on it. Have a good flight."

Sinclair replaced the phone upon his desk once more, reclined into the soft backrest of his chair, and for a short time, stared back out at the sky through the broad, office window.

II

Sebastian Klyne entered the lobby of his apartment building. He had left a local bar relatively early after having a single drink with a friend and, though the night was yet young, he had decided to head home nonetheless. There were a few people standing next to the elevators, waiting for one to descend, and he nodded a greeting to a man he recognized – a tenant whom he believed resided on the fourth floor. Sebastian walked towards the elevators and stood next to the little group. The elevator arrived on the ground floor heralded by a strident ping, and the polished metal doors slid open. A young couple exited the elevator, and when they cleared the doorway, the other waiting tenants filed into the elevator behind them. Sebastian followed them in, turned, and pressed the button for the ninth floor.

When the elevator reached his floor, Sebastian promptly stepped out into the carpeted hallway and made his way towards his apartment at the end of the hall. As he approached the door to his apartment, he removed his keys from his pants pocket. They jingled as he lifted them, and he sifted through them in search of the apartment key. He reached the door to his apartment, unlocked it, and replaced the keys into his pants pocket. He noted that the lock had turned rather loosely as he turned the key, but soon dismissed the thought. Sebastian pushed the door open gently and stepped into his apartment. The living room was dark, but not a perfect dark, for the city lights seeped through the closed blinds, so that the window frames and patches of the ceiling and walls were ever so faintly illumined. Sebastian's eyes had not yet adjusted to the darkness, yet he had the sense that something was different in the apartment, that something was amiss. He turned, took a single step to his right, and flicked on the lights.

The lit room revealed the presence of three men. The one that caught his eye first was the big man who had a handgun leveled at him in an outstretched hand. Startled, Sebastian tried his best to quell the icy pang of fear that had suddenly twisted his insides. He quickly glanced at the other two men, then returned his sights to the unmoving gunman. The man had a shaven head, broad shoulders, and a dark, open jacket. In fact, all three men wore jackets of some kind, presumably to conceal the weapons they undoubtedly carried. The second man, one of lesser stature who sported a thin goatee, and who had been sitting next to the big man in Sebastian's armchair, casually rose to his feet. Both men were squinting slightly in the newly lit room. To the left of the door, a stocky pit bull of man, who had been leaning against the wall with a gun in hand, stepped towards Sebastian and gave him a hefty shove in the back with the heel of his thick palm. As Sebastian stumbled forward, the stocky man slammed the apartment door closed and locked it. Sebastian kept his feet, but found himself standing disquietingly close to the big man's gun. Beyond the unwavering barrel, the big man's face was expressionless in a cold, threatening way.

"Who are you," demanded Sebastian, his manner wary and ill at ease.

"Well..." the big man replied indifferently. "I'm the guy with the gun."

Sebastian's mind was a whirlwind of thoughts, all of them means by which he might escape his present situation.

"Is this a joke?" said Sebastian despairingly. "Did some of my boys at the station—"

"Nah..." interrupted the big man, "trust me, things are pretty serious for you right now, Sebastian. How about you raise your hands and interlock your fingers over the back of your head."

Gone was the meager hope that he might simply be rid of his present circumstance. The lingering denial Sebastian had felt dissipated as he actualized the reality he faced. Sebastian raised his hands and placed them behind his head. However, before he interlocked his fingers, he turned a small dial on his watch with a quick, subtle movement of his thumb and forefinger. The gentle twist caused a mechanism behind the dial to unlock, whereupon Sebastian inconspicuously pushed the dial into its housing, activating the device Dr. Ling had installed beneath the face of the watch. The device was a small transmitter, which signaled that

Sebastian was in a situation both inescapable and dire. It also allowed his location to be pinpointed and tracked from a remote device, which Dr. Canterberry and Gabriel each possessed. Having successfully activated the transmitter without rousing the suspicions of the three men, Sebastian seamlessly segued the movements of his hand into the interlocking of his fingers.

"Now, get on your knees...slowly...and keep your hands locked up behind your head," continued the big man. Sebastian lowered to his knees grudgingly. The big man signaled the stocky man with a flick of his head in Sebastian's direction, following which the stocky man approached Sebastian from behind and proceeded to frisk him. He frisked Sebastian roughly with a single hand, while, with the other, he pressed his gun into the small of Sebastian's back.

"This has gotta be some kind of mistake. I haven't..."

"No mistake Sebastian...trust me," interjected the big man.

"Right," Sebastian muttered with evident disdain as he averted the big man's steady gaze. Sebastian's muted sarcasm earned him a heavy kick to the back from the stocky man behind him. Sebastian's body jolted under the blow and he pitched forward onto the floor. His arms flung out in front of him instinctively, but the kick was so forceful that he still landed roughly upon his hands, forearms, and stomach. He heard the stocky man speak with a thick New York accent behind him.

"Stay down'n don't bitch."

The man who had been sitting in Sebastian's armchair, the only one of the three who did not have a gun trained on him, left the big man's side and lowered himself next to Sebastian. He dug one of his knees into Sebastian's spine as he forced Sebastian arms behind his back. Sebastian resisted at first, but realized the futility of it and let his hands be placed behind him. The man pinned Sebastian's arms against his back and held them there while the stocky man dropped to a knee beside Sebastian and palmed the back of Sebastian's head. The stocky man pressed Sebastian's face against the tile floor and held him there. Breathing alone was made awkward by the force with which the stocky man held Sebastian's head and neck against the floor, and he gritted his teeth as his facial bones ground against the tile.

Sebastian did not see the big man produce a small syringe from the inside pocket of his jacket, nor did he see him remove the plastic top that covered the needle. Unbeknownst to Sebastian, the big man approached him and crouched next to him. What

Sebastian did register, was the sudden, sharp prick of the needle as it was jabbed into his neck. Sebastian cursed and squirmed, but the other men held him down. Shortly, his vision began to cloud and darken, and he became unable to hold a coherent thought. Soon after, his eyes began to close, and he succumbed to the tranquilizer.

"He's out," said the man pinning Sebastian's arms. He released Sebastian and stood, looming over the stilled body. The stocky man tucked his handgun away beneath his jacket and then reached into his jacket pocket. From within the pocket he removed a conical, paper party-hat. He withdrew it by the thin, elastic chinstrap attached to the bottom of the hat, so that once it was clear of the pocket it dangled mockingly above Sebastian's head. Staring down at Sebastian's unconscious form with a trace smirk upon his broad face, the stocky man spoke in a muted, sardonic tone.

"Party time, buddy."

While the stocky man remained hunched over Sebastian, the big man turned from the others and headed towards Sebastian's refrigerator. Once there, he opened the refrigerator door and stooped to examine its contents. The big man reached into the fridge and took out a beer bottle. Holstering his gun, the big man twisted the cap off of the bottle. The hiss of escaping gas from the freshly opened bottle was quite audible in the now silent room. The big man walked over to where Sebastian lay and poured beer over Sebastian's neck and collar. He then put the bottle to his lips and drank nearly half the bottle's remaining content with evident zeal. The big man sighed his approval, wiped his lips with the back of his hand, and glanced at his two compatriots.

"All right...let's get outta here."

* * * *

Two young men entered the ground floor lobby. Save for the two men, the lobby was empty, and so the two men did not quiet their uncouth discussion. One of them, a blond, fair-skinned man, held the glass door open for his friend as he prattled on about the night's exploits jocularly. The other young man, who had a tattoo on his forearm, and was perhaps of Latin decent, followed his friend into the lobby laughing heartily.

"Forget that," said the blond man as they proceeded with their conversation beyond the lobby door, "that chick was dirty."

"Yo, she weren't that bad man. It's not like you're tryin' to make her your girl, or nothing," the tattooed man replied to his friend.

"Whatever, man...you're a freak," the blond man said laughingly. As the two young men chuckled and bantered, a sonorous ping sounded within the lobby and, an instant later, the elevator door slid open. A large man with a shaven head, and a shorter, stocky man emerged from the elevator. Between them, his arms draped over each of their shoulders, was a man wearing a red, conical party-hat. It appeared that the man with the party-hat was completely inebriated, for the two men were holding him firmly to prevent him from sliding off their shoulders. Their drunk friend's head was hung at his chest, and he seemed incapable of moving his legs. The two men supporting him bore his entire body weight, allowing only the tips of the man's shoes to drag across the lobby floor. A fourth man with a stylish goatee, who was evidently part of the group, had slipped out of the elevator behind the first three. The smell of alcohol on the intoxicated man was strong, as he had apparently overindulged. Both of the young men were distracted from their aimless conversation by the drunken spectacle. The young man with the blond hair stared at drunken man's limp and seemingly senseless body, then glanced at the big man with the shaven head.

"Wow...he's really out of it, eh?" the blond man observed. The big man gave a friendly wave of his free hand, in which he held a beer bottle.

"Yeah...well...he can't hold his liquor for shit. It's not the first time we've had to baby this pansy," the big man replied with a smile. The young man laughed, as did his tattooed friend.

"We got that friend, too," said the blond man with a knowing grin. "Well...take care y'all."

"Cheers," the big man replied with yet another genial wave of his beer bottle.

The young men then made their way towards the elevator and watched on amusedly while the big man and his stocky companion hauled their drunken friend through the lobby. The man with the goatee strode out in front of the other three and opened the lobby door for them. A moment later, all four men had disappeared from view into the night.

III

The third floor was dimly lit and utterly silent, typifying a usual night within the hallways of the restricted level. His open coat flowing subtly behind him as he moved, Gabriel walked through the hallway with little more noise than a fly treading over paper. The carpeted hallway stretched out before him, softly illumined by a yellow-orange glow from the row of pot-lights above. Up ahead, on the right side of the hall, was the thick, metal door that led into the cryolab. In actuality, the cryobank occupied little more than a quarter of the space in the sizeable laboratory, and was isolated within a Plexiglas encasement. The remaining area was equipped with other necessities, much of which were the result of expressed requests made by the obsessively thorough Dr. Ling. A small, square window was built into the burnished surface of the cryolab door, and from the little aperture, pale light from within the lab poured onto the adjacent hallway wall.

Gabriel surmised that Dr. Ling was working late, as he often did when on the brink of some new discovery. Gabriel approached the laboratory door, squinting as he stepped into the light being cast by the cryolab. Inside, the laboratory was well lit by fluorescent bulbs, which emphasized its immaculate cleanliness. Gabriel's pupils contracted into the tiniest of pinpricks within his yellow-gold eyes as he peered through the little window. As he expected, Dr. Ling had remained in the laboratory beyond his usual hours, and was bent over a lab table gazing into a microscope, his thick glasses pressed against the binocular lenses.

Gabriel turned from the window and continued on down the hallway. Having returned to the facility only a short time ago following a brief night's roaming, Gabriel planned to attend to certain of his administrative obligations. However, as he proceeded through the hallway, a small pool of warm light, which flooded out onto the hallway floor from beneath the broad, wooden double doors of the library, diverted his attention. At present there were only four people who were even granted level-three clearance, he being one of them. He had just passed Dr. Ling in the cryolab: Sebastian was not at the facility, and Dr. Canterberry was working on the south side of the facility in the ward.

Like the cryolab, the library was located on the north side of the uppermost floor, and it would have been impossible for Dr. Canterberry to have reached the library without first crossing his path. Something beyond the door moved, causing a shadow to briefly sweep across the pool of light at the base of the doors. Gabriel paused for a moment and then, with gravely narrowed eyes, he approached the library doors noiselessly. Where most other doors on the third floor required keypad access, or were locked at the very least, the library doors were usually left unlocked. Slowly, Gabriel pushed the door halfway open, and then, turning his shoulders, slipped into the library, closing the door softly behind him. The lights in the library were capable of being set to various degrees of intensity to accommodate both his nocturnal eyes and the less sensitive eyes of the others.

Strangely, the lights had been left quite dim, so that the library was lit solely by a soft, ubiquitous, amber glow. For a moment, Gabriel stood statue still in the small foyer of the library, his eyes scouting the darkest corners of the room and peering through the rows of books into the shadow-cast isles between the few standing bookshelves in the library. Aligned in tight series with their spines facing outward, the rows of densely packed books made it impossible for Gabriel to see beyond the second of the partition-like bookshelves. Almost entirely concealed behind the small succession of bookshelves was a miniscule reading lounge, which spanned from beyond the last of the bookshelves to the far wall. To the left of the foyer were two cubicles, each equipped with a computer and LCD monitor for access to the electronic library.

The library itself was relatively small, owing primarily to the fact that another library of sorts was adjoined to it. Within this separate room were a store of books and writings from bygone ages, along with other aged documents and artifacts. In essence, the adjoined room was a vault, accessible only through a thick metal door located on the far wall, which was hidden from sight behind a large painting. Unlike the primary library, this secondary library required a key-code access and was always locked.

Slowly, silently, Gabriel stalked forward, his eyes darting about the dimly lit room. Seeing nothing, he sniffed the air as he edged on, while his ears attended to the slightest disruption of the pristine quiet within the library. The air offered a strange scent to his nostrils, familiar, yet foreign and subtle in degree. Gabriel's brow furrowed curiously. The scent evoked a surge of memories, which surfaced in his mind as clear, vivid images, so that even before he heard the faint rustle from the little lounge beyond the bookshelves, he knew what it was that had made it. Gabriel went deathly still, and his gleaming eyes widened. Alert and intense, they scoured what area of the lounge they could observe beyond the bookshelves, but Gabriel saw nothing that begged inspection of his sharp eyes.

His eyes then narrowed once more, and the muscles of his jaw went taut, making the hardened look upon his face all the more menacing. After some moments, another vague rustle issued from the lounge, prompting him to steal towards the far end of the library afresh. His gait was resolute, yet he proceeded with frightening stealth. As he passed the rows of bookshelves to either side of him, he would peer into the darkened isles with sidelong glances, though he knew full well that what he sought lay beyond them. In nearing the last row of bookshelves a greater portion of the lounge was revealed to him, yet still he saw nothing. Gabriel's pace slowed to a predatory stock, and he crept forward. Inches from the last row of shelving, Gabriel heard the faintest of scratches, like that of an insect upon a windowpane. Upon hearing this whisper of sound, he hesitated there only for a brief moment before stepping out from behind thc wall of bookshelves into the lounge.

The furnishings of the reading lounge consisted of two love seats and an armchair, each facing a central coffee table around which they were equidistantly placed. The back of the armchair faced the bookshelves, and was situated not a couple of meters from the last of them. Unmoving, Gabriel simply stared with a forbidding expression upon his face, for sitting in the armchair, his long raven-black hair flowing over his back and shoulders, his body draped in a long, black, leather coat, was the ancient master of Rosslyn Castle: the lord Moxica.

His profile clearly visible from where Gabriel stood, he was poised with his elbow rested gently upon the padded armrest. In his pale clutch, he held a book; it seemed so utterly fragile in his monstrous hand. With the forefinger of his free hand, he skimmed along the lines of print, the sharp, black-clawed tip of his finger softly grazing across the page. Moxica's bestial eyes calmly followed the path of his ringed forefinger over the page as he read, seemingly unaware of, or indifferent to Gabriel's louring presence. When finally his forefinger reached the end of the page, Moxica slid the talon of his thumb beneath the paper and turned the page. The paper rustled delicately as it was turned. Moxica paused for moment, casually staring at the print upon the new page. In a voice that resonated with the same deep, even tone Gabriel remembered, Moxica spoke, his eyes still fixed upon the page.

"Dis book," said he, as he gently placed the fingertips of his free hand upon the page, "presents an interesting take on a particular historical event...interesting...but not entirely accurate." Moxica slowly turned his head from the open pages and finally met Gabriel's hostile gaze. "I remember de way it was...I...was der." Moxica apprised him loftily, his interest in the book itself appearing to wane.

Gabriel studied Moxica's face. It had aged. The changes were relatively subtle, yet Gabriel perceived them. The bone structure appeared more pronounced, more bestial in nature, and the whitish flesh was perhaps less taut. Gabriel noted the evident wisps of white hair, which streaked the undersides of the long black mane that cascaded from his temples; no longer pulled tightly from his brow and tied high upon his crown in an arcing plume, it fell as it may about his shoulders as smooth, pitch drapes of mane.

"So, my friend, have you made your peace with your God? Do you yet see de truth of your existence?" Moxica's searching stare bore into Gabriel until the ancient lord seemed to find the answer he sought. "I see dat you have," Moxica mused knowingly. "It is plainly seen in your eyes. Your hunt for vengeance has lost its luster, yes? Its meaning? And you have not yet taken your own life as you so adamantly swore. Good...good," Moxica observed, crooning his last words.

"How did you get into the building?" Gabriel said dismissively. Moxica gave Gabriel a mildly amused look that seemed to suggest that the answer was self-evident.

"Hmm...likely in de same fashion dat you enter dis place... when you choose to enter unseen." Moxica fell silent for a brief moment – his eyes left Gabriel's briefly as he nonchalantly looked about the room at nothing in particular. "You have done well to procure yourself dis place." Moxica commended him, alluding to the entire facility with a subtle, sweeping gesture of his hand. "And to have hidden in plain sight both yourself and all dat you have amassed," rather abruptly, Moxica's frightening aspect grew quite solemn, "but in dis age of men, my friend, such as we cannot remain in de same place indefinitely. You will be found out, my friend, and dey will hunt you as you hunt dem."

"I have taken measures to insure both my safety and my privacy," Gabriel assured him. "This place is legitimate. On paper it conforms to the legalities of all relative bylaws and regulations; it is government contracted, and I have insured that it is protected in layers of red tape."

"Dat may be, but I found you, and so can dey," Moxica said solemnly. Unmoving where he stood, Gabriel eyed Moxica flintily.

"Who exactly do you mean by...they? The FBI?"

"Indeed, some of der rank may hold positions within such institutions, but those I speak of belong to a group both more eclectic and select. Many of dis enclave can trace der lineage and wealth back to a time before even you were born. Dey are a congregation of elite persons in de society, people of affluence, influence and power. Dey have access to near limitless resources for der purposes, and it is dey who are de true government, de true masters of dis nation," explained Moxica in his erudite manner.

"I know how this all works, this society, this world. I know the minds and tendencies of its peoples. I may not have walked this earth as long as you have, but I am old enough to have seen this nation built, watching from the shadows."

Ever so subtly, Moxica leaned towards Gabriel, his thick, clawed forefinger raised languidly in point of fact.

"And from de shadows, dey built dis nation."

"Slaves and tireless workers built this nation," Gabriel said flatly.

"Semantics, my friend," Moxica replied. "Regardless of your sanctimony. I am simply illustrating de capacities of what you may soon face."

Sensing the gravity in Moxica's tone, Gabriel remained silent for a moment, and with a dour look upon his face, waited to hear what else the ancient lord might divulge. Seemingly cognizant of the meaning behind Gabriel's sudden silence, Moxica continued.

"Dey are de Illuminati, a modern offshoot of de Templar order I served in days of yore."

"Why should they concern me?" Gabriel finally inquired. "If they can't find you, then why do you believe they could find me?"

Moxica held Gabriel's eyes in a steady, meaningful gaze.

"Dey did find me," said Moxica with a portentous edge to his voice. "Truly, dey very nearly killed me. Dey broke into my chamber high above de city streets, cornered me in de very place I sought respite through de hours of day. Dey came at nightfall with many men, specially trained and well armed. Der was no way out save through dem, and so even as I sought escape, der searing bullets tore into my bare flesh."

"Yet, you escaped," said Gabriel, denoting the obvious to prompt the ancient lord into disclosing the means of his escape.

"Ah...well...I remembered your particular means of escape from my castle tower and decided to...emulate...your method," Moxica answered with a trace smile. Gabriel recalled the events leading to his desperate flight from Moxica's tower centuries ago and unconsciously glanced at his once-severed right hand. Moxica placed his forefinger thoughtfully upon one side of his face, with mild amusement still expressed thereon.

"I must say, it has grown back quite well," Moxica mused. Gabriel ignored the wry comment. Clearing his mind of archaic memories, Gabriel looked up at Moxica once more.

"Why have I never encountered these...Illuminati?" Gabriel asked.

"Perhaps you have in one fashion or another and simply did not know it," suggested Moxica. "Dey adhere to de method of de secret society established by de Templar."

Staring down at the carpeted floor, Moxica paused, evidently lost in thought. Presently, he met Gabriel's gaze anew with a look of purpose upon his fierce countenance.

"At Rosslyn Castle I gave you some insight into my past, and how my fate became intertwined with dat of de Templar. Perhaps it is time I revealed more to you, so dat you may understand dat which you will likely face, and why it is dey seek you."

"It was in 1118 dat De Knights Templar were established by Hughes De Payen, the first grandmaster of the order, along with Andre De Montbard and seven other knights...de very same knights who stumbled upon me in dat cave whilst I lay in stillness. In Jerusalem, de Templar protected de Christian's pilgrimage routes within de Holy Land. As I told you long ago, it was I dat led dem to what is known as de Stables of Solomon. Der dey appropriated a trove of ancient documents and artifacts, and staggering fortune in riches.

"With myself among der rank to guide dem unseen, de Templar became a powerful order dereafter. De Templar held great might in de east for near two hundred years. I have told you de Templar persecution birthed of de envy of kings and clergymen throughout Europe. Dey fled to Scotland because it had been placed under papal interdict at de time, and so we took refuge in de lands of St. Clair and Robert de Bruce. Scottish and Templar families were soon bound by marriages, and so select Scottish clans, namely de St. Clairs, shared in de knowledge and riches of de crusades. A few of de foremost members of de Illuminati hail from dese clans of Scots, and dis is how dey acquired der means, how dey were afforded der ascension into power."

"I remember hearing of this St. Clair clan long ago," Gabriel interrupted, his eyes reminiscent. "Rosslyn Castle was kept by the St. Clairs, was it not?"

"Indeed," answered Moxica. "Dey ruled de surrounding land."

"From what I observed those many years ago, you seemed to have held a position of significance, you undoubtedly held some rapport with the St. Clairs of that time. What did you do to fall so far out of favor with them?"

"I?" posited an apparently amused Moxica, pleading what Gabriel thought might have been disingenuous innocence. "Nothing. I was never really in der favor, nor did I have a true rapport with dem...not with de St. Clairs, nor even with de first of de Templar with whom I made a pact. Only a select few of de inner circle even knew of my existence, and those dat were aware of my presence did not know de full truth of my nature. Der tenuous loyalty was wrought of fear and greed. Dey had use for me, and I made use of dem...nothing more. Der greed is de reason dat dey took me into der rank in de beginning, and actuated by dis same vice dey hunt for me now."

Moxica leaned forward and placed the book he had been reading on the coffee table before him; he then sat back into the armchair once again. Gabriel observed him in silence.

"Since de beginning of de pact, I had anticipated dat der loyalty would falter once those who served to benefit by me became wealthy. It is for dis reason dat before I led de first Templar to de treasure hordes of Jerusalem, I had secreted away a portion of wealth for myself, along with de most sacred and most valuable artifacts of de caches: de Spear of Longinus and de Holy Grail itself among dem. De artifacts dat I secured and hid, were to be my last bargaining chips should de greed of de Templar and der families of succession be tempted to betray me. As I alluded to when first we met, it came to pass dat I became de keeper of de Grail, and only I knew where it was hidden. Numerous times dey requested I relinquish it to dem. First dey begged, then in later decades dey urged, der greed slowly outweighing der fear with each passing generation."

"Someone conspired against you," Gabriel presumed.

"Ah...yes...dat was de Scottish Lord Henry De St. Clair, de sixth Henry of de St. Clair line...de man who sailed to de New World before Christopher Columbus had ever been born."

Though practically imperceptible, Gabriel's face contorted in a mild expression of disbelief, the incredulity of which did not escape Moxica's perceptive eyes. Moxica gave a subtle lift of his eyebrow.

"It is de truth, my friend, he had all de means he required for de voyage. He was made Earl of Orkney, Baron of Rosslyn, Pentland, and Cousland. With titles of such distinction, he easily financed his journey; also, through his ancient Norse lineage, Henry was privy to information regarding overseas passage to de New World. Besides dis, he also acquired de secreted maps of Phoenician voyagers, whose charts and routes were part of a horde I led de Templar to in Jerusalem, under de Dome of de Rock; and so my friend, Henry, first disembarked to de New World in 1396. When he returned, he spoke to me in brief of his tales, and of de goods he had fetched."

Moxica paused as he brushed a long, silky lock from his face and ran his pale fingers through one side of his lengthy, black mane.

"Anyhow," said Moxica with a dismissive sweep of his clawed hand. "On de eve of his second voyage to de New World, Henry sent a company of men to my chamber, soldiers under his command. Der task was to force me into disclosing de location of de Grail. Dey were to torture me, hold me captive until de whereabouts of de Grail were ascertained, and kill me when de Grail was in der possession. At least, dis is what I...coerced...from de one soldier I had not yet killed...before I killed him."

"And St. Clair?" Gabriel inquired with genuine interest.

"Later on...I killed him, too." Moxica replied dispassionately. "What I learned nearly five centuries later, was dat Henry had kept some kind of record of his less public affairs, a diary of sorts perhaps. If I had known of dese records at dat time, I would have destroyed dem. I could have saved myself much hardship. Dis document contained de locations of a few caches of Templar spoils which Henry had secretly hidden in de New World for safe keeping, for he had planned to return to de New World and settle der indefinitely. Dese were riches he had retained after much of de Templar spoils had changed hands to de Scottish families after de inception of Scottish freemasonry in de mid fourteen-hundreds. De document also contains references to myself...descriptions... mention of my clandestine function, and Henry's general perceptions. In short, it revealed secrets dat only a few living persons knew, secrets dat I believed had died with dem in de decades dat followed."

His manner outwardly pensive, Moxica inspired deeply and repositioned himself upon the suede armchair.

"Through de years, de St. Clair name changed to Sinclair...it still refers to de same familial line of course. De Illuminati are led by a descendant of de Sinclairs. His name is Andrew Sinclair. In truth, he is an illegitimate heir of a bastard line of de Sinclairs. Unlike de Sinclairs who were abound in de history texts, Andrew Sinclair was de progeny of a spurious succession of Sinclairs descended from William...a succession whose lineage had been deliberately withheld from historical records. William De St. Clair... or Sinclair," Moxica clarified, "de builder of Rosslyn Chapel, had an affair with an unwed woman of comparatively meager status. However, she was no peasant woman, and was thus treated with a modicum of respect. De bastard child of der union was thus born into some financial stability albeit a forced and surreptitious fortune. De bastard Sinclair lived in de shadow of the legitimate lineage of Sinclairs, but managed to procure himself a considerable living, keeping ties with de powerful Sinclair families as best he could; ties which faded when one of the bastard line of Sinclairs eventually sailed for America.

"Eventually, one of dese Sinclairs obtained Henry's journals, and de bastard line of Sinclairs gained immense wealth. I was already in America at dat time, and I eventually learned of de Sinclairs presence. I began to observe der activities, gaining knowledge of der methods and secrets, knowing dat sooner or later I would find a way to regain my former wealth from dem...a great fortune, much of which I had been unable to transport with me to de New World. Ironically, what I sought to regain was a portion of de same wealth dat I myself had discovered in Jerusalem," stated Moxica, letting slip a faint sigh in mock exasperation.

"For some time, my methods of observation were crude and unpracticed, unaided by de growing technologies which I could have had at my disposal but for my initial reluctance to understand dem." Moxica chuckled softly at himself in retrospect. "I was so remiss as to have let Andrew Sinclair catch a glance of me through his bedroom skylight when he was but a mere boy. I thought little of de incident and eventually dismissed it; but as I have learned, de now senior Andrew Sinclair has not. I had taken up de alias John Smith so dat I might safely exist in de system; I thought it to be a common enough name to allow me to blend into the American populace without detection...still I was discovered by Sinclair, and another of de Illuminati, on more den one occasion. Following de encounter I spoke of earlier, de one I barely survived, dey thought me to be dead. Der efforts to apprehend me slackened, and so I found some reprieve from der hounding. It was in dis time dat I learned how to truly hide myself within de system, and how to watch de movements of de Illuminati unseen. For nearly two decades I have not engaged dem; I have simply observed what institutions dey control, and what persons of influence are part of der rank. I keep dese enemies closer than I have ever kept any other."

"Does Andrew Sinclair know exactly what you are? I mean...do the Illuminati actually know about the vampire species?" Gabriel asked unsurely.

"No...no dey simply know of me, and systematically attempt to find a means of locating me. As for de vampir...in your lifetime you have decimated der number...though I suppose I had a hand in dis as well, in de time dat I sought vengeance after I was changed. As scarce as de vampir are, and so naturally illusive, few will ever know dat dese creatures truly exist. Dey have become so much more intelligent," Moxica remarked before shooting Gabriel a telling glare. "And dey are so much more dan de beasts you thought dey were when you hunted dem."

Gabriel disregarded Moxica's last words.

"If Sinclair doesn't really know what you are, if you are so certain you can evade the Illuminati, and if you are keeping tabs on their activities, then why are they such a concern? If they believe you to be dead then let them continue to think so."

"Ah," Moxica asserted softly. "Dat is de problem. Dey no longer think me dead."

"So...you were subsequently seen then?"

"No," Moxica answered in a portentous tone. "You were seen, my friend."

Gabriel's brow furrowed, making his eyes little more than fiery slits.

"What?" he voiced in disbelief.

"Yes...some months past now," Moxica explained. "You were spotted running about on a rooftop in de midst of a large-scale police matter. De sighting was likely filed in a post operational report and reviewed by someone to whom your description was meaningful...meaning your description was noted by one of de Illuminati's vigilant eyes. Eventually, Sinclair himself requested de report. De point is, with you having been seen, de Illuminati have redoubled der efforts to search me out. You see, my friend, dey believe you to be me, and in being seen, you have effectively narrowed de focus of der search, and in attempting to find what de believe to be me, they would have inevitably found you. Your being seen is how I learned of your presence here, dis is how I was able to find you, and dat is why I have come to warn you."

Gabriel's face bore a stony, yet troubled look, but when he spoke his voice retained its composed tone.

"Why are they so persistent, why so determined to find you?"

"Because I am a threat to dem." Moxica replied plainly. "Because I am something dey cannot control, or monitor, because of de knowledge and wealth I possess, which make me all de more powerful in dis modern world...and," added Moxica, arguably somewhat self-amused, "because much of said wealth...was gained at der expense."

"You stole from Sinclair...directly?" Gabriel inferred.

"Yes," answered Moxica placidly, as he raised a hand to inspect his black claws, "It is de premiere reason dey even began to hunt me. However, dey remain most uninformed of—"

Quite unexpectedly, a muted, continuous series of monotone beeps issued from Gabriel's person. Moxica fell silent, and with an expression of modest curiosity, glanced at an area near Gabriel's waist, his keen ears pinpointing the exact source of the sound.

Gabriel's eyes fell to the beeping device that was concealed behind the flowing length of his black coat. He peered at Moxica for an instant, and then, rather abruptly, turned from the ancient lord. Moxica remained seated in the plush chair, and calmly observed Gabriel with a knowing air. Gabriel reached under his coat along his beltline to the rear of his waist, and felt for the small, black, neoprene sleeve fastened there. From the sleeve, he withdrew the rectangular device that had been encased within, and then produced the device from the depths of his coat, holding it delicately in the palm of his pallid hand. The device was relatively thin, with a series of small buttons at one end, and a screen comprising the majority of the remaining surface area. The screen displayed a GPS grid, an abstract, winding system of streets and highways. On one of the highways, a red pinprick of light flashed on and off in synchronization with the beeps that issued from the device itself. Gabriel pressed a button on the device and the incessant beeping ceased. The little red dot however, seemed to be in motion along a stretch of highway, represented on the screen as a gently meandering, yellow filament. To the bottom left of the screen were two vector gages, their numeric values, registering to the meter, increasing steadily.

"You appear somewhat unsettled, my friend," Moxica said

from behind him.

With his back still turned to the ancient lord, Gabriel responded following a moment's silence.

"I have a matter to attend to."

"I have learned," Moxica said probingly, "dat Sinclair planned to apprehend and interrogate a man he suspects might possess valuable information pertaining to my whereabouts...or yours really, as it where," said Moxica thoughtfully, "an Officer Klyne."

Gabriel's head whirled round, and he stared into the face of the ancient lord from over his shoulder, his piercing, yellow eyes glaring fiercely.

"Ah," Moxica mused perceptively. "You do know of dis man. I reasoned dat you might, though I hoped it was not so."

The fire in Gabriel's eyes appeared to ebb, and he turned fully to face the ancient lord once more.

"You seem able to acquire detailed information regarding the Illuminati's internal activities," Gabriel marked with a certain expectancy in his expression and tone.

"I have my methods," Moxica admitted. "But I have as much reason to inform you of dem as you have reason to tell me what lies in de room secreted behind dat artwork," he reasoned, as he casually pointed to the large painting upon the far wall of the library.

Gabriel glanced past Moxica at the painting beyond, and then stared into the eyes of the ancient lord. Gabriel's countenance belied the true measure of his astonishment. Still, a subtle, perspicacious half-smile crept over Moxica's pale lips.

"If you recall," Moxica explained, "when first we met, you saw fit to kill me without cause, and so I have no real reason to trust you with all of my secrets."

Even as Moxica spoke these words, a faint buzzing sound made itself known, though to their sensitive ears, the muted sound seemed to fill the library. Gabriel held Moxica's animal stare as he reached beneath his coat a second time with his free hand and snatched up a vibrating cell phone from his coat pocket. Finally breaking gaze with the ancient lord, Gabriel glanced down at the caller identification, and then raised the phone to his ear.

"Nigel," said Gabriel somberly. Dr. Canterberry's voice issued from the cell phone, and though faintly garbled, it was clear by his tone and the rapidity of his speech that the doctor was panicked.

"Gabriel! My remote transceiver just activated, did—"

"I know," Gabriel interrupted, "mine did as well."

"Bloody hell!" Dr. Canterberry cursed. "Right...ahm...I'll go ahead and bring round the GTO from the garage then?"

"No," Gabriel responded briskly, "you endangered yourself enough last outing. Tonight I go alone."

With his usual poise, Moxica rose from the armchair, the movement prompting Gabriel to lock his wary eyes upon the ancient lord afresh. Moxica took a single step away from the chair, and in that selfsame step, turned to face Gabriel head on. Gabriel noted that beneath the black leather of his long, flowing coat, he possessed the same powerful musculature as when first they had encountered one another.

"Yes...well," Dr. Canterberry faltered anxiously, "ahm... Godspeed."

As Gabriel returned the phone to his inner coat pocket, Moxica approached, and then came to a standstill next to him.

"I have watched Sinclair's movements for some time, but I would not confront de Illuminati without cause. Now dat dey search me out once again however, de circumstance has changed. Der is no doubt dat it is dey who have detained your Officer Klyne. I hope, for your sake, dat he is as loyal a pet as were my past stewards," said Moxica grimly, "for dey will exercise der authority in cruel fashion should he not immediately bend to der will."

"I don't plan on having to find out."

There was an edge to the usual timbre of Gabriel's voice, and with those words he turned towards the library doors.

"I assume you can find you own way out," Gabriel said harshly, his back to the ancient lord. Moxica, who seemed to study Gabriel for a moment, presently followed him through the rows of bookshelves towards the door. Moxica's gait was leisurely and unhurried, and he observed Gabriel with apparent curiosity. Gabriel's pace quickened, and distancing himself from Moxica, he soon reached the library doors. As he pushed one door open with the hefty thrust a single arm, he heard Moxica address him from within library. The imposing, worldly quality of the ancient lord's voice resounded from behind him, and for an instant, Gabriel paused in the doorway, the white palm of his outstretched arm rested against the open door.

"You think it best to risk yourself for one, insignificant man... one who, in de end, will mean nothing to you. His life, when compared to yours, is like de blink of an eye. What worth has he? Truly?"

"I often think of the past. It's hard not to...I am forced to remember it so perfectly," said Gabriel, his voice a hushed rumble, his feral, unblinking eyes staring out into the dim hallway. "Already too many innocents have died because I have lived."

With that, Gabriel slipped into the hallway and headed for the armory, a small room on the north side of the facility. His coat began to splay out behind him as he quickened his pace further still. He rounded a corner and as he strode through the darkened hall towards the armory, he heard the distant sound of the latch upon the library door: a faint click as the door swung closed. He did not look back over his shoulder, for he knew he would see nothing but an empty hallway behind him. He knew that Moxica was gone.

* * * *

Inside the armory, Gabriel pulled off his coat and flung it aside onto a gun wrack. Around him, upon similar wracks, was an assortment of weapons spanning each of the four walls. These ranged from ancient swords, spears, and the like, encased in glass for preservation, to advanced ordnances. Gabriel slipped on a dragonskin bulletproof vest, fastened it, and then slung a large, black, leather shoulder holster across his chest, overtop of the vest. He then snatched up an automatic weapon and slid it into the leather sheath. The gun was relatively small for an automatic weapon, as it was meant to be held in a single hand. Jutting some ten inches from the base of the breech was a sizeable magazine that curved slightly towards the muzzle, which itself was equipped with a thick silencer.

Gabriel fastened another holster around his waist and equipped it with a loaded handgun. He quickly strapped a tight-fitting ammunition satchel over his free shoulder so that the satchel hung at his back, and then grabbed a few other small implements before adorning his black coat once more. Thereupon, he turned and headed to his personal lift; the single, slender, metallic door of which could be easily missed within the armory, obscured as it was between two munitions racks.

The lift descended below ground, bringing Gabriel to his private garage, a discreetly hidden subsection of the underground parking garage. The burnished door slid open, and Gabriel stepped out of the lift into the garage. He walked alongside a row of impressive, gleaming vehicles, each parked at exact angles along one side of the garage, their fronts facing outwards. Under the dim, yellowish glow of a series of ceiling lights, Gabriel placed a glossy, black helmet over his head, his face hidden behind the inky tint of its lustrous face-shield. Thereupon, Gabriel leaped astride the seat of a customized, racing motorcycle, which had once read Kawasaki Ninja before its sleek, black paint job. Gabriel clasped the handlebars in his white hands, and an instant later, the engine roared to life beneath him.

* * * *

Outside the facility, the moon and stars shone in the still blackness above, and in the distance, spanning the western horizon, a dark mass of storm clouds slowly and ominously rolled towards the eastern sky. The night was relatively quiet, the streets barren. Litter and leaves tumbled along the pavement under sway of a gentle breeze. The dampened whine of an electric motor sounded from beyond the broad, segmented, metal door that led to the underground parking garage of the facility. Almost simultaneously, the garage door began to rise, and the rumble of another motor roared over the whirr of the first. The rising door revealed the mouth of the sloping entrance into the underground lot. The smooth, concrete walls of the tunnel beyond were illuminated by a source of light approaching from inside the tunnel.

Gabriel shot out of the tunnel upon the black motorcycle, and then decelerated the vehicle as he neared the wrought iron gates. The headlights flooded the entranceway with beams of light, the reflections of which gleamed upon his helmet. Behind him, the metal door had begun to close once more, and no sooner did it touch down upon the pavement, than the wrought iron gates began to open. Gabriel leaned forward on the seat, bracing himself for the acceleration of the vehicle. Even before the gates were completely open, he twisted the throttle and surged through the gap. Gabriel peeled out onto the street and then pinned the throttle. The drone of the engine grew increasingly louder and higher in pitch as Gabriel sped away on the vehicle, his black coat bulging and finally flailing out behind him under the mounting velocity. The noise of the engine tapered into a soft, distant hum as Gabriel careened around a corner onto the main road and raced out of sight.

In an unlit alleyway opposite the facility, a set of lights suddenly flickered into existence, accompanied by the rumbling ignition of another engine. The sound resounded throughout the alleyway, its brick walls aglow with light. Where moments prior, there had been nothing but darkness to the naked eye, a figure took form, and from within the alleyway, another rider emerged. He was adorned with a black helmet, red, archaic, lion decals spanning either side. Flowing out from beneath the helmet came long raven-black hair, which spilled over the top of the rider's lengthy, black coat like inky silk. The rider cruised out into the middle of street atop a charcoal-silver Ducati, and there came to a brief stop. Balancing the temporarily inert vehicle upon a single leg, the rider slowly turned his head, seemingly gazing down the empty street the way that Gabriel had past. With a gentle turn of the throttle, the rider set the Ducati into motion once more and wheeled the vehicle towards the main road at the end of the block. Rising in pitch, the engine roared, and the Ducati hurtled forth, causing the rider's capacious, leather coat to flap in the wind behind him like the wings of bat. The rider turned onto the main road and accelerated in the direction in which Gabriel had gone.

IV

The first thing that Sebastian Klyne became conscious of was the sensation of movement. His eyelids felt unnaturally heavy, and his mind particularly sluggish. His thoughts seemed to fluctuate between being cogent and nonsensical in nature. Presently, he registered a gentle, yet incessant vibration all around him, accompanied by a deep, muted droning, presumably the sound of an engine. He noted he rested against a soft, velvety backing, and reasoned that he was in a moving vehicle, likely the back seat of a car. He was even more certain of this fact when he felt that he was buckled to the seat by a seatbelt.

Sebastian, who had been slumped over to one side, began to raise his head, and slowly sat upright. He forced his bleary eyes to open but saw nothing but blackness. He felt the heat of his breath roil about his face, and he realized that his head was covered by a cloth or mask of some kind. Sebastian found that his hands were cuffed behind his back, and so he could not remove the mask, nor alleviate the discomfort in his strained shoulders. He suddenly remembered the danger he was in, and an instantaneous rush of adrenalin roused him from his groggy state. He strained against the cuffs and shouted manically.

"Where am I!? Where are you taking me!?"

Sebastian heard a movement to his left, and then felt a

tremendous impact on the left side of his face. He reeled sideways and grimaced as his head struck what he assumed was a rear window. He face throbbed painfully, and his head felt shaken.

"Shut ya mouth, or ya get it again y'understand?" said an aggressive voice from beside him. Given the tone and the thick New York accent, Sebastian guessed it to be the stocky man. Sebastian righted himself once more.

"What the hell do you want with me!?" Sebastian yelled. The stocky man struck him again and Sebastian lurched to his right and thumped against the rear door. He felt warm blood welling in his mouth from a searing gash on his lip. He remained apprehensively curled against the door, attempting to protect his head from the Stocky man's fists in case he lashed out at him yet again.

"Whadid'I just say, uh? Now shaddup!" The stocky man barked sharply. Sebastian remained where he was and said nothing. From the front of the car he heard a hushed, callous chuckle.

"Yeah...stay!...g'boy." The stocky man commanded him mockingly.

The passage of time thereafter was agonizingly slow. The three men barely spoke, and when they did, they were brief and vague, so that Sebastian could glean nothing from their words. Some time later, Sebastian felt the car decrease in speed and turn off what he could only assume was a highway. Finally, the car stopped, and Sebastian heard the bustle of movement along with the sound of car doors being opened. He heard a click from the vicinity of his waist; the stocky man had removed his seat belt. Quite suddenly, the car door he was propped against was yanked open, and a set of strong hands seized him about the collar before he toppled out of the car. Sebastian was hauled out of the vehicle, whereupon, he was grabbed by another of the men in addition to the first. Pulling him by his fettered arms, the two men hurried him over what sounded and felt to be hard soil, flecked with gravel. They towed Sebastian a short distance from the car and then came to a stop.

"That Klyne?" a man whose voice he had not heard before asked.

"Yeah," the big man answered from what seemed a few feet in front of Sebastian, nearly as far away as the other man who had spoken, "he came to a little earlier than expected. The boss inside?" he asked almost rhetorically. The other man did not give any verbal response that Sebastian could hear, but Sebastian heard the scrape and clink of a key being slipped into a lock, and the clunk of a bolt being shifted within the mechanism. He heard the sound of a door being opened before he was abruptly dragged forward once more and forced through a doorway.

* * * *

Director of National Intelligence, Andrew Sinclair, had arrived at Fort Hamilton earlier in the day, well before the black ops team arrived. He had been provided temporary lodgings at the fort, a small, private dwelling reserved for guests of his distinction. When his team arrived, they were given similar consideration, save that they were allotted rooms at the Fort Hamilton Inn. Sinclair's arrival at the fort was a momentous occasion, and so, as per his prior arrangement over the phone with the Garrison Commander, he had been immediately accommodated.

The Garrison Commander was, of course, left unapprised of Sinclair's actual intent, in spite of his station. Indeed, Sinclair had insisted that his brief stay at Fort Hamilton be unpublicized, and that all civilians and personnel stationed at the fort remain uninformed of his presence and the presence of his team. Solely out of necessity, Sinclair had informed the Garrison Commander that three of his agents would be transporting a detainee for interrogation, and requested the use of a building removed from the civilian population. The Garrison Commander had promptly sanctioned the use of an old building near the bluff as a detention center. The structure, which might have once served as a munitions depot, had a single entrance that led into a single, narrow hallway, to which old storage rooms were adjoined.

With a sturdy, black briefcase in hand, Andrew Sinclair walked down the narrow hallway towards the hefty, wooden door at the end of the hall. The young black ops soldier who was posted at the door stiffened when Sinclair rounded the corner into the hall from the entranceway, and he issued the seasoned director a salute.

Two additional black ops soldiers were stationed outside, guarding the sole entrance to the remote building. A short distance from the structure, which served as Sinclair's detention center, a further two soldiers had been holding palaver with the pilots and gunner of Sinclair's helicopter; however, they had likely joined the rest of the team at the inn. The pilots and gunner were to remain with the helicopter, which had been set down in a clearing next to an unpaved area beneath the highway, a storage yard of sorts in appearance.

Sinclair returned the soldier's salute perfunctorily, and then slid his free hand into his pants pocket. He wore a steel-grey, fitted suit, accented with a blue tie, his demeanor as formal as his attire. Sinclair's footsteps echoed through the hallway, nearly drowning out the electric buzz of the old florescent lights, which were positioned longitudinally on the intrusively low ceiling above. He produced a key from his pants pocket and handed it to the young black ops soldier when he came abreast the young man.

"Lock up after me," he ordered curtly.

"Yes, sir," the black ops soldier responded obediently.

Sinclair reached for the tarnished knob of the wooden door, and gently pushed the door open to reveal a small, dimly lit room, the meager light of its single hanging bulb glowing eerily upon the rough, concrete walls. The room was barren save for a small table, which was wedged into one corner near the door, and a hefty, wooden chair that had been placed in the very center of the room. Sitting in the chair, with a black, felt bag over his head, was Sebastian Klyne. His hands were cuffed behind his back with the plastic flex cuffs one of the agents had bound him with, so that his arms and rear torso were tightly pressed against the backrest of the chair, effectively fettering him to it. His ankles were bound to the legs of the chair with several layers of duct tape. Sebastian's head was tucked into his chest, likely to protect his face, as his body had abruptly tensed defensively when Sinclair had opened the door.

"What now," Sebastian said, "one of you going to bust my teeth in?"

Sinclair's face remained impassive, and he stepped into the room, closing the door behind him.

"I don't even know what this is about....I don't know what you guys want from me," Sebastian continued.

Sinclair regarded the young officer, who was shaking his head despondently, as though he were still in disbelief of his plight. An audible clunk sounded from behind Sinclair, as the soldier in the hallway locked the door. Sinclair turned from Officer Klyne and walked towards the little table in the corner. He then lifted his briefcase and placed it upon the table. Sinclair entered a combination into its brass locking mechanism and then opened the briefcase. He pulled out a manila folder with a few sheets of paper inside it, and laid it next to the briefcase. With one hand still clasping the open top of the briefcase, Sinclair then turned his attention to the little, metal case that had lain beneath the folder. Presently, he released the briefcase, turned around, and took a few steps towards Officer Klyne. Sinclair stood a few feet in front of the wary officer, who, by his body language, was cognizant of Sinclair's proximity. Sinclair stared down at the young officer, as though he were contemplating the man's fate.

"Officer Klyne," Sinclair addressed him coldly, "what do you know about a man named Smith?"

"What?" asked Sebastian with genuine confusion. "I don't know what you're talking about."

"Fair enough," Sinclair responded with a reptilian calm. "Then what do you know about a wealthy man with particularly pale skin?"

"I...really don't know what the hell you're talking about," Sebastian faltered.

"Well, we'll just see about that now, won't we, son?" Sinclair said grimly. He turned and walked to the table once more. He reached into his briefcase and snatched up the metal case. He laid the case on the table and opened it. Inside, embedded in soft, white foam, was a syringe and a tiny vial of pellucid liquid.

"I respect the fact that you're a dutiful defender of the peace, Officer Klyne, and that, son, is the only reason why I'm not gonna beat the piss outta you just yet." Sinclair explained as he delicately lifted the vial and syringe from the case. He rested the vial on the table while he removed the top from the syringe to expose the needle, and then took it up again in his free hand. Sinclair punctured the plastic top of the vial with the needle and drew up nearly half the liquid within the vial into the syringe. This done, he returned the vial to the case, turned, and slowly walked towards Sebastian with the syringe upright in his hand.

"I'm gonna give you a little injection of Sodium Pentothal. It's what you call truth serum. We'll see if that doesn't free up your tongue some."

* * * *

Gabriel barreled across the Long Island Expressway at breakneck speed. The highway lights reflecting upon his tinted face-shield appeared as mere wisps of illumination along its glossy, black surface, as he whizzed by an innumerable series of light posts. It was the dead of night, yet a scant assortment of vehicles remained on the highway, and he weaved through them as he hurtled along. Gabriel glanced down at the remote transceiver, which was mounted upon a customized fixture on the console. The numerical values of the two vector gauges, mainly the horizontal, were decreasing markedly, and yet their incremental decline seemed agonizingly slow to Gabriel. He kept vigilant watch of the gauges as he swept along the highway, insuring that he was tracking Sebastian's transmitter signal with the utmost precision. The GPS display on the remote transceiver evidenced that Sebastian was still in motion westward, and was undoubtedly being transported along the expressway.

Gaining steadily on Sebastian's signal, Gabriel hoped to reach the young officer before he exited the highway into the dense street system of the metropolis, where tracking him might prove more painstaking. He was unsure of Sebastian's circumstance and condition, but assumed that he was being transported against his will. Presently, the vector gauges registered a sudden decrease in the speed of displacement of Sebastian's signal relative to Gabriel's position. Gabriel's tracking device recorded Sebastian moving in a southerly direction for a time, and then westerly once more. Not long thereafter, the average speed of Sebastian's signal displacement slowed again, until finally, the gauges no longer registered any displacement at all. The tiny, flashing dot representing Sebastian's position, remained inanimate upon a fixed point on the screen.

Gabriel lifted his eyes from the screen, and he weaved through a series of cars. Beyond them, the highway was barren. Once past the meager traffic, Gabriel wrenched the throttle to its limit with a flick of his clawed hand. The engine roared, and the motorcycle lurched forward beneath him, rearing in the slightest with the sudden acceleration.

Gabriel tore across the empty highway, the strident hum of the motorcycle echoing softly as his form grew indistinct in the distance.

When the GPS on Gabriel's transceiver had ceased to register any movement of Sebastian's transmitter, the signal had reported to be broadcast from a location south of the 278. The transmitter signal indicated a point a short distance east of where the 278 merged into the Verrazano-Narrows bridge, which spanned the Narrows of the Upper New York Bay. According to the map abstract displayed on the transceiver screen, Gabriel was rapidly closing on the location from which the transmitter was broadcasting.

Gabriel surmised that if he traveled west on the expressway any longer, he might overshoot Sebastian's location. He veered off the highway at the next exit and headed southward, navigating by the readings of the transceiver.

It was not long before he reached what, at first glance, appeared to be a military community, or compound of sorts. It might have spanned a kilometer or so, and the Narrows bordered the western fringes of the area. According to the position of the flashing dot on the transceiver screen, Sebastian's transmitter signal appeared to be emitting from within the area – in the northwest quadrant. Without an initial verification from the device, Gabriel inferred that the site was Fort Hamilton, and even before he neared the place, Gabriel switched off his headlights. His eyes darted about beneath his tinted face-shield, assessing the area, devising where he could cache his motorcycle and how he might best enter Fort Hamilton unseen.

He cruised through a side street, and then onto Shore Parkway. The parkway, which skirted the shoreline of the Narrows, effectively semicircled the fort. Time was of the essence. Accordingly, Gabriel did not travel the road long before choosing an area to suit his purpose. He slowed his motorcycle near the southern fringe of Fort Hamilton Park, and the noise of the engine ebbed to a deep rumbling. When he felt sure that he was watched by none, Gabriel wheeled the bike off-road into forested terrain. Unable to drive through the dense patch of wood past a certain point, Gabriel let the motorcycle come to stop a few meters into the forested area. As the vehicle began to tip, he extended a single leg. His foot, which bore his weight and that of the motorcycle, came to rest upon the forest floor with a soft thump. In the same instant, he turned the grumbling engine off and swung his other leg off the seat of the motorcycle so that he came to stand abreast it. He undid his helmet and pulled it off with a single hand.

For a moment, as he held the motorcycle upright with his free hand, Gabriel stood still in the sudden quiet of the dark forest. His ears pricked, he sniffed the air, his nocturnal eyes scouring his surroundings. Satisfied, he proceeded to roll the motorcycle into a thick plot of bush, and set it to rest there upon its kickstand. He hung his helmet from one of the handlebars and then, using both hands, he detached the remote transceiver from its fixture upon the console. This done, He turned and headed south, following Sebastian's transmitter signal upon the device in hand.

V

As per Sinclair's instruction, delineated to them via Kenton Bruce, the three agents had utilized a nondescript vehicle for their undertaking. A short distance from the makeshift detention center, whereto they had brought Officer Klyne, the three agents loafed momentarily next to the grey, Ford sedan. Dark, rain-heavy storm clouds loured above, a thick, drifting canopy that swallowed up the light of the moon and stars. The verdant hues of the grass and trees were indiscernible, so black and colorless were they in the darkness. As such, the glowing embers of the big man's cigarette lit his face pronouncedly, the smoke rising in winding plums about his shaven head. The big man squinted his eyes within the acrid pall of smoke, as a stub of dry ashes flitted down to his shoes and upon the grass beneath him.

The man with the goatee leaned against the back door of the car with his hands in his jacket pockets, and from where he stood with his back against the window, he watched the fumes of the big man's cigarette rise and then disperse above. His eyes remained lifted skyward, while the stocky man, who was partially sitting, partially propped atop the hood of the car, continued his tirade regarding the New York Jets, pausing only to take another sizeable bite of a hotdog he had purchased that night. The big man observed his heated compatriot amusedly, though only half listening to the stocky man's criticism of the Jets' defense.

"It's gonna pour," the agent with the goatee said gloomily, his eyes lowering to the big man once more, "you wanna get back to the hotel? We've been up too long anyway and I need some fuckin' sleep."

Before the big man could say a word, the stocky agent spoke up with a large bolus of chewed hotdog bulging out one side of his mouth.

"Wha?...you can't see I'm still eatin' over here? Come on bro, enjoy da down time," the stocky agent said boisterously.

"If we had to wait for you every time you were eating we wouldn't get jack done. How many dinners you eat anyway, Valentino?" the agent with the goatee asked sassily.

"Ey...that's how it's done. Small meals, lots of 'em, high protein."

The agent with the goatee shook his head, inwardly amused by the stocky man's volatile personality. The big man gave the agent with the goatee a wry look.

"Yeah, yeah...whateva, ladies," the stocky agent remarked after observing the taciturn communication between his colleagues. "I'm done anyway."

The stocky agent swallowed the masticated contents that were causing his cheek to bulge, and then stuffed the remainder of the hotdog into his mouth, finger feeding the last of it in with his meaty digits. Chewing in a most bovine fashion, the stocky man lifted himself from the hood of the car and began to make his way around the front of the vehicle to the passenger seat.

Standing next to the driver's side door, the big man took one last drag on his cigarette, then extended his arm and flicked the smoldering butt away. Behind him, the agent with the goatee had opened the rear car door on that same side.

A sudden, low, yet rapid rush of air, scarcely audible even in the still quiet of the night, whisked into existence behind the three agents. No sooner did the big man register the soft noise at his back, than he heard a wet, hollow thud resound from behind him. The big man spun around as his compatriot's body was hurled forward with brutal force. He turned about in time to see his compatriot's body dashed against the inner side of the open rear door. The man had been propelled headlong with such strength that his head smashed through the window, accompanied by an eruptive shower of fragmented glass. Hinges creaked and cracked as the metal components deformed, and the door all but gave as the man's body was dashed against it. The man's body slid out from within the dented window frame, wherein his head and chest had thrust through the glass, and he collapsed to the ground lifelessly.

In the same instant, the big man perceived a large, dark blur of movement mere feet beyond his felled compatriot. His eyes lent greater focus to the moving thing, but he was only able to catch the briefest glimpse of a daunting figure clad in black before it rushed towards him with shocking speed. The big man was unable even to raise his arms in defense before the shadowy assailant struck him with such power, that he felt his face cave with a sickening, agonizing crack. The big man's head reeled under the force of the blow, and his senseless body was flung from where it had stood.

Startled by the sudden bedlam from off to his right, the stocky agent, who had only just rounded the front of the car, whipped his head about and stared frantically over his shoulder. His eyes focused themselves in time to witness the big man lift a few feet into the air. The big man's body seemed limp, and though his back faced the stocky agent, his head and torso had begun to fold over backward in the air at an unnatural angle; enough so that the stocky agent could see the big man's disfigured face, from which arced a heavy spattering of blood. The big man landed on the hood of the car with a weighty thump, then rolled off the hood and toppled to the ground a short distance from the stocky agent's feet.

The stocky agent quickly glanced up from his fallen compatriot. Before him, threateningly poised beyond the front end of their car, was a man dressed in black, his form somewhat obscured in the darkness by a long coat. The stocky agent had only caught a brief glimpse of the assailant, before the strange man leaped at him from where he stood. The moment of the sudden, swift pounce seemed to slow, as he watched the man in black rise into the air. The man soared over the front end of the car, his limbs extending like a lion on the hunt at the penultimate moment between predator and prey.

"What'da..." he managed through the partially chewed food in his mouth, as he attempted to reach beneath his jacket for his side arm. Unable to properly grasp his gun in time, and caught off guard by the sheer speed of the attack, the stocky agent raised his arms in a boxer's guard to protect his head as he attempted to evade the pounce; but the man in black seemed to possess a preternatural physicality, and he caught the stocky agent in mid stride. The man in black took him high upon the chest, and collided into him with an impetus that rattled him painfully throughout. The stocky man felt his legs kick out from under him, as he was hammered backward. For a moment, they flew through the air together, the man in black atop him.

His pain was compounded when the man in black drove him into the ground, concussing him. Disoriented and winded, his body half limp, he skidded over the grass on his back, the man in black still upon him. He had only slid a few feet when a sudden vice-like grip upon his neck brought him to an abrupt halt. He felt an immense pressure building in his head, and felt as though his eyes had begun to bulge. Through his clouded, spotty vision, he could make out the large, tenebrous form of the man in black, who now stood astride him in a deep animal crouch. The man in black was deathly still as he loomed above him, save for his free hand, which appeared to hurl something aside, though he could not be sure, so distorted was his vision. With one hand grasping the man in black's wrist, the stocky man reached for his side arm a second time with his other hand, but his fingers found no gun in the holster.

Panicking, the stocky man instinctively grabbed the man in black's wrist with both hands, attempting to tear the fearsome clutch from his throat, but he could not so much as budge the man's rigid arm. On the contrary the man in black's grip seemed to strengthen if anything, and the stocky man simply stared up at his assailant wide-eyed. The haze in the stocky agent's vision began to worsen, enough so that beyond the man in black's outstretched arm, the man's face was made an indistinct, menacing obscurity. In a voice that instilled greater fear his heart, the man in black finally spoke.

"Car keys," said the man in black in chilling tone.

"Th...th...there in...Victor's jacket...th...the...big guy," he clarified, gasping in response. Even as the last word escaped his lips, the man in black's terrible grip suddenly tightened about his throat. The stocky agent writhed in agony, struggling to free himself, but to no avail. He felt a horrible series of crunches from within his throat, and he was crippled by the disorienting pain therein. As the pressure in his skull mounted to a torturous degree, his vision clouded into blackness, and he abruptly lost all thought.

* * * *

The storm clouds above began to darken increasingly, so heavy with moisture that they could no longer hold aloft the rain cumulated within them. Outside the makeshift detention center, a lightning bolt blazed into existence, illuminating the area, as though an ephemeral, argent sun had been awakened above. Thunder followed the twining bolt, a deep rumble that resounded across the firmament. Presently, a light rain began to fall. One of the two black ops soldiers, a middle-aged man with a stubbly beard, gazed up into the black sky. The raindrops spattered upon his black, MICH military helmet, upon his corresponding black military accoutrements, and upon his upturned face. Blinking in the falling rain, the middle-aged soldier cursed softly.

The soldier to his right chuckled dryly, a sarcastic chortle demonstrating his mutual disagreement with the rainy weather, which was essentially a curse in itself. Overtop of their Kevlar vests, both soldiers carried assault rifles suspended by harnesses, which were slung about their shoulders so that the weapons hung at their firing sides. The middle-aged soldier looked down at his weapon and watched the rain run down its waterproofed surface to the barrel.

"Seriously though," said the other soldier, continuing a conversation they had been having a few moments prior. "Who do you think this guy is? Gotta be something big...leader of a terrorist cell...espionage...hadda be something like that to warrant all this." He speculated, gesturing to their immediate surroundings with a general sweep of his hand.

"Could be," replied the middle-aged soldier. "But you never really know. That's the point, that's why we're here, because something's gotta happen that nobody is supposed to know about, and the less they tell even us...well...that's just all the more people that don't really know what the hell's goin on," the middle-aged soldier remarked, finally looking up from his weapon. The rain began to fall in torrents, filling the air with a reverberant, pattering staccato, as it struck the roof of the structure behind them. The middle-aged soldier looked skyward once more, blinking furiously in the incessant rain.

"Aw, crap," he muttered miserably, "this is definitely not lettin' up any time soon."

A second bolt of lightning flashed in the night sky, an instant of brilliant light that flooded the darkness afresh. In that instant, only a short distance from the structure, the existence of a lone, onrushing figure was revealed by the sudden radiance. Thunder clapped above, and the bolt evanesced in the black firmament. The cloak of darkness returned to the world, consuming any trace of the ethereal figure.

"What!" the other soldier shouted over the noise of the rain.

"I said," the middle-aged soldier raised his voice, as he bowed his head and wiped the rain from his eyes, "this is definitely not letting up any—"

The middle-aged soldier cut himself short, for subsequent to brushing his hand clear of his eyes, he glanced up in time to see his comrade in mid-flight out in front of him. The soldier's body had gone slack, and it thumped against the wet ground haphazardly. Dumbstruck, he watched as the body rolled rag-doll-like until it came to rest face down in the soaked grass. The middle-aged soldier quickly regained his wits, and was immediately aware of the large, black form that stood where his comrade had been moments before. In the corner of his eye, he perceived a sizeable male figure, shrouded in a black coat, which swayed in the wind and rain. Before he could fully raise his weapon, or even turn to face his comrade's assailant, the man in black seized him by the throat and slammed him into the wall, pinning his back to the cold stone with fearsome strength. Though protected by his helmet, the soldier was still jarred when the back of his head struck the wall.

Grimacing, his eyes nearly clenched shut, the soldier felt his weapon wrenched from his hand as though he were a child. When his eyes managed to focus themselves he found himself face to face with the man in black. The man glared up at him from under his brow, his longish, black hair hanging in wet locks over his ghostly face. Most harrowing were the man's eyes, which appeared unnatural even in the darkness, and seemed to shine like amber gems from beneath the man's hanging locks. The man's grip was excruciating, like a metal clamp compressing the soft of his neck. When finally the strange man spoke, his words were brief, his timbre both eerie and menacing.

"How many more of you inside?" the man in the black coat demanded in a harsh whisper.

"Y...you have no idea what you're walking into pal...you're as good as dead if you try anything here...cause there—"

"How...many?" the man in black repeated with a chilling viciousness, his grip tightening further still. The soldier's eyes began to water and redden, each eye a bloodshot sphere of bulging, intertwining vesicles.

"I..." the soldier rasped. "I ain't gonna t...tell you shit," he asserted weakly. The soldier watched in utter horror, as the man's lips curled back to display sharp, bestial fangs. A low, grating, animal growl rose over the sound of the falling rain, filling his ears and perfusing him with abject dread. Clutching him about the jaw line, the strange man lifted the soldier from his feet, keeping him pinned to wall so that his body scraped against the wet stone as he was hoisted by the throat. The soldier felt as though the man might crush his jawbone and throat, and he winced with pain. The primal sound emanating from deep within the man in the black coat seemed only to intensify until the man held him aloft by a single hand. The man in the black coat spoke one final time, his voice so bestial, that the soldier wondered if what he now faced were a man at all.

"Yes," the man in the black coat contended softly with a dreadful snarl, "you will."

Petrified with fear, the soldier gazed helplessly into the man's horrible, burning eyes.

* * * *

Though the walls of the hallway dampened the noise, the young black ops soldier could still hear the sound of thunder from within the makeshift detention center. However, he heard nothing from beyond the door, which remained some ten feet behind him. Earlier, he had heard an indistinct murmuring from within the room, and he had heard some slight commotion from the room as well. Since that time, all had fallen rather silent, save for the storm outside. A certain amount of fatigue had befallen the young soldier. His mind began to wander and his thoughts grew less cogent. The rumbling thunder became a lulling, background noise and his alertness dwindled.

Quite abruptly, something like a subdued thunderclap reverberated through the hall. The young soldier lifted his head and froze for a moment, wondering if what he had heard were not simply another boom of thunder. Reassessing the noise he had heard, with his now more wakeful mind, he reasoned that the sound had originated from too close a proximity, and it struck him as having been too brittle and dull a noise to have been thunder. Suddenly stricken by the paralysis of uncertainty, the young soldier remained unmoving as his eyes searched the hallway for some sign of disturbance. His eyes fell to the entranceway, which intersected the hallway a short distance from where he stood.

In the same instant, something large and silent burst into the hall from the entranceway. It moved with such swiftness that the soldier was barely able to conceive it a man until it rounded the corner towards him. The moment the man appeared in the hallway, he had seemed to slash at the length of dual fluorescent lights and exposed wiring above him with a quick, subtle swipe of his hand. There was a loud shattering of delicate glass and an abrupt darkening of the hallway, as a few panels of light flickered out of existence above. The remaining lights beyond the entranceway, partially lit and partially silhouetted the onrushing man. Recouping from his initial start, the young black ops soldier instinctually raised his weapon and hurriedly opened fire.

The intruder had already more than halved the distance between them and, unsettled by the man's fierce rapidity, the soldier fired recklessly. Undaunted, the man charged on, simply springing aside from the line of fire, so that the largely errant bullets whizzed harmlessly past, close to where had been. Automatic fire rang out in the hallway, accompanied by a cacophony of ear-splitting cracks, as bullets bore into the surrounding concrete, each impacting with a distinctive plume of pulverized masonry.

As the man sprang to one side of the hallway, he extended a leg to the wall, making contact against it with the sole of his boot. The man's body began to tilt in the air even before his foot touched the wall, his head and torso keeling to the opposite wall to avoid contact with the low ceiling. Amazingly, the man took a few quick steps upon the wall itself, and by this method, closed on the soldier. The young soldier attempted to follow and overtake the man's erratic movements with a steady barrage of fire, but he scarcely had time to swivel his torso and adjust his aim before the man lunged at him from the wall.

The man alighted upon the ground alongside him in a low crouch, and simultaneously thrust out a single hand with inhuman speed, seizing the barrel of the gun before the soldier could mow the man down with a sweep of the firing weapon. The man halted the movement of the soldier's assault rifle, and began to wrench the weapon from his grip. The young soldier did his utmost to hold on to his assault rifle, causing the weapon to discharge a few stray bullets into the door. The man in black tore the weapon from his hands so violently that it unbalanced him, enough so that he was unable to remain facing the man in black as he regained his footing. The very instant he was forced to give the man his back, he felt the man's hand meet the back of his neck, with impetus enough to pitch him forward and jolt his brain into disarray.

Held upright by the scruff, he skimmed the floor with the tips of his boots as he was driven into the adjacent wall. He was able to raise his arms in an attempt to mitigate the severity of the impact, but the man in black propelled him into the wall so mercilessly that his arms buckled, and his front slammed against the concrete. He felt a number of his teeth cave and chip, and he had the wind knocked out of him. The man in black pinned him face first against the wall, clenching him by the base of his skull, his grip excruciating. The soldier felt warm blood well in his throbbing mouth and then trickle down his chin. He grimaced in pain, but his eyes remained open nonetheless. He saw that one side of his face was pressed against a small metal sign, which was screwed into the wall at each of its rounded corners. Upon its glossy surface, he caught a dull reflection of his assailant.

A large, menacing figure, the intruder had stood to his full height behind him. He saw only the briefest glimpse of the intruder's face, for the man quickly lifted his gaze from the young soldier and looked off searchingly towards the wooden door. Brief as it was, he thought there had been something eerie about the man's face, though he could not immediately place it. Momentarily numbed by a sudden feeling of impotence, the soldier simply endured his pain, and continued to regard the man's reflection warily. With a forceful, yet somehow insouciant, rearward flick of his arm, the man tossed the soldier's assault rifle well beyond the entranceway. The soldier heard his weapon clatter against the concrete until it slid to a stop on the hallway floor. Still staring at the door, the man seemed to sniff the air for a moment, and then abruptly turned his malevolent gaze upon the black ops soldier once more.

* * * *

Sinclair leaned against the little table, his arms crossed patiently. Having observed Sebastian until satisfied that the officer had succumbed to the Sodium Pentothal, Sinclair glanced at his watch and then lifted himself from the table upon which he had been lounging. Still bound to the wooden chair, Sebastian moaned wearily, the sound muffled by the felt bag covering his head; addled by the drug, his head hung listlessly at his chest. Sinclair turned from Sebastian and began to gather the manila folders he had strewn on the table. He had returned the syringe to its metal case a short while ago, and it lay closed on the table; this he picked up in his free hand. Save for the gloves, which he still wore, he replaced the contents of his briefcase as they had been, and then reached out to close it. As he set his hands upon the open briefcase, he heard what he thought to be a crash from the hallway, but he could not be certain, for the noise was muted by the heavy wooden door. He turned his head towards the door and went still for a moment, listening attentively for any further racket. Quite suddenly, the distinctive sound of automatic fire resounded from beyond the door. Sudden though it was, the abrupt burst of gunfire did not endure more than a couple of seconds.

Sinclair moved clear of the doorway reflexively and withdrew from the table as fast as he could manage, pressing his back against the wall to the immediate left of the door. Almost immediately after the gunfire ceased, a second burst of automatic fire, even briefer in duration than the last, rang out from beyond the door. Simultaneously, three holes erupted in the door, propelling bits of splintered wood into the room. Sinclair recoiled from the door even further, and then stared at the ragged holes in the wood perplexedly. In the relative silence that followed, Sinclair became aware that Officer Klyne had begun to babble under influence of the Sodium Pentothal. He momentarily turned his attention to the young officer.

"G...Gabe... comin' now.......y..you...can't...s...stop...im."

Sinclair's face tightened gravely. He returned his attention to the bullet holes once more and, skirting the wall, quickly moved towards the door. He leaned into the doorway and stooped, leveling his right eye to one of the bullet holes. Closing his other eye, he squinted through the hole, which accentuated the wrinkles of his face. Even as his monocular vision came into focus through the hole, he perceived some large, silhouetted thing hurtling through the air towards him. He only managed to catch a fleeting glimpse of it, before it occluded the hole he was peering through as it slammed against the outer side of the door. Precipitated by a heavy bang, the wooden door rattled violently. Sinclair jerked his head back; even as he did, he knew that what he had seen flung into the door was the body of the black ops soldier stationed in the hallway.

Sinclair leaned into the doorway again to peer through the bullet hole. The soldier had fallen away from the door, for his view through the hole was clear once more. The hallway was darkened, and some of the above lights that still functioned were strobing faintly. Sinclair's throat went dry; his heart began to pound, his fingertips went cold, and his stomach fluttered timorously. There, in the center of the hallway, stalking towards the door, was a man with a ghostly, white face, dressed all in black. Most harrowing of all were his yellow, animal eyes, which, even in the dim light, stood in stark contrast to his ashen face and black locks, like hot embers.

The moonlit image of the white-faced man he had seen in the skylight above him as a child sprang to his mind from the repressed recess in which it had been harbored. What he now saw before him was, and yet, was not, the face he had seen in the skylight those many decades ago, but its staring eyes burned with the same piercing, unnerving intensity. Sinclair froze. As he approached the door, the white-faced man suddenly cast his terrible gaze at Sinclair, as though he had sensed he was being watched through the hole in the door. Numbed with dread, Sinclair willed his fear-stiffened body to move, and he took a few hurried, clumsy steps away from the door. Sinclair stumbled backward and fell to the floor on his back. Off to his left, Officer Klyne had begun to mutter something else, but Sinclair did not truly hear him. Frantically, Sinclair dug his right hand into the pocket of his steel-grey blazer and retrieved a cellular phone from it. Still half lying on his back, he activated a speed dial number on the touch screen and then lifted the phone to his ear.

Another, louder bang issued from the door, and it shook as though it might rent under the force being delivered from the other side.

"Commander!" Sinclair shouted desperately in a hoarse, half whisper. "The target is here! Assemble your team 'n get to my position stat. And get that goddamn chopper in the air! Do not lose the target! I repeat do not..."

Another resounding bang from the door, as it was rattled upon its hinges, accompanied by the strident crack of splintering wood. Sinclair rushed to his feet and retreated from the door until he backed into the far wall. Again the door was bashed with tremendous force; the wood nearly split in two, and the heavy door flew off its metal hinges. The door smacked against the concrete floor and slid to a stop near Sinclair's feet. In the doorway stood the white-faced man, who glanced at Officer Klyne and then leveled his eyes upon Sinclair with malignant intent.

"I...I'm just the doctor," Sinclair implored falsely, as he raised his arms in surrender, watching as the white-faced man glanced at the latex gloves he wore. "I just monitor the patient as ordered, I—" He cut himself short as the white-faced man moved towards him, his frightful eyes regarding him almost searchingly. The man stopped mere feet from Sinclair, peering down at him as if deciding his fate. The white-faced man seemed to snarl, and then he lashed out with deadly speed, striking Sinclair with the back of his pale fist. Unprepared for the sudden blow to his skull, Sinclair's head reeled to one side as he toppled against the wall behind him, and he fell to the floor in a sprawling heap.

VI

The rain had begun to subside somewhat: a substantial drizzle as opposed to the prior downpour. The light rain pattered against the rotor blades, fuselage, and windshield of the helicopter, a gentle, hollow sound to the ears of the three uniformed soldiers inside it. In the cockpit, the pilot gazed through the window at nothing in particular. The once dry, dusty ground of the storage yard, upon which he had brought the helicopter down, was so dampened by the rain that the surface had a mud-slicked look to it. The pilot's eyes moved from the rain-soaked ground to the abandoned cars and trailers, to the storage crates, and to the various oddments clustered about the fringes of the little clearing. High above and just north of the storage yard, spanned the 278, supported by immense, lofty pillars, which subtended the underbelly of the curving highway.

The three soldiers: the pilot, his copilot, and a door gunner, who had also functioned as additional protection for Sinclair, were engaged in intermittent, casual conversation to pass the time. All three had removed their helmets, and were positioned as comfortably as possible in their rather cramped quarters.

"Okay screw it...whatever," the gunner suddenly exclaimed. "I gotta take a piss, I don't care."

With that, the gunner lifted himself from were he sat and shuffled towards the open doorway on the side of the helicopter, leaving his compatriots smiling in amusement. Slipping past the harness and heavy machine gun mounted in the doorway, the gunner leaped down from the helicopter and landed on the muddy ground with a wet, viscous thud. He trotted off a short distance from the helicopter, and then undid his pants to relieve his swollen bladder.

"Hooooowaaa!" the gunner whooped with some showmanship intended. Through the sound of the falling rain, he heard the pilot's radio crackle to life. A stern, edgy voice was addressing someone, perhaps all of them, he supposed. He could not distinguish any of the words however, garbled and vague as they were from his position. The gunner turned his head towards the helicopter, peering over his shoulder at his compatriots. As he turned, he did not perceive the thing that slipped past him in the darkness but a few meters away, a silent shadow within shadow. Still staring into the doorway of the helicopter, the gunner managed to discern that he was being waved in, or so he thought. Confirmation came in the form of a raucous yell from the pilot.

"It's go time! That was the commander! Move yer rusty ass!"

"For the love o—" The gunner rushed his process, hiked up his pants and sprinted back to the helicopter. The pilot had already started the helicopter, and the blades had already begun to revolve by the time the gunner was back inside. The other soldiers had already put on their helmets, and the gunner followed suit. He then propped himself on the high seat behind the heavy machine gun, strapped himself into the harness so that he was securely positioned in the doorway, and then grabbed the mounted gun with both hands. The oscillating drone of the helicopter grew louder as the blades whirled to speed and the men were forced to shout at each other to be heard over the noise. When finally they achieved lift off, the pilot flicked on the helicopter's floodlight.

* * * *

Unseen, he watched them from the darkness, as he had done for some time. He slinked through the shadows towards them, weaving amidst the odds and ends littering the fringes of the storage yard until he was a short distance from them, whereupon he went still as stone. He watched as the helicopter rocked, wavered, and then began to lift from the muddy ground. His muscles coiled, readied to launch him forth when so desired, but he waited patiently for the perfect moment, as he always had. His keen eyes observed the way the pilot orientated the helicopter as it began to hover and drift, anticipating its flight path. Quite abruptly, he sprang to life, darting forward with amazing speed.

Knifing through the darkness, he was a near-indistinguishable wraith as he set out on an intercept course; intuiting the helicopter's trajectory, he closed upon it, careful to avoid the light. At full sprint, he vaulted onto the top of a parked trailer, and had barely alighted upon it before bounding to the lofty top of a stack of crates. Without a moment's hesitation, he glanced upwards and leapt towards the night sky. It was as though he were suddenly weightless, so effortlessly did he lift towards the darkened firmament; and with a single, white hand outstretched, Moxica's phantasmal form rose through the air towards the passing helicopter.

The door gunner had turned to the pilot when, quite suddenly, the helicopter lurched to one side; it jerked enough that if the gunner had not secured himself in the harness, he might have fallen out of the helicopter. His startle reflex was to tighten his grip on the mounted gun. He cursed, and his head spun to face out the doorway once more, his wide eyes staring down at the dark ground below as the helicopter righted itself. He noticed something large, or at least a portion of it, moving below him, beyond the threshold of the doorway. It seemed to be a fabric of some kind, and he wondered if the pilot had caught one of the landing skids on some sort of flag or banner. The gunner leaned out of the open doorway as far as the harness would allow him, attempting to ascertain what had caused the helicopter to rock as it had.

As he peered over the lip of the threshold, an icy chill ran down his spine, knotting his guts; for what he saw, climbing the landing skid mere feet beneath him, was a strange, pale-faced man in a long, black leather coat, which, like the man's lengthy, raven-black hair, flailed in the rain and wind. Even more distressing, the man had leveled a handgun at his head, the barrel of which was equipped with a robust, cylindrical silencer.

The gunner's head shuddered violently, and his body went limp, hanging in the harness like a dead animal in a net. There had been a sound like a marble being dropped in a large, clay cup, seemingly inaudible over the noise of the helicopter. Nonetheless, the copilot had heard or seen something that caught his attention and, having just recovered from the helicopter's sudden lurch himself, he turned his head towards the gunner.

"O'Connell?" he exclaimed confusedly from where he sat, his voice nearly unintelligible over the noise of the helicopter. The soldier stared at the gunner's, lifeless body, which hung like a marionette in the harness. Though the gunner's back was to him, his head was lolling to one side, and he noticed that a stream of blood was running down his face, and that a few rivulets of blood were trickling down from under the gunner's helmet. Even as the grim reality of the situation dawned on the copilot, an arm swung up into the open doorway from below, the monstrous, ashen hand of which seized the support of the machine gun. The soldier's jaw went slack, and he stared at the hand wide-eyed, with some disconcertion.

"Jesus...Cappello!?" The soldier called the pilot by surname, shouting more as an alert to the pilot of the presence on board than an inquiry of what to do. The soldier fumbled to unfasten his safety belt, and bolted upright from his seat in order that he might reach the sidearm at his hip unhampered. Faster than he could reach for his firearm, a large man half hauled, half vaulted himself into the helicopter, alighting in the doorway in a low, animal crouch. He was fearsome to look upon, and even beneath his long, black, leather coat his frame spoke of a heavy, powerful physique. Stepping out from the cockpit, the copilot tore his sidearm from its holster and lifted it towards the man, but even before the weapon was leveled at him, the man lunged at the soldier with serpent-like quickness and grasped the copilot's gun hand at the wrist.

It was then that the pilot peered over his shoulder to see what was causing the commotion. He turned in time to see a huge man rush his copilot. The man moved with such speed that the pilot was barely able to perceive what had occurred behind him.

The man's strength was immense, and the soldier's arm buckled under the force of the charge such that his own firearm was shoved into his chest as the man drove him into the far wall of the compartment with a harrowing, guttural growl. The helicopter rocked slightly as the soldier's body was slammed against the inside of the fuselage, and the pilot frantically turned to the controls once more.

Wincing with pain, the soldier found himself pinned to the wall by the man's sole, outstretched hand. The soldier felt the man's agonizing grip crushing the bones of his hand, and groaning, he looked down and saw that his hand was being held against his chest such that the barrel of the gun dug into the soft flesh below his chin. He glanced up at his attacker's face and saw only a cold, merciless, feral stare that haunted his very being. With an ominous glint in his strange eyes, which shone like amber-stained glass, the man crushed the soldier's hand further still, forcing the soldier's forefinger down upon the trigger.

The gun fired, and the soldier felt a searing pain tear through his neck. His mouth opened as if he might speak, but only a raspy, gurgling sound came forth from his throat, accompanied by a small spray of warm blood. Still pinned against the wall he could do nothing but stare into the cruel, unchanging eyes of his killer, who simply stared back at him with a physiognomy most pallid, stern, and emotionless.

Hearing the gunshot, the pilot wheeled his head about once more, and saw the strange man in the black coat release his bloodied compatriot – only to strike him down with such force that the soldier's helmet flew off into the back of the compartment, where it clattered about until it spun to a stop on the floor. The soldier's dead body dropped onto the seat and then slumped to the assailant's feet, revealing a gruesome indentation where his jaw had been caved in. With mounting panic, the pilot watched as the assailant turned to face him, lifting a handgun that he had not previously seen in the man's right hand. He reasoned that it had been somehow concealed in the dimness by the man's long, black coat. Obligated to keep the helicopter aloft to preserve his own life, the pilot stared helplessly at the fearsome man who stood mere feet behind him, unable to, nor given the time to fathom what had just occurred.

The man held the firearm level with the pilot's head, and the pilot stared nervously into the hefty silencer mounted on the barrel of the gun. The man stood still as a statue, his long jet-black locks flickering gently in the wind from the open doorway. It was then that the pilot saw the man's eyes, whose searing stare was nothing short of daunting.

"What...the...fuck?"

"I...am Moxica," the man said in reply, his tone impassive, his timbre an imposing resonance, "and your life is only valuable to me so long as you guide dis machine precisely as I command."

"Okay," the pilot acquiesced, momentarily raising his hands from the controls to indicate his surrender, "but my commander will know something's wrong and they'll—"

"Dis means nothing to me," the man interjected balefully, his eyes burning with contempt. "Now...bring me into de air."

The pilot half nodded, half stammered his compliance, and turned back to the control panel. He did his best to keep sight of the strange man, glancing at him out of the corner of his eye as inconspicuously as he could.

Still aiming his gun at the pilot's head, Moxica took a step towards the open doorway and, subtly cocking his head to a side, eyed the dead gunner in the harness. He reached out with his clawed hand and unbuckled the body from the straps. With seemingly callous indifference, he allowed the dead gunner to fall from the helicopter out into the rainy night, and plummet to the ground below. The ancient lord then fastened himself to the harness. With a single hand, he firmly took hold of the heavy machine gun mounted before him, keeping his own weapon leveled at the pilot all the while. Like a falcon poised upon the verge of a lofty cliff, he scoured the darkened expanse below him. His sharp, nocturnal eyes pierced through the night, revealing to him the world below like a starlight device, even as the helicopter ascended into the night sky.

* * * *

He had fully intended to kill the old man; doctor or not, unwitting or not, the old man was, at least in part, an accomplice to Sebastian Klyne's abduction, and evidently a tool of the Illuminati Moxica had spoken of. Furthermore, the old man had laid eyes upon him, and in close proximity. Still, in regarding the helpless old man, some glimmer of conscience had stayed his killing instinct. It had not seeded his compunctions enough however, to stay a single swing of his fist.

Gabriel turned from the old man's unconscious body and hurried towards Sebastian Klyne. He crouched next to Sebastian and slid his hand beneath his coat, reaching behind his back. He produced an antiquated knife from beneath the folds of his coat, and proceeded to hew Sebastian's restraints with an evident sense of urgency. Having cut Sebastian loose from the bonds that had fettered him to the chair, Gabriel rose to his feet.

Standing over Sebastian, Gabriel yanked the bag off the young officer's head and cast it aside while keeping Sebastian propped against the backrest of the chair with his opposite hand, which clutched Sebastian about the shoulder. Sebastian's head hung limply, and Gabriel cupped the young officer beneath the jaw and lifted his head, careful not to scratch Sebastian's face with his claws. Sebastian's face showed signs of battery, and his eyes were somewhat unfocused and only half open. Sebastian uttered a soft moan.

"Sebastian," Gabriel called him by name, as he examined the young officer's swollen face. Sebastian moaned once more, and then finally spoke.

"Huhhhh...G...Gabe?" he murmured questioningly, gazing up at Gabriel with a glassy expression.

"You've been drugged. Can you stand?" said Gabriel, with uncompromised severity.

"Uhhhh...I...think," Sebastian faltered momentarily.

Gabriel knew that they did not have time to waste, for the gunfire he had drawn would have alerted any number of personnel stationed at the fort. With this in mind, he dismissed Sebastian's attempt to reply, seized him beneath the arms and hoisted him to his feet.

"Hold on," Gabriel advised with a grim voice. He then dipped below Sebastian's chest and scooped the stricken officer onto the breadth of his shoulders.

* * * *

The cargo van veered off road and rumbled over the grassy landscape towards the remote structure in which the detainee, Officer Klyne, was being held. The commander of the black ops team ordered the soldier driving to turn on the high beams, and the headlights instantly flooded the dark expanse before them with a more penetrating luminosity. The beams lit the drizzling rain, which crossed before the headlights at an angle, like a thin, flitting haze.

The remaining five black ops soldiers waited in composed anticipation, sitting on benches that were bolted in place along either wall within the van's interior.

"There it is," said the commander, indicating the structure to the soldier at the wheel with a brief point of his forefinger. They were still some distance from the structure, and the headlights had not yet evinced the building's exterior. As they drew nearer, the commander squinted past the rain-specked glass and through the watery streaks left by the windshield wipers. The furthest reaches of the high beams had begun to bathe the distant building in the slightest glow. What the commander noted first was that the two soldiers of his team that were supposed to be stationed at the door for the current rotation, did not seem to be present. He wondered if perhaps he had missed them at first glance, for the building was yet vague ahead of him, somewhat shrouded in the all but moonless dark. His eyes searched the front of the structure, the visibility improving as the increasing proximity of the van cast greater light upon the building.

Quite suddenly, the door to the building swung open, whereupon a man in black darted out of the shadows that filled the doorway. The man in black appeared to have another man draped over his shoulders, in the same fashion that an old shepherd might carry home a stray lamb. Even carrying the seemingly limp body, the man in black moved with astounding swiftness. Still in motion, the man in black appeared to give the van a fleeting glance before abruptly turning his head from the lights of the closing van.

"What in the..." the driver trailed off as he spotted the man in black.

"Step on it!" the commander shouted, treating the driver's query as rhetorical.

The commander watched as the man in black swept across the face of the building and then careened around the stone wall, his long, black coat trailing out behind him as he slipped out of view behind the corner.

The commander recalled a description he and the rest of the team had been issued during their mission briefing. This, coupled with the urgent deployment order he had received over his phone not minutes ago, made it clear that the fleeing man in black was their target. Ironically, their target, the very objective of their mission, had come to them, evidently to the purpose of liberating the detainee, Officer Klyne, whom the commander had identified as the man the target had carried off on his shoulders.

Now only a short distance from the structure, the commander perceived what he had failed to see before. Some ten feet in front of the structure was DeSantos, one of the black ops team who had been posted at the door. His still body lay on its side, nearly prone, his clothes soaked with rain. As the headlights of the approaching van began to suffuse the area with light, the commander saw that, closer to the door, another soldier lay in the wet grass, this one face up in the falling rain. It was Wells, who had also been posted at the door. Wells' mouth hung agape, and rain-diluted blood stained his weathered face, which was twisted in a grievous expression.

"Jesus," the soldier at the wheel murmured,

"Keep driving," the commander barked resolutely. "I'll radio in for medevac, though it don't look like a hospital'd make a damn bit of difference to 'em anyhow," he remarked, as he gazed over the morbid spectacle before him. "The target's our priority, we stay on 'im." The commander glanced upwards through the windshield, his eyes searching the sky. "Where the hell is that goddamn helo?" he cursed exasperatedly.

The van reached the remote structure, then rumbled past, and the area was swallowed by dark of night once more.

* * * *

Gabriel's legs pounded against the wet earth, a liquescent bloom of water droplets erupting from beneath his boots with each powerful stride. He raced along the side of the old building and plunged into the night beyond.

In moments, he reached the car that the three men who abducted Sebastian had used, their bodies still indiscriminately scattered about the vehicle. He held Sebastian atop his shoulders with one hand while he opened the driver side door with the other. Gabriel bowed his head and let Sebastian's body roll down from his shoulders, over his tucked head, and into the crooks of his waiting arms. When Gabriel lifted his head, he noted the flood of light that suddenly broke out from the other side of the building behind him. The luminance wavered and shook in tandem with the rising sounds of an engine and rattling machinery

– the lights from the pursuing van. Gabriel turned back to the car, stooped into the doorway, and leaning in, half placed, half tossed Sebastian into the passenger seat. Sebastian grunted as he flopped into the seat, and with a soft groan turned to Gabriel, who had already slipped into the driver's seat.

"Gabe...I...I'm sorry...I don't know wha...what happened...I couldn't...."

Gabriel slammed the driver side door closed, reached beneath his coat into an area near his waist, and removed a set of keys.

"It is no fault of yours," said Gabriel, as he started the car.

"I didn't...I didn't tell them anything," Sebastian insured him devoutly. "I swear to God."

Gabriel looked Sebastian in the eyes, and then, with the subtlest movement of his head, gave the young officer a meaningful nod.

Leaving the headlights off, Gabriel pressed the gas pedal and the car lurched into motion, the wheels tearing up the wet earth beneath them. He had not traveled far when, looking into the rearview mirror, he saw the big cargo van surge out from behind the building with a burst of light that set the area aglow. Gabriel let his eyes fall from the rearview mirror as his pupils contracted into tiny, black motes, and he squinted slightly to shield his sensitive eyes.

"Wha...what's going on? Who are these people?" Sebastian asked concernedly.

"Perhaps later," Gabriel said in an even tone, as he stared straight ahead through rain-spattered windshield. The car fishtailed as Gabriel headed the vehicle westward, and Sebastian toppled against the passenger side door, bumping his already bruised head.

"Ow," Sebastian muttered dryly through his swollen, bleeding lips, as he reached for the seatbelt and buckled himself in.

Gabriel drove with purpose as he raced the car in towards his entrance point, unwavering in his course. He drove both on and off road, barreling through what he was not forced to circumnavigate. Sebastian braced himself as Gabriel tore across Fort Hamilton, the van in dogged pursuit some distance behind them.

* * * *

Inside the van, the black ops commander peered through the window into the side mirror next to him. He saw flickering lights in the distance behind him. He could not be sure of their source; perhaps the military police platoon that remained on sight at the fort. Either way, the target's incursion into, and subsequent flight from Fort Hamilton had not gone unnoticed by local personnel, and it seemed a response team of some sorts had been mobilized.

"Aw, Christ!" the commander profaned. "This was supposed to be covert, this mission is fallin' apart."

"Looks like the local law is gonna get themselves involved," the soldier at the wheel said after a quick glance into the rearview mirror.

"Then we better get to the target first, or we ain't getting our full dues," came the commander's astute response. "Keep on 'im."

VII

With the New York Bay ahead, Gabriel drove the car past the boundaries of Fort Hamilton. They approached Shore Parkway and the car rocked and bounced as it was forced over uneven terrain. Gabriel swerved the battered, mud-spattered vehicle onto the parkway, the tires screeching as they found purchase on the wet pavement. Fighting nausea, Sebastian looked over at Gabriel. Dulled as he was from the drugs he had been administered, there was a wide-eyed, albeit vapid and slack jawed expression of shock upon his face, a definitive testament to Gabriel's terrifyingly reckless driving.

Gabriel sensed he was being regarded and turned his head from the road to find Sebastian staring at him, a stunned and partially reproachful look upon the young officer's face.

"Y...you know, Gabe," Sebastian slurred. "Some of us h...haven't gotten to live..." he paused to hold back his gorge, "...into our hundreds yet." Sebastian said sardonically. For a moment, Gabriel simply stared into the young officer's eyes with a flinty expression and then he returned his attention to the rain-slicked road.

After traveling the parkway for only a few moments, he abruptly veered the car towards a wooded area along the side of the road. Gabriel plowed the car through bushes and low-hanging branches, which scraped and rattled against the sides of the vehicle. Gabriel had only driven a short distance into the wood before he reached an impasse where the trees grew more densely, and there, he brought the car to a sudden halt.

"Let's go," Gabriel said calmly, as he removed the keys from the ignition. Gabriel opened the car door and then hurriedly exited the vehicle, slamming the door closed behind him. Sebastian followed suit as fast as he could manage. He pulled himself out of the car in time to see Gabriel's obscured form moving briskly amidst the trees beyond the car. An instant thereafter, Sebastian lost sight of him in the darkness. Sebastian closed the passenger side door and blundered into the wood after Gabriel as fast as he could. He found Gabriel sitting astride a motorcycle. Gabriel tossed something large and rounded in his direction, and though it thumped against his chest, he was able to catch it in both hands before it fell to the ground. Sebastian inspected the glossy, black object, and saw that it was Gabriel's helmet. Contemplating what this signified and entailed, he looked up at Gabriel with a somewhat worried look upon his face.

"Ohhh shit," he muttered under his breath.

* * * *

The soldier at the wheel had watched as the target drove onto Shore Parkway, whereupon he had temporarily lost sight of the fleeing car, for the target somehow drove the vehicle through the darkness without the use of headlights.

The black ops commander cursed and leaned forward in the passenger seat, squinting through the windshield to regain sight of the target. When the cargo van reached the parkway, the soldier at the wheel followed the target onto the road. As the van rumbled onto the parkway, the commander saw brake lights some distance ahead and watched as the fleeing car careened off road once more, and plunged out of view into a wooded area by the roadside.

"The hell is he doin'?" the black ops commander remarked.

The van soon reached the plot of wood, and the soldier at the wheel swerved from the parkway towards it. The van rocked as it descended into a slight ditch, and then began to ascend a gentle, grassy incline into the wood. The high beams illuminated the dark wood, filtering through the leaves and trees to create a patchwork of light and cast shadows. The soldier slowed the van, for not fifteen yards ahead, semicircled in a small alcove of trees, was the car in which the target had escaped. The vehicle seemed to have been abandoned. The driver and passenger side doors of the car were closed, but the glare on the rear windshield made it impossible to ascertain whether or not the target and Klyne were still in the vehicle. At the commander's order, the soldier brought the van to a stop behind the car.

"What is..." the commander trailed off momentarily as he heard the strident whir of an engine a short distance off to the right of the van. The sound was quite audible even through the tinted windows and over the idling van. The commander turned his head towards the passenger side window, peering into the darkness outside the flood of illumination from the headlights. There, he saw something sweep past behind a line of trees. He followed its movement through the fringe of the dark wood towards the road behind them, and finally witnessed a motorcycle burst forth from the wood with two riders astride it.

"Get back onto the road!" the commander barked with some urgency, still staring out the passenger side window.

"Jesus Chr—" the soldier at the wheel began to exclaim, having heard the drone of the motorcycle engine himself.

"Go, go, go!" the commander interjected, exhorting the soldier, who had already begun to reverse following a single glance at his side mirror.

The commander watched as the motorcycle traversed the ditch behind them and motored onto the parkway. Before the motorcycle roared out of view up the parkway, the commander noted that the man in black astride it was indeed the target, and the man in the helmet seated behind him was not doubt Klyne.

The van accelerated backwards cloddishly and peeled onto the road. The soldier put the van into drive and the tires screeched as the van lurched forward and rumbled up the parkway in pursuit of the motorcycle.

* * * *

Gabriel headed north on the parkway. He drove without a single light to guide him, not even the brake lights were active. It was another of a handful of specifications that Gabriel had requested be part of the vehicle's customizations. With all the motorcycle's lights disengaged, Gabriel, Sebastian, and the bike itself were difficult to make out in the dark, even as they swept over the near-barren road. Gabriel peered over his shoulder beyond Sebastian, gazing down the stretch of road behind him. Though it was some distance away, the van had set after himself and Sebastian once more. He knew they could not see him in darkness from such a distance, but he maintained his speed. The parkway began to curve, and here he slowed in the slightest, not wanting to sling Sebastian from the seat. Sebastian's arms ringed his waist, and he would feel the young officer's grip loosen now and again, and then suddenly tighten as Sebastian struggled to combat the effects of the drug.

Gabriel faced forward once more and spotted a vehicle moving into the road in the distance. It was so far ahead that, in the darkness, it would be completely imperceptible to Sebastian. Gabriel's eyes however, functioned with remarkable nocturnal proficiency, and his pupils dilated slightly as his gleaming eyes magnified and then brought into focus that which had moved into his path in the distance ahead. It was a police car, and Gabriel watched as the officer within positioned the vehicle at the juncture between Shore Parkway and Gowanus Expressway, creating a partial roadblock where the two roads merged to become the 278. This officer was clearly the first to arrive on the scene, but Gabriel knew others would soon join him, for the southeast was suddenly teeming with flickering police lights, which had begun to filter out of and appear around the periphery of Fort Hamilton.

Indeed, even as he neared the parked car, he spotted another cruiser on approach. For a moment, Gabriel debated an evasive detour, but with the bay to his left, and other units quickly closing on his relative position from the right, circumventing the roadblock would not necessarily be advantageous. The van in pursuit behind him was evidently not associated with local law enforcement. It likely carried more of the heavily armed soldiers he had been forced to dispatch earlier, and behind them he would only find more of the police contingent. He was effectively being channeled northwards, and decided he would stay his course and attempt to slip past the roadblock rather than risk entrapment contending with the trained soldiers on his trail, or the mobilized units behind them. As the soldiers had likely been employed under Sinclair, the man Moxica had spoken of, keeping local law in the chase would, at least for the time being, hamper their no doubt separate agenda.

Up ahead, the officer had switched on the cruiser's lights, which set the pavement below aglow with flickering colors. It was then that Sebastian noted the vehicle stationed on the parkway.

"Um...Gabe," he shouted through the helmet as best as he could manage, his voice significantly muffled by the full face-shield, "You...you see...cop car right?"

Taut with perplexion, Gabriel's aspect had hardened, and he did not acknowledge Sebastian's alert. His rescue of Sebastian Klyne had been reckless; under sway of a sense of morality, he had, to a degree, compromised the logic and patience he usually employed in such infiltrations. He had taken a much greater risk to himself and his clandestine existence than he would typically allow. Still, that he himself might be apprehended did not cross his mind, but to escape with Sebastian by his side, and with the young officer in such a state, he was not as certain.

Gabriel inhaled calmly, and then lowered his head into the wind. He twisted the throttle and the motorcycle surged forward.

Sebastian, who had been about to address Gabriel a second time, remained silent and tightened his grip around Gabriel's midriff.

* * * *

Upon hearing the whine of an engine, the officer in the police car took his eyes from the few cars that were traveling the expressway and turned his attention to the parkway. He saw the lights of a vehicle some distance away, but the sound he heard seemed to be originating from a closer source.

"Where is that noise...?" he did not complete his query, murmuring more to himself than to his partner.

His eyes searched the road, but he saw nothing. He looked to his partner for confirmation that she had heard an approaching vehicle as well.

"No idea, I don't see anythi—" she began. "Wait...look, look," she said suddenly, pointing across her partner's chest towards the parkway. The officer's head whirled back to the parkway. Straining his eyes, he caught sight of something in the road. Nearly amorphous in the darkness, even under the staggered roadside lights, it was already quite close and approaching expeditiously. The drone of the closing ambiguity mounted exponentially and an instant later, a motorcycle bearing two riders shot past the stationed cruiser in blur of motion. The two officers had barely time enough to react before the motorcycle grew somewhat obscure once more as it swept onto the 278 heading northbound.

Siren wailing and lights glaring, the cruiser radioed in an APB and then set off after the motorcycle, followed closely by the speeding cargo van.

* * * *

Were it not for his extraordinary vision and practiced ability to intuit what attempts might be made to apprehend him en route, he would likely have been unable to evade capture for so prolonged a time. Skillfully avoiding roving police cruisers where he could, he traveled north on 278. However, he had not been able to elude the officer that had followed him from Shore Parkway, and two more police cruisers had joined the chase. Gabriel contemplated exiting 278 and losing them in the city streets where he was so adept at vanishing into the night, but he knew he had no time to deviate from the highway. Moreover, he still had Sebastian's fate to consider. Of this, however, he was certain; he must do whatever was in his power to shake the police cruisers from his trail, for even now they were no doubt reporting his every move to dispatch.

Gabriel glanced into the side mirror and observed the small motorcade trailing him. The officers' faces were tense with concentration, for they were driving their vehicles at a dangerous speed to maintain their proximity to him and keep in eyeshot. It was because he drove without light that they attempted to keep so close – undoubtedly concerned they might lose him to the darkness should he get too far ahead. He began to devise how he might use this relative proximity against them. His head cocked to one side in the slightest as he looked at the wet road in the mirror, assessing the distance between himself and the cruisers. His gleaming eyes still staring into the side mirror, he slowed the motorcycle as he reached under his coat towards the concealed ammunition satchel strapped to his back.

A moment later he withdrew his hand, a rounded metallic object clutched in his white palm. Gabriel peered back over his shoulder past Sebastian's hunched figure. Beneath the helmet, Sebastian was watching Gabriel as intently as he could in his muddled state. Gabriel held the motorcycle steady with a single hand, as he outstretched the other low to the glistening pavement, which whisked by below as a blackish blur. He took one last instant to gauge the distance between him and the pursuing cruisers, and then flicked the pin free from the grenade with the claw of his thumb. He held the grenade a half-second further, and then gently let it slip from his fingers. Gabriel turned back to the road ahead as the grenade clunked, bounced, rattled, and scudded over the pavement behind him.

Sebastian, who initially had not even been aware Gabriel had removed something from beneath the coat, turned his head as best he could to watch the grenade roll away towards the foremost of the pursuing police cruisers behind them. The original cruiser was in the center lane, and was situated between the other two police vehicles, which were somewhat staggered on either side behind it. The tumbling grenade was suddenly illuminated by the headlights of the police car and Sebastian watched as the cruiser drove over the spinning explosive. The grenade ricocheted off the inside of the cruiser's right, front tire, and then disappeared into the shadows beneath the front of the car.

Gabriel peered into the side mirror once more, in time to see the grenade detonate beneath the middle car. There was an explosion of flame, smoke, and debris from beneath the front of the cruiser, and it shuddered visibly under force of the blast. Shrapnel burst against the metal frame below and into the engine. A few fragments of the detonated grenade tore up into the hood, deforming the metal and shattering the windshield. A portion of one front tire was rendered little more than melted, mangled rubber overtop of the nearly exposed hub, which sent up a spray of yellow sparks as it made contact with the pavement. The cruiser swerved erratically, and suddenly veered into the path of another police car.

"Oooh boy," Sebastian muttered to himself concernedly, as he witnessed one police car plow into the side of the smoking cruiser that had swerved into its path. Metal twisted and dented as they collided, and the smoking cruiser jounced off the front end of the other police car, which fishtailed and then slammed into the median almost head on. The initial impact between the two vehicles caused the smoking cruiser to spin abruptly and violently in the opposite direction, hurtling the battered cruiser towards the remaining police car.

Startled by the explosion, the officer inside the remaining police car swerved towards the shoulder reflexively in an attempt to steer clear of the sudden wreckage. Driving at the speed he had been, the car skidded wildly. The officer attempted to regain control of the car, but to no avail. The cruiser ultimately crashed sidelong into the adjacent highway girder, and came to a grinding, screeching halt alongside it on the roadside.

Sebastian watched as the smoking cruiser spun to a stop in the road with a squeal of tires, whereupon licks of flame flickered into existence beneath the crumpled hood. Sebastian turned from the three downed cruisers, which had already begun to shrink into the distance behind him.

Gabriel had been about to draw the automatic weapon beneath his coat to incapacitate any of the police cars that might have driven past the explosion unscathed. Instead, he replaced his hand on the handle bar and accelerated the motorcycle once more.

Behind them, the van weaved through the wrecked cruisers and did not slow in the least.

Just as he had done with his caches in a time long past, he had created for himself a handful of small, hidden dens to which he could retreat if need be, small safe-houses of sorts; and just as he could, with profound clarity, still envision the rolling lands of Northumberland from times of yore, he recalled much of the city, much of the country, with a photographic memory. Gabriel perused his vast store of memory, examining where he might go, for he could not head back to the facility with so hot a pursuit on his trail. The difficulty was that he was north of all his dens, save one that he had established in Toronto, but he could not risk a border crossing at present.

A distant sound from the south took Gabriel from his thoughts, a faint sound which Sebastian could not yet detect. A deep whirring had made itself known in the night sky, and Gabriel looked up into the firmament behind him. The clouds had begun to disperse and diffuse in the slightest, partially revealing the moon and the few scattered stars. Gabriel immediately spotted the distant helicopter and wondered if it had been deployed to find Sebastian and himself. However, flying as it was in a northeasterly direction, the helicopter increasingly diverted from overtop of 278, distancing itself from Gabriel. Using his own raptorial vision as a measure, Gabriel knew that he and Sebastian were beyond the range of sight anyone aboard the aircraft would be capable of; and so he continued northward, secure in the knowledge that he had not been spotted by the eye in the sky.

Gabriel saw the second helicopter before he heard it, a dark speck set with flickering lights in the northern horizon ahead. Though there was ample time to change course before it reached him, reach him it would if he continued northbound, for it flew south along 278 on an intercept course. Clearly, the pilots had been informed of his last known coordinates and heading via police radio, and now sought to catch sight of him once more. Should the helicopter spot himself and Sebastian, and fix its searchlight upon them, the aircraft would be nearly impossible to shed if he intended to keep Sebastian safe by his side. Consequently, he did not continue northwards, but headed westward towards

Manhattan when he reached 495, seeking to elude the helicopter by traveling underground through the Queen's Midtown Tunnel. Gabriel sped across 495 until he neared the tollbooth, whereupon he slowed the motorcycle, activated its lights as not to arouse further suspicion, and then reached into the inner pocket of his coat. Beyond the booth, the road sloped downwards, descending below ground into the cavernous tunnel.

The tollbooth attendant, a scrawny man with an unbecoming, scraggly moustache and thick, broad-lensed glasses, discreetly thumbed through one page of the open comic book that lay on the desk beside him. Magnified by the glasses, his eyes widened as he read through a particularly suspenseful scene. The tollbooth attendant looked up from the comic when he heard the sound of an approaching engine. He wondered how he had not noticed the motorcycle when he had glanced at the road moments ago, and he watched as the motorcycle approached the booth. There were two men atop it, one without a helmet. The helmetless rider, a daunting-looking man in a black coat, pulled up to the booth fast enough that the tires of the motorcycle emitted a brief squeal as the vehicle came to an abrupt stop at the booth, startlingly close to the attendant's window. The rider, his head lowered so that his rain-soaked hair hung in black tendrils over his face, did not look at the attendant head on. Indeed, the rider appeared as though he had not turned his head from the road, but the man's attentive poise led the attendant to feel as though the rider's eyes were examining him from beneath the quivering, wet locks.

"Um..." the attendant stammered initially, as he began to lift a cupped hand to accept the toll, his enlarged eyes blinked nervously within his disproportionately large frames. There was a faint rustle of wet fabric as the rider's left hand shot out towards him. The hand hesitated over his for the barest fraction of a second and then withdrew from the window of the booth, as quickly as it had come. Upon hearing a soft tinkle, the attendant felt something settling in the palm of his cupped hand. He looked down at his hand to see that the rider had already placed the toll in his palm. Dutifully, the attendant pressed the button to raise the gate. The strident drone of the motorcycle engine caused him to look up once more, and he lifted his eyes in time to see the motorcycle accelerating towards the Queens Midtown Tunnel. Blinking confusedly, he stared after the two men, his cupped hand still held out in front of his chest.

Some moments later, a few seconds before the motorcycle vanished into the tunnel, a large van roared towards the tollbooth from whence the motorcycle had come.

* * * *

Gabriel and Sebastian whisked through the Queen's Midtown Tunnel, the pitched whine of the motorcycle engine resounding within the hollowed expanse. After some time, the road began to incline, and presently, they ascended above ground once more. Gabriel exited the tunnel into Manhattan, and headed north afresh on 3rd Avenue. As ungodly an hour as it was, slight traffic seemed to have collected on the road, slowing their progress. Even Gabriel, with his penetrating vision, was unable to ascertain what had occurred up ahead to cause the untimely congestion, for two trucks, one in either lane, were obstructing his line of sight. Still well aware that he had been unable to shake Sinclair's mercenaries from his trail, Gabriel whipped his head around and glanced over his shoulder. The large cargo van was indeed on approach behind him, and closing quickly, for it had not yet been hindered by the slim traffic. Though it was night and the van still some eighty meters behind him, Gabriel could see the two soldiers through the windshield. Through the dim glare of the city lights upon the glass, he observed expressions of anticipation upon their faces, and watched as the helmeted soldier in the passenger seat began to ready an assault rifle in his eager hands.

Gabriel looked forward once again and hesitated only briefly as his eyes examined the congested stretch of 3rd Avenue before him. Sebastian had noted that Gabriel had turned to look over his shoulder again, and he turned his head rearward himself. He saw the van immediately, and turned to Gabriel. Before Sebastian could utter a word, Gabriel wrenched the throttle and abruptly turned the motorcycle to the left. The motorcycle lurched into oncoming traffic and Gabriel crossed through the honking vehicles onto the opposite shoulder of the road. Switching the motorcycle lights off once more to effect evasion of his pursuers, Gabriel pinned the throttle and sped the motorcycle northward on the shoulder with oncoming traffic rushing past him on his right. Behind him, the van veered across the road as well, and it rumbled onto the shoulder behind him.

Turning left when he reached 42nd Street, Gabriel tore through the intersection, deftly navigating through the thinning traffic while a fretful Sebastian clenched him tenaciously about the waist. He maneuvered himself onto the right side of the road, heading westward on 42nd Street.

Gabriel spotted the police cruiser ahead well before he reached Park Avenue, and hoped he could turn onto Park Avenue before the officers spotted him. The cruiser was heading in his direction from the opposite lane. The officers within were staring out over the wet road and were noticeably on edge. Gabriel kept the vehicles lights off as he raced across 42nd Street. The squad car was still some distance from Park Avenue as Gabriel veered off 42nd Street. As he whisked past the intersection, Gabriel turned to the cruiser and locked his lurid eyes upon the officer's, as if willing them not to see him. Before he could disappear on Park Avenue, the officer in the passenger seat caught sight of him. The officer's face grew instantly severe and his eyes widened. Silent even to his ears, Gabriel observed shouted words mouthed beyond the windshield as the officer pointed at him emphatically.

He careened onto Park Avenue, heading north once more. As the colored lights atop the police cruiser flickered to life, and its siren wailed into existence, Gabriel's ashen lips curled in the slightest, an atavistic snarl of displeasure that revealed the sharp tips of his alabaster fangs. Before he raced out of sight behind the Grand Central Terminal building, he saw one of the officers in the cruiser barking vehemently into the police radio.

The buildings and skyscrapers along either side of the road, their lit windows stark against the night sky, loomed and then diminished behind him as he passed them by. Gabriel knew he had mere seconds before the cruiser turned onto Park Avenue in pursuit, and he veered onto a one-way street in attempt to evade his pursuers, traveling into oncoming traffic once more. There were a scant few cars on the street, however, and he accelerated westward across 48th Street, wrenching the throttle enough to make the motorcycle rear from the pavement. The city rushed by Gabriel in a blur of towering infrastructure and lights, under which his pupils would contract in the yellow of his eyes. Gabriel arrived at Madison Avenue; he turned right, heading north along the wet road. He did not see the police cruiser in the side mirror, and was quite sure he had shaken the officers, for the moment.

Quite suddenly, the roar of an engine rumbled in Gabriel's attuned ears from somewhere off to his right. He turned his head in the direction of the sound as he hissed by the small intersection of Madison and 49th Street, another one-way street. There he saw what had made the sound, and saw it speed towards the intersection against the designated direction of the street. His face taut, Gabriel shot a glance into the side mirror and watched as the dark van careened out onto the road behind him from the mouth of 49th Street. Now little more than a dozen or so meters behind him, Sinclair's mercenaries had managed to close the distance Gabriel had been able to gain between them since Fort Hamilton. He observed the soldier in the passenger seat through the windshield. The mercenary's eyes were fixed upon Sebastian and himself as the man began to roll down the passenger side window, an assault rifle brought to the ready in his opposite hand.

Gabriel looked up at the road ahead and then back to into the side mirror, whereupon he saw the soldier lean his head, right arm, and shoulder out of the window; the soldier then proceeded to train the assault rifle on them, squinting along the sights of the weapon. Gabriel steered the motorcycle out of harm's way, just as the sound of automatic fire reverberated throughout the street from behind him. Some distance ahead of the motorcycle, the pavement erupted in a series of bullet holes. The stray bullets struck the ground with deafening cracks, lifting small plumes of dust and rocky debris from the gouges they chipped in the road. Maneuvering the motorcycle so abruptly that Sebastian had to cling tightly to Gabriel to keep from being hurled from the vehicle, Gabriel quickly veered to the far left side of the road so that the soldier would be forced to fire awkwardly across the windshield to achieve any sort of angle that would allow a clean shot.

He glanced over his right shoulder at the van in time to see the soldier in the passenger seat hauling himself out the window, enough so that the mercenary's head and shoulders rose above the roof of the van. His lower half braced against the inside of the van, the soldier propped himself on his elbows overtop of the roof and the upper portion of the windshield, his weapon in hand.

He saw the soldier leveling his weapon at him once more, this time from overtop of the van.

"He's gonna fire again!" Sebastian yelled from within the helmet, evidently having also seen the soldier clamber to the roof of the van.

Gabriel faced forward, and his eyes fell to the narrow intersection ahead. To his left, the intersecting street ran out of view between two immense structures. Gabriel knew he could not evade the marksmanship of a trained soldier with an automatic weapon for much longer, especially not atop the motorcycle. He accelerated towards the intersection hoping to careen out of the line of fire behind the nearest of the large buildings on the left. He noted that the narrow street which crossed Madison Avenue ahead was 50th Street, which was yet another one-way street. As close as he was to the street, he could not see along it, for the corner wall of the large building nearest him obscured his view. However, he did not hear the sound of oncoming vehicles emanating from beyond the corner of 50th Street, and so he initiated his left turn through the intersection at speed, leaning heavily into the bend.

Even as he surged into the turn, he heard the sound of the soldier's assault rifle resound afresh. The soldier continued to unload his magazine as Gabriel swerved towards the one-way street. Overtop of the discharging assault rifle, Gabriel could hear a flurry of bullets whizzing past him, the errant bullets bombarding masonry somewhere off to his right as he turned onto 50th Street. A moment before Gabriel could slip out of the line of fire behind the building, a bullet shattered the left side-mirror of the motorcycle. In almost the same instant another bullet struck the base of Gabriel's neck. The bullet tore into his flesh with a sickening, wet thump and erupted from within the dense muscle and soft tissue with a sanguineous spray.

Gabriel's head shuddered under the impact of the bullet, and his body seized. He winced, and as he was still gripping the handlebars, his reflexively-tensed body caused the motorcycle to swerve far too suddenly. The tires screeched as the motorcycle wobbled and then fishtailed out of control. The motorcycle keeled as the rear tire lifted, and the motorcycle was suddenly flung sidelong across the street. Gabriel and Sebastian were hurled clear of the street and tumbled brutally over the broad, concrete sidewalk beyond the curb, while the motorcycle flipped end over end on the street, bits of it scattering over the pavement. The motorcycle fell to one side and then skidded into the curb, while Gabriel and Sebastian rolled onto the concrete grounds of a massive edifice.

Grimacing, Gabriel was slow to rise, but he rose all the same, the back of one hand the only evidence that his tough skin had been scraped by the concrete after being flung from the motorcycle; but he was certainly not unscathed. He clutched his neck with a single hand, and felt freshets of his warm, rubescent blood streaming between his white knuckles from the grievous bullet wound by his throat. He was well aware that a vital artery in his neck had been ruptured, for he could feel the lifeblood pulsing forth from his body and rushing over his now gore-slicked hand. The pain was intense, and he could hear his heart pounding in his ears. He had already recovered from a brief disorientation, but a few of his limbs still ached, compounding his pain. Gabriel took a few steps towards Sebastian, who was sprawled on his side.

Sebastian lay unmoving at his feet, the black helmet scratched on the crown and side, a trickle of blood running down Sebastian's neck from beneath the helmet. It appeared that Sebastian had not escaped the soldier's fire either, for his sweater was torn where a bullet had bore into his shoulder, the fabric soaked by the blood from the open wound. There was still life in Sebastian however, for his chest still rose and fell. Gabriel knew he must carry Sebastian to safety regardless of his own wound, and he looked to the colossal edifice beside him thinking to take sanctuary within it. It spanned the entire block. He observed the ornate masonry, the large stained-glass windows along the expanse of its side, its dual leveled rooftop high above – each level fenced by a myriad of exquisite, spine-like spires, and he immediately recognized St. Patrick's Cathedral – most markedly denoted by its two lofty, neo-gothic steeples which, from his perspective, rose into the night sky from the far end of the cathedral, beyond the rooftop.

There was a sudden screech of tires from behind Gabriel, and he spun around stiffly, instinctually bearing his fangs in a menacing snarl as he reached beneath his black coat.

The van rumbled through the intersection towards 50th Street, the soldier in the passenger seat still poised with his gun mounted atop the van. The van was headed directly towards him, and the soldier, who was now only half propped atop the van, trained the sights of his weapon on Gabriel yet again. Still clutching his bleeding wound, Gabriel hauled his automatic weapon from its holster beneath the confines of his coat and leveled it at the soldier in one outstretched hand.

Hurried by Gabriel's sudden draw, the soldier opened fire hastily, sacrificing his aim for a prompt offensive. Gabriel dropped to one knee, staring down the barrel of his weapon with the cold stare of a cobra as he held the soldier in his gaze with eyes that amplified, then enhanced the image of their quarry. Even as the soldier's assault rifle discharged, Gabriel opened fire: a muffled automatic discharge through the thick silencer. Wounded as he was, he did not flinch in the face of a spread of bullets meant for him. The errant bullets hissed by him and overtop of him, buffeting against the cathedral wall and the concrete grounds, yielding tiny, powdery plumes of debris upon impact.

A sudden, strident staccato rang out in the street as the van was riddled with bullets. The windshield shattered, and the hood and roof along the passenger side were abruptly perforated with bullet holes. A few bullets struck the soldier's bulletproof vest, while two bullets tore through his left arm and another gouged his helmet as it grazed past his head. The soldier toppled from the roof of the van, but managed to keep from falling out of the passenger side window. The bloodied soldier ducked down below the dashboard as best he could, while the soldier at the wheel, who was attempting to duck behind the dashboard himself, swerved off 50th Street, seeking cover from Gabriel's deadly barrage.

As soon as the van swerved out of view behind the east end of the cathedral, Gabriel holstered his weapon. He cast his piercing gaze down upon Sebastian, and then quickly reached down towards him. Gabriel grimaced as he lifted Sebastian's limp body from the concrete in his powerful arms, blood still flowing from the gruesome, swollen hole in his neck. He dipped his head, hoisted Sebastian over his shoulder so that the young officer's upper body hung at his back, and then he rose to his feet. Though Sebastian lay upon the shoulder opposite the side of the bullet wound, the young officer's incidental weight upon Gabriel's neck was agonizing. Gabriel heard doors opening and frantic footfalls from behind the east end of the cathedral, followed by vehement shouts. He knew it would only be seconds before the armed mercenaries from the van rounded the corner of the cathedral, and he knew that they would open fire on sight. Gabriel turned from his assembling pursuers and lunged into a flat out sprint.

* * * *

Gritting his teeth from the excruciating pain, the black ops commander pressed his back to the somewhat rounded end of the cathedral that faced Madison Avenue; his left arm, shot and bloody, hung dead at his side. Above him, lengthy stained glass windows adorned the stone, and some of the masonry behind him had been left with bloody smears across it where his wounded arm had brushed against the rounded wall. The commander peered out from the behind the wall and witnessed the target slip out of view behind an extravagantly designed, spire-crowned, cubic outcrop, which jutted out from along the length of the cathedral wall. The commander cursed under his breath in disbelief. He had been certain he had shot the target down, yet the target had risen and fled once more, while carrying the detained officer no less.

The black ops team fell into formation against the wall behind him, and disposing with hand signals, he barked orders with a particular edginess, brought upon by the debilitating pain spreading from his arm and a disquieting gut feeling within him. As he was unable to hold his assault rifle in both hands, the commander ordered another soldier to assume the lead, and filed in behind the team's formation as they rounded the corner in pursuit of the fleeing target.

* * * *

Gabriel raced along the side of the cathedral, his legs pounding against the concrete with astonishing speed. The profuse bleeding from the wound on his neck had begun to subside somewhat, as his vampiric platelet cells commenced a rapid coagulation within the wound sight, but he could feel a certain infirmity from the blood loss. The pain had also begun to lessen, though his breaths were yet labored and rasping. It pained him to breathe, but he kept on, running parallel to 50th Street, skirting along the side of the cathedral beneath a series of immense, stained glass windows. He heard distant sirens warbling in the night air, the ominous sound seeming to come from all directions, all closing upon him. He gauged the distance of the sirens ahead, and then those of others around. His eyes stared wildly from beneath black tendrils of hair, his mind assessing his possibilities with Sebastian over his shoulder in this increasingly dire predicament. Thereupon he made up his mind and sprang upwards towards the stone wall, one leg extended towards it. Incredibly, even with Sebastian draped over one shoulder, Gabriel lifted from the ground like a panther.

The wall was not flush. Smooth, slender ribs of masonry projected from the wall at regular intervals, interspersed between each of the large stained-glass windows above. The ribs thickened into long, rectangular columns at the level of the window sills, and then tapered into spires high above at the plane of the lowest and outermost roof level. It was the side of one such stone rib, near the base of the cathedral, that Gabriel's outstretched foot found purchase upon. In the same moment that the sole of Gabriel's foot struck the masonry, he propelled himself up into the air higher still. With a powerful thrust of his single extended leg, he leaped for the broad sill of one stained-glass window. Gabriel rose into the air like a dark angel.

He alighted upon the great stone sill in a deep crouch, clutching one side of the stone frame with his free hand to keep himself from toppling backward off the sill. The strain of the feat caused a renewed pang of pain to emanate from his wound. The wound, the bleeding of which had abated markedly, burbled forth a brief gush of sanguineous fluid. Gabriel roared in pain as his hardened musculature clenched with the effort, a daunting, bestial sound, more animal than man. His claws grated against the cold stone as he regained his usual balance; his other hand cupped around Sebastian's waist to brace the young officer against his shoulder and keep him from falling to the ground below. Gabriel rose to his full height upon the broad sill and released the side of the window frame.

The intricately crafted stained-glass window was mere feet from him, and he seemed to stare through the beautifully colored glass. The window itself was at least as wide as he was tall, and the rounded peak of the window reached high above him. Below the floral, stone tracery near the cusp of the window, the stained-glass was divided into three large, exquisitely painted panels. These were demarcated by two stone mullions, which descended from the tracery above. Gabriel eyed the thin, widely spaced, metal bars which ran transversely across the colorful pane, assessing their strength. Still eyeing the window, Gabriel coiled into a poised crouch with Sebastian angled away from the pane. With startling quickness, he lunged at the window, raising his forearm to protect his face as he thundered into the stained glass with force enough that two of the transverse bars caved and then gave, battered free from their anchor points in the stone frame. The stained glass shattered into glinting, colored shards, as Gabriel leaped through one of the outer panels from the stone sill.

* * * *

The seven remaining black ops soldiers ran along the cathedral wall in pursuit of their target. Hearing sirens, they moved quickly, intent on subduing, or dispatching the target before police arrived and cordoned the area. His weapon readied at chest level, the soldier, whom the team commander had ordered to lead the assault in his stead, rounded the cubic outcrop beyond which the target had disappeared moments before. Athletically inclined, and influenced by the adrenaline of the moment, the soldier had not noticed the distance he had but between himself and the other soldier's behind him. Consequently, he was the first to cast a glance along the expansive south wall of the cathedral beyond the cubic outcrop. He had heard a strange bestial sound as he rounded the outcrop, and so he lifted his gaze, spotting the series of large stained-glass windows high above on his right, which were interspersed by rising stone projections adjoined to the masonry.

These all but impeded his view of the windows at the angle from which he observed them, and so it was only by chance that a fleeting movement in one of the stained-glass windows caught his eye, and he shifted his gaze towards it. He heard the sound of shattering glass, and watched as the last of a dark form crashed through one of the large longitudinal panes, next to one of the stone mullions. The trailing end of a long black coat vanished into the cathedral through the broken window. A moment after the target had slipped out of sight into the cathedral, the rest of the black ops team rounded the cubic outcrop and filed in behind him.

* * * *

Heralded by a myriad of colored, jagged, glass shards and bits of masonry from where the bars had been ripped from the stone frame, Gabriel was vaguely silhouetted in the large stained-glass window as he hurtled through it, high above the white marble cathedral floor. Still clutching Sebastian to his shoulder, Gabriel seemed to hang in the air for a moment before he began to descend to the cathedral floor with the fragmented glass. The metal transom that traversed the glass panel at the level of Gabriel's shin did not buckle under his charge, and it unbalanced him, causing Gabriel to pitch forward as he plunged through the window. Gabriel twisted cat-like in the air, righting himself so that he might land upon his feet. He landed in a deep crouch amidst a shower of colored shards, which tinkled as they broke and scattered over the smooth, burnished floor.

He could not keep his feet however, and he collapsed to his knees under Sebastian's weight, splaying an outstretched hand on the floor to keep himself from toppling over completely. Still protected by Gabriel's helmet, Sebastian's head rapped against the floor with a soft clack between his own limp arms. Gabriel felt a sharp pain in his forearm and side, and wondered if he had not incurred a hairline fracture at either location from busting through the metal bars. The bleeding at his neck had ebbed into thin rivulets, which wound down his throat and beaded into tiny, vermillion globules before dripping to the floor. His head hung, Gabriel took a moment to breathe, and watched the droplets splatter like tiny scarlet stars upon the marble floor. Pushing himself to his feet once more with his free hand, Gabriel rose, staring about the cathedral through the damp locks of hair that had fallen in his face.

The cathedral was serenely quiet. He saw that the vast interior of the cathedral was shaped in the general form of a Roman cross and that he had entered the cathedral from the side, next to one of the transepts. Perhaps ten meters ahead of him, spanning the nave and separated by a central isle, two parallel rows of wooden pews stretched from his left to the foot of a set of stairs some distance to his right. The stairs led to the chancel and the high altar of the cathedral, which was ringed by white pillars all around, save where the stairs climbed up to meet it. An ornate, gothic, wooden paling of sorts also ringed the altar; lofty, rounded, varnished pickets, bridged along their tops by intricate woodwork, the palings occupied the gaps between the pillars. The pillars, rounded and longitudinally grooved with decorative flutes, merged seamlessly into arching buttresses within the domed portion of the cathedral ceiling, which hung like a concave canopy high above the alter.

Behind him, built within a series of alcoves in the wall, were a succession of small chapels. Each chapel was immaculate and unique in design. The cathedral was dimly lit, but warmly so, bestowing a divine ambiance to each chapel, and to the entirety of the ostentatious cathedral. Flickering within tiny, colored, glass cups of melting wax, the flames of rows of small candles bathed areas of the cathedral in their rich, wavering glow. Gabriel glanced over the chapels and stained-glass windows along the far wall beyond the pews, and then turned his head and looked to the far end of the cathedral, opposite the altar.

Some height above the front entrance of the cathedral was a balcony of enormous proportions. It was a squared, solid mass of shellacked wood, embossed with magnificent chisel work along the bottom of the barrier, which enclosed the balcony. The huge balcony overhung the wall above the entranceway, and towering from atop the balcony were the great pipes of the organ. High above the balcony, higher even than the rising, silver pipes, was a soaring rose window. The stained glass set within the tremendous, rounded aperture, was made multifaceted by intricate, stone tracery, and the tinted light passing through it was a celestial blue, or rather, an amalgamation of celestial blues.

Adjusting his grip of Sebastian's unconscious body, Gabriel broke into a run towards the center of the nave. Along either side of the nave, a colonnade of monolithic, white pillars rose to the lofty ceiling. These stretched from the either side of the balcony, to the foot of the altar and chancel, subtending the roof of the cathedral. Gabriel sped past one of the large pillars into the nave. When he reached the first row of pews, he jumped onto one of them and sprang from it into the center isle between the two rows of pews and support pillars. He alighted upon the marble floor and immediately bolted towards the colossal, wooden doors at the front entrance. He hastened over the smooth floor of the center isle, pews whisking past him on either side with increasing frequency as he raced towards the front entrance. Tiny pinpricks of light had begun to appear in his field of vision, but he dismissed them as he had done his pain. He left the pews and the altar behind him, and closed on the front entrance. As he neared the great wooden doors he heard urgent shouts from outside. These were accompanied by blaring sirens, which seemed much closer than they had been when he first heard them.

Gabriel knew he needed a moment of respite: time for his body to verge upon homeostasis and heal. His lurid eyes searching wildly for a means of escape, he glanced up at the balcony a short distance ahead, which projected out over the front door like a promontory. He eyed the furthest of the large pillars to his left, one of the two that rose to the ceiling a short distance from the sides of the balcony. With mounting speed, he sprinted towards the pillar. When he was close enough to the entranceway that he was almost underneath the balcony, his eyes fixed themselves upon a single point above the base of the pillar. Securing Sebastian against his shoulder, Gabriel abruptly bounded from the marble floor with a pounding thrust off a single leg. He rose some ten feet into the air, hurtling towards the pillar at an extraordinary speed. As he had done outside the cathedral wall, Gabriel extended his other leg as he traveled through air, so that when he reached the pillar, he met the smooth, white surface with the sole of his boot.

No sooner did his foot make contact against the pillar, than he sprang off it, propelling himself upwards with all the power his dense, tensile muscles could summon. He grimaced as a sound of inhuman effort was forced from his lungs, and he soared up towards the balcony. He extended his body to its limit, stretching his free arm to the fullest as he reached out for the base of the balcony with his ghostly hand. At the very height of his astounding leap, his fingers barely reached the base of the balcony, and he was unable to grab the aesthetic, shallow lip, which ran along the base of the balcony. As he and Sebastian began to fall, he lashed out frantically with his free hand to take hold of the first in an array of praying angels carved into the underside of the balcony, just beneath the lip. Gabriel clasped the wooden statuette tenaciously, and his short, blackish claws dug grooves into the sculpted, varnished wood. Swaying pendulously, he hung from the base of the balcony, perhaps some thirty feet above the cathedral floor.

Sebastian's torso still hung limp at Gabriel's back, and droplets of blood, which had pooled around the gunshot wound in Sebastian's shoulder, dripped from his torn, blood-soak clothing and fell to the marble floor.

His face taut with effort, Gabriel glanced upwards and, for a brief moment, stared at the tranquil angel from which he hung. He willed himself to dismiss the throbbing pain radiating from the aggravated, bloodied gunshot wound, and noted that the urgent shouts he had heard moments ago from outside the cathedral had began to intensify.

To brace himself against the balcony, Gabriel swung one foot up onto the wooden lip so that he was nearly upside down, keeping Sebastian firmly anchored to his shoulder as he did so. Then, in a display of phenomenal strength, he began to pull himself and Sebastian upwards with his one outstretched arm. The strain on his body was tremendous and he grunted between his gritted teeth. Beneath his garbs, his sinewy muscle stood out beneath his white skin, and his veins swelled, forcing a gush of fresh blood from his wound once more. Gabriel heaved his chest above the level of the lip, and suddenly reached upward with the same hand that had held the wooden angel. His arm moved like a whip, and before gravity could claim him, he caught hold of a protruding piece of woodwork an arm's length above the lip. Using the woodwork as a handhold, and straining himself anew, he hauled himself and Sebastian higher up the elaborate, wooden barrier, enabling himself to lift both feet to the lip.

A sudden boom erupted from somewhere in the entranceway below him, the sound resounding heavily throughout the quiet cathedral. He heard heavy doors give, then swing open with an echoing bang. Hearing the sound of footfalls rushing over the marble floor from underneath him, Gabriel pulled himself into a difficult crouch, his legs wide spread to allow his feet solid purchase on the narrow lip. He drew himself as flat as possible to the outer rim of the balcony, but Sebastian's dangling lower body acted like a wedge between him and the wooden barrier, and the heels of Sebastian's boots unavoidably clicked against the sheer, wooden surface before them. Gabriel glanced below him and saw the first of Sinclair's mercenaries move into view from beneath the balcony. He knew that he and Sebastian would be easy targets should the soldier's spot them. He lifted his eyes to the brim of the barrier and poised himself to spring up into the balcony.

* * * *

Below, the black ops team had begun to fan out into the cathedral, their formation silently communicated by a series of hand signals. As one of the soldiers crept out from underneath the overhanging balcony, he spotted spatters of blood on the cathedral floor beyond the entranceway. There he stopped, and he heard a faint scrape from somewhere above him. He turned and then looked up, tilting his head back to better observe the towering heights of the cathedral. The soldier's eyes widened as he witnessed the target leap straight up from a narrow ridge along the face of the balcony's enclosure, with Klyne over his shoulder. Before he could react, the target outstretched his free hand and, clutching the top of the wooden barrier for leverage, vaulted sidelong over the enclosure. Even as the target swiveled to land in the balcony, the soldier raised his weapon.

"Up top!" the soldier yelled vehemently. The soldier opened fire and, taking their cue from the soldier, the rest of the black ops team rushed out from underneath the balcony, turned, and raised their assault rifles to join the barrage.

* * * *

As Gabriel alighted on the balcony floor, the sound of automatic gunfire rang out from below, echoing loudly inside the cathedral. A flurry of bullets cracked against the outer face of the lavish, wooden barrier, and ricocheted stridently off the exposed organ pipes, which, situated against the wall at the back of the balcony, rose high above the balcony floor. Gabriel dropped to a knee, seeking cover behind the wooden enclosure. He let Sebastian slide from his shoulder, and the young officer slumped against the inside of the barrier, the helmet gently clacking against the varnished wood. A shower of splinters erupted from the barrier where bullets had struck it along the top. As the slivers of wood rained upon Gabriel's stooped head and back, he reached under his coat with both hands. He quickly produced his automatic weapon in his right hand and another grenade from his satchel in his left. Subtle musculature around Gabriel's ears caused them to move in the slightest as he deduced where the men were positioned down below by their sound. Gabriel flicked off the pin from the grenade with the sharp claw of his thumb and held the grenade a few moments longer. Then, with a quick flick of his wrist, he tossed the grenade over the wooden barrier.

Revolving slowly, the grenade soared out into the open air above the cathedral, and then, almost ominously so, began to drop towards the cathedral floor. The black ops team had ceased fire, but in the dimness, none had seen the rounded, metal thing lobbed from atop the balcony. As the grenade descended towards the floor near the center isle, one of the soldiers managed to spot the small explosive as it fell. The soldier's eyes widened.

"Grenade!" he yelled at the top of his lungs, as he bolted from the center of the nave. An instant later, the grenade detonated, mere feet above the cathedral floor. The soldiers attempted to dive for safety, but some were unable to escape the explosion. Following the explosion, Gabriel rose from behind the wooden barrier and swung his gun over it, leveling the weapon at the stricken men below. He observed them through the thin cloud of smoke created by the detonation. Two soldiers lay moaning and bleeding out on the cathedral floor, their limbs and faces mutilated by shrapnel. Another soldier hobbled out of view beneath the balcony. Three were crouched down behind pews and one other stood with this back propped against one of the large, white pillars to the left of the balcony.

Gabriel saw that one of the men squatting behind the pews was the soldier who had shot him from the passenger seat of the van. One arm hanging uselessly at his side, the man was wincing, and he had not yet spotted Gabriel through the smoke. Gabriel leveled his weapon at him and opened fire. The man's body shuddered as bullets tore into the unprotected areas of his upper body and thumped against his Kevlar vest. Errant bullets rapped against the pews and the man keeled over amidst a hail of fragmented wood, sheered from the riddled pews. Holding the trigger, Gabriel swept his gun to one side, catching another soldier in the enfilade.

With a groan, the soldier collapsed between pews, clutching his chest near the underarm. The once-quite cathedral reverberated with the sounds of war.

"Fall back! Fall back!" the soldier behind the pillar shouted with a tone of underlying angst. Gabriel aimed at the soldier and opened fire a second time. A volley of bullets struck the pillar with ear-splitting cracks, leaving rounded cavities in it, from which burst small palls of dust and debris. The soldier pressed his back to the pillar as flat as he could manage, squinting as flecks of marble flitted past him. The remaining able-bodied soldiers rushed out from cover and fired up at Gabriel as they retreated beneath the balcony. Gabriel dropped to a knee behind the barrier, as the soldiers' bullets peppered the wooden construct afresh. Pulling a second magazine from beneath his coat, Gabriel quickly reloaded his weapon.

He heard the soldier's footfalls, and ascertained that the entire team of mercenaries, what was left of them, had withdrawn from the nave, back into the entranceway. Gabriel replaced his weapon into its holster and turned to the great organ behind him. Above the organ were its enormous burnished pipes, rising longitudinally from above the organ itself. These were aligned in series, and so large and so many were they, that the pipes were arranged in five distinct sections, demarcated by wooden, columnar, partitions, lavishly embossed with stately saints and splendid engravings. The tallest was the middle section, which rose, what Gabriel guessed to be, more than some thirty feet or so.

The relatively symmetrical lateral sections were not so tall as the middle section, but in totality were wider and spread from the middle section like concave wings, mounting in height at either end. The entire construct was as large as a suburban home, and built so close to the wall as it was, it reached the base of the immense rose window near the ceiling of the cathedral. The construct was primarily composed of exposed piping, save where it was bridged and encased, along the top and bottom, by elaborate, sorrel woodwork; specifically along the top of the piping, where the woodwork was so luxuriant, grand, and organic, it seemed to be made of lacquered coral.

Gabriel could hear the mercenaries regrouping in the entranceway below, and knew it would not be long before they found their way to a stairwell that would bring them to the level of the balcony. He placed a hand to his wounded neck. Though it was still raw and painful, the bleeding had abated to a trickle. He felt the instinctual compulsion to feed burgeoning within him, and he could hear his heart beginning to pound in his ears. Still resting upon a single knee, he closed his eyes and breathed in deeply, ousting the impulse. He removed his hand from his neck and let it rest upon his thigh. Bowed as though in prayer, the fingertips of his other hand gently placed upon the balcony floor, Gabriel went utterly still, forcing himself to take a moment's respite. His breaths were slow and deep, and his heart rate slowed in turn. His momentary stasis enabled the profound regenerative ability of his body to take effect with considerably greater efficiency, and his wound ceased to bleed entirely, as the wound site coagulated with raw tissue.

Gabriel opened his eyes and turned to look behind him once more. He gazed up at the lofty rose window above the organ pipes, observed it a moment longer, and then turned to Sebastian. Leaning forward, he took hold of Sebastian's wrist and pulled his slumped body away from the wooden barrier. Gabriel slipped his head beneath Sebastian's underarm, and then scooped the young officer onto his shoulder as he had before. As he rose to his feet, he lifted one arm and hooked it around Sebastian's waist. He then turned to the great organ. Securing Sebastian upon his shoulder he took a few steps towards the organ, and then sprang from the floor of balcony, alighting atop the organ like a cat on a window sill. Lifting his gaze, Gabriel lowered himself into a crouch, the dense, coiled muscle of his legs readied to spring. He leapt from the organ, lifting himself and Sebastian straight up into the air towards the immense wall of organ piping.

Running parallel along the lower bridge of woodwork encasing the base of the pipes, were two narrow ridges, much like the lip carved along the outer face of the balcony barrier. Reaching up with his free hand as he rose, Gabriel clasped the uppermost ridge in a vice-like grip and the hard, black claws at his fingertips dug into the varnished wood. Almost simultaneously, his feet found purchase upon the lower ridge, and he was able to cling to the base of the construct. He paused there for a moment, as he slowly removed his right hand from Sebastian's waist, freely balancing Sebastian's limp body over his right shoulder. He lifted his right hand, and took hold of the upper ridge alongside his other hand. Gabriel looked to the upper reaches of the towering pipes and began to climb.

He used one of the deeply embossed, columnar partitions as a hand-hold, scaling one side of the middle section of the towering wall of organ piping. Once past the ridges, he braced his feet against decorative wood and exposed piping alike, using his legs as best he could to help him climb, as might an ape. Careful not to move in such a way that would cause Sebastian to slide from his shoulder, he ascended hand over hand at a steady pace, hauling them both towards the rose window above. Gabriel left the balcony floor far below, and soon reached the palatial crown of woodwork that bridged the top of the piping. There, the ornate woodwork made for easier climbing, and Gabriel quickly reached the apex of the construct. From the very top and center of the broad, wooden crown, rose a large, winged angelic form.

Gabriel took hold of the tall, wooden statue and heaved himself upward, so that he was just able to lift one foot onto the top of the wooden crown. He replaced his right hand atop Sebastian's waist to secure the young officer to his shoulder; then, holding the statue, he hauled himself and Sebastian up with a thrust of the leg he had placed upon the crown, and he rose to his feet alongside the winged statue.

Gabriel's eyes lifted, and he gazed at the immense rose window before him. Separate from the rectangular portion of the window below, the rose window was delimited by a large, circular section of stone tracery, its diameter at least twenty-five feet across. Thick, stone tracery wound its way over much of the rose window, giving the stained glass an intricate floral design, and delineating the colored panels into a myriad of petal abstractions. The rose window lay only a short distance beyond the top of the organ pipes, a gap Gabriel could easily clear with a single bound, even while carrying Sebastian. Gabriel let his free hand drop from the statue, and then leapt from the organ pipes towards the rose window. He landed on the bottom portion of the encircling tracery, and he clasped a segment of the intricate, floral tracery above with his free hand, keeping himself from simply toppling backwards. Once balanced, he lifted his right hand from overtop of Sebastian once more, and with it, took hold of another segment of stone tracery.

What meager luminance passed through the rose window, from the city lights beyond, was tinted cerulean by the stained glass. In the gentle glow, Gabriel's whitish skin was colored a faint, misty blue. The rose window was so large, that nearly each of the petal abstractions was large enough for him to pass through, which had been his intent since leaping up to balcony. Gabriel glanced down at one of the largest petal abstractions nearest him, primarily blue in color, with spots of red and yellow. His ears pricked as he did, for he heard distant footfalls from below, and surmised that Sinclair's remaining mercenaries were ascending a stairwell to the balcony. Still staring at the petal-shaped panel, Gabriel released the tracery with his left hand, drew back his arm, and clenched his hand into a fist.

Gabriel swung his fist into the glass panel, pounding the stained glass with his white knuckles. A portion of the floral panel shattered upon impact, sending a hail of tinted shards out into the night air beyond. Gabriel withdrew his hand from the gaping, jagged hole he had punched in the glass. He struck the smashed panel a further three times using the ridge of his forearm, shattering the remaining stained glass within the petal-shaped panel. Storm wind blew in through the newly made opening to the outside world, wavering Gabriel's hair. Within the petal-shaped portion of the tracery, all that remained of the beauteous stained glass were small ragged shards, which jutted from the fringes of the stone tracery. Protected by the sleeve of his black coat, Gabriel forcefully ground his forearm along the inner rim of the panel, abrading the last bits of glass from inside the aperture. The vestiges of the stained-glass panel broke off with soft, tinkling cracks, like the sound of ice giving under foot. The serrated glass snagged a few small tears in the sleeve of this coat, leaving tiny scrapes in his tough skin.

The aperture was too small for Gabriel to fit both he and Sebastian through comfortably, or efficiently, and so, gripping the young officer by the back of his pants, he pulled Sebastian down from his shoulder. He allowed Sebastian's body to slide down his chest and fall astride his lifted thigh, whereupon Sebastian's unconscious body slumped against the rose window. Gabriel hooked his hand behind Sebastian, clasping him about the back of the neck beneath the helmet to support his head. Guiding his head, Gabriel lowered Sebastian to the glassless panel and maneuvered his head and shoulders through it so that Sebastian eventually toppled backward, the upper portion of his torso hanging out beyond the threshold of the stone panel. With nothing to support them, Sebastian's head and arms lolled awkwardly in the night air high above the street level.

Gabriel heard the mercenaries' footfalls. By their sound, they were seconds from reaching the organ balcony via the stairway, forcing Gabriel to move with even greater haste. His right hand still gripping the stone tracery on the inside of the rose window, Gabriel conveyed Sebastian's supine body through the stone panel by his belt buckle, and then by a single leg. With so much weight depending out in the open air beyond the window, Sebastian's body suddenly slid from within the panel, threatening to fall to the paved cathedral grounds far below. Gabriel quickly seized him by the ankle, halting the young officer's headlong fall.

His arms dangling towards the pavement, Sebastian's body thumped against the outer face of the cathedral, and the back of the helmet clacked against the stone tracery that wound its way over the length of connecting stained glass below the great, rose window. Gabriel knew he did not have time to haul the young officer onto his back. Instead, he stooped low, and still holding the stone tracery above him on the inside of the rose window, he ducked his own head and shoulders through the panel. Clasping the inner tracery with one hand and suspending Sebastian by the ankle with the other, Gabriel slung one leg out over the threshold of the panel and stole forth from the rose window.

* * * *

The soldiers burst out onto the balcony with their weapons raised at chest level. To their consternation, neither the target, nor the escaped officer was to be found on the balcony. The soldiers filed out over the balcony, their eyes wide and searching. High above them, a dark silhouette in a long coat climbed out of view beyond the azure stained-glass of the rose window, carrying with it another silhouetted form, which, swaying upended beneath the first, was lifted out of sight above the rose window a moment later.

VIII

Gabriel climbed towards the roof of the cathedral. Gritting his teeth under the immense strain, he lifted himself and Sebastian upwards in increments using the incredible contractile strength of his free arm and surrounding musculature. Bracing himself against the face of the cathedral with his legs, and using them to help him climb as best he could, he hoisted Sebastian's limp, dangling body up the face of the cathedral, as a leopard might haul its prey to the canopy of a tree.

Some distance to either side of him, the two giant steeples, which were built into the front face of the cathedral, rose high above the roof – spear-like monoliths that seemed to touch the black, clouded sky. The cusp of the smooth, stone frame, which domed the rose window, projected so far from the top of the stained glass, that Gabriel was forced to climb towards one of the steeples in order to continue his ascension. A strong wind blew across the face of the cathedral, howling as it rushed over the old masonry, causing his dark locks and his long, black coat to billow under its sway. The night air was cool, and the blaring sounds of the sirens he had heard earlier echoed through it from the base of the cathedral. Glancing down, Gabriel saw a gathering multitude far below: a myriad of flickering, glowing lights, a score of police cruisers, interspersed by uniformed officers that had exited their vehicles.

They seemed a world away from him. The din from below was accompanied by another noise he had detected from within the cathedral, a closer noise that emanated from the night sky itself. He had heard it before escaping through the rose window, and now, the oscillating drone of the helicopter filled his ears. Presently, it came round the side of one of the towering steeples, its floodlight sending a visible, expanding beam of luminance down towards the street below. The helicopter banked and flew in a loose arc across the face of the cathedral. As Gabriel climbed, it appeared as though the helicopter might fly past him, but before it slipped out of sight beyond the opposite steeple it began to slow and finally hovered in one spot high above the cathedral. Gabriel turned his head towards the helicopter and stared deep into the eyes of the pilot through the glossy windshield. He saw that the pilot had spotted him, and turning back to the intricate masonry before him, he began to climb once more with redoubled effort, forcing himself through the inhuman strain. The spotlight, emitted from the floodlight of the helicopter, lifted up the face of the cathedral towards him, and before Gabriel could make it to the cathedral roof, the floodlight shone upon him, and he was caught in the center of the brilliant beam.

To nocturnal eyes that amplified the most meager ambient light, that could see in near absolute dark, the floodlight of the helicopter was an overwhelming luminosity. A bestial sound rumbled in Gabriel's throat as his vision was bleached into a blinding albescence, his pupils contracting into nothingness, leaving naught but the yellow, liquescent, irises that had held them. Grimacing so fiercely that his ivory fangs were bared, he clenched his eyes shut and tucked his head beneath his outstretched arm. His eyes ached with a deep, pulsating pain, and it was as though he could still perceive the intensity of the spotlight, even through his closed eyelids. Gabriel knew that he could not simply remain clinging to the masonry as he was. Admittedly, he had begun to doubt that he could make good his escape, especially with Sebastian as dead weight in tow. In addition, he felt as though his strength had ebbed, and the desire to feed compelled him from deep within once more.

Inspiring deeply, Gabriel willed himself onwards. Using what portion of the masonry along the face of the cathedral that he had consolidated to mind, he began to climb blind, using internalized images from his photographic memory stores as a source of sight. Still, he could only climb up the face of the cathedral at a crawl, his ascent made slow and tentative by his sudden blindness.

Beyond the beating sound of the helicopter above him, rose another, almost identical, oscillating drone, and though he could not see it, Gabriel could hear that a second helicopter was on approach. Blind and nearly helpless where he clung to the masonry of the cathedral, Gabriel cursed himself inwardly for allowing himself to be made so vulnerable – so exposed to a world which, for the most part, knew nothing of his existence. Lunging upwards as best he could, his free hand lashed out for a small, decorative ridge in the stonework that he envisioned should be there. Indeed it was, but his perception of its distance from him was not exact, and he felt his claws rake harshly against the masonry and then slip from the stone outcrop. Gabriel reached out frantically with his free hand, his claws grating against the stone as he suddenly dropped from where he had clung. An instant later, his pale hand found purchase on another piece of decorative masonry, and he seized the projecting stone in an iron grip.

Still clutching Sebastian by the ankle, he stopped their brief fall and felt the dislocating force of the abrupt halt throughout the span of his arms and chest. Grunting, he kept his grip on the wall and repositioned his feet against the face of the cathedral. Still caught in the spotlight, Gabriel heard the second helicopter closing on his position, and then, to his alarm, the booming, staccato discharge of a heavy caliber weapon resounded from somewhere above. He heard the strident pings and cracks of bullets ripping into metal, and an instant thereafter, he was suddenly aware that the spotlight was no longer centered on him. Squinting and blinking involuntarily, Gabriel forced his eyes open. His eyes were both sore and hypersensitive, and white spots dotted his field of vision. Yet through his obscured vision, he perceived a helicopter knife out into the night sky above him from beyond the roof of the cathedral. As it passed overhead, Gabriel observed a series of muzzle flashes strobe from the side the helicopter, and saw that it was firing upon the helicopter that had caught him in the floodlight.

Gabriel turned to the other helicopter and witnessed it being incessantly riddled with bullets. The fuselage was pocked with bullet holes, and the helicopter had begun to whir and smoke. Through the shattered glass, Gabriel saw that the pilot had been caught in the barrage, and his body, perforated with bullet holes, was slumped over the control panel. He watched as the smoking helicopter listed and sank from the air, turning in a slow spiral as it fell to the street below. The other helicopter soared past the cathedral, past the plummeting helicopter and over the top of a nearby building.

Gabriel's vision began to clear and he recommenced his ascent of the cathedral with renewed fervor. As he neared the rooftop, he heard the sound of the helicopter mounting behind him. He turned from the cathedral wall and saw that, like the first helicopter, it too had banked, and was circling back towards him in a tight arc. It was then that Gabriel, his vivid, golden eyes piercing the night air, gazed skyward and saw who it was that stood in the doorway of the approaching helicopter.

* * * *

From the darkened sky above, he watched the spiraling helicopter fall to the street below and crash into the wet pavement. A ball of flame erupted from the belly of the riven fuselage, while broken blades and metal oddments flew from the demolished aircraft. The police officers nearest the downed helicopter had taken cover behind their vehicles. He watched as, following the crash, they rose to their feet and stared in disbelief at the flaming wreckage, which cast the surrounding area in a rich, wavering glow. The winds above rustled through his black mane, and it succumbed to the gentle gale, flailing to one side like a long, silken pennant. The once Lord Moxica stood in the open doorway of the helicopter like a brazen, dauntless centurion, holding the mounted machine gun before him in the clutch of one powerful hand. His other hand, outstretched towards the pilot, still held the large handgun.

"Steer de craft back round," Moxica demanded in calm, icy tone, without so much as a glance in the pilot's direction. In the cockpit, the pilot peered nervously over his shoulder at the large silencer that was leveled at him by the eerie man behind him. With a near imperceptible nod, he turned back to the control panel and began to turn the helicopter around. Moxica stared down upon the rabble below like a royal falcon on the wing, his eyes, which shone like yellow sapphires, glared at the throng with vengeful intent. Lowering the heavy machine gun, Moxica opened fire into the street below. The night sky was filled with the thunderous staccato of the machine gun once more, and a cascade of spent shells rained down from the firing weapon. A sweeping line of fire tore across the street amidst the police officers and their vehicles. The heavy-caliber bullets struck the pavement with a series of rapid, deafening cracks, instantaneously lifting tall flutes of dust and rubble from the battered street. All around the foot of the cathedral, officers took cover yet again, as a furious barrage of devastating bullets hailed down upon them. Many of the cruisers were riddled with gaping holes, and a few burst into flame. The linear onslaught ripped through the police cordon with devastating effect.

Though his body shook with the expeditious discharges of the machine gun, the steel mount it was set upon, and great strength of his rigid arm and grip, steadied the weapon before him. Moxica continued to fire as he drew near the cathedral anew. Below, uniformed officers continued to scatter and dive for cover. A few, their bodies torn by bullet wounds, toppled dramatically like mangled rag dolls, falling dead in the enfilade. Inundated by the unrelenting cannonade from above, the scene below was thrown into chaos, and the stricken throng lost sight of the man in black most of them had witnessed clinging to the cathedral wall above. Moxica lifted his piercing eyes from the bedlam in the street and caught sight of Gabriel. He watched as Gabriel took hold of the large spire next to one of the towering steeples and then hauled himself onto the roof with a single arm. Moxica lifted his hand from the mounted machine gun and addressed the pilot, his eyes observing Gabriel as the vampire lifted the young man, Klyne, to the rooftop as well, heaving him up by the ankle.

"Bring me across...der," Moxica commanded, pointing out the open doorway with a clawed forefinger.

* * * *

Sebastian had begun to groan as Gabriel reached the top of the cathedral wall. At first it had been a single, breathy noise, but it had quickly become less intermittent, as Sebastian began to stir from his comatose state. Having hoisted him to the roof by a single leg, Gabriel took hold of Sebastian, righted him in his arms, and laid the young officer on his back atop the black roof. The rooftop slanted upwards towards a central ridge, and Gabriel had to hold Sebastian to keep the young officer's body from sloughing off the roof. Hunkering next to the Sebastian, Gabriel cupped the back of the young officer's neck, propping his head up with the palm of his hand.

Gabriel noted that his free hand had begun to tremble, a sign that he had incurred significant blood loss, affecting the endurance of his prodigious muscle. Staring into the glossy face shield of the helmet, Gabriel called the young officer's name.

"Sebastian!" he exclaimed, assessing the young officer's coherence. Sebastian moaned languidly, but he was still not lucid. Gabriel looked up abruptly and spied the remaining helicopter as it passed over the cathedral. It banked a second time, and by its trajectory, Gabriel anticipated that it would take another pass, close to where he now crouched atop the roof. Indeed, after circling, the helicopter proceeded on a straight path that would fly it directly across the face of the cathedral. Gabriel saw Moxica standing in the open doorway of the helicopter. Their eyes met and, severe and expressionless as their aspects remained, it was as though there were some unspoken understanding between them. The helicopter drew near and Gabriel watched as the once Lord Moxica extended a bestial, pale hand into the night air and beckoned him with a slow, distinct, inward curl of his clawed fingers. Still staring into the ancient lord's eyes, Gabriel bowed his head in the slightest, conveying to Moxica the subtlest of acknowledgements.

Finally breaking gaze with Moxica, Gabriel quickly gathered Sebastian in his arms, slung him over a shoulder once more, and hurriedly climbed the sloped roof to the top of the central ridge that ran along the rooftop. Once there, Gabriel turned to the dark, western horizon beyond the front face of the cathedral. To either side of him, the lofty, pointed steeples loomed overhead, and mere feet from him, the front face of the cathedral rose to a peak where the central ridge of the roof met the gothic, cathedral face. Situated between the monolithic steeples, the peak overhung the rose window below it, and atop the peak, was mounted a cross of beauteous design.

Gabriel looked to the helicopter once more, gauging it as it began its sweep across his field of vision. His eyes moved to

Moxica, who watched as Gabriel took a few, measured, deliberate steps backward along the ridge. The sound of the helicopter filled Gabriel's ears, and his heart began to pound in his chest. He breathed in deeply and then slowly exhaled, while his eyes followed the helicopter as it closed upon the face of the cathedral some dozen feet from and above the rooftop.

For a moment, Gabriel was stone still, poised to spring forth like a waiting panther. The helicopter neared closer still, and suddenly, Gabriel lunged forward. With mounting speed, and with perfect balance, he raced along the ridge at an astonishing pace. He reached the verge of the rooftop in an instant, his eyes riveted upon the base of the helicopter as it finally swept across one of the giant steeples.

Moving at unprecedented speed, his face taut with strain, Gabriel leapt from the peak of the rooftop, skimming past the mounted, stone cross. With Sebastian upon his shoulder, and his black coat trailing out behind him, Gabriel rose from the cathedral as though he were weightless. Outstretching his free hand, he soared towards the passing aircraft and, for moment, seemed to slow as he sailed into the night air. At the height of his leap, at the penultimate moment, he seized one of the metal landing skids, which ran along the base of the helicopter. Gripping with all the might his free hand could muster, his white palm clamped over the metal skid like a vice.

Jolted by the momentum of the aircraft, Gabriel swung like a pendulum by his single arm, and he felt a sharp pain shoot through the extended limb. A primal sound issued from Gabriel's throat, and he winced with pain. Still, he clung to the skid, holding Sebastian tightly to his shoulder as they dangled below the helicopter. Swaying to and fro, Gabriel peered down at the tumult near the foot of the cathedral, and listened as the wailing sirens and commotion below grew fainter in his acute ears, swallowed by the whirling blades of the helicopter above him. Presently, he lifted his head, gazing up at the helicopter and then at Moxica, who still stood above him within the open doorway. Moxica casually eyed him, and gave him a knowing look. He then turned to the pilot in the cockpit and uttered a single word.

"East," Moxica bade, his voice a calm and yet commanding resonance.

* * * *

A number of police officers witnessed the helicopter depart overhead. Before it evanesced into the darkness above, some perceived the tenebrous form of a man in black, climbing from the landing skids of the aircraft towards the fuselage itself. Growing smaller as it flew towards the east, it began to climb into the night sky, leaving the cathedral behind. The helicopter became obscure as it soared into the distance, until finally, it was indistinguishable against the darkened firmament.

Chapter Seven

Sins of the Past
I

Andrew Sinclair placed the document he had been reading on the large, wooden desk. He propped both elbows on the desk, and with a forceful sigh of fatigue, he closed his eyes and gently rested his face in his palms. There he remained for some time, breathing deeply into his cupped hands. His head was heavily bandaged from his ordeal at Fort Hamilton the previous night, and the severe concussion he had sustained gave him bouts of dizziness, nausea, and a throbbing pain at his temples. One side of his face was discolored and swollen, made black and blue by the bruised tissue and bone.

Beyond the window, the estate was quiet. It was one of the reasons Sinclair had retreated to the smaller study on the upper floor instead of working in his father's old study on the main floor; the silence was soothing to his recent discomfort. Though it was an uneventful night in the mansion, he did not want to be anywhere near his hired help, nor even hear the incidental, dutiful sounds of their domestic activities. Also, he had found that his eyes were bothered by bright light as a result of the concussion, and not expecting his attendants to operate in near darkness, it had simply been another reason for him to retire to his secondary study.

He had placed a lamp on one corner of his desk. It was equipped with an adjustable stand, and a conical, metal lampshade, under which was a halogen bulb. He had bent the lamp away from himself to a noticeable degree, and it was currently the only source of light in the room, causing it to be dimly lit. He had been ordered to sleep in brief increments by his personal doctor, and so, understandably fatigued as he was, his mind was often a sea of non sequitur thoughts.

The faintest of clicks sounded from the latch of the closed door to his left. To his right, the broad window dimly and vaguely reflected the black, wooden door. In the reflection, the gold handle upon the door began to turn every so slowly. Lost in thought, Sinclair did not hear the subtle click, and remained seated in the ovular-backed, wooden chair. In the reflection upon the window, the door began to open gradually, and presently, a soft creak issued from the hinges. Somewhere amidst his weighty thoughts, Sinclair detected the quiet sound, registering it enough that he opened his eyes, slowly lifted his head from his hands, and gingerly turned to the door.

He had expected the door to be closed, with perhaps an attendant in the lit hallway on the other side about to inquire something of him. Instead, he found the door swung wide open, and the hallway beyond, dark. Yet it was what loomed within the doorway that caused his eyes to widen in alarm and his innards to twist into cold knots of fear. Sinclair's mouth went dry, and he froze where he sat; for, standing in the doorway, shrouded in shadow, was a fearsome man with broad, powerful shoulders, and a long, black, leather coat that skimmed the hallway floor. He wanted not to look upon the man's face, but could not help but do so, and when he did, he saw that it was the face he had dreaded to see. Smooth, black hair flowed like ink down past his shoulders, emphasizing the man's eerie, unreadable, whitish face. Distinctive as the man's features were, this was not the assailant who had incapacitated he and his men at Fort Hamilton. However – and the truth ate at him – he knew in his heart that this was the harrowing face he had seen in the skylight, those many years ago: John Smith, the white-faced man.

Sinclair gazed helplessly into the man's eyes, and was met by a piercing, feral stare. The man's golden eyes seemed to burn like seething embers, and their stare pervaded his being with abject terror. Sinclair watched in horror as the living nightmare that had haunted his mind since childhood took a single step over the threshold and into the study with him. The silence in the room was chilling, and for a moment, the two simply stared at one another. Finally, the white-faced man spoke, breaking the silence with the forbidding voice of a vengeful god.

"It has been many years, Andrew Sinclair, but I have not forgotten your scent, I...have forgotten nothing, I...remember all. You hunted me, you stole from me, you sought to destroy me."

Sinclair felt his heart rise to his throat as panic gripped him tighter with each word the white-faced man spoke.

"I, dat, from de darkness, watched dis age of man birthed, have survived peril beyond your understanding. I......am Moxica," said the white-faced man, his voice suddenly bestial and harsh, "and I shall walk dis earth long after you are dust claimed by de soil."

Cold silence held the room once more, and then the man addressed Sinclair one final time.

"If you have words, speak dem now, for you are not long for dis world."

With that, the white-faced man who called himself Moxica, took another, slow step into the study, and reaching out beside him with a pale, monstrous hand, closed the door behind him.

II

Having woken from his quiescent state, Gabriel left his chamber and made his way through the hallway of the facility. Save for a few blood packets he had taken from the lab, he had not fed since his rescue of Sebastian Klyne two nights prior. There had been much to attend to when he returned to the facility after learning what he had from Moxica – matters of the utmost urgency to safeguard himself and the new facility to which, in secret, they would soon be moving. On the night he had liberated Sebastian, he had made it back to the facility a little before sunset, and so, he had taken the following night to manage the pressing affairs. That night, the urge to feed had been present, distractingly so, but, for the most part, he had restrained himself from the compulsion. He had healed completely during the diurnal period leading up to that night, nonetheless, at present, he could no longer repress the instinctual side that had so become a part of who he was. Still, he maintained his usual composure, for he had weathered this impulse near its apogee many times before, a discipline practiced both out of necessity, and for the sake of his remaining humanity.

Gabriel walked through the dimly lit hallway, and rounded the corner towards the south side of the facility. He soon reached the third floor lounge that had been built into the alcove in the hallway, and was about to pass it by when something upon the large, glass coffee table caught his eye. The thing was laid flat across the length of the glass table, and its own considerable length had a lustrous sheen, for it held the soft glow of the pot lights above. Gabriel came to a dead stop alongside the open lounge. His amber eyes widened in the slightest, his mouth loosened as though he might speak, his face the picture of disbelief, for there, rested upon the glass table, was a sword, its design intimately familiar, its condition pristine. Gabriel's eyes ran along the great length of the broad blade to the elaborate, silver guard, a twining, metal composition like silvery briars, a guard which, like two crescent moons sprouting from the long hilt, curved up towards the blade. Awed, Gabriel took a few slow steps towards the sword, towards his sword, the ancient blade his father had given him in his youth so very long ago.

Standing next to the glass table, Gabriel reached down with his right hand and took the sword by the hilt. He held it aloft for a moment, his eyes never leaving the blade. He felt its familiar weight and balance in his hand, and a deluge of memories from a distant past, some unsettling and grim, some spirited and wondrous, flooded his mind. Slowly, Gabriel lowered the sword and rested the flat of the blade in the upturned palm of his left hand. There was a far off look in his lurid eyes, as they looked over the length of the great Tizona. The blade was now a relic of the past, and he wondered why Moxica had even kept his sword. Ages ago, he had tried to take Moxica's life, and still the ancient lord had sought him out, warned him of imminent danger, and perhaps even saved his life. Moxica was still much a mystery to him, yet he could not help but feel that the intentions of the ancient lord were honorable.

Gabriel lifted his eyes from the sword and looked down both ends of the hallway. As he had expected, it was empty. He did not know when Moxica had come, but as to how, he had his suspicions. A trace smile appeared upon his pallid face, and he gazed back down at the sword in his hands.

* * * *

Dr. Canterberry opened the door to the brightly lit ward. He was careful not to bang the quaint tray he held in his left hand in the doorway, lest he spill the tea he had just prepared, along with the tea set he balanced upon it. Once through the doorway, he looked up from the tray and gave Sebastian a cordial smile. Sebastian, who had been asleep a short while ago, was sitting upright on the hospital bed, and greeted the doctor in kind.

"Hey, doc," Sebastian addressed him with a dry, tired voice. Sebastian's face was badly bruised, and he had received stitches to seal the wounds on his shoulder where the bullet had entered and exited. He wore a tank top, and his bare shoulder was wrapped with blood-dampened gauze.

"Well," said Dr. Canterberry in good humor, "here we are

again."

Sebastian smiled and made a face that admitted the unfortunate comedy of his being tended to in the hospital bed once more.

"Though this time round," Dr. Canterberry continued, "I would thank you kindly not to jab my own pen at my jugular."

The wrinkles at the corners of the doctor's blue eyes betrayed his amusement, and Sebastian chuckled weakly. Dr. Canterberry walked to Sebastian's bedside and placed the tray on the small bedside table.

"Earl Grey?" Sebastian asked, managing to lift an eyebrow against the swelling on his face.

"Of course...piping hot, too," Dr. Canterberry replied as he lifted the teapot and began to pour the tea, though the aromatic steam rising from the teacups was proof enough that it was at a scalding temperature. An audible vibration suddenly made itself known, followed by a melodious piece of classical music, Mozart. Dr. Canterberry reached beneath his white lab coat and into his pants pocket. He removed his cell phone from his pocket and lifted it to his ear.

"Hello," said Dr. Canterberry, his eyes staring off at nothing in particular.

"Nigel," came Gabriel's hard, somber voice over the phone. "We are going to have to change the locking mechanism on the rooftop entrance again before the move.

"Why," Dr. Canterberry commented, "was that sinister fellow here again?"

"Yes," Gabriel replied calmly.

"Good Lord," the doctor exclaimed, "that is rather unnerving news."

"Perhaps, but I don't believe he means us harm," Gabriel advised.

"Yes...well...be that as it may, for those of us who are not highly evolved killing machines ourselves, and who often work up here alone, at night, it is not particularly comforting to have some enigmatic, nocturnal predator lurking about in gloom with oneself unseen. Gives me enough of a bloody start bumping into you in the hallway. Speaking of which, I don't know why it is that you must move without a bloody sound when you walk throu—"

"Nigel," Gabriel interrupted the fulminating doctor. "I'm going out."

Dr. Canterberry paused and blinked a few times, considering the meaning behind his employer's words.

"Em...right...well...happy hunting then," he stammered, his manner returning to its usual amicability. Dr. Canterberry remained on the line for a moment longer, but as he expected, as he was accustomed, Gabriel was gone.

* * * *

In the armory, Gabriel placed his cellular device into a pocket. Standing still for a moment, he stared up at one of the weapon racks. He had placed his old sword amongst his collection of ancient weapons and, for a short time, he gazed at it. Then, he turned from the weapon, passed through the munitions racks, and entered his personal lift. At the touch of a button, the metal door slid closed, and with a grating whir, the lift descended.

III

Though he did not feel it as such, the air was cool, and a gentle breeze blew through it. High above, the sky was cloudless and clear, revealing a perfectly black expanse, laden with brilliant stars. Standing atop the verge of a midsized building, Gabriel scoured the darkened city before him. The city lights infiltrated the purity of the night with the faintest, ambient glow, which, to Gabriel's vampire eyes, lit the world around him as though it were day. The sounds and scents of the city lifted from the small side streets below, readily discerned by his acute sensorium. He was partially attentive to that which his senses perceived, and partially lost in thought. Unmoving in the dim moonlight from above, he had remained stone still for some length of time, like a gargoyle upon the edge of an edifice. He thought about what had been in his distant past: what changes had befallen the world since then, and what might be. A nostalgic stream of crisp, clear memories drifted through his mind. He thought of those whom he had held dear, those that were now long dead.

He soon tired of his doldrums and began to scour the streets for the drug dealers and gang-related rabble he often preyed upon. His ears detected a soft, rattling sound and, some distance away, something appeared from around the far corner of a building, catching his attentive eyes. It was the front end of a shopping cart, laden with an assortment of scrap, and Gabriel watched as a homeless man slowly pushed the metal cart along a wall. Gabriel focused his vision upon the homeless man. The man was hunched and disturbingly thin, his clothes tattered and soiled. From beneath a grubby tuque, course, greyish bits of hair hung down over a weathered, creased face. Leaving his cart, the homeless man began to amble about the street and sidewalk, gingerly stooping to pick up worthless odds and ends, each time staring at what he had found with an idiotic, toothless grin.

Gabriel noted the poor wretch's unbalanced, teetering gait, as the homeless man returned to his cart to cache his worthless oddments. The man was not of sound mind and was clearly unable to properly care for himself. As he stared at the helpless wretch, a predatory instinct burgeoned within him, and he leaned over the verge of the building, poised as if he might leap to the tall streetlight overhanging the pavement below.

It was then that he detected the faintest of scents upon the wind. It was thin in the air, and ephemeral at best, yet it stirred a host of macabre memories, a roiling stream of dark, ancient images that haunted his mind. Gabriel's eyes widened and their golden centers seemed to glow like dim embers. Averting his gaze from the homeless man, Gabriel searched the city streets beneath him, his eyes darting about as they fossicked the darkness below.

The vaguest of movements from the street level caught Gabriel's attentive eyes, and he immediately turned towards the moving thing he had perceived between two buildings. Yet, with the omission of the bumbling, muttering homeless man, and bits of trash blown about by the wind, all else in the street was still. Similarly unmoving, Gabriel observed the dark mouth of an alley, wherein he had seen the thing that had stirred.

Silent, Gabriel stared into the shadow-filled alley, his eyes examining the darkness. Though it was partially concealed by the corner of the nearest building, Gabriel made out an obscure figure in the shadows. The figure appeared to be hunched, or rather crouched within the mouth of the alley. From what Gabriel could see beyond the corner of the building, the figure wore a frayed, threadbare, hooded sweater, and a long, oversized, ragged coat, which, perhaps once tan in color, was now darkened with patches of grime. At first glance, the motionless figure appeared to be another of the homeless: a poor wretch of a man, quickly passed in the street by the privileged. The vagrant's face was entirely hidden by the shabby hood of the sweater, but he appeared to be staring out over the street. Remaining deathly still, and hunkered quite low to the ground, the hooded vagrant looked as though he were watching the homeless man across the street quite attentively.

Gabriel remained perfectly still himself, and continued to observe the hooded figure from his perch upon the edge of the rooftop. Some moments passed, and finally the vagrant moved once more, taking a single step out from within the mouth of the pitch-dark alley. The hooded figure seemed tentative to leave the shadows. Where he sat crouched between the threshold of shadow and street light, the vagrant slowly, nearly indiscernibly, looked out to one end of the street and then the other, as though ascertaining that the street was empty, save of course for the witless homeless man on the other side of the street. This done, the hooded figure stared out across the street as before and, from Gabriel's perspective, seemed to lock his sights upon the ambling destitute anew. Gabriel could not see the vagrant's face within the hood from where he stood atop the building, but he still intuited that there was something strange, even eerie about the vagrant – something troublingly familiar.

It was the way the hooded vagrant had moved: the practiced manner with which he skulked forth in the darkness; his silence, his crouched, almost predatory poise; the way he seemed coiled and ready to spring at the slightest sound. Gabriel knew that what he saw before him was the source of the trace odor he had detected in the air. Undeniably, it had been the scent of those creatures that he had hunted in an age long past, the creatures whose virulent blood had forever changed his very being.

It was not without some disbelief that he observed the hooded figure below. He recalled the genocide he had waged in Europe – remembered how he had all but exterminated the archaic race of vampires. He had hunted them so relentlessly, that he had once thought them too few to recover from the brink of extinction. Yet, some years ago, he had found living specimens of the ancient breed that had endured in Europe, and here before him now was another of their kind. He could not help but think of the female vampire and her youngling, though he knew that through the ages that had passed, they would have withered with age and were both long dead now.

He had admitted it to himself before, and he did so again; Moxica had been right; they were more than beasts, and more intelligent than he had ever conceived. They seemed to mimic human beings to such an accomplished degree, that they learned from the behaviors of their prey, thus growing more proficient as sentient creatures; creatures towards whom he no longer held true malice, for he understood their function, their place in the world. Centuries ago, Gabriel had seen the rudiments of culture develop amongst these creatures, and now it seemed, though he knew not how, that the vampires had not only survived, but found their way across a continent.

Still crouched where it had gone motionless, the eerie, hooded figure continued to hold the homeless man in a steady gaze. Gabriel noted that the figure had begun to sway in the slightest, slowly rocking from side to side, seemingly taking in the ambient sounds of the city, and the scents in the air. When the homeless man caused the lid of an aluminum garbage can to clatter upon the street as he rifled through a bag of rubbish, the figure's hooded head cocked to one side quizzically, and the eerie vagrant went still again.

Presently, the hooded figure began to creep forth from where it had been stilled, stalking towards the homeless man from the opposite side of the street. Moving with progressive haste, the hooded figure slinked into the street, the dim luminance of a distant streetlight tingeing the hooded figure with a soft, rich, amber glow.

It was then that the wind changed, and shortly thereafter, the hooded figure came to an abrupt halt. The hooded head bobbed now and again, and Gabriel watched as it began to sniff the air. Gabriel knew that the thing had now caught his scent in the changing wind, and he looked on as the hooded figure's head began to swivel in his direction, still sniffing at the air like a jackal on the prowl. Its attention momentarily diverted from the homeless man, the figure turned its hooded head. It was not long before the figure slowly lifted its searching gaze to the spot where Gabriel stood on the building.

A pair of vivid, feral, yellow eyes rose up at him from inside the shadowy hood, glinting in the soft light; yet fearsome as they were, they bore a quality of uncertainty, perhaps even apprehension. Gabriel saw the bestial face within the hood. He observed the thick, whitish skin, and the heavy facial musculature beneath the pale flesh, most pronounced near the brow, temples and jaw. The menacing visage merely confirmed what Gabriel had known already, and he met the vampire's unblinking, questioning stare. For a tense moment that seemed to linger in time, each held the fierce, raptorial gaze of the other. Staring at Gabriel searchingly, the hunting vampire let its maw fall open, and a harsh ululation rang out from its throat. Perhaps it was a warning, a vocal claim over its hunting grounds, and perhaps, thought Gabriel, it was speech, a greeting of sorts from a lonely soul. Gabriel did not answer. He simply regarded the creature below, his eyes gleaming balefully. The vampire stared back at him, waiting.

Meanwhile, unaware of the nocturnal encounter, the bumbling homeless man returned to his shopping cart. After placing a single, dirty sock into the cart, the homeless man sidled to the back of the cart and began to push it along the sidewalk, muttering and humming to himself contentedly.

Hearing the rattling cart and idle rambling, the vampire turned from Gabriel and stared after the homeless man. It watched as the poor wretch wheeled the rusty cart past the wall and into an alley. The homeless man wandered out of view behind the corner of the wall and the vampire turned back to Gabriel. It held Gabriel's impassive gaze for a few moments with what might have been an expression of indecision upon its face; then it curled back its lips and bared its fangs in a vicious snarl. Turning from Gabriel, the vampire darted away in utter silence, scampering across the dimly lit street like a wraith. It reached the alley in an instant and eagerly scurried into the darkness.

Gabriel watched as the vampire slipped of view beyond the corner of the wall and into the alley. It was not long before a feeble, dry scream sounded in the night air. The cry was brief and abruptly silenced, leaving the streets quiet and barren once more.

For a short time, Gabriel stared out over the city, the wind ruffling his black locks and causing his long black coat to billow and flail. He turned from the verge of the roof and began to walk away along the rooftop. His pace quickened until he broke into run. He swept across the rooftop until he reached the opposite end, whereupon he leaped out into the night. Like a dark specter, he soared through the air and then began to fall from a breathtaking height, his coat lifting in dark folds like pinions. With a thump and a crunch of gravel, he alighted upon a neighboring rooftop. No sooner had he come to ground, than he lunged forth into the night once more and, coursing above the sleeping city, he soon vanished into the darkness.

About the Author

Joshua Martyr was born and raised in Toronto Canada. He earned his Specialized Honours degree at York University and received his Bachelor of Education from OISE at the University of Toronto in the disciplines of Physical Education and English.

In addition to being an athlete of some distinction, Joshua is a lover of the world's many animal species and of its untamed wildernesses.

Also by Joshua Martyr

Genesis of The Hunter Book 1
by Joshua Martyr

eBook ISBN: 9781615721214
Print ISBN: 9781615721283

Genre: Dark Fantasy
Sub Genre: Horror
Novel of 101,351 words

The world cradling humankind is yet to be understood. Much of its archaic beginnings linger within the mind upon a plane of postulates, mystery and uncertain truth, the voice of myth from times long past. In these legends are glimmers of truths dismissed as lore.

This is such a story: the origin of a legend that spans from distant past to the present day, the origin of the vampire. Alluring and suspenseful, it is the dark, epic chronicle of a man changed in nature and body. Once a sentinal of a prosperous settlement, he is forced into a nocturnal existence, and instinctually compelled in ways that he fears will cost him his very humanity. He gained an unnatural longevity, and while the ages pass, the modern world develops around him. His existence is discovered by an old organization whose siege even he shall be hard pressed to survive.

More from Damnation Books:

Sepulchral Earth
by Tim Marquitz

eBook ISBN: 9781615720767
Print ISBN: 9781615720750

Genre: Horror
Sub Genre: Dark Fantasy
Novella of 12645 words

Two years after the furious dead rose up to murder the living, the remnants of mankind face a brutal extinction. Wretched and broken, trading humanity for life, the survivors suffer under the inevitable shadow of death.

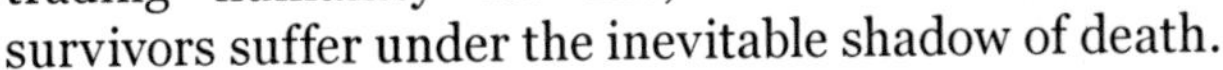

Aided by friendly spirits, the necromancer Harlan Cole wages war against the merciless forces of the undead. Driven to bring peace to the souls of his wife and daughter, Harlan vows to return the dead to their graves, or join them trying.

LaVergne, TN USA
18 October 2010
201308LV00001B/2/P